Praise for *Dylan*:

"Admirand does an excellent job of setting the scene with her amazing flair for scenery and description... Readers will be left panting."

—*RT Book Reviews*, 4½ stars

"Hot, sexy Texan cowboys who know what they want and go after it with both hands."

—*Fresh Fiction*

"If you want a story that's got heat, heart, and a little mystery to keep you guessing, then you need to read *Dylan*."

—*Long and Short Reviews*

"First Tyler and now Dylan—I do not know how much more a girl can take, but I am ready to find out."

—*Coffee Time Romance*

"The characters are great and memorable... and a multidimensional plot kept my interest... The ending was inspired. I've already fallen in love with younger brother, Jesse. If you enjoy a good contemporary Western romance, pick up this series!"

—*Night Owl Reviews*

"A fun, seductive story line... Makes me want my own _____ ward to the last installment."

—*Bookloons*

D0957277

"The characters are well written, the hero being the serious down-home cowboy with thick skin and a soft heart."

—*Romance Fiction on Suite 101*

"Oh yeah! Hot, sexy, and stunning."

—*Seriously Reviewed*

"Admirand has a sassy writing style that is simply irresistible!"

—*Huntress Reviews*

"A witty story of love, romance, and raw sensuality."

—*Eva's Sanctuary*

"This story… enhanced my love for the handsome cowboys. I'm already going through Garahan withdrawal!"

—*Book Obsessed Chicks*

Praise for *Tyler*:

"Steamy… The passion is electrifying."

—*RT Book Reviews*

"Fantastic… multifaceted and interesting."

—*Night Owl* Reviewer Top Pick

"An interesting, potent, provocative love story. Perfect for those who love cowboys and strong men."

—*Love Romance Passion*

"Tyler and Emily's story is wonderfully written with loads of humor, spicy romance, and good old-fashioned charm that makes it a pleasure to read and impossible to put down until the last page is turned."

—*Reader's Entertainment*

"A great present-day Western story full of handsome, witty, sexy, hardworking cowboys, beautiful, witty, smart, sexy, hardworking women, and a passion for work, life, and love."

—*My Book Addiction and More*

"Down-home country and downright sexy... Every touch drives you to want more, page after page."

—*Coffee Time Romance*

"Very vibrant, full of life, and easily relatable."

—*Romance Fiction on Suite101.com*

THE SECRET LIFE OF ·COWBOYS·

Jesse

C.H. ADMIRAND

sourcebooks
casablanca

Published by Sourcebooks Casablanca, an imprint of Sourcebooks, Inc.
P.O. Box 4410, Naperville, Illinois 60567-4410
(630) 961-3900
FAX: (630) 961-2168
www.sourcebooks.com

Printed and bound in Canada
WC 10 9 8 7 6 5 4 3 2 1

Chapter 1

JESSE GARAHAN HIT THE GAS AND BREATHED IN THE hot Texas air. He loved the feel of the wind in his face and the engine rumbling beneath him as the hot sun smiled down, trying to parboil him to the driver's seat.

He'd left the ranch in two pairs of very capable hands—his brothers'. Tapping his fingers on the steering wheel, he wondered if he could find a wild woman like the one Garth Brooks was singing about on the radio. Hell—he didn't have time for romance right now, too much to do and not enough time to get it done in. Setting that thought aside, he concentrated on the road ahead of him and coaxed as much speed as possible out of his truck.

Flooring it, tearing ass along the road to town, he grinned. He loved driving and figured he missed his calling, having to work at the ranch with his brothers—but Garahans stuck together no matter what, and as long as the ranch still had life left in it, a Garahan would be running it. With enough work for ten men, most days he and his brothers were worn to the bone, but not ready to roll over and give up.

A speck of color off in the distance at the side of the road had him cutting back on the accelerator. Could be one of the Dawson sisters; Miss Pam had told him she'd been having a bit of trouble with her old pickup. Slowing it down, ready to lend a hand, he sucked in a breath and held it. Steam poured out from under the hood of a car that a very curvy, compact, jean-clad blonde was opening. When he noticed the rag in her hand, he knew what she was going to do.

"Damn fool woman!" He feathered the gas for more speed, cranked the wheel hard to the left, whipping the car in a perfect one-eighty. Gravel spit out from beneath his tires as he skidded to a halt behind her vehicle.

When she jumped back with a hand to her heart, he threw the truck in park and swung his door open with enough force to move the dead summer air like the early morning breeze coming across the pond at the Circle G. Stomping over to her, he grabbed her by the elbow and pulled her off to the side, out of harm's way.

When she yanked free of his hold, he was more than ready to read her the riot act. Drawing in a deep breath, he was about to let loose when he heard a little voice calling.

"Mommy?"

"Lacy, honey, I told you to stay in the backseat until I fixed the car."

Looking down, he noticed a pint-sized cowgirl staring up at him, her big blue eyes wide with wonder. Not much surprised Jesse Garahan, but the little bit of a thing, no bigger than a fairy, was wearing pink—from the top of her head to the soles of her feet—and stood out like a swirl of cotton candy at the county fair.

"Go on back now; I have to thank the man for trying to help us." The woman's voice was firm, but the little girl wasn't listening. Before he could process that fact, the vision in pink was tugging on his jeans and asking, "Are you a good guy or a bad guy?"

He shook his head at the incongruity of the situation. He'd intended to put the fear of God into the woman foolish enough to open the cap of her overheated radiator while she stood in front of it, and instead here he was staring down at the tiniest, pinkest cowgirl he'd ever seen.

"I uh…" He didn't know how to answer. If he'd done what he'd intended to do—yell at her mother—the little girl would probably be crying now, and positive he was a bad guy. "I stopped to help."

When the little one nodded but refused to let go of his jeans, the woman came closer and soothed, "He's a good guy, honey."

The little girl tilted her head to one side and frowned up at him. "But he gots a black hat—Gramma says good guys wear white hats."

Jesse chuckled. "Is your grandmother a fan of Gene Autry or Roy Rogers?"

Her little head bobbed up and down, and her cowgirl hat slipped off her head and would have hit the ground if not for the bright white cord attached to it. She was still looking up at him when she said, "Uh-huh."

"That was a long time ago, and only on TV," the cowgirl's mother told her. "The good guys wear white or black hats now."

The little one bobbled and grabbed a hold of his leg with both little hands and whispered, "Daddy wears a black hat."

He didn't need to know that. Concentrating, he couldn't figure out a way to delicately loosen the little one's grip without scaring her. Her mother surprised him by kneeling next to him. Looking down at them, he remembered the times his mother had gotten down to eye level with him when he'd been scared as a kid. It always helped ease most of his worries—except for the biggest one—why wasn't his father coming home?

To keep from letting his mind go down that rocky path, he focused on the still-steaming engine and grumbled, "Don't you realize how dangerous it is to open the cap on an overheated radiator?" He'd learned that particular lesson from his grandfather years ago; his pride had taken a direct hit, but he hadn't ended up disfigured from steam burns.

The blonde's head snapped up and their eyes met. He couldn't help but notice the frosty blue daggers pointed directly at him.

"I was going to be careful to keep the cap facing away from me." She cupped her hands around her daughter's where she still held tight to his leg, and urged, "Come on Lacy, you can let go now."

To his relief, the little one finally did as she was told. When her mother lifted the itty-bitty cowgirl up in her arms, he relaxed. The only kids he came into contact with were the handful of teenagers who came out to the ranch, working off a debt they owed to his older brother Tyler and his fiancée, Emily.

"But, Mommy," she whispered, "I gots to ask him."

He was standing close enough to hear. "Ask me what?"

"Are you a real cowboy?"

Before he could answer the little girl added, "I never seen one in my whole life!"

"Your daddy's a cowboy."

"Nuh-uh." Lacy shook her head. "He rides bulls, not horsies, 'member, Mommy?"

Jesse couldn't keep the chuckle inside; the rumbling sound seemed to capture little Lacy's interest because she poked her tiny pointer finger in the middle of his chest.

"Lacy, what did I tell you?" Looking up at him, the blonde's eyes were troubled. "I'm sorry. She's curious about everything. We're working on keeping our fingers to ourselves." She smoothed a hand over the flyaway hair on the top of Lacy's head and said, "Aren't we, sweetie?"

"I was trying to find the sound, Mommy," the little girl admitted. "His lips din't move."

Not much touched his heart since the woman he'd been planning on marrying changed her mind, but this miniature cowgirl had the walls surrounding it cracking. He smiled down at them and it felt good inside. "Name's Garahan, ma'am," he said, tipping his hat to the little lady. "Jesse," he said, staring into the mother's cool blue eyes.

Her cheeks flushed a tender pink, reminding him of the sweet peas climbing on the fence by the back door that his new sister-in-law, Ronnie, had planted. "Pleased to meet you, Mr. Garahan."

Lacy bounced in her mother's arms. "Me too, me too!"

Her mother hugged her daughter and looked up at him; her slow smile stole the breath from his lungs. He'd seen a lot of pretty women in his time, and loved his fair share, but something about the pair in front of him just got to him on a level he didn't quite understand. It was new to him, and he wasn't quite sure how to react or what to say. Lucky for him, the little one kept babbling about cowboys, black hats, and funny rumbling sounds until his brain kicked in and he realized he'd been staring at the little one's mother.

She kissed the top of her daughter's head, and he'd swear he heard another crack echoing deep inside of him.

"Does your mommy have a name, Miss Lacy?"

The girl beamed up at him and nodded.

Satisfied that he'd find out the woman's name, since she hadn't offered it yet, he grinned and Lacy answered, "Mommy."

He pushed his Stetson to the back of his head and let out a breath. "Hel—er, heck, Miss Lacy, I already knew that."

She tilted her head to one side and studied him for a moment. "I like him," she said in a stage whisper. "Even if he wears a black hat like Daddy."

The look of sadness in her mother's eyes was swift and filled with pain. "We'll talk about that later, sweet pea." She looked at him and said, "My name's Danielle Brockway, and you already know this little cowgirl is Lacy."

"Pleasure to meet you both." And it was. When the two were laughing, it was contagious, and for the first time in weeks, he felt lighter, happier. Wanting to keep the feeling going just a bit longer, he nodded toward her overheated car. "Can I give you and Miss Lacy a lift into town?"

"Shouldn't we crank open that cap first?"

He shook his head. "It'll cool off better if you let it sit. I'll stop by on my way back to the Circle G and check the radiator and coolant level for you. Where can I drop you ladies off?"

When she looked at him and then over her shoulder, he knew she was going to refuse. She shifted Lacy in her arms and reached into her back pocket and pulled out her cell phone. After pressing a couple of buttons, her troubled gaze met his. "The battery's dead."

"S'OK, Mommy." Lacy patted her on the cheek. "You can plug it in the car, 'member?"

She hugged her daughter with just a hint of desperation. "I don't have a charger, Lacy honey, this is our new phone. We had to give the other one back."

Her gaze shot to his, and he knew she hadn't meant to mention that last little bit of information. No surprise—women liked to talk, except when a man was trying to find out what he wanted to know. Then all of the sudden, a woman had nothing to say. Her eyes filled with sadness, and for reasons he couldn't understand or explain, he wanted to do something to help.

Why did they have to give their damned phone back?
Where the hell is Lacy's daddy?
And why is Danielle sad?

Before he could ask, she was thanking him for his time and trouble. "We'll be fine. My uncle will be worried if we don't show up soon; he'll come looking for us."

"And he'll know just where to look because?"

The light of irritation in her pretty blue eyes made him feel a whole lot better. He liked a woman with a little temper but as of late preferred redheads to blondes. Blondes only led to trouble. He'd better be wary around this one.

The longer he stared at her, he noticed there was something familiar about her. "I'm trying to help you," he ground out. "Not hurt you."

Had they met before? Had he broken a promise or, worse, her heart? A feeling of dread swamped him.

"Who's your uncle?"

She shrugged and Jesse was starting to get a clearer picture about these two damsels in distress: Lacy's daddy wasn't in the picture; they'd traveled far enough driving a car that either had little or no maintenance done on it or had a crack in the radiator—either option would cause the car to overheat. He wondered if her uncle had any idea that she and Lacy were headed into Pleasure to visit with him.

He asked again, and this time she answered. "James Sullivan, he owns—"

"Sullivan's Diner," he interrupted. *Crap.*

"Thank Mr. Garahan for stopping to help us, Lacy."

"But I..." His words died in his throat as the little girl practically leaped out of her mother's arms reaching for him. "Whoa there, little filly," he warned, taking a step closer.

Breathless belly laughs had the little girl tumbling further out of her mother's arms. He reached for Lacy as her mother changed her grip to keep her daughter from falling on her head. Jesse was faster. And before his head could warn his heart to be careful, the ladies were cradled in the protective circle of his arms, warming him from the inside out.

"You saved me!" The little girl's squeal of excitement was a totally foreign sound to him. Uneasy and unsure of the feelings he wasn't used to experiencing, he settled her safely in her mother's arms and stepped back.

But the pint-sized cowgirl wasn't through. "Leggo, Mommy. I gotta thank my hero."

Jesse rolled his eyes, another phenomenon; men didn't roll their eyes. Hell, he'd only been in the company of these two females for fifteen minutes and already he was acting like someone else. Shaking his head, he held up his hands and said, "My pleasure, ma'am."

Lacy seemed disappointed, but he had other worries on his mind. "You can use my phone." He reached into the breast pocket of his shirt, then offered it to her. "Call your uncle."

He thought she'd refuse and wondered what it was about him that worried her. Most of the women in town were happy to have his help—some more than others. After a few moments, she finally reached for the phone and dialed.

He was surprised when she handed the phone back to him. "Uncle Jimmy wants to talk to you."

He took the phone, met her gaze, and smiled. A deep, gravelly voice on the other end demanded to know what the hell happened and who the hell he was talking to. Putting himself in the other man's shoes, he calmly answered, "This is Jesse Garahan, Mr. Sullivan." He waited for the owner of the diner to say something about the time he and his brothers got caught stealing a pie from the windowsill of the damned diner.

It wasn't long in coming. "What the hell did you do to my niece's car? Don't think I don't remember you and your brothers, Garahan." He felt like he was a kid again, caught with the pie in his hands. Tyler had passed it off to Dylan, and Dylan to him as Sullivan was hollering at them from inside his diner. They'd nearly gotten away, but Jesse had tripped and fallen on top of the pie. They'd had to make it up to Sullivan; their grandfather had insisted.

To this day, he always steered clear of the diner. Too bad. Jimmy Sullivan made the best damned pie in Pleasure.

"Did you hear me?" The man's question brought him back to the present.

"Yes, sir. I'm sorry, sir. I was driving by on my way to town and noticed them stranded by the side of the road. Their car overheated. I'll check things out later. Yes," he answered, wishing he could ease the frown lines between her eyebrows. "Not a problem, I'll make the time."

After reassuring her uncle that he wasn't going to go back and steal her car, or let her stand by the side of the road baking her brain in the hot Texas sun, he handed the phone back to her. "Your uncle wants to talk to you."

She narrowed her eyes and frowned up at him. He shrugged and walked back over to her car. It should be cool enough to add more fluid to the radiator by the time he was on his way back to the Circle G. Damn but her uncle had a way of making him feel like an irresponsible kid again. Lost in thought, he didn't hear her approach.

"Mr. Garahan?"

He looked over his shoulder. "I guess you don't remember me... I'm only a couple of years older than you. Call me Jesse."

She squinted at him. "Vaguely."

Once he'd made the connection, he remembered meeting her at Dawson's; she'd been pestering her uncle for a chance to ride a real horse and not a stupid old pony. The memory made him smile.

"Jesse, then," she grumbled. "If you're sure it's no trouble, would you please drop us off at my uncle's diner?"

"None at all, ma'am." Placing his hand beneath Danielle's elbow, he led her toward his truck. "Can you slide into the middle, Miss Lacy?"

"Uh-huh!"

He waited until they were settled on the front seat before he closed the door and rounded the cab to get in the driver's side. The odd thought that he'd like to keep them and bring them back home to the Circle G had him shaking his head as he slid onto the seat. Closing the door, he waited while Danielle buckled the seat belt around her daughter and then herself, before he put the truck in drive.

Cruising along the road at a more sedate pace, Jesse had the feeling that these two ladies had just changed his life. While they chattered back and forth about the hole in the knee of his jeans and the smear of dirt on his shirtsleeve, he wondered if it was too late to head for the hills and regroup. Women were trouble, and in pairs—dangerous.

He shook that thought from his head. Garahans don't back down and they sure as hell don't retreat. He gripped the steering wheel tighter and concentrated on getting them into town so he could drop them off at Sullivan's Diner. Distance was required if he was going to clear his mind and deal with his reaction to the ladies.

———

Danielle Brockway dug deep for the smile she needed to reassure little Lacy that everything was going to be fine. The big man sitting just inches away from her was just this side of intimidating and wasn't the type of man to be ignored for long. The fierce frown furrowing between his brows wasn't making it easy for her. She wished she could remember meeting him. A quick glance down and she knew it didn't matter how angry or brooding the cowboy appeared, or if she'd known him for years; for her daughter's sake, she'd dance in the truck bed or on the roof of the cab if it would make Lacy smile.

"Mommy, how come we're in Mr. Garahan's truck?"

"Because ours overheated, sweetie."

"He's not a stranger, right, Mommy?"

"That's right," she said, smoothing the hair out of her daughter's eyes. "He knows Uncle Jimmy." She straightened the bubblegum pink cowgirl hat that had been a gift from Lacy's father. Her little girl slept with it clutched in her tiny hands... every night... as if that would bring her daddy back or change his mind.

Lacy had turned inside out with pleasure when her ex had shown up with his parting gift. Lacy hadn't understood at the time that he wasn't coming back. Urging Lacy closer, Danielle relaxed when she felt the warmth of her daughter's little body go slack against her side.

"She's plumb tuckered out." The deep rumbling voice rolled over her like a slow moving wave coming in from the Gulf. She shivered in reaction.

An odd feeling combined with the rush of love she felt for her daughter, a feeling so strong, her head felt light. Breathing deeply, hoping the feeling would subside, she realized that she'd felt something similar once before—trouble was, it had led her to heartache. Lacy mumbled in her sleep and Danielle shook her head. No, that wasn't exactly true; while they had had some difficulties that led to her ex's cleaning out their joint savings account, he'd given her a gift beyond compare. She had a beautiful little girl, who up until he decided he wanted to pursue his bull-riding career solo—without strings or family weighing him down—had been the light of her ex's life.

It had been next to impossible to explain that Lacy's daddy wasn't coming back—ever. The little girl had adopted the same stubborn mind-set Danielle had had since a child—if she wished hard enough for anything, it would happen. She stopped wishing sometime last year. Hard work and determination made things happen.

She brushed her hand on Lacy's cheek, reveling in the familiar silky soft skin and the way her daughter snuggled closer. She might regret her husband's financial decision to invest their life savings in an RV so he could travel the rodeo circuit in style, while she and Lacy lost their home, but she'd never regret giving birth to the only miracle in their lives. Heck, it was only a house, four strong walls on the outside, broken on the inside—like Danielle—since Buddy Brockway lit out toward Amarillo.

"So are you just stopping by for a visit?"

Distracted by the dark feelings swamping her, she shook her head.

"If you don't want me to run off the road, Dani darlin', you'll stop shaking your head and answer me."

Heat of a whole other kind filled her belly to bursting. She tried to tamp down the feelings that roared to the surface with the low, rumbled nickname. He was just being polite by trying to keep his voice down so as not to wake Lacy. He didn't pitch it that way so that it would distract her with feelings she had no business feeling—so soon after her ex. Down that particular road was a wreck of *Titanic* proportions. She had no intention of ever going that way again—but Lord, she was tempted.

Digging deep for the control that had helped her show as little heartache as possible when her ex was packing his brand new RV, Danielle forced a smile. "Sorry, Mr. Garahan. Lacy and I are staying for the summer."

She didn't want the man to know her whole sorry story; she'd nearly slipped when she'd reminded Lacy about the new phone. No reason to confide in a stranger—no matter that she'd decided to trust him because her Uncle Jimmy knew him. It was too hot outside to let Lacy bake in a car that had no air-conditioning with an engine that had decided to call it quits—just like… Stop thinking about that man and blaming him—marriage is a two-way street.

She'd known he wasn't ready to settle down and start a family, but thought he'd change his mind when she told him the good news. Well, she'd been wrong about that too; he had urged her to terminate the pregnancy, citing his budding career as a bull rider and the fact that he was too young to be tied down.

Now that she thought about it, he never asked her how she felt about having a baby once she'd told him she was keeping it. A soft, snuffling sound had her returning to the present and the reality that one simple slipup resulted in—the fairy-sized cowgirl snuggling on the front seat of another handsome-as-sin cowboy's battered pickup truck.

When would she ever learn? Maybe she was destined to make choices that seemed wrong at the time, but ended up with rewards that she'd reap for a lifetime. Her little girl was proof of that. Would there be a reward for getting to know Jesse? Stealing a glance out of the corner of her eye, she got sidetracked by the breadth of his shoulders, the strength in his arms, and the size of his hands as they gripped the wheel. Biting back a moan of sheer pleasure, she could just imagine that getting to know him better would be just this side of amazing, but could she risk letting her head follow where her heart led again?

"Vacations are nice," he offered. "Haven't taken one myself since—well, hell," he laughed, "ever!"

"I find that hard to believe," she soothed, "everyone takes time off now and again, especially during breaks from school."

He glanced in her direction and then back at the road ahead of them. "Easter break and summer vacation meant more time helping our grandfather keep the ranch running smoothly. When you own a spread and raise cattle and horses, you pretty much work twenty-four/seven."

She looked down at the sleeping angel by her side and smiled. "A lot like being a parent."

He chuckled. "I guess it is. Don't have much experience in that area, though."

He frowned, and she wondered what direction his thoughts were headed. She didn't have to wait long to find out.

"I don't know much about kids and can't tell just by looking. How old is she?"

"She'll be four on her next birthday."

He grinned but didn't look away from the curving road. "Sure is tiny… but a pistol for her age."

"Nothing wrong with being a bit on the feisty side."

Jesse stole a look at her this time. "I like women with a little P and V in them."

She shook her head. "What does that stand for?"

"Piss and vinegar."

"Lovely."

"Hey, it was one of my grandfather's favorite say-ings—he had quite a few."

"I'm sorry."

"For?"

Reaching across the sleeping child between them, she touched his elbow. "Your loss." The warmth radiating through the worn fabric of his shirt surprised her, but not as much as the tingling sensation zinging through the tips of her fingers where she touched him. *Careful,* she thought, *this man could be trouble.*

"Thanks."

The simple word pleased her. It had been some time since a handsome man had thanked her for anything. Wrapping the feeling close to her heart, she let the motion of the truck and the rumble of the engine lull her to a semi-aware state. Just ahead was the turn-off Uncle Jimmy had reminded her about. It had been years since she'd seen him and still more since she'd had a vacation—time off, since it wasn't technically fun time. Her plan was to find a job in Pleasure. Knowing she'd have a safe place for her and Lacy to stay for the next little while eased the guilt she still felt for having to up-root her daughter.

"Are there a lot of employment opportunities in Pleasure?"

His quiet laughter caught her off guard. "Well now, there's always work in Pleasure, Texas, especially if you're a rancher, but do you mean paying jobs?"

She crossed her arms beneath her breasts and was about to give the man a snappy comeback but didn't want to wake Lacy. Letting concern for her sleeping child flow through her, she redirected her ire. "Yes, that's what I mean."

He shrugged. "Don't rightly know, but if anyone has their finger on the heartbeat of this town, it's Mavis Beeton. It's hard to say where she'll be this time of day; the woman's a mover and a shaker. I can ask over at the feed store after I drop you off at Sullivan's."

Gratitude soothed the rest of the feathers he'd unknowingly ruffled, but added yet another aspect of the man that appealed to her—his compassion for others. Lord, she'd better be careful to watch her step and guard her heart. She had a feeling that this was one cowboy she'd like to get to know better. For her sake and Lacy's, she'd best remember that history had a way of repeating itself.

Danielle let her mind drift as the scenery slipped past them on the ride into town. Fence posts, grassy land, and barbed wire blurred, merging until she was only aware of colors and shapes. Sounds became muffled and indistinct. Relaxing for the first time in days, she closed her eyes and let her worries go.

"Danielle."

The most marvelous scent clouded her mind. It was a combination of fresh-mown hay and sun-warmed male, with a hint of horse. Sighing in contentment, she lingered in a state of semi-awareness, soaking up the odd feeling of being protected.

"Dani darlin', wake up."

The rumbled request jarred her awake. *Oh God!* She'd fallen asleep, with her precious child between herself and a virtual stranger. Even though her uncle knew him, and Jesse swore they'd met, she should have been on her guard, vigilant and protective. There were no excuses that she could think to offer.

"I'm so sorry!" She sat up and groaned, "I didn't mean to—"

"You were exhausted," Jesse interrupted. "Not a crime in this town." His smile was slow and easy. "I'd wanted a quiet ride into town, and after the both of you stopped snoring, it was."

Mortification crept up from her toes; she could feel her skin flushing as her emotions ran the gamut between embarrassment and self-directed anger. "I normally don't close my eyes during the day," she began, and then what he said sunk in. "Did you say snore?"

His chuckle was beginning to lose its appeal. "Yes, ma'am. You two could be in the Olympics, tag-teaming, if snoring was a sport."

"Mommy?"

Lacy waking up saved the man from a verbal tongue-lashing, and prevented Danielle from having to apologize for something else. "It's all right, honey, we're here."

Jesse had already closed the door on his side and rounded the truck cab to open the passenger door. She wasn't sure if he was being gentlemanly or getting out of striking range. She wouldn't have hit him—although the urge to smack that grin off his face had crossed her mind before she tamped it down—but she wasn't prone to violence, so she let that unfamiliar thought go as soon as it occurred to her.

Focusing on what was important, she smoothed the hair out of her daughter's face and settled Lacy's cowgirl hat back on her head. "Are you ready to see Uncle Jimmy?"

"Can I have pie?"

The deep laughter echoing hers warmed her heart. "I think that can be arranged, sweetie. But first we need to thank Mr. Garahan for rescuing us."

Lacy nodded and scooted across the seat following her. Danielle stood and scooped her daughter into her arms. Before she could open her mouth to speak, Lacy beat her to it. "Thanks for saving us."

If she hadn't been watching him closely, Danielle would have missed the odd look in their rescuer's dark eyes. It was an emotion she hadn't seen in a man's eyes in a long while. Too nervous to put a name to the emotion or admit that a similar one was sweeping through her, she added her thanks.

"My pleasure, little lady," he replied, touching the tip of his finger to Lacy's button nose. "It's part of the Cowboy Code to rescue damsels in distress."

Gratitude filled her, but the look in Jesse's eyes haunted her, reminding her of the rift in her life and the gut-burning knowledge that Lacy's daddy had signed over his rights to be a part of Lacy's life along with the dissolution of their marriage. Deep down she knew why—he simply no longer cared about either one of them.

"What's a code?" Lacy asked.

Pushing his hat to the back of his head, he grinned. "It's like a law or rules that us cowboys have to follow."

"Mommy gots rules—no stuffing frogs in my pockets."

Their eyes met over Lacy's head. Danielle saw his facial muscles twitch and knew he wanted to smile, but he kept his expression serious for Lacy's sake.

He nodded. "Well, your mom's right, you don't want to squish 'em, do you?"

Lacy shook her head.

"I bet I have more rules to follow."

"Why?"

"I'm bigger," he said with a laugh.

Lacy frowned. "Tell me another one."

He grinned at the little girl. "A cowboy should never shoot first—"

"Do you have a gun?" Lacy wiggled in her mother's arms trying to see if he did.

"Yes, ma'am," he answered, his lips twitching. "I keep a shotgun under the front seat. Pleasure's been known to have wolves, coyotes, and snakes."

Danielle's heart began to pound at the thought. Why hadn't she remembered that they were going to be living in the country and not the urban life she was used to?

"Did you shoot anybody today?"

Jesse laughed a full, rich sound that vibrated from deep within his impressive chest cavity. "Uh... no, ma'am. I only shoot to protect our herd."

"Do you have buffalo?"

Watching the way her daughter lit up like a firefly at twilight as Jesse answered her, Danielle realized just how deeply the scars her ex's leaving would go. It was just a matter of time before Lacy would start coming home with tales of other kids' dads taking them places, showing them how to play ball or ride a horse. The list would be endless, and her guilt for having failed to save her marriage, thereby keeping Lacy's daddy as an active part of their little girl's life, would be soul deep.

"Don't you want to know the rest of the rule?"

Without thinking Danielle answered first, "Yes."

His eyes twinkled as his beautifully sculpted lips slowly lifted into a smile that had her heart picking up the beat, pounding in her breast. He winked at her, and said, "Well, there are a couple of cowboy codes out there, but my grandfather was real partial to Gene Autry, so he had us memorize the list as kids: never hit a smaller man or take unfair advantage."

Disappointment arrowed through her. "So you're saying that it's a Hollywood thing, this code?" She couldn't believe it; she'd thought it was something handed down from generation to generation.

"It was one we could relate to, having watched videos and DVDs of *The Gene Autry Show* as kids." Looking up into her eyes, he added, "We never met our great-grandfather, but he had a set of rules that was handed down to us. The list is similar. Not as well-known, but the heart of the list is the same."

"If I don't shoot nobody, can I be a real cowgirl?" Lacy's gaze was riveted to Jesse's, waiting for his answer.

"Well there, little filly, you've already got the boots and hat, all you need is a horse."

Her daughter giggled and bounced in Danielle's arms. "I wanna ride. Will you teach me... pretty please?"

He hesitated and she hoped her daughter wouldn't have a hard time when Lacy realized that they probably wouldn't be seeing their rescuer again. Ranchers were busy people and normally didn't have time during the middle of the day to visit. Once Danielle explained her situation to her uncle, she and Lacy would be busy too. The hard part would be convincing her uncle that she wouldn't let him take care of them indefinitely.

As if he'd read her mind or heard her unspoken

thoughts, Jesse looked at her and rocked back on his boot heels. "Well now, that depends on your mother."

Unexpected. She looked down into Lacy's upturned face and wondered if she could trust this man with one of her daughter's dreams. "If you're offering to teach Lacy, we'd be obliged, but I don't have a lot of extra cash right now—"

His frown was fierce and Danielle wondered about the temper that might go along with it. The Irish were known for their hair-trigger tempers. Her ex had had one; would Jesse?

It simmered in his gaze, and he clenched and un-clenched his hands before putting them in his pockets, as if needing to do something with them. Their eyes met and she sensed that Jesse had better control of his temper. Relief flowed through her.

"Lessons are free," he said to Danielle. Turning to Lacy, he added, "I'd be happy to teach you, Miss Lacy."

Lacy placed her hands on either side of her mother's face and turned Danielle's head until they were eye-to-eye. "Can I, Mommy, can I, can I?"

Danielle chuckled. "I don't see why not, but we don't have a horse, sweetie, or a car."

Lacy slid one hand around her mother's neck and leaned the side of her little head against Danielle's. "Do you got horses in your herd?"

Jesse smiled. "We have horses, but our herd is made up of longhorns, beef cattle."

Lacy's eyes grew wide. "Can I see 'em? Can we ride now?"

He chuckled and shook his head. "I've got to get on over to Dawson's and then on to Harrison's feed store to take care of business. From there I have to check your car and then I've got to get on back to the Circle G to help my brothers in the south pasture."

Lacy's shoulders slumped and Danielle's heart ached for her. This was how it had always been with Lacy's father. She wanted to blast the man for raising her daughter's hopes but didn't have the chance because Lacy spoke up.

"Maybe tomorrow?"

He seemed to be thinking about it. "We usually finish our daytime chores around supper time. I might be able to squeeze in some time for a lesson before the evening chores."

"OK," Lacy said, before asking, "all right, Mommy?"

"We don't have a car right now, honey. Maybe another time."

Jesse nodded. "Your car is probably just low on coolant, but how about if I come into town and pick you ladies up? I can give you a tour around the ranch and then show little Miss Lacy how to ride." He tipped his hat forward and touched the brim. "If you ladies will excuse me, I've got to head on over to Dawson's."

"Promise?" Lacy called out.

"Yes, ma'am!" he answered before getting into the truck and driving away.

Danielle and Lacy watched their rescuer drive away. When he was gone, Lacy patted the side of Danielle's face to get her attention. "Mommy, is it tomorrow yet?"

Chapter 2

DANIELLE KNEW JUST HOW HER DAUGHTER FELT—AS if someone had given them a shiny, red balloon and then let all of the air out of it. Sighing, she wished it was tomorrow already too, but knew that wishing and hoping didn't always get you what you need in life. She bent down and scooped Lacy into her arms, and finally looked at the building where Jesse had dropped them off. The weathered clapboard siding needed a fresh coat of paint and had her wondering if her uncle's business was doing well. She should have thought about that before making the long drive to Pleasure.

A niggling worry started to unsettle her stomach. It had been a long time since she'd spent a couple of summers here, when her parents were trying to sort out their marriage. Her uncle had kept her busy and given out hugs of encouragement while he taught her how to make pie.

Time had a way of passing by quickly. She hadn't seen him since she'd fallen hard and fast for that sweet-talking, bull-riding cowboy. Once the doctor had placed her newborn baby in her arms, everything else ceased to exist... ceased to matter. Lacy was her world. Maybe that was one of the reasons her ex had become distant; maybe she should have paid more attention to him.

"Mommy," Lacy piped up. "I'm hungry."

Danielle buried the worries and problems she could no longer do anything about deep, and focused her attention on the light of her life. "Why don't we go on in and say hello. I haven't seen my uncle in a long time," she said. "And I know he'd love to meet you."

"'Cause I'm 'cocious?"

"That's right, baby girl, you are precocious."

"Mommy," Lacy said again as they paused halfway up the steps, "what's 'cocious mean again?"

"Too smart for your own britches but cute as a bug," a deep voice boomed from just inside the screen door.

Danielle smiled. "Uncle Jimmy!"

Her uncle opened the door wide, and swept the two of them into his beefy arms, hugging them both tight, until Lacy started squirming. "You're squishing me."

He eased up on his hold and chuckled. "Sorry," he said, setting them both back on their feet, "but I'm just plum tickled that my favorite niece stopped by and brought an itty-bitty cowgirl to visit me."

Standing back and holding the door open wide, he ushered them inside. Danielle's gaze swept the room. Everything looked just the same and felt like home. "So," she said slowly, "do you have any chocolate pie?"

Jimmy laughed and grinned down at them. "I might have baked one this morning and whipped up some cream to make it pretty… just like someone I know likes it, but I think introductions are in order first."

Danielle gave herself a mental head slap. "Sorry, it's been a rough morning and a long trip." Squatting down next to Lacy, she eased the hat from her little girl's head and smoothed the hair off her face. "Jimmy Sullivan, I'd like to introduce you to my darling daughter, Lacy

Brockway." Straightening up, holding Lacy by the hand, she smiled. "And this is your Uncle Jimmy."

"Unca Jimmy, don't you 'member if you baked pie?"

"Uncle Jimmy's just teasing because he knows how much I love his chocolate pie."

"My mommy bakes pies too."

"I taught her the secret to my famous piecrust when she was just about your size." He led them into the kitchen, settling them at the oak pedestal table while he opened cabinets, gathering plates, cups, and utensils. "I could teach you too."

Lacy was watching Uncle Jimmy move around the sunny room like a baby bird, curious and hopeful that she'd be fed soon. "OK." After a moment, her daughter couldn't contain her excitement. "Are you gonna feed us pie? Do you gots any other flavors 'cept chocolate?"

Jimmy looked over his shoulder at Danielle and the little girl perched on her lap and shook his head. "You sound just like your momma." His sigh was heartfelt. "She was no bigger than a minute the first time I saw her."

Lacy grabbed her mother's wrist and twisted it so she could see the watch Danielle always wore. Staring at the watch face, she wrinkled her nose and said, "Gosh, that's little."

He agreed. "But pretty as a June bug."

Her daughter giggled and settled against her, relaxing. Danielle's eyes filled and she had to blink the moisture away. She didn't want her uncle to suspect that all was not right with her world.

"I like bugs."

"Wouldn't be any grandniece of mine if you didn't," Jimmy said, walking over to the table with a pie in each hand. "Now then, ladies," he rumbled, "time to decide if you want chocolate or cherry."

Lacy looked from one dish to the other and then up at him. "Can't I have both?"

"A woman after my own heart," he rumbled, setting the pies in the middle of the table. "How big a piece can you eat?"

Danielle grinned. "She can have a sliver of each." When her uncle started slicing into the first pie, she added, "I'd like the same too, please."

After he served up two plates of pie and poured out two glasses of milk, he sat down across from Danielle and crossed his arms in front of his broad chest. "I'm delighted to finally meet my grandniece, and I only have one question—what took you so long?"

Danielle had called every couple of months and sent pictures in between those phone conversations, but it wasn't the same as visiting. "We were just so busy." That sounded like a lame excuse, but it was all she had to offer without telling her uncle about the whirlwind romance, the unplanned pregnancy, and the devastating divorce. Their eyes met and she realized she didn't have to explain anything after all.

"I knew it would take some time before you came on out for a visit. Times are lean and you were so wrapped up in being a new mother that you weren't thinking about much else, let alone your crusty old uncle."

Danielle blinked back tears for the second time in the last half hour. "You are not crusty and I was so busy, I couldn't see straight. I'm sorry."

He just smiled and shook his head. "New parents are supposed to be caught up with their little ones. Don't you worry none, June bug. I figured I'd see you sooner or later, and until I did, we had our talks on the phone and I had the pictures you sent."

Screwing her courage up, she met her uncle's gaze and confessed, "Buddy left us."

He nodded. "Not surprising. That young man's first love was and will always be the rodeo. She's a tough mistress."

"I know." Her ex was like a shooting star. Blazing hot and glorious while he was in her life. Now that he'd moved on, only a trace of him was left behind—their beautiful daughter. And for that she'd be forever grateful. "It's hard."

While they ate, she wondered where she would go from here. What would lie ahead for her and little Lacy? She had no intention of living off of her uncle; she needed a job. Time to tell him, before he started making his own plans; her uncle had a way of taking over.

Danielle wiped Lacy's mouth with a paper napkin. "I've really missed you and your pie, Uncle Jimmy."

"I liked the chocolate best," Lacy confided as she reached for her milk.

He was smiling when he said, "Nothing I like better than feeding people who appreciate good food."

While he and Lacy chatted, she wracked her brain but couldn't think of a way to casually ask about finding work. Better just to ask and get right to the heart of the matter. "So, I understand there's a lot of work in town if you're a rancher."

Jimmy nodded. "We have a number of ranches on the outskirts of town. Beef cattle mostly, but some raise horses too."

"But what about other jobs?"

Looking from Danielle to her daughter, her uncle sighed. "You just arrived." He frowned at her. "Are you going to be difficult?" She shrugged and he sighed loudly. "Times are a bit lean right now, but I could ask around, introduce you to folks you haven't seen in a decade."

Danielle smiled. "Thanks, Uncle Jimmy."

He pushed his chair back to stand. "No arguments now, but you and little June bug are staying with me."

"Just until we get on our feet." Danielle hugged her baby girl to her heart.

"We'll see," was her uncle's cryptic reply. "Come on, ladies, I'll give you the grand tour of Sullivan's."

While Uncle Jimmy led them through the kitchen to the front of his diner, Danielle wondered if he'd heard the scuttlebutt about her ex and how well he'd been doing since their divorce. With her mind on other things, she didn't hear Lacy talking until her daughter tugged on her hand.

"Mommy!"

"I'm sorry, sweetie, I was letting my mind wander."

"You two ladies must be tired. I can show you around later."

"No, it's fine, Uncle Jimmy." Danielle reached for Lacy's hand. "We'd love to see the rest of the diner."

He stared at her, and for a moment, she thought he'd argue, but something in her gaze must have convinced him she was on the level with him. "Follow me."

They walked through the swinging doors to the main dining room, and there it was, just as she remembered— the etching on the plate glass window facing the street. "I know you told me the last time I spent the summer with you, but how old is that window?"

Jimmy smiled. "'Bout seventy or eighty years old. That's the first thing I saw when I pulled up out front—the etched glass. Had to have the place; didn't know what I'd turn it into, but I had a couple of ideas."

Lacy looked from her mother to Uncle Jimmy and scrunched her nose. "That's really old!"

They both laughed at the innocence of youth. "Yes, it is, little lady."

Letting her glance sweep the room, Danielle noticed the oak tables, set in various groupings of two, four, and six. Right in the middle of every table was a glass bottle filled with colorful flowers. "I love the wildflowers in the mismatched jars."

"Hobby of mine, collecting old condiment jars. Some are clear, brown, blue, or green. I like 'em all." He shook his head. "It's a lot of work, though, cutting all those damned flowers and changing them in and out of those jars every couple of days."

Lacy tugged on her mother's hand until Danielle bent down. She cupped her hands around her mother's ear and whispered, "Unca Jimmy just said a bad word."

Danielle smiled and said, "Yes, he did, sweetie."

"Sorry." He shook his head. "I'm not used to little ones. I'll have to pay better attention."

"S'OK, but you'd better 'member. Mommy's strict about bad words."

Her uncle didn't laugh at her daughter, and she remembered that he had never laughed at her—he'd laughed with her plenty of times, but never at her. Just one item on the long list of reasons she loved her uncle and had always felt welcome here.

"Can I see upstairs?"

Her uncle hesitated. "It's mighty hot up there today, maybe we can come back later tonight when the sun's gone down for the night or first thing tomorrow."

Lacy followed behind her mother like a little puppy, stopping where she stopped, touching what Danielle touched. She was proud that her little one mimicked the way she did things, knowing that she was setting an example that Lacy should and would follow.

"We're not sleeping here?"

Jimmy shook his head. "Not in the diner. I've got a house just outside of town, on a nice quiet dead-end street. No streetlights, so you can see every single star that'll be shining high in the Texas sky come evening time."

Lacy hung on every word and Danielle's heart filled with admiration for her uncle. He always knew just what to say and how to say it so people—the tall and the small—relaxed in his company. It was his gift.

Thinking of his way with people, she looked down at her watch and wondered where all of his customers were. "How come there are no customers?"

He shrugged. "Afternoons are real slow in town, but things pick up later in the week. I'm mostly busy with the breakfast crowd these days, so I close up right around three o'clock every day."

"So you're OK then? The diner's doing well?"

He brushed a strand of hair out of her eyes and pressed his lips to her forehead, then did the same with Lacy. "I'm fine and the diner's doing better than good. You can stop worrying about your old uncle now."

Relief filled her, tangling with the raw feelings roiling inside of her for having to leave the town she'd spent the whole of her married life in. She needed to recharge, but now wasn't the time. She had her daughter to think of first. At least Lacy had one parent who cared.

Setting those dangerous thoughts aside, she smiled up at Uncle Jimmy. "I'm glad; it's a full-time job just worrying about Lacy, let alone my favorite uncle."

"I'm just about finished up here. I need to straighten out the kitchen and make sure I have everything I need for the breakfast crowd."

"Can I help?" Danielle asked.

He nodded. "Of course, just like always."

She smiled when Lacy cried, "Me too!"

Uncle Jimmy's booming laughter filled a part of the void inside of her. *It is going to be all right.* She let Lacy pull her toward the kitchen.

Chapter 3

JESSE GRINNED AS HE OPENED THE DOOR TO DAWSON'S. Some things never changed and it lightened his heart. Life seemed to be passing him by out at the ranch, with his brothers settling in with the women they'd chosen to spend the rest of their lives with. It was good for them, but not for him.

A creature of habit, it was a little unnerving to have female voices added to the mix in the mornings. He missed the days when he and his brothers would wake up and either say good morning or punch one another on their way to the coffeepot. Not that they'd fight that early in the day every day, but at some point in every day, the Garahan brothers had been known to blow off a little steam. A nice fistfight usually did the trick.

But now his brothers were different. If he had to put his finger on it, he'd say they were content, happy—and smiling all the damn time! It set his teeth on edge each and every morning when his brothers came downstairs with shit-eating grins on their faces. He knew they'd both had themselves a time the night before—hell, he had ears… and their women had lungs.

Disgusted with the train of his thoughts, he focused on his surroundings and the fact that the entrance to the hardware side of Dawson's. Barrels lined up lying on their sides, each one filled with nails, screws, nuts, bolts, or washers. He breathed in and the air smelled the same.

He couldn't put his finger on it, so he closed his eyes, took another sniff, and grinned. "Fresh-cut pine, kerosene, and oil, same as always."

"Well which one do you want?" A familiar voice interrupted his trip down memory lane.

His eyes shot open and he grinned. "Actually, I'm here to pay down our bill, Miss Pam."

The older woman waved her hand in his general direction. "I know you're good for it. You can always count on a Garahan."

His throat tightened as gratitude swamped him. He nodded until the emotion eased up and he could speak. "You know it, but it's been too high and we've been working hard to bring it back down to a controllable level."

"Times are tough all over, Jesse. That's why us town folk have to stick together to help out our neighbors—the ranchers."

As if she could sense that her words affected him, she reached out and patted him on the arm. "Well, come on back to my office and we'll settle up what you've got with you today and see where the Circle G Ranch is on my books."

He touched the brim of his hat. "Much obliged, Miss Pam."

They made their way past the strategically stacked displays of varnish and paint, Jesse making a mental note to pick some up in a couple of weeks—that is, if Dylan's current side job paid him on time. His brother still took on a job or two as a carpenter for hire in the evenings. He grinned; that was how Ronnie had met his older brother, when he'd agreed to do the repairs to her shop after some local teenagers had destroyed the place.

When Jesse and Miss Dawson reached the back of the store and her little hole-in-the-wall office, he started to sweat. He hated owing people but knew they'd never keep the ranch going without Miss Dawson extending them credit. Shoving those thoughts aside, he said, "It's not a lot—"

"Whatever you have is fine with me," Pam told him. "It's the principle of the thing that's important here. You and your brothers have an open tab and you're paying on it, whatever you can, whenever you can." She crossed her arms in front of her, as if daring him to contradict her.

His momma raised him right. "Yes, ma'am." They settled up and he tipped his hat. "Thank you, Miss Pam."

She shook her head at him. "You know that makes me feel really old when you call me that."

He shrugged. "Old habits die hard. My grandpa would have smacked me in the back of the head if I didn't pay proper respect to you."

Her sad smile had him realizing he and his brothers weren't the only ones who missed Hank Garahan. She blinked and cleared her throat. "Well now. What else can I do for you today?"

He put his hands in his back pockets and rocked back on his boot heels. "Could you or your sister use another clerk here at Dawson's?"

He guessed from the surprised look on her face that his question hadn't been what she'd been expecting from him. "We've only got two part-timers on my side of the store, but in a pinch, there are times I could use one more body. Why?"

He shrugged. "Just asking."

She wasn't having any of it. Frowning up at him, she

started tapping the toe of her boot. "You'd best tell me now; you know I'll find out as soon as Mavis drops by. The woman knows everything."

That had him grinning. He'd been hoping to run into her at Dawson's. "I stopped to help someone on my way into town. Her car overheated."

"And she's looking for work in town? A stranger?"

"She is now but didn't used to be." He shifted from one foot to the other, unnerved by her close scrutiny.

"Well, this is like pulling teeth. Save us both the time it'd require for me to keep asking while you keep hemming and hawing, and just tell me."

He laughed and told her what happened on his ride into town.

"Well then, she's got to be Jimmy Sullivan's niece Danielle, the one who married that bull rider a few years back. Jimmy's right proud of her, though she hasn't been to see him in half a dozen years."

"Well, since you know her," he began, intrigued by the prospect of keeping the curvy little blonde close by so he could get to know her better, "do you know of anybody in town with a job opening?"

"Like I said, my side of the store—the hardware side—doesn't really need too many people working at one time, but on the food side—my sister's side—well now she just might need a new cashier," she said, tapping her cheek with her finger. "Let's go ask her."

A half an hour later, Jesse had planted the bug in enough ears about Danielle Brockway looking for a job that the network of busybodies should be on full alert and looking. His work here was done, but now he was an hour or so behind schedule.

Thinking and driving, he nearly shot past the disabled car at the side of the road. Pulling a quick one-eighty, he put it in park and walked over to Danielle's car. As expected, the engine block had cooled enough that it was easy to see what had caused the vehicle to overheat: she was low on coolant and the engine nearly seized. Ranchers were pretty much a self-sufficient bunch; since that one time he'd cooked the engine and cracked the head on his grandfather's truck, Jesse made sure he always had a gallon of water and couple bottles of 10W40. He always took care to keep his engine running cool and lubed. It was too expensive to keep replacing the damned heads all of the time, and unless you had a connection over in Mesquite, you paid through the nose for a new one—forget about the price for a new engine block; he'd park the darned truck and go back to riding his horse everywhere rather than pay for a new engine.

He'd have to ask Tyler or Dylan to help him drop off the car tonight. It would be really late, but at least he'd more than fulfilled his promise to the ladies... well, one of his promises. He called Sullivan's Diner and left a message for Danielle that her car was good to go and that he'd drop it off later.

Life was funny; today was the first time Sullivan had spoken to a Garahan in fifteen years and all because Jesse had stopped to do a good deed. Maybe Sullivan would give him a clean slate. *Yeah,* he thought... *not happening.* Chuckling to himself, he got out, opened the gate, and drove on through. Putting the truck in park, he let his mind drift while he got out to shut the gate.

When the ranch house came into view, he just had to stop and stare. Emily and Ronnie must have been at it again. Flowers spilled out of planters at the foot of the front steps and there were planters sitting on top of the porch railing.

He shook his head. "Man… what is it with women and flowers? Couldn't they plant trees instead? We could use the shade over by the barn where the old Red Oak died."

No one was around when he pulled up out back, so he didn't bother going inside. Once he'd saddled up, he rode out to the southern pasture to catch up to his brothers.

"'Bout time you showed up, Bro," Dylan called out. "We needed you about an hour ago."

"Sorry, had to rescue a damsel in distress on my way into town."

When he didn't say anymore, his brothers gradually made their way over to where Jesse was checking the herd. With a brother on each side of him, he felt hemmed in. Familiar with the tactic, he pulled back on the reins, but his brothers had anticipated the move and boxed him in.

Tyler grinned at him. "Is she a redhead?"

Dylan shook his head. "Bet she's got long dark hair, like my bride."

Jesse wanted to hang on to the irritation building inside of him, fan the flames until he could work up to a serious mad, but the way his brothers started arguing over which hair color was the sexiest had him chuckling.

"You're both whipped and don't even know it."

"No way," Tyler disagreed.

"Who's whipped?" Dylan demanded.

Jesse just shook his head and his smile widened. "The two of you. Hell, no sense trying to pretty it up when the proof is staring you in the face. Those two women—really fine women I might add—have the both of you wrapped up so tight around their fingers it's a wonder either of you can breathe."

Tyler's face turned an interesting shade of red while Dylan's jaw clenched. *Now we're getting somewhere*, Jesse thought. *Both brothers ready to take a swing at me. Hell yeah! I'm ready to rumble.*

But before he could tense up, preparing to fight back, Tyler and Dylan did something completely out of character for either of them—they shrugged and eased away from Jesse. *Damn.*

Mumbling to himself, he urged his mount over toward the group of steer on the next rise—just part of the job, ensuring that their herd was in prime health. Every once in a while, one of their animals would show signs of lameness and they'd have to do a careful inspection of the animal's hooves, checking for the cause of the injury. Most often it was caused by a rock, a bit of wood, or a thorn. Removing the object and cleaning and trimming the hoof before using antiseptic was the rule of thumb on the Circle G. They didn't prescribe to the notion of additives in their herd's feed, so their only other choice was to call the vet—that was expensive and used for rare instances where there really was something that the brothers couldn't handle.

Breathing deeply, Jesse surveyed the land around him and smiled. They'd continued the Garahan tradition of cultivating their pastureland with a mixture of native grasses: little bluestems, Bermuda grass, crabgrass, millet, and love grass in the warm season, and cereal rye, rye, and wheat in the cool season for extended spring grazing.

They'd never really been certain about Grandpa's

insistence that the love grass would encourage fertility and the millet would discourage prussic acid. But their herd produced healthy offspring every spring, and they'd been careful not to plant any sorghum or Sudan grass, both known to contain prussic acid—the deadly, fast-acting plant toxin—so there hadn't been a reason to doubt his word.

"And most folks think a cowboy's life is easy." Still smiling, Jesse made his way through the longhorns grazing peacefully on the rise. Satisfied that everything was normal, he moved to the next section he'd been assigned that morning. Danielle and Lacy weren't far from his thoughts. Distracted, he fought to regain his balance by drawing in a breath and looking around him. A deep calm washed over him, because as far as he could see lay Garahan land. Pride filled him. They were holding on to the Circle G and contributing to the heritage of the great state of Texas by continuing to raise longhorns. They'd thought about crossbreeding, but in the end hadn't because so many of their herd's qualities were appealing; longhorns are intelligent, gentle, and long lived. The cows are productive and protective, while the bulls are strong and sturdy with lean, flavorful beef. Though he'd learned early on that they weren't pets, he had named a few when he was younger.

Even though the calving season was over, they were still vigilant, as far as keeping an eye out for the calves that would somehow manage to get caught in places they couldn't get out of. They were easy to find, because the calf's mother would either be doing her best to extricate her young or bawling like crazy to let one of them know there was a problem.

A man of the land and committed to their way of life, Jesse wondered what it would be like to have a woman by his side, just as determined. Would she be like Emily—not all that savvy when it came to raising stock but an absolute whiz with accounting and pinching pennies? Maybe she would be more like Ronnie, a great cook but also at home in the saddle.

His thoughts drifted back to the pretty little blonde and her pink, pixie daughter. Something about Danielle as an adult reminded him of her when she was younger. The sound of rapidly approaching horses drew him back to the present. He turned toward the sound. "What's up?"

"Didn't you hear us calling you?" Dylan demanded.

He shrugged.

"We're finished out here, heading back to the ranch." Tyler asked, "You coming?"

"Yeah. Herd looks good."

"It was a productive spring," Tyler agreed. "Now all we have to do is keep our eyes peeled and our ears on."

"We'll be ready for trouble," Dylan said. "Not that we expect any, but it pays to be ready for anything."

"Have we alienated anyone in town lately?"

Dylan grinned. "Weren't you the last one in town, Bro?"

Jesse shrugged. "I paid down some of the feed bill and what we owed at Dawson's."

Tyler was watching him like a hawk about to snag a fat mouse on the fly. "You didn't stop off at the bank to pick a fight with Mike Baker, did you?"

"Hell no," Jesse grumbled. "I haven't talked to him since before his sister tried to get her hooks into your hide a little while back."

Tyler clenched his jaw.

Dylan snickered. "She was persistent. You have to give her that much."

"Just don't let Emily hear you say that," Jesse warned. "She's a mite protective of our big brother."

That had their brother relaxing his facial muscles, easing the tension in his jaw. "Works both ways."

Jesse picked up on the possibility that there had been trouble in town at the Lucky Star. "Did someone try to break into the club again?"

Dylan shook his head. "Not that we've heard. That new dancer Jolene hired seems to be working out."

Jesse was ready, willing, and able to step into his brother's shoes—make that spandex briefs—if the ladies over at the Lucky Star needed him, but so far they hadn't needed him to. "Maybe I should call her."

Tyler grinned. "Jolene is a woman of her word; she'll call if they need you, Bro. Besides," he said, turning his horse toward home, "things are mighty busy around here. We need you. Jolene understands."

Bummed that he was the only Garahan who hadn't been up on the stage and the recipient of all of that feminine adoration rankled, but he wouldn't let his brothers know or they'd ride his case mercilessly. Hell, he would if the tables were turned—it's what brothers do.

"No problem." He waited a moment then followed after his brothers. They hadn't asked about the woman he'd rescued on the way into town. He figured they knew he *wanted* to tell them about Danielle… *the bastards*. He grinned.

The closer they got to home, the more he was convinced that they were messing with him—what else was new? He was the youngest, low man on the totem pole, the one who always had to ride shotgun so that he could get out and open and shut the gate.

"Hell."

By the time he'd made it back to the barn, he was only five minutes behind his brothers and the last to care for his horse.

As he walked into the kitchen, Dylan was leaning with his back against the counter and boots crossed at the ankles. "She was a blonde, wasn't she?"

Jesse laughed. He couldn't help it; he'd won their little game because Dylan asked before Jesse could offer any information about the damsel in distress. "And had a way of filling out her jeans that would make a man sit up and beg."

"That good?" Tyler asked, pulling a casserole dish out of the refrigerator before turning toward Dylan. "What was it that Ronnie said was in this dish again?"

"Stuffed eggplant."

"Mom never made anything with egg plants in it," Jesse grumbled.

"It's got nothing to do with eggs, brainless," Tyler added. "I've only had it breaded and fried. What's it stuffed with?"

Dylan grinned. "Really gooey, tasty cheese. Try it," he urged his brothers. "It tastes great."

"That's because Ronnie cooked it."

Dylan shrugged. "My wife's a great cook."

The brothers agreed she'd saved them from starvation and Jesse's rotgut chili.

"Yeah," Jesse said, "but she can't make chili."

Dylan grinned. "She's been working on perfecting a recipe—just for you."

"Really? Cool." Nobody'd done that since their mom had died. Their mom knew what each one of them considered his favorite meal, pie, cake, cookies, snacks, and flavor of soda. She was one in a million. Sometimes he missed her so much, his chest ached.

He rubbed at the dull, hollow feeling creeping inside of him. Hard to believe it had been nearly twenty years since she'd been gone. He'd buried the hurt deep, so it wouldn't catch him off guard as often as it had when he was a kid, but that didn't mean he didn't think about her or feel her loss.

"Hey," Dylan said, poking him in the back, "you don't need to eat it if you don't want to. There's plenty of leftovers or sandwich fixin's in the fridge."

Jesse blinked and frowned at his brothers. "Did you try it yet, Tyler?"

"I'm getting to it."

"It's even good cold," Dylan said, grabbing a clean fork, spearing the eggplant, and shoving it toward Jesse.

He took it, stared down at it, then shrugged and grabbed the fork. Bold, spicy flavors danced on his tongue, mingling with cold cheese he couldn't identify and what he guessed was the innocuous taste of the eggplant. "Not bad." He grinned. "It'd probably taste better if we nuked it." Moving out of striking range of Dylan's long reach, he washed up and dug into the casserole and heaped some on a dish.

With the hot, fragrant plate of cheese-filled eggplant in front of him, Jesse realized that he owed Emily and Ronnie; they'd brought a sense of hearth and home back to the Circle G. The only thing missing was a woman he could call his own.

"Hell," he mumbled, forking another bite of food into his mouth. "Don't need one."

Tyler tossed a hunk of bread at Jesse. "What don't you need?"

Jesse saw the movement out of the corner of his eye, reached up, snagged the bread with one hand, and stopped the plate of butter Dylan had slid toward him with unerring accuracy. It was good to be part of the family, even if he was feeling a little left out as of late.

"Nothing. Hey, Dylan, where's Ronnie today?" Jesse asked.

"Getting ready to open up for business next week."

"The shop looks great," Jesse said. "If I hadn't seen the damage myself, I never would have believed it."

Dylan grinned. "It brought the woman I love into my life."

Tyler chuckled. "And here I thought it was when you tossed your lasso around her."

"Yeah," Jesse answered, "and reeled her in!"

Dylan accepted their ribbing good-naturedly. Hell, everything about his brother seemed to be positive and upbeat since he married Ronnie DelVecchio. *Go figure.*

Turning to Tyler he asked, "Is Emily coming home late tonight?"

The satisfied smile on the oldest brother's face should have annoyed him, but instead, he was happy for him.

Tyler finally answered, "I'll be driving into town to pick her up at closing time."

"What about you, Dylan? Are you driving into town to pick up your wife?" Jesse got a kick out of saying that; she was the first Garahan bride for their generation and kind of cool.

Dylan locked gazes with Tyler, and Jesse knew what his brothers were thinking, planning, and going to be doing a few hours from now. "Damn!"

"Go find your own woman," Dylan said.

"Maybe I've already found one."

"Really?" Tyler tried to sound disinterested, but Jesse could tell he finally had the attention of both brothers. No small feat.

"Hey, I already told you all about her."

"The hell you did," Dylan grumbled. "Wait—was this the damsel you saved this morning riding into town?"

Jesse smiled. "So you were listening."

"Hell, Jess," Tyler ground out. "We always hear you. Sometimes we pay attention."

Dylan leaned back in his chair. "So she's blonde, curvy, and pretty?"

"'Bout covers it," Jesse said, "well, except for little Lacy."

"She has a pet named Lacy?"

Jesse grinned and pushed away from his place, sighing in contentment because the food had been great and filled the hole in his belly. "Nope, a little pink cowgirl. I need one of you to follow me to Sullivan's so I can drop off her car."

His brothers grinned at one another, and Tyler drawled, "It'll cost you, Bro."

It was after ten when they dropped off the car.

Chapter 4

RIDING TO HER UNCLE'S HOUSE, DANIELLE WAS THINKing about how much her life had changed since the last time she'd stayed with her uncle. She'd finished school, graduated with honors, met and married the love of her life, and was a mom.

But what she'd felt for her ex paled in comparison to the residual effect the tall, dark, and handsome cowboy who'd rescued them had on her. But right now wasn't a good time to let herself be distracted by another cowboy. She had more important things in her life to worry about now: Lacy, first and foremost. Everything else just wasn't important.

But the dark-eyed, dreamy cowboy filled her mind again, and for a brief moment, she wondered what it would be like to be held in his arms again. That brief touch, when he'd reached out to save Lacy from falling out of Danielle's arms, was imprinted on her heart. He'd been strong, solid, and larger than life—heaven help her, it felt as if they belonged there.

But there were things to consider, other than where she'd begin if she had Jesse all to herself for just ten minutes... you could pack a lifetime into ten minutes. But would she really have the nerve to ask him to park his boots under her bed? The image of his broad-shouldered frame standing in the doorway to her bedroom had her breath catching and her heart tumbling.

"Mommy?" Lacy tugged on her sleeve. "When will we get there?"

Danielle buried the image and glanced over at her uncle. "Five minutes?" She waited for a sign from him that she had been right.

He smiled. "You still remember."

She reached across Lacy's head to lay her hand on his forearm. "I spent the best summers of my life here with you."

It had always been that easy for her; their relationship had been based on love and trust from the time she was old enough to toddle into his waiting arms... and then he fed her pie. Life without pie wasn't any kind of life at all. For those that hadn't experienced manna from heaven—aka Sullivan's chocolate pie à la mode—it was something that could not be explained. One had to experience firsthand the taste sensation of flaky perfection filled with smooth chocolatey goodness, finished off with his special whipped topping, a combination of crème fraîche—which tastes similar to sour cream but not quite as sour—and heavy cream.

Perfection. There just wasn't anything else that she could think of to explain the tasty goodness and sensation of the chocolate filling melting on her tongue.

"Mommy?" Lacy asked as they turned onto the familiar road.

"Yes, sweet pea?"

"Can we go to the Circle G tonight? I wanna see cowboy Jesse."

Her heart stopped, then slowly, painfully, started beating again. Why should the mere mention of the man's name affect her? She swallowed and shook her head. "Not tonight. Jesse had work to do and didn't have time to give us a tour of the ranch, remember?"

Lacy's sigh was loud enough to have Danielle and her uncle looking at one another and grinning. "But I wanna learn to ride a horse."

Danielle was amazed that Lacy remembered the name of Jesse's ranch but not surprised; her daughter listened to everyone and everything around her, sometimes hearing things Danielle wished she hadn't. Hoping to redirect Lacy's line of questioning, she asked, "How about if we promise to visit Jesse out at his ranch, but wait for him to call us?"

"Do you know his number?"

Danielle laughed, while her uncle asked, "Little June bug, do you always pester your momma like that?"

Lacy stopped squirming on the seat and gave her undivided attention to her great-uncle.

"I just want to see him again, Unca Jimmy."

"I've known him a lot of years and am pleased to say that he has worked hard to overcome the first impression I had of him."

"Really?" Danielle asked. "What did he do to give you a bad impression?"

He smiled and shook his head as he pulled into the driveway.

Since he wasn't going to answer, she reminded Lacy, "Besides, it isn't polite to just show up somewhere without an invitation." She hoped that would be the end of it, but the man was a definite distraction.

"But he did invite us, 'member?"

Danielle sighed. Obviously she wasn't the only one captivated by their cowboy hero. "He did, but he also said he'd pick us up. So let's just wait for him to call us, OK?"

"We're here," her uncle announced, getting out of his truck.

Danielle and Lacy slid across the seat and got out, walking hand-in-hand up the front porch steps. A wave of nostalgia swept up from her toes, and from an adult point-of-view, she realized just how wonderful it had been to be able to spend summer vacations in Pleasure, her home away from home.

"Why don't you ladies go on in and make yourselves at home?" Her uncle grabbed the two bags they had brought with them.

"You've already made us feel that way," Danielle reminded him. "How about if I see what's in your fridge and decide what to make you for dinner? You've been cooking since sunup, haven't you?"

His grin said it all and transported her back in time. No matter what happened during those long days of summer, he had the patience of a saint and a smile that would set hearts aflutter—well, at least that was what some of the ladies downtown used to say.

"How come you never married?"

He paused on the stairs and looked over his shoulder. "No one asked me." Laughing, he made his way to the second floor. He'd probably put their things in the back bedroom, where the morning sun would peek in their window and wake them.

"How come nobody asked Unca Jimmy to marry them?" Lacy was frowning up at her. "I like him."

"I don't know. He is a good man and would make a good husband." Opening the fridge, she contemplated

the contents and decided she would pick up some groceries for her uncle in the morning. Tonight, they'd feast
on leftovers. Pulling a few containers out, she was surprised to see Lacy staring at the staircase.

"Hey, don't worry, sweet pea," she soothed, setting
the food on the counter. "We'll be all right."

"I was thinking 'bout Daddy," she said without turning around. "Was he a good husband?"

Danielle paused to consider her words carefully. She
didn't want to say something that her little girl would
misconstrue. Her relationship with her ex had been
difficult toward the end, but he was still Lacy's father.
Walking over to where Lacy stood, she knelt down so
they were eye level. "He was the best he knew how to
be. We can't ever ask anyone to do more."

Her daughter seemed satisfied with the answer.
"Maybe Unca Jimmy wanted to bake pies and sell them
more than he wanted to be married."

Relieved that Lacy understood, she agreed. "He
makes the best pie."

"The secret is in the crust," his deep voice called out
from the top of the stairs. "You two look as if you are
either plotting to take over the world," he said, walking
into the kitchen, "or planning to meddle in my life."

"We were talking about Daddy."

"Ah." He looked at the containers lining the countertop
and then back at Danielle and Lacy. "Hungry, ladies?"

Grateful for the distraction, Danielle answered,
"Well, not really, but I thought it would help to know
what I could either heat up or cook for dinner. You
worked at the diner half the day, it's my turn."

"You know, Lacy," her uncle said, turning toward his

grandniece, "this is just one of the things I love about your mommy—her willingness to pitch right in and get to work."

Lacy scrunched her face up and Danielle knew her daughter was considering her uncle's words. "Mommy always works hard, Daddy says too hard." When she grew quiet and frowned, Danielle knew it was time for a major distraction. Lacy had already cried buckets when her ex walked out of their lives. She would do everything in her power to keep a smile on her daughter's face.

The promised trip to visit the Circle G would be perfect, now if only the cowboy would keep his word. Hope blossomed in Danielle's heart. It was a good start.

———

Jesse wandered out to the barn to make sure the horses were bedded down for the night. A rancher always took good care of his animals, especially the mount who worked with him every day, all day. He remembered a couple of ranch hands who had worked for his grandfather when he was younger, who hadn't followed along with old Hank's rules about caring for the Circle G's horses.

Once a ranch hand broke a rule, he was gone, no second chances. As far as his grandfather was concerned, if you didn't take proper care of the horse you rode, you could take your sorry hide elsewhere and find work. Funny thing was, once a ranch hand was let go from the Circle G, no one else would hire him—or ask why he was let go. The town of Pleasure respected Patrick Henry Garahan. It was that simple. Hank had let the ranch hand go and that was reason enough not to hire him.

Jesse had checked the horses earlier but made the rounds one last time. "Plenty of fresh water," he said aloud to Dodge. His horse whinnied softly, pushing against Jesse's shoulder. He reached out and stroked the broad handsome face that watched him, the wisdom of the ages in his luminous, dark eyes.

He always felt better after talking to his horse. "I can't help but be jealous of my brothers." Dodge nudged him again. "How do I know I haven't already met 'the one' and lost her?" Slumping his shoulders he turned to go, but his horse had other ideas, grabbing the back of Jesse's worn cotton shirt with his equine teeth.

Momentarily confused, he stopped and turned to look over his shoulder. The sound of fabric tearing had him sighing. "Damn it, Dodge," he grumbled. "That was my last clean shirt." Knowing his horse had an irascible temperament—just like his own—he retraced his steps and scratched the horse behind his ears. When he butted up against Jesse's chest, he knew what Dodge wanted—more one-on-one time. With no other chores left for the night, he gave his horse his full attention.

"Are you sure you weren't female in a former life?"

The horse snorted and Jesse laughed as Dodge bathed Jesse's face with hot, moist horse-breath. He remembered the first time he sat on a horse, his grandfather had lifted him up to sit in front of his dad in the saddle. Jesse had known right there and then that no matter where in Texas he lived, he would always own at least one horse. His life wouldn't be worth spit if he didn't have one of those strong, graceful, hardworking animals in his life.

Thinking about riding with his dad had him smiling and suddenly his mind detoured and settled on a little pink cowgirl who waited *all* her life to meet a *real cowboy*. Still stroking the blaze between Dodge's eyes, Jesse's mind changed direction and settled on a sweetly curved divorcée with tawny blonde hair and soft blue eyes. "Trouble ahead, Dodge," he murmured, giving his horse one last pat.

"Just because I saved Danielle from serious injury earlier today is no reason to be thinking about her." But while he walked through the barn, double-checking latches on the stalls, his thoughts kept returning to the two damsels in distress who'd fallen asleep on the truck ride over to Sullivan's Diner. He slowly grinned, remembering the sound of their soft snores filling the cab of his truck. Struck by the thought that he wanted to see them again, he started going over the next day's never-ending list of chores in his head, all the while wondering how he could wheedle a chunk of time out of his day to drive on into town to pick them up… because he couldn't wait to show them around the Circle G tomorrow.

His head told him to slow down, but his heart told him to downshift and gas it, because even though there were dangerous curves ahead, he knew they'd be sugar-sweet and just ripe for the tasting. "Whoa!" he mumbled aloud coming to a halt. "Hell." That's what women were on your heart, and other parts of your body, once they moved on to greener pastures. That was the one lesson he learned when Lori left him for the second time.

Walking back over to the house, he decided he wasn't ready to turn in yet, so he settled on the porch swing and gently pushed off. The soothing motion, moving back and forth in the cool night air, was just what he needed. He remembered the night and the fight that had smashed the slats of the bench apart. He was glad Dylan had been able to repair the gift their father had built for their mother before he'd been deployed; if he hadn't, the guilt would have eaten them both alive.

Life was precious. He and his brothers had learned as children that it didn't matter if you were ready for what lay ahead of you or not; sometimes life came at you with both barrels, and as his grandfather often said, *"Best you be ready, boys."*

But was he ready for the subtle changes a certain divorcée and her little girl might make in his life? His body stood at attention and said, *Hell yeah*, but his heart put up both hands and said, *Whoa!*

Distracted, disturbed, and discouraged, Jesse stopped swinging. "A cold one would be good right now."

As he walked to the back door, a feminine moan of ecstasy drifted toward him on the night breeze. He gritted his teeth and reached for the door. He missed the soft touch of a woman but it probably wouldn't kill him. Admitting that it had been a while longer than either of his brothers thought wouldn't happen in this lifetime. After all, a Garahan had his pride to think of—that and his reputation in certain circles in town.

He slammed the back door and felt perversely better for having given it an extra push. Grabbing a hold of the refrigerator door handle, he yanked and pulled it open. He knew he should calm down, but the frustration had been building inside of him for about a month now. He'd known something was up, but Lori hadn't wanted to confide in him… and then she was gone.

Opening the bottle, he tipped his head back and drained a third of the bottle in one big gulp. "Damn shame that I couldn't have fallen in love with someone like Emily or Ronnie."

Thinking about the two newest additions to their life out at the Circle G, he wondered if he would have noticed someone special. He'd been so hung up wanting someone he couldn't have that he probably wouldn't have noticed if the woman came wrapped in a bow with a note that said, "I'm the one you've been waiting for."

Snickering, he lifted the beer to his lips and sipped. The cool, yeasty flavor had his taste buds cheering. Sometimes there wasn't anything better than a cold longneck.

The breathy moans were getting louder. Shaking his head, he drained the rest of his beer. "Gotta find me a woman—fast, before I lose my friggin' mind!"

Trudging up the stairs, he headed to his room. A shaft of moonlight lent an eerie glow to the darkness, and he could just make out the balled-up sleeping bag on his bed. Why bother to put clean sheets on the damned bed if he wasn't sharing it with anyone? Only women cared about that kind of thing. Well, now that the ladies had moved out to the ranch, his brothers had started to care too.

"I don't," he repeated loudly enough to be heard down the hallway if his brothers had been listening—which he was certain they weren't. They were too preoccupied. "God, I'm going crazy. Do. Not. Go. There."

Heaving a sigh of resignation tinged with frustration, he smoothed out the sleeping bag and zipped it shut so it would lay flat. He'd have to wash his sheets eventually; for now, the sleeping bag would do. It was too hot to sleep inside of it, but it would be more comfortable than the old mattress he never had the time or funds to replace; its lumps were hard to ignore. Most nights he was too tired to notice, but tonight, he wasn't tired and they sure as hell would keep him awake.

Pulling the T-shirt over his head, he tried not to think about being the only Garahan presently sleeping alone. His frustration level wasn't at the critical point yet, but he had a feeling the more time he spent around Danielle, the higher it would go. She had curves in all the right places.

Hell, one thought led to another and pretty soon he was hard, hot, and horny. "Damn." He hadn't had a case of SBS in a long time. Snickering, he remembered the first time Tyler used the phrase when they were teenagers and it had been especially true; Sperm Backup Syndrome wasn't pretty, and the reason he was so grouchy lately. The need to find a willing woman speared through his insides, twisting his guts and other parts into knots.

Unzipping his jeans, he stepped out of them, leaving them right where he could reverse the movement at first light—saved time getting ready in the morning.

Naked and aching, he rubbed his hands over his face. "I can't just ride into town and pick up the first woman I see and ask her to do a little mattress dancing."

"Sure you can," the devil on his right shoulder said, poking him in the cheek with his pointy, red pitchfork.

"No you can't," the angel on his left shoulder insisted, plucking a soothing note on his tiny golden harp.

Man, he was insane. "Damn. Too bad this wasn't the good old days, when a man could do whatever he wanted and damn the consequences."

But his mama, and then his grandfather, raised him

right, and he knew he couldn't or wouldn't even try. He'd had sex for the sake of release, and while it felt really great at the time, there was just something missing. Then, he'd thought he'd found the perfect woman... but it turned out Lori only wanted to be friends. After meeting Danielle and Lacy, he wanted to spend more time with them. Who knew where it might lead?

He crawled onto the bed. With a sigh, he settled on his back, stacking his hands beneath his head. The shaft of moonlight wasn't as wide as it had been before. It was getting late if the moon was moving beyond his bedroom window.

"Women!" Rolling over, he pushed up off the bed, punched his pillow a couple of times, and settled on his side. Exhausted from a hard day working the ranch, Jesse closed his eyes and tried to will himself to sleep, but the pretty blonde with eyes the color of cornflowers had him rolling back onto his back.

Staring up at the ceiling, he sensed that Danielle was a woman who could take his mind off his troubles, but she wasn't the "let's get it on and move on" type; she was the "white picket fence and forever" type. Closing his eyes, he imagined little Lacy taking a hold of his hand and asking, "What's wrong with forever?"

Chapter 5

"HEY, ARE YOU SICK?"

Jesse ignored the voice and rolled onto his side.

"If you want this cup of coffee, you'll get your scrawny butt out of bed, Bro."

The scent of fresh-brewed coffee wafted toward him. He opened one eye and saw his older brother standing by the bed, holding two steaming mugs. "Why couldn't it have been Emily or Ronnie bringing me coffee?"

Tyler frowned down at him. "Because the ladies know two very important facts about the men in this family."

Jesse ran a hand through his hair and then over his face. Sitting up he asked, "What's that?"

Tyler grinned. "We sleep in the raw, and we do not share our women."

"Hell, Ty," Jesse ground out reaching for one of the mugs. "You see one man naked, you've pretty much seen all there is to see."

His brother chuckled. "Some of us are more gifted than others, Bro. 'Bout time you realized that."

Ignoring the taunt, Jesse sipped and sighed. All he needed to get through the morning's list of chores was a hearty breakfast, then he'd be good to go till noon. As the caffeine worked its magic, he focused on his goal for the day—finish up so he could drive into town and pick up Danielle and Lacy.

"Breakfast in five. We've got hay being delivered this morning; you want to wait for it?"

"No problem. The truck's running a bit rough; I can look at it while I'm waiting, but I'll be heading into town this afternoon... I've got a promise to keep."

His brother waited for him to explain, but instead Jesse asked, "Hey, are you and Dylan moving the herd today?"

Tyler shook his head. "Think we're good for a little while longer, maybe next week or so."

"Good to know. Are we going to put the word out, or are you going to call Timmy and his buds?"

"Already took care of it. Timmy and a few of his friends will be here when we need them. They'll be helping out this morning checking for strays and riding over to the pastureland we'll be moving the herd to in order to check it out."

"I guess it was a good thing you were the one who caught them trying to break into the Lucky Star that night. Anyone else might have tried to convince the ladies to press charges and you wouldn't be able to call on those kids to help... to return the favor."

Tyler's smile was slow, thoughtful. "Luckiest day of my life was the day Jolene hired me and I saw Emily for the first time."

Stepping into his jeans, he opened his top drawer and sighed. "Hey, Ty, I'm borrowing a pair of socks."

"No prob." Tyler headed for the stairs.

Wearing boots without socks was a mistake Jesse only had to make once, when he was thirteen and thought he knew it all. The blisters had popped right away, but the infection had lasted a whole lot longer. His grandfather had been serious as a heart attack about him not putting his boots back on until everything healed.

"Smart man," he admitted out loud, grabbing a pair of clean socks from his brother's drawer and walking back to his room. He scooped up half the pile of dirty clothes and headed toward the laundry room. After sorting the dark colors from the whites—as he'd been asked—he ran back upstairs for the rest of the dirty clothes.

"Mornin', Em," he called out to the redhead standing in front of the stove, cooking. Contentment filled him and he couldn't hold back the sigh. "You sure are a pretty sight first thing in the morning, darlin'."

She turned and smiled at him, and he was struck again by how lucky his older brother was. As far as he was concerned, Emily Langley was the pick of the litter. "Better not let Tyler hear you trying to sweet-talk me."

"I haven't even gotten started yet," he said. "I dropped off some laundry—" he began only to be interrupted by her.

She looked at the armful and frowned up at him. "I don't mind doing laundry, but you're making more work for me by not remembering to bring it down at least once a week."

"I'm sorry, Em. It's just that I'm dead on my feet at night and don't remember until I'm getting dressed in the morning."

"And have to dig through the dirty pile to find something to wear?"

"How did you know?"

She started to laugh. He really hated being laughed at and wanted to be mad at her, but just couldn't—the sound of her laughter in their kitchen reminded him of their mother.

"A blind woman might not notice that smear of God knows what across the front of your shirt," she said. "I'm not blind."

They were still laughing when Tyler and Dylan walked into the kitchen. Tyler frowned at him and grumbled, "Get your own woman, Jesse."

Feeling good, he replied, "Why? Emily and Ronnie are perfectly happy to feed me and wash my clothes."

Tyler's hand shot out, but Jesse had enough caffeine in his system to dodge the blow. "Hey, you should be in a good mood."

"Oh yeah," his brother said, "and why's that?"

"Hell," Jesse said with a glance in Emily's direction, "I'm not deaf you know."

The sound of her sharply indrawn breath had him dancing backward in case his brother decided to throw another punch. "One of these days, Jess," Tyler warned.

Feeling pretty good that he'd dodged what would have been a wicked jab to his shoulder, he asked, "Why not today?"

"Tyler," Emily warned, stepping in between the brothers. "Breakfast is ready." She stood on her toes to press her lips to Tyler's cheek.

"We've got more work than we can handle today," Tyler ground out. "I'll have to wait till later to beat the crap out of you."

If looks could kill, Jesse would have been six feet under. Knowing when to play with fire and when he was about to get burned, he got a plate, walked over to the counter, and started to fill it. "Thanks for cooking, Emily. This looks great."

But she was preoccupied wrapping herself around his brother. Since Tyler and Emily weren't paying any attention to him, he shrugged and sat down to dig into his meal. By the time he was on seconds, Dylan and Ronnie walked into the kitchen looking loose and limber.

"Hell. I'm going out to the barn." Grabbing his Stetson off the peg by the back door, he slapped it against his thigh, pushed the back door open wide, and let it slam behind him.

By the time he reached the barn, he realized that he was acting like a jerk. No use riling the horses just because he had trouble sleeping—and the need to sink into the warm and welcoming depths of a willing woman.

"Fuck me."

The heart of the matter was a whole lot more basic than love. "A man has needs," he muttered to himself as he grabbed the bridle and reins from the hook on the wall and his saddle from the tack room. "Won't matter unless I can find a woman interested in being a really close friend with benefits."

He gently offered the bit to Dodge and praised him when he took it between his teeth. "I know you'd rather forego the hardware, but it comes in handy out there on the range."

Smoothing the blanket across his horse's back, he made certain there were no wrinkles before he laid the saddle on top of it. With a friendly pat to Dodge's belly, the horse let go of the breath he held and Jesse was able to tighten the cinch.

He'd learned the hard way that horses had a sense

of humor when they didn't particularly want to be saddled. Vaulting into the saddle and having it shift off to the side when the horse let out its breath had been a source of entertainment for his brothers, but his ten-year-old pride had taken a direct hit. Worse than his injured pride was the fact that his grandfather had not been amused and rode Jesse's case for the next few weeks, until he had proven that he wouldn't make beginner mistakes again.

Leading the horse out of the barn, he had his foot in the stirrup when Tyler called his name.

"What?" He had a list a mile long of things he had to tackle before he showed up at the diner. He needed to get going.

"Did you forget about the hay delivery this morning?"

Hell... He had. "Yeah." He dismounted and led Dodge over to the corral. Once his horse was inside, he walked back into the barn and grabbed a bridle off the wall. Whickers of interest and impatient stomps greeted him. "Yeah, I know you guys are ready to get a move on." Stopping by the first stall, he greeted Wildfire. "I know Dylan already fed you, so let's get goin'."

As he led each of the horses out to the corral, he wondered if the hay delivery would be on time or late like the last one. Depending on who was delivering the hay, the Circle G was either first on the list, if it was coming from the west, or last on the list if coming from the east. Either way, his morning was already kicking into high gear. He'd have to keep moving if he was going to keep his promise and teach a little cowgirl how to ride.

—⁓—

Danielle loved the quiet of early summer mornings. Her friends back home thought she was odd, getting up with the birds, but since Lacy had inherited the same gene, it worked out well for them. Lacy usually started waking up when the first bird called at around four thirty in the morning. If Danielle was lucky, Lacy wouldn't come looking for her until at least five.

Smiling, she scooped grounds into the old fashioned percolator her uncle favored. Checking the clock on the stove top, she lit the burner and figured she had about twenty minutes left of quiet time before her little Texas tornado came downstairs.

Uncle Jimmy had been firm about not wanting to see them at the diner until after eight. They'd talked about it last night, and just as she'd remembered, there was no budging her uncle once his mind was made up.

Moving around his kitchen was like living a memory. Glass-fronted cabinets and heavy earthenware mugs and plates were still mixed in with the largest collection of mason jars she'd ever seen. Danielle was comfortable here, just as she'd been as a child.

Finding what she needed, she set the table for the two of them and started making breakfast. Hers was simple. She needed protein to keep moving until lunch so scrambling a couple of eggs and toast would work for her, but before she started melting butter in the frying pan, she rummaged through the canvas shopping bags they'd brought with them and found Lacy's favorite marshmallow and oat cereal. Setting it by the pretty red bowl and mason jar, she was suddenly starving.

The coffee was ready by the time she'd finished cooking. "Perfect timing." Fingers crossed, she hoped Lacy would sleep for another fifteen minutes, giving her time to sit on the back porch and enjoy the new day.

Having grown up watching birds, she recognized the calls of a chickadee and house finches. Sipping her coffee, she watched a blue jay swoop low to check out the feeder. Her uncle had filled the feeder the night before, and the bird's scratchy call as he flew off to spread the good news that breakfast was served had her wondering if the smaller birds would have a chance to get any of the seed.

Putting her feet up on the railing, she let her mind wander while the backyard birds kept her company. A certain tall, dark, and handsome cowboy filled her mind and she wondered if he'd keep his word to Lacy, or if he'd be just another sweet talker like her ex. "I hope for Lacy's sake he doesn't forget."

Cup empty, she placed it on the floor beside her. Closing her eyes, she let the warmth of the day and the background music of the birds soothe her frayed and tired nerves. If she could start each day out here, she just might be able to tackle every new problem that she knew would arise.

Uprooting her daughter hadn't been her choice; she hadn't had one, thanks to the thoughtlessness of one man. "People just don't think," she murmured.

"What people?"

Her eyes shot open and she sat upright. "Lacy, honey, I didn't know you were standing there. When did you get up?"

Her little girl stood in the doorway, dressed in her

favorite pink princess nightgown and little pink boots with her cowgirl hat hanging down her back. "Just now. I'm hungry."

Danielle rose to gather her daughter in her arms. She loved the way Lacy would giggle when she hugged her close. "Did you wear those boots to bed again?"

Lacy squirmed and Danielle set her on her feet. "Nuh-uh," she answered. "Not all night, Mommy."

"Want some cereal?" She grinned when Lacy's eyes went round with wonder.

"You 'membered to bring it!" She dashed inside, climbed onto the chair, and poured herself a bowl, managing to get most of the cereal where she wanted it—in the bowl. "Thanks, Mommy," Lacy said, between chews.

"How about a glass of milk?"

Lacy nodded and Danielle poured.

Spoon poised in front of her mouth, Lacy frowned. "That's a jar."

Danielle laughed. "Uncle Jimmy likes to use them for glasses."

Lacy shook her head. "He's funny, but I like him."

Smoothing the flyaway strands, she echoed her daughter's sentiment. "He likes you too."

"Where is he?"

"Over at the diner, serving breakfast."

Lacy stopped eating and set her spoon down. "Shouldn't we help him?"

"We will, but he wanted us to rest up before going over to the diner." Danielle paused. "Oh no. We don't have a car."

Lacy shook her head. "Sure we do, 'member? We drove it here yesterday."

"It's probably still on the side of the road where we left it."

Her daughter frowned up at her and shook her head. "I heard Unca Jimmy talking to someone last night."

Danielle smiled and said, "That was me."

But Lacy just shook her head again and wiped her mouth with the back of her hand. When Danielle opened her mouth, intending to remind Lacy she should have used the napkin by her plate, Lacy sprang up and reached for her mother's hand. "Come on."

Caught up in her little one's enthusiasm, she let herself be led to the front door. Lacy tugged her mother with one hand and pushed the screen door open with another. "See, Mommy?" She pointed toward where their car was parked.

"I had no idea that he dropped the car off."

"It's part of the Code."

Distracted, she looked down at Lacy. "What code?"

With a dramatic sigh, the little one shook her head. "Mommy, you gots to listen when people talk."

Well, that was like the pot calling the kettle black. "Which people?"

"Cowboy Jesse."

"Ah." It all made sense now, something Jesse had said yesterday had stuck with her daughter; undoubtedly it had to do with being a cowboy. "Which part of the Code? He said a lot yesterday."

"He promised he'd fix our car. Cowboys keep promises."

The only other cowboy she'd known was her ex, and he certainly hadn't kept any of the promises he made to her. "Well, Jesse certainly kept this one, didn't he?"

"So we can go help Unca Jimmy?"

"I think you'll need to get dressed first."

"But I am dressed," Lacy insisted, stomping one tiny pink boot in frustration.

Danielle fought against the urge to smile—no use encouraging bursts of temper just because her daughter was so adorable when she was riled. "You can't wear your pajamas all day, sweetie. Get dressed."

Reluctantly, Lacy turned in a swirl of candy-pink cotton, but did as she was told and headed for the stairs. Danielle waited until she heard Lacy stamping her little boots along the hallway above her before she let her laughter go.

"My little hardheaded angel."

Five minutes later, the kitchen was put back to rights and her daughter was clomping back down the stairs, calling, "Ready, Mommy. Can we go now?"

Anxious to get started on the next phase in their lives, she followed her cowgirl who now sported a T-shirt with a race car on it that said "Go fast or go home!" with matching shorts. Danielle winced at the choice, but was a firm believer in letting her daughter choose what she wanted to wear most of the time.

The green and brown camouflage colors clashed with Lacy's pink boots and hat, but asking her to change would set the tone for how their day would go and definitely not in a good way. Remembering her mother's advice to pick her battles wisely, Danielle smiled, took her daughter's hand, and headed out to the car.

Chapter 6

JESSE STARED AT THE PHONE IN HIS HAND, SHAKING HIS head. "Well, damn."

"Hey, Garahan!" a voice yelled. "You still there?"

Swallowing against the lump of emotion in his throat, Jesse held the phone against his ear. "Yeah, but could you repeat that last part one more time?"

The deep chuckle from the other end had Jesse wondering if he was going insane. Either that or someone was playing a cruel joke at his expense. "You heard me right. Doctor's orders, I have to give up driving for the next few months. This last concussion was a bad one."

His hands were shaking, so he dug deep for control and cleared his throat. "Why me? We haven't hung out in town since my grandfather died."

"Yeah, about that," Slim said. "I'm sorry I didn't come around to see if you needed help, but—"

"Hey, you came to the funeral. I get it. Everybody's got stuff, lives to lead." Jesse thought about it; he'd been so wrapped up in his own misery after losing his mom and then his grandfather that every ounce of his energy had gone into working with his brothers to keep the ranch going.

"OK, so are you interested in driving my car out at Devil's Bowl?"

"Hell yeah! What do I have to do? Do I have to come up with the entrance fee?"

"I'll front you for the first race, but I expect you'll clean up if you still drive the way you used to. You can take next week's fee out of your winnings."

Everything Jesse ever wanted was being dangled in front of his face; all he had to do was say yes. *Is this a test?* Should he be double-checking with Jolene to see if she needed him? Hell. A chance like this came along just once—if you were lucky—real lucky. "I'll need a helmet."

"You can use mine. If it doesn't fit, I can get my hands on one for you." Slim paused. "You'll be doing me a favor, man. I've invested a lot of money in this car. If you drive it for me until I can get back behind the wheel, my car will still be out on the track, keeping my sponsor happy. So don't think it's all one-sided."

Jesse agreed.

"Meet me out at the track tonight for a couple of practice laps."

"I'll be there."

Jesse's childhood dream of racing cars filled him to bursting and it was only after he'd disconnected that he'd remembered—Lacy.

The whine of a diesel engine downshifting caught his attention and had him swearing. Their delivery of hay was right on schedule. Mentally shifting gears, he was back in rancher mode when the truck pulled up their driveway.

He'd have to figure something out for tonight. He never broke a promise before, but now, because he'd been distracted by the possibility of fulfilling a long-ago dream, he'd given his word twice for the same evening.

Hell, he'd have to work quickly if he was going to

squeeze a trip into town to stop at the diner and explain to two ladies why he'd be putting off Lacy's riding lesson one more day.

A few hours later, he was finally able to put the first part of his plan into action. Pulling up outside of the diner, he got out of his truck and wiped his suddenly damp palms on his thighs. *Hell.* The prospect of seeing Danielle had him acting like a teenager.

Grumbling beneath his breath, he opened the door and walked in. He could hear voices coming from the kitchen, but no one was in the front of the diner, and that's when he remembered that Sullivan's closed early these days.

The voices sounded as if they'd moved further away; he opened the doors to the kitchen and walked in. Looking around he was taken aback—it was empty. "Well, hell." The back door was propped open with a wooden crate and he could hear the sound of a truck's engine idling.

But now what? He strained to listen, but he couldn't hear much over the engine. Maybe they were all outside; he started toward the door, but then hesitated. He really didn't want to interrupt if they were receiving a delivery, knowing how hectic that could be.

He could walk straight through to the back, but he really didn't want to have an audience when he talked to Danielle. Although it seemed as if they'd buried the hatchet yesterday, there was still a chance that her uncle probably still harbored resentment toward him.

Jesse glanced around him and saw a clipboard and pen hanging from a cup hook on the back wall. Hastily scribbling a note to Danielle, he told her he was sorry he missed her, but something had come up and he wouldn't be able to give Lacy a riding lesson tonight. Promising to see her tomorrow, he left the note in the middle of the butcher-block table and pushed through the doors into the dining area. A gust of air swept past him into the kitchen, but he didn't take the time to notice.

"I've been waiting all of my life to get behind the wheel of a race car out here." Jesse looked around him and said a silent prayer. *Lord, don't let me blow this chance.* So much was riding on him. Slim was counting on keeping his car in contention, having it racing Saturday nights even though Slim wouldn't be driving.

Then there was the Circle G; they needed to keep paying their debts down or else they could still lose the ranch. What the hell would they do then? Garahans had been working the land and driving the herd for more than one hundred fifty years. He and his brothers had other talents, but not that they could focus on twenty-four/seven, like they had to do with ranching.

Tyler had brought in a substantial sum while he worked over at the Lucky Star. Dylan added his portion by filling in for a few nights, but the bulk of what Dylan kicked in came from his side work as a carpenter.

Jesse wondered if he could win enough racing to make his contribution count. Hell, it was his turn, but things were pretty quiet over at the Lucky Star. The new headliner seemed to be working out just fine, so there was no need for Jolene to call on him for help. Too bad; he really wanted to have his turn up on that stage.

His cell phone buzzed in his shirt pocket. He took it

out, checked the number, and grinned. "How the hell are ya, Tom?"

His cousin chuckled. "It'd take a couple of pints to tell you."

Jesse asked, "So are you and your brothers in?"

Tom hesitated. "Something's come up… only Mike and I will be there."

Jesse sensed something serious had happened, so he asked, "Did I miss something on the news?"

His cousin sighed. "It hasn't hit the news yet, but it's bad, Jesse. Real bad."

"Who was hurt?"

"Pat," Tom said. "But it's more than Pat's body that's hurt."

From the break in his cousin's voice, Jesse knew that whatever fire the youngest Garahan had been fighting had taken a toll on his cousin. "You'll let me know if you need us to do anything." It wasn't a question.

"Count on it, Cuz."

"When's your flight?"

"Mike and I are flying out in two weeks. We both had some vacation time, so we decided to take it out at the Circle G." Tom paused, then asked, "Is that OK with you?"

"Are you kidding? It'll be like when we were kids and Mom—"

Tom waited a few minutes and then finished what Jesse hadn't been able to. "Used to threaten to pull her hair out, riding herd on all us kids."

"Yeah," Jesse said, relieved that his cousin understood. "Have you heard from Sean?"

"He and his brothers can't get away, but I heard from Ben and Matt."

Before he could answer, he had to wait for the race car coming around the bend to pass by. "Yeah?"

"Are you out at Devil's Bowl?"

He grinned. Leave it to his cousin to pick up on the background noise. "Yep, but if I tell you anymore, I'll have to kill you."

His cousin hesitated as if he was actually considering taking that chance. He finally laughed and said, "They'll be coming in the day after Mike and me."

"So the Murphy side of the clan can't make it, but the New York City Garahans and Colorado Justiss cousins will be here?"

His cousin laughed. "I, uh, had to pull some strings to convince the lawmen they needed to be in on the event."

"Did you tell them that we aren't doing anything indecent? We're just gonna be up on stage wearing, jeans, boots, hats, and vests?"

"That was the problem, seems our Colorado cousins don't usually go around in public with their shirts unbuttoned, let alone not wearing them at all."

Jesse tried to cough to cover his laughter, but in the end, just let it loose. "It's for a great cause."

Tom hesitated, then asked, "So how many single women do you figure are in town?"

It wasn't what he asked, but the tone of his cousin's voice that had Jesse pausing to consider his answer. "Hell, a bunch. Do I need to get the details?"

"Yep, or else Matt and Ben won't fly down."

"Are you kidding me?" Jesse couldn't believe his stubborn Colorado cousins wouldn't just come when he called for help.

"Yeah, Ben said something about the last time they

came down, a bar fight, and redheaded twins visiting from out of town."

Jesse whistled low and sighed. "That was one hellacious long weekend. Tell Ben not to worry. There are more than enough single females in Pleasure."

It was Tom's turn to laugh. "Matt said they only want to hear about the single ladies over twenty-five."

"That a fact?"

"Yep, I'm guessing they're pressed for time and don't really care about the important stuff, like what the women look like and their hair color…"

When Tom let his comment fade out, Jesse started thinking; maybe all of his cousins really needed this break for more reasons than just to help their Texas cousins out. "Don't worry, there are enough single women in town to attract and distract."

"All right. Talk to you later."

"Thanks, Tom."

"No problem, but you'll owe us."

Jesse sat staring at his phone. He didn't mind owing any of his cousins. They were family and families stick together through good and bad, thick and thin.

"Hey, you ready to race or not?" Slim sounded ready to roll.

Jesse's blood was pumping so hard, he wondered if his friend didn't hear it. "Why don't I just show you how ready I am?"

Slim grinned. "Grab your helmet and meet me in the garage."

Following along behind, he felt his adrenaline kick start as he got into the car and punched the gas, racing around the oval at a speed just this side of insane. His tires sprayed dirt as the car dug into the groove and found the sweet spot right before he gunned it on the straightaway.

———~~~———

"Man, Slim, your car has balls."

His friend grinned. "And a hell of an engine." They tinkered under the hood until Slim finally straightened and said, "Let's not mess around with a good thing or Bo will kill us. 'Bout ten minutes till you've got to get over in the lineup. You ready?"

Jesse wondered if his friend felt this adrenaline rush before he raced. He tried to ignore it and concentrate. "Yeah, I'm ready."

"Let's do it."

The first few laps Jesse kept falling behind, until he realized that he wasn't pushing himself or Slim's car to the limit. *Have faith in yourself, Son.* His grandfather had said those words so often, Jesse heard them in his head whenever he was up against something he wasn't sure he could handle.

Gritting his teeth, cutting the wheel, he goosed the gas pedal, moving past the car in front of him. *One down, five to go.* Concentrating, aware of everything around him—the car, the track, the other cars—Jesse gave one hundred and ten percent and flew across the finish line to the roar of the crowd.

Stunned, he stared at his hands where they still gripped the wheel and wondered if he'd imagined that he'd crossed first.

"Hell of a finish, Jesse!" Slim unhooked the netting from the window frame and leaned in the car to take his hand. "Best decision I ever made putting you behind the wheel."

Wiping the sweat from his eyes, elation swept up from his toes. "Can I drive again next Saturday night?"

Slim laughed and leaned his elbows on the window. "If you want to win again next weekend, you'd better be here practicing this week."

With a grin, Jesse agreed; he was tired, sore, and couldn't stop smiling. He'd tested his mettle against the track and had come out on top.

"You tweaked more speed out of that car than I've been able to," Slim said. "How'd you do it?"

"I'm not sure I can explain it," Jesse said, "but I can show you again."

Slim laughed. "I need to get under the hood with Bo. Let's do this again tomorrow night. Does that work for you?"

Jesse hesitated. "How late will you be here?"

"You've got something else going on?"

Jesse raked a hand through his hair and looked down at his feet. Would Slim understand if he told him about Danielle and Lacy? Was he crazy for even considering putting his friend off or selfish for putting off the Brockway ladies?

"Look," Slim said, "don't worry about tomorrow night. It'll give Bo and I a chance to give the car an overhaul after the way you were screaming around the track tonight. How 'bout the day after?"

Relief swamped him and had him looking back up at Slim. "Thanks, man. It's a long story and I didn't want you to think—"

"That you weren't committed to racing my car?" Slim finished for him.

Jesse nodded.

"Hell, Jesse. I've known you since forever and know how badly you wanted to race cars back in high school. If things had been different—"

Jesse's gaze met Slim's and the other man fell silent, but Jesse knew he'd been about to say: *if your parents and grandfather hadn't died.*

"So we're good?" Slim asked.

Jesse nodded.

An hour later, he held his winnings in his hand. Four hundred thirty-nine dollars and twelve cents. Driving back home to the Circle G, he marveled that he'd earned so much for doing what he loved. "A.J. Foyt move over, there's a new Texan who's gonna break some speed records out at Devil's Bowl Speedway."

Thinking of his Houston-born hero, he wondered if he'd be able to earn enough to pay down the feed bill and the mortgage. It felt good to be contributing like his brothers had. They'd done their part working a second job to help keep the ranch going; now it was his turn, and he surely did it his own way... behind the wheel of a race car.

Jesse couldn't get the awesome feeling of being behind the wheel, driving in the dirt out of his mind. But it was different than he'd thought all those years ago. As a kid, he'd wanted this chance so badly that he thought he'd go crazy knowing it wasn't gonna happen. Now that it had, things were different. He wasn't the same kid he'd been. Nothing shook your foundation like losing a favorite family member, but his grandfather had stepped up to the plate when their father had died all those years ago, then again when their mom was killed in that wreck. Old Hank had simply taken the rest of the burden of raising three hoodlums—as he liked to call Jesse and his older brothers—all on his own. When his grandfather died, Jesse felt as if he'd aged twenty years. He and his brothers had lost everyone; now they only had each other.

As he neared the turnoff to the Circle G, he realized that while he'd been working the ranch alongside his grandfather and brothers, something had happened to that childhood dream of racing cars... it had been tempered with a bone-deep commitment and love for the land he drove toward—Garahan land, as far as he could see.

Satisfaction settled inside of him as he pulled up to the gate. He stared at their family's brand, the *G* inside the circle, and knew there was more here than just their land and the herd—it was a way of life that had become ingrained in him over the years. He might like to flirt with the idea of giving up ranch life to pursue driving full time, but it was a pipe dream and not one that really mattered anymore. But the chance to drive out at Devil's Bowl was something he'd take on, just so that years from now he'd have no regrets... no what-ifs.

Shaking his head, he got out and opened the gate. Driving through, he wondered if Danielle was upset that he hadn't been able to pick them up tonight. But he'd done the right thing and left her a note, so she couldn't be too upset, could she? Females were persnickety sometimes. He'd learned that from his grandfather, and there wasn't a hell of a lot that the old man had ever been wrong about.

Feeling pretty good about himself, he let his mind wander as he let himself in the back door. His life had taken a turn for the good yesterday when he'd stopped to help out a stranger. Didn't that beat all that they'd known each other years ago?

Parking by the back of the house, he noticed a light had been left on in the kitchen for him. It was either Emily's or Ronnie's doing; his brothers wouldn't have thought to leave one on for him.

Tossing the money on the table, he started to walk away and decided to leave a note. *For the feed bill.* "Let them wonder where I got it from." He yawned. "I'm gonna hit the hay."

He trudged upstairs and thought about sitting down halfway up; he was done, but he dug deep for the strength and got to the top and walked to his bedroom. He took off his shirt and tossed it to the floor. When the buttons clicked on hardwood, he paused, confused.

Half asleep he laughed when he remembered that he'd finally listened to Emily and delivered his laundry. Opening the button and unzipping the fly of his jeans, he let them fall into a heap by the bed. With a sigh of relief, he scrubbed his hands over his face and rolled his shoulders. Sliding between the sheets, the scent of sunshine and clean air surrounded him. "Thanks, Emily," he sighed and drifted off to sleep.

Chapter 7

"Hey, you plannin' on sleepin' in?"

Jesse opened one eye and couldn't focus, so he closed his eye and rolled over.

"We're burnin' daylight, Bro."

Pulling his pillow over his head, he mumbled, "Fuck off."

The scraping sound didn't register until Jesse's elbow and hip hit the floor and the mattress landed on top of him. He woke up fast and shot out from under the bedding swinging. His jab connected with Dylan's jaw. The satisfying sound of fist meeting flesh had the blood in his veins singing and his heart pumping. It felt good. Real good.

"What the hell is wrong with you?"

Tyler's question caught him off guard and Dylan's uppercut connected solidly to Jesse's chin. Momentarily stunned, he swayed on his feet before his brains unscrambled and he could think again. "All I said was fuck off." He fingered the sore spot on his chin. "Since when is that a crime?"

Tyler shoved at Dylan, shook his head, and said, "Isn't... well, it wasn't before—"

Irritation shot up from Jesse's churning gut. "Don't even go there if you're gonna say it used to be OK before Emily and Ronnie moved in."

Tyler closed his mouth, looked at Dylan, and shrugged. "Coffee's hot."

His damned brothers grinned at one another, stepped over the wreckage of Jesse's room, and walked out the door, talking about the herd, fences that were down, and supplies that needed to be picked up in town.

The sun hadn't even started to show on the horizon; it was still dark. A glance at the clock and he could see that it wasn't even half past four. The heat of his temper fizzled out. He needed caffeine if he was going to refuel his mad and get to work. Hefting the mattress back onto the box spring and frame, he cursed his brothers again. "Those sheets were clothesline fresh, damn it."

With a quick flick, he had the sheets free of any dirt he'd tracked in last night from the speedway. Tossing them on the mattress, he didn't bother to remake the bed; he was already one cup behind his brothers.

Grabbing his jeans off the floor, he pulled them up and reminded himself to thank Emily for the clothes that had been neatly folded on his dresser top. Dressed, he headed downstairs where the sumptuous scent of fresh-brewed coffee and pan-fried steak had his stomach rumbling.

Both brothers were crowding their women close enough to have Jesse wondering if they needed birth control. He almost asked, then remembered the clean clothes, and said, "Thanks for doing my laundry, Em."

She slipped out of Tyler's arms and smiled at him. "Don't you just love the way they smell when they've been dried on the clothesline?"

"Yeah." A glance in his brother's direction had him wondering why he was looking all pissed off at him. Still sore that they'd dumped him out of bed, he added, "Thanks, Em. You are the best!"

Just to test his theory that his brother was jealous,

Jesse moved toward Emily to hug her. He swallowed a chuckle as the muscle beneath Tyler's left eye began to twitch. If he wasn't so hungry, he might have pushed his brother even further by kissing Emily—he missed their morning rumbles in the kitchen.

His stomach growled again and he focused on the food. "Hey, Ronnie, you save any steak for me?"

His sister-in-law pushed the hair out of her eyes and nodded. He almost laughed because that same hank of hair slid back in her face. He had a feeling Dylan was the one responsible for her delightfully disheveled appearance. She finally got her hair tucked behind her ears and reached for an empty plate. After she filled it with pan-seared steak, eggs, and potatoes, she handed it to him.

"You are an angel, Ronnie."

"Hey." Dylan moved closer, staking his claim and outlining his territory. If his brothers had their way, no one would get within three feet of their women. Normally he felt crappy about being envious of them all the time, but today was different—he had two pretty women waiting on him to finish his chores so he could pick them up and bring them out to the Circle G.

If he played his cards right, he'd be kissing Danielle's delectable lips this afternoon. He wondered if they'd be honey sweet or berry tart?

"Are you all right, Jesse?"

Emily's soft voice jolted him to the present and the realization that he hadn't moved. "Uh, yeah." He walked over to the table and sat down. "Just low on caffeine."

Magically, a cup appeared at his elbow—milk and two sugars, just the way he liked it. He drank some down before looking up. "Thanks, Emily. I could have

gotten it." The grim look on Tyler's face nearly had
him giving in to the laughter building inside of him.
It was just too hard to hang on to being mad when
there was breakfast a man could count on to carry him
through till noon, coffee just this side of perfect, and
pretty women smiling and smelling like—he paused
and, before his brothers could stop him, leaned toward
Ronnie first and then Emily, breathing deeply. The
ladies were an intriguing combination of rain-washed
lavender and lemons.

With a grin, he plowed through his meal while his
mind wandered and he wondered what scent Danielle
favored. Damn, he couldn't remember. He'd have to get
real close to her again and find out. He'd better get a move
on with his chores and volunteer to head on into town to
get the supplies. "So, need anything at Harrison's?"

"Nah, Dylan's got it covered. You and me will be
riding fences today."

"Sorry, Bro. I've got plans for this afternoon."

"Change 'em," Tyler grumbled.

"Can't," Jesse answered, surprised that he was
in such a good mood. Was it the prospect of seeing
Danielle again, or teaching a certain little cowgirl how
to ride? Probably both, he reasoned before looking at
both brothers.

Dylan asked, "You got a special reason to want to head
into town?" His brother's gaze was watchful, interested.

He shrugged, got up, and rinsed his plate and utensils. As he put them in the dishwasher, he looked up and
caught Ronnie's nod of approval. He winked at her and
hotfooted it out of Dylan's reach. Damn, but his brothers
were touchy where their women were concerned.

As the door closed behind him, he realized that he couldn't wait to bring the Brockway ladies to the ranch and see how they fit. He was smiling as he made his way over to the barn.

Dodge whickered a welcome as Jesse made his way toward his horse's stall. His horse nudged him while Jesse placed the bit in his mouth and the bridle into place, keeping Jesse's mind occupied and off of the dangerous subject of women. It wouldn't be smart to be distracted working around large animals.

"Dodge, there's a little lady who would love to meet you."

His horse nodded and whinnied, and Jesse couldn't help but smile. Humming to himself, he checked the cinch and mounted his horse. Right on cue, Tyler opened the back door and before Jesse could look away, the oldest Garahan gathered his woman into his arms and held her tight, burying his face in her curly red hair.

"Damn," Jesse rasped. "To be loved like that." *Hell*, he thought, *to love like that*. It must have been what his parents had shared before his dad had gone on that fateful mission to Beirut.

He wondered if Danielle was the one… he had a feeling she might be and wondered if she would be willing to take a chance on another cowboy. Shaking his head, he wondered what the hell was wrong with him. He was starting to sound like an old woman. With one last look over his shoulder, he rode out, ready to tackle the first of the day's jobs. Tyler would catch up and they'd plow through their never-ending list. One thing was certain— come four o'clock that afternoon, he would be driving into town.

—◦◦◦—

"Mommy, when's he coming?"

Danielle sighed and finished combing Lacy's hair. "I'm not sure, sweetie, but you know he's a busy man, with so many longhorns to look after."

Lacy's mouth was set in a firm line. Recognizing the look, Danielle tried to dig deeper for the patience to deal with the fallout of one more sweet-talking cowboy who hadn't kept his word.

"But he was 'sposed to pick us up yesterday." Lacy was pouting, and Danielle didn't blame her daughter.

"I know it's hard to understand, Lacy," she soothed, digging deeply to find the patience to come up with an explanation for why Jesse had stood them up. "But sometimes grown-ups have to do things they don't want to do in order to make the time to do the things they want to do."

"I 'member. You said that when Daddy left."

Danielle's heart clenched and a wave of cold swept up from the tips of her toes. "That's right, sweet pea. He left us, but I'm still here."

Lacy reached out and wrapped her arms around her mother's neck. "I love you."

Tears burned the back of her eyes, but Danielle blinked them away. "I love you back."

Letting go, Lacy spun around and clomped toward the doorway. "Can we have pie for breakfast?"

This time, Danielle laughed out loud. "Maybe a sliver, you little rascal."

Lacy danced out the door and down the hallway. Danielle could hear her daughter singing to herself, just slightly off key, and the words hit home—hard. "Save a horse, ride a cowboy."

Thank goodness her little girl had no idea what those words really meant; she just liked the tune and the beat that accompanied it—well, that and it was about Lacy's favorite thing in the whole world... cowboys.

Following along behind, she hoped she'd be able to keep her daughter busy enough over at the diner to have her forgetting about a certain dark-eyed cowboy for the rest of the morning. Danielle had thought Jesse would have kept his word. He seemed so down to earth, so connected, not superficial. *Maybe something had come up.* But he hadn't called or left her a note.

By the time they were cleaning up from the lunch shift, she knew it was going to be difficult to interest Lacy in anything else. Her daughter talked to everyone who came into the diner, pleased to be Uncle Jimmy's little June bug and setting the napkins rolled around utensils at every table. Her daughter's voice always increased in volume when she was excited, so it was easy to keep track of the conversations her little one was having with the patrons of Sullivan's Diner. Every one started or ended with her tale of being rescued by the biggest cowboy she'd ever seen.

The people in Pleasure were as friendly as she remembered, from her times visiting as a child, and treated Lacy as if she were someone special. There were quite a few long looks in her direction when they thought Danielle was too busy to notice, but she noticed all right. She'd heard from her uncle that the speculation was already running high as far as Jesse Garahan and Danielle were concerned.

A sliver of awareness raced up her spine. He was a

man worth getting to know, but if he didn't show up, how could she? Then another worry took hold: when he got here, would he want to stick around?

Once they'd bid the last customer good-bye, they got to work cleaning up and setting up for tomorrow morning. It was hard, honest work—a lot harder than her office job had been. That had only taxed her brain and stressed her out, worrying whether or not she'd get home from work in time to pick Lacy up from day care. Compared to worrying about Lacy, manual labor was a cinch.

"Do you mind if Lacy and I leave the diner before closing tomorrow?"

Her uncle looked up from grill he was scraping. "Sure thing. Have you got a date?"

The look on her face must have been priceless, because he started laughing deep, belly laughs.

"No, but I thought I'd head on over to the Circle G ranch and see if I can't talk a certain cowboy into keeping his promise to my little girl."

Her uncle looked over his shoulder to where they'd left Lacy and nodded. "Might be a good idea, else little June bug just might start asking one of my regulars to drive her out there."

Danielle laughed despite her uneasiness discussing Jesse. "She's pretty obvious."

"Like her momma—with a one-track mind."

Danielle smiled. "You could always figure out a person's motives five minutes after meeting them." Trusting her uncle to tell her the truth she asked, "Do you think Jesse is like Buddy?"

Her uncle emptied the griddle's grease trap and wiped his hands on a towel. "In some ways yes, in others, no."

"Great." She walked over to where Lacy stood looking out the window. She didn't think her daughter noticed her, so she was surprised when Lacy turned and asked, "Do you think he'll 'member about his promise?"

"It takes a lot of time and hard work to keep a ranch going," Uncle Jimmy said. "There is the herd to take care of and the horses that they use when working the herd."

"How come you know so much 'bout ranching, Unca Jimmy?"

He smiled. "I've lived in Pleasure most of my life and have friends that took over the running of their family's ranch."

Lacy was quiet on the ride home and went to the living room to watch television rather than keep them company in the kitchen. In between rolling out crust and worrying about broken promises, Danielle tiptoed down the hallway. As she'd hoped, Lacy had fallen asleep. Since she looked comfortable, she let her be.

"She all right?"

"Yes. I just wish Jesse had kept his promise and stopped by."

"Well now, I'd say that maybe you and my favorite grandniece are a mite impatient."

"Uncle Jimmy—"

"Don't Uncle Jimmy me," he said, brushing the flour from his hands. "I'm not pleased that he didn't call to explain himself, and will have something to say to him if and when he shows up, but sometimes emergencies happen—especially out on a ranch."

"Maybe you're right," she admitted. "There might be a perfectly good reason why he didn't show up."

By the time he'd put the last batch of pies in the oven,

Danielle was washing the last of the mixing bowls when Lacy wandered back in. "Can I help?"

"You're just in time to help us decide what to fix for dinner."

"Hamburgers!"

"Sure," Uncle Jimmy answered.

"Lacy and I can make Gramma's short-cut baked beans."

Her uncle smiled. "That would be great. I've got some canned pork and beans in the pantry. What else do you need?"

Danielle wished she'd thought to unpack her file box of recipes; now she'd have to recreate it from memory. "Onion, butter, and brown sugar."

"No chili powder?"

She grinned. "Dad can't eat hot spices anymore, so Mom adapted her recipe so he could eat it."

"Do you need any help?"

"It's our turn to wait on you." She wondered if she and Lacy would have coped as well if they didn't have Uncle Jimmy. "How about if you take a break and go on out to the back porch?"

He hugged Lacy first and Danielle second. "You cook, I clean."

She shook her head. "We'll talk about that later. Right now, you deserve a nice long break while my partner and I fix your supper."

"Call me if you need me."

"We will," Lacy called out. Watching him leave, her daughter turned and asked, "Did Jesse call yet?"

The urge to smack her forehead with the heel of her hand was so strong, she almost gave into the need, but at the last minute, she dug deeper and found the patience to simply shake her head and not give in to the frustration. "Not yet."

Was it wrong to pray that Lacy would wait until tomorrow to ask again?

Throwing herself into dinner preparations, she helped Lacy form the round meat patties and set them in the fridge to keep cool while they sautéed the onions in butter.

"How do you know when they're done?"

"See the part of the onion we didn't use?"

"Uh-huh," Lacy answered.

"Now look at the onion I've been stirring."

"It looks different."

"Exactly," Danielle said, pleased that her daughter was observant. "Just a little more time so the onions are translucent and we'll add the brown sugar until it gets all melted and smooth."

"Do I like onions and sugar?"

Delighted with her little one, Danielle answered, "You love them, especially in Gramma's special beans."

Scrunching up her nose as if she wasn't quite sure, Lacy shrugged. "When will they be ready?"

"Hmmm, how does Gramma know when they're ready?"

Lacy considered the question, and like a flower, her face bloomed with a smile that seemed to glow from within. "She tastes it!"

Smart as a whip and cute as a button.

Lifting the wooden spoon to her lips, Danielle taste tested the mixture. "Hmmm… just right."

"That's what Gramma always says."

"Then it must be ready," Uncle Jimmy said, walking back inside.

"Do you want to heat up the kitchen some more?" Danielle asked. "Or do you want to cook those burgers outside?"

"Let me fire up the gas grill. It'll be hot in just a few minutes. Besides," he said, looking at the beanless pot, "don't you need to let the beans soak up some of that saucy stuff?"

"That's next."

Lacy nodded. "Know what, Unca Jimmy?"

He got down to her level and asked, "What?"

"Mommy taste-tested it and it's good. Know how I know?"

He shook his head. "Tell me."

"She didn't make a funny face, so it must taste good."

Putting his hands on his knees, he straightened up and walked over to the frying pan. "Can I try it?"

Danielle handed him a teaspoon. "Sure, but you can't fiddle with it till it's on your plate."

He frowned at her but dipped his spoon in and scooped up the sauce. He touched the tip of his tongue to it. "It's not too hot." While they watched, he sampled the mixture and smiled. "It's good."

"'Course it is, silly," Lacy said. "Mommy's a good cook."

He nodded and grabbed the kitchen matches. "I'll light the grill. Be right back."

Later that night, when she was tucking Lacy in, her daughter asked, "If I'm really good tomorrow, Mommy, do you think cowboy Jesse will come and see us?"

"Oh, sweet pea." Danielle struggled to hold it together and not break down and cry. "He's just busy, honey, that's all."

"Are you sure? 'Cause daddy said he couldn't stay 'cause of me."

Danielle's heart broke. "Lacy, that's not true."

"He said he din't want to be my daddy anymore. I heard him!"

Gathering her daughter in her arms, she pressed her lips to the top of Lacy's head. "He didn't mean it that way."

"He said it," Lacy insisted.

"But—"

"Am I bad?"

This had gone far enough. Even though her uncle was right, she should be patient, she couldn't let her daughter worry that Lacy was the reason her daddy had left, or the reason Jesse had yet to fulfill his promise.

That her daughter would even think that cut a hole in Danielle's heart until it bled. "No. You are not bad. You are my perfectly wonderful, beautiful, talented daughter and the light of my life."

"But Daddy said—"

"Daddy left me too, sweetie."

"So, maybe cowboy Jesse isn't mad at me?"

Holding Lacy close, she whispered, "He isn't mad at you, and you know what? We're going out to the Circle G tomorrow."

"We are?"

"Yes, ma'am. So close your eyes and get plenty of sleep because tomorrow will be a really big day." She settled Lacy under the covers and kissed her forehead. "I love you, sweet pea."

"I love you back, Mommy."

The rumble of deep voices surprised Danielle as she was coming down the stairs. Her heart fluttered when

she recognized Jesse's smooth baritone. *He was here!*
Taking a deep cleansing breath, she prayed she would
keep her cool and not demand he tell her why he hadn't
kept his promise to Lacy.

"Hello, Jesse."

His eyes met hers and something shifted deep inside
of her. She felt different when he looked at her. Not
quite able to put her finger on just what it was, she told
herself she would worry about it later.

"Lacy will be so sorry she missed you," she said.
"She was really looking forward to it."

"I'm sorry I got held up today. I was shooting to be on
my way to town by three o'clock this afternoon," he said
with a shake of his head. "But we had a steer go loco on us."

"Loco?"

"Crazy," Jesse and her uncle said at the same time.

"What happened?"

"Damned steer broke through a section of fence we'd
just repaired and we had to chase down the rogue and
his buddies."

It seemed like a reasonable excuse, but the fact remained
that Lacy had been just as heartbroken yesterday when he
didn't show up. Although she hadn't wanted to bring it up,
she just couldn't get the image of her little one's sad face
from her mind. "About yesterday—" she began.

He pushed his Stetson to the back of his head and
smiled down at her, a look of relief on his face. "I'm
glad you understood why I didn't want to interrupt."

"Interrupt?"

"When you were all out back with the delivery." He
frowned. "Didn't you understand my note?"

Perplexed, she asked, "What note?"

"I left you a note on the table explaining that something came up and I'd be stopping by this afternoon for Lacy's lesson." He paused then shook his head. "Only, damned if I couldn't get away like I'd hoped."

"So you left me a note," she repeated, unable to hold back her smile. When he echoed that smile, she asked, "Did you leave it in the mailbox?"

It was his turn to frown. Funny, but up until that point, he seemed pretty relaxed. "I took a piece of paper off the clipboard and left the damned note in the middle of the table."

She looked at her uncle who shook his head. "Well, we didn't find anything."

He took his hat off and worried the brim with his hands. "Then Lacy and you thought I forgot about you?"

Uncle Jimmy patted her on the back, winked, and then left them alone.

Not trusting her voice or wanting him to know how close to tears they'd both been, she shrugged and a lock of hair tickled her nose. She tossed her head to get it out of her eyes, but it slid back down in her face.

Jesse reached out and smoothed the strand behind her ear. Pins and needles of awareness prickled just beneath her skin where his fingers had brushed against her.

Her sharply indrawn breath had his gaze zeroing in on her face. "You two were on my mind all day." Something dark and desperate bubbled in the depths of his eyes as he rasped, "I never break my word, Danielle."

"I was hoping you wouldn't," she admitted. She didn't know what else to say. She'd been so churned up before he arrived and now that he was here, she was all but tongue-tied.

As if he could sense the turmoil within her, he closed the gap between them and slid his arms around her. Her breath caught as the blood rushed through her veins.

"Dani darlin'," he whispered, pulling her flush against him until she could feel the pounding of his heart. Her gaze flicked to his and he lowered his head. "I've been dying to taste you."

"Oh, I—" Jesse's lips claimed hers and every thought drained from her head as his mouth took command of hers in a devastating kiss.

He slid his hand down to the small of her back and pinned her to him, the hot, hard length of him straining against the denim that held him in check. Her startled cry was echoed by the triumph in his as his tongue swept into her mouth to tangle with hers.

———

He would never be satisfied with one mind-blowing kiss. Delving deep, he stroked his hands up and down the curve of her supple spine, stopping to mold her curvy backside with his hands. When she gasped a second time, he swept his hands up her sides, cupped her face, and tipped her head back. "I want more."

Desperate to take, a heartbeat away from sweeping her into his arms and kidnapping her, he drew up short when a jubilant voice cried out, "Cowboy Jesse!"

He dropped his hands and turned just in time to catch the tiny missile aimed at his knees. He bent down and snagged Lacy before she banged her head on his knee bone. "Hey there, little darlin'."

"I knew you'd come," she crowed as he lifted her up into his arms. "I told Mommy you would."

Dazed from the absolute trust shining in her blue eyes, he looked from daughter to mother and shook his head. "I always keep my promises."

"But you din't yesterday," Lacy reminded him.

"I left your mommy a note at the diner."

"I knew it!" The little girl shocked the shit out of him when she threw back her head and gave a rebel yell. He couldn't help it; he laughed and suddenly Danielle and Lacy were both in his arms, laughing with him.

The bottom just dropped out of his stomach as his world spun in circles and his heart skidded closer to the edge, like he had out at Devil's Bowl.

"Can we go riding now?"

Touching the tip of his finger to the end of her turned up nose, he shook his head. "The horses have all gone to bed for the night, but I wanted to ask if your mommy could bring you to the ranch tomorrow afternoon."

"Yes!" Lacy answered for her mother.

"Well, I—"

"Yes," her uncle added from the living room.

"I guess it's settled then," Jesse said, running the tip of his finger along the curve of Danielle's cheek. "Say yes, Dani. I've got something I need to do tomorrow night, so if you drive out in the afternoon it'll save me time so I can squeeze in a lesson before dinner."

When she hesitated, he tucked her hair behind her ear and tipped her face up. The look in her eyes warned him not to kiss her. Hell, he never liked being told what to do. He claimed her mouth with a swift kiss that was over far too soon.

"You don't kiss Mommy like Unca Jimmy does." Lacy punctuated that statement with a giggle.

"I sure hope not, little lady," her uncle called out from where he stood in the doorway.

Unable to help himself, Jesse pressed his lips to Lacy's forehead. "Is he the only man who kisses your mommy?"

He thought he heard Danielle grumbling under her breath, but was distracted when Lacy answered, "Uh-huh… 'specially since Daddy left us."

"That's enough for one night, Lacy." Her mother shifted until Lacy was back in her arms, and she stepped out of Jesse's. "Time for bed."

"Can cowboy Jesse tuck me in?"

Every drop of spit dried up in his mouth. He couldn't have answered even if he wanted to, so he did the next best thing and nodded. Following behind them, he grabbed the handrail to steady himself as they ascended the stairs.

A night-light shone from the open door at the end of the hallway. Walking toward it, he wondered if this was a passing fancy or if Lacy would want him to stick around and tuck her in every night. Damned if that thought didn't appeal almost as much as getting his hands on Danielle—only the next time he got his hands on her, there wouldn't be anything to stop him from satisfying his bone-deep need to make love to her.

Danielle settled Lacy under the covers, kissed her cheek, and turned to reach for his hand. She squeezed it—maybe it was her way of letting him know it was OK with her that he be in her daughter's bedroom like this, about to take part in their nightly ritual.

His throat tightened, but he ignored it and bent down to kiss the tip of Lacy's nose. She giggled and wrapped her arms around his neck and kissed his cheek. "I love you, cowboy Jesse."

A lump the size of Texas filled his throat as moisture filled his eyes. His voice useless, he answered her the only way he knew how, by wrapping his arms around her tiny little frame and hugging her close. The precious life in his arms snuggled close as if she were settling in for the night.

"All right, sweetie, Jesse has to go home and get some rest if he's going to be getting up at dawn to take care of the ranch animals."

Grateful that she intervened, yet at the same time sorry that he had to go, Jesse eased back from the little one and brushed the hair out of her eyes. "Sleep tight."

"...and don't let the bedbugs bite!" Lacy finished, smiling as she closed her eyes.

Jesse didn't know how long he would have stayed there if Danielle hadn't grabbed a hold of his hand and given it a tug to get him moving. When they were in the hallway, she stopped and looked up at him. "Thank you, Jesse."

After the outpouring of affection he'd received from both of the Brockway ladies, he was the one who should be down on his knees thanking her. "I didn't do anything special," he finally grumbled.

"There's where you're wrong," she told him. "You just proved to my daughter that a man can keep his word and can be trusted." She lifted her hand to touch his face but hesitated, drawing back at the last moment.

He snagged her hand in his and brought it to his lips. "You and Lacy are something special," he rasped. "I can't wait until you come out to the Circle G. There's so much I want to show you."

"Tomorrow," she whispered, tilting her head back.

"Tomorrow," he rasped, sealing his words with a kiss.

Chapter 8

JESSE SMILED AND TOUCHED THE TIP OF HIS TONGUE TO the back of her knee. The soft, sweet moan of pleasure was his cue to begin licking a path up her toned and tasty thigh. His fingertips circling her hipbones had her squirming and shifting. He smiled as he pressed his lips to the top of her thigh and inhaled her sweet, subtle scent, reminding him of—coffee?

"What the hell?"

"'Bout time you woke up, Bro." Tyler held out a mug of coffee.

"Explains why her thigh smelled like coffee," he mumbled, reaching for the cup.

Tyler grinned. "Sounds like you had a good time last night."

Jesse drank deeply and sighed. His brain would start working by the time he got to the bottom of the mug.

Tyler was leaving when he turned back. "By the way, where'd the money come from?"

Jesse wondered how long it would take before somebody asked him. He wasn't sure why, but he didn't want to say anything just yet. He shrugged in answer.

After a few moments of silence, his brother took the hint and left. Getting out of bed, he stepped into his jeans and pulled on a pair of clean socks. Man, he'd have to do something special to thank Emily for doing his wash.

What, he had no clue, but he'd think of something. Right now he had to get a move on.

"No rest for the wicked." He pulled on a clean shirt and his boots, and was ready for the day.

Over breakfast, Dylan asked him about the money, but he ignored him. He'd have to change tactics by tonight, because the longer he held out, the more his brothers would try to pry the truth out of him. It wasn't a big deal, just something he wanted to keep to himself just a little longer.

"Talked to Tommy yesterday," Jesse said to change the subject.

Tyler reached over to squeeze Emily's hand and explained, "He's one of our New York City cousins."

"The fireman?" Ronnie asked.

"One of them. He and his three brothers are firemen."

"Yeah." Jesse grinned. "Pat and John can't make it, but Tom and Mike will be here. They're coming in a week early."

"Maybe they could help move the herd. Did you ask them about it?"

Jesse scooped up a mouthful of fluffy scrambled eggs and nodded.

Dylan asked, "What about the Justiss side of the family?"

"Matt and Ben will be here, but they, uh—" He looked from Emily to Ronnie and back and shrugged.

Tyler caught Jesse's look and nodded. Jesse was glad his brother understood; where Matt and Ben were concerned, there had to be women involved. Not that they expected their Garahan cousins to line up dates for them; they just liked to know the lay of the land and availability of female distractions in the vicinity of the ranch. Time was always at a premium when they visited, especially since they spent a good chunk of each visit working the land with their cousins.

"Something wrong?" Emily asked.

"Maybe we can help," Ronnie offered.

Jesse smiled into his cup. "Uh, no thanks. Got it covered."

"Well," Emily said, "if you change your mind."

He set his mug down and stood up. "I'll let you know. Thanks again for the clean clothes."

She smiled. "My pleasure. Do you have any for me today?"

He shook his head. "No, ma'am, not yet." He grabbed his Stetson off the peg by the back door. "Maybe tomorrow."

"You'll tell us eventually where the money came from?"

Tyler's question had him pausing to answer. "I didn't steal it. Can't you just accept it and let it go?"

"For now," Dylan agreed.

Relief arrowed through him. A reprieve... for now.

"Danielle and Lacy will be stopping by this afternoon. Will you and Ronnie be here?"

Emily smiled and said, "We'd love to meet the ladies responsible for turning your head."

"Who said anything about that?" Jesse grumbled.

Emily just smiled. "Tell them we can't wait to meet them."

Jesse shrugged and followed his brothers out to the barn.

———

"So what's up with Matt and Ben?" Tyler asked as they rode out to the west of their land.

Dylan moved closer so he could hear their conversation.

Jesse shrugged. "They just wanted to make sure there were females over the age of twenty-five."

It was Tyler's turn to laugh. "Something must have happened since we saw them last."

Dylan chuckled. "Yeah," he snickered, "they got older."

Jesse started to laugh. "Maybe he remembers the last time they were here—and what happened with the Johnson sisters."

"Yeah," Tyler said. "Those two were set on meeting up with two real, live U.S. Marshals."

"Where did they get those police-issue handcuffs?" Jesse asked.

Tyler shook his head.

"Well, they returned the favor when you went up there a few years ago." Dylan smiled. "When they sicced those redheaded sisters on you."

Tyler shuddered. "Maybe I have a way to get even with them. I think Jolene could help with a couple of names." Jesse smiled. This was gonna be fun. "They have a couple of regulars that would be just what the doctor ordered for our cousins the lawmen."

"They'll be pissed." Dylan was smiling.

"Yeah," Jesse said. "We haven't had a good old fashioned donnybrook with our cousins in a long time."

"That's because the last time, Ben broke your nose and you couldn't ride herd with us for a couple of days."

"So I owe him." To Jesse's mind, it was that simple.

Riding side by side, the brothers were united in their quest to outdo their know-it-all cousins from the Rockies.

Tyler looked up and smiled. "It's gonna be a good day."

"Always a good day when you can spend it in the saddle, riding our land," Dylan added.

"We're burning daylight." Jesse squeezed his thighs against his horse, urging more speed from Dodge as they rode away from the sunrise.

Hours later, exhausted, needing to refuel, they rode back to the ranch house. Giving their horses a much-needed break, they rubbed them down and set them loose in the corral. Ready to grab some grub themselves, they filed into the kitchen and opened the fridge.

Jesse pulled out a tall glass pitcher of iced tea and rasped, "Bless you, Emily." He tipped back his head and lifted the pitcher high—

"Damn it, Jess," Tyler grumbled coming in behind him. "Get a glass."

Dylan chuckled. "Saw him kissing Dodge this mornin'."

Jesse stretched his arm as far as it would go and poured icy cold tea down his throat. Wiping his sleeve across his mouth he grinned. "And my lips never touched the pitcher."

Tyler shook his head. "Baby brother's got talent."

Dylan grabbed for the pitcher, but as he lifted the pitcher, Tyler shoved a glass at him.

Shrugging, he poured a glass and passed the pitcher. By the time it made it back to Jesse, there was less than half a glass left. "Hey—"

"Ronnie said she was leaving us some salads and sandwiches and not to touch the casserole filled with meatballs and sauce."

Jesse's eyes widened. He'd do just about anything for his sister-in-law's meatballs. "I'll bet she didn't count 'em when she was making 'em." He pulled out the macaroni and potato salads and handed them off to his brothers. With a quick glance over his shoulder at Dylan, he grinned and said, "She'll never know."

As if that decided it, Tyler said, "I'll grab the forks."

"One meatball each," Dylan warned, "or Ronnie will know we snitched some."

Jesse agreed. "I'll fill in with sauce so she can't tell where we took them from." Working as a team, the brothers each took a turn spearing a cold meatball covered with sauce. "Man, Dylan, when you get tired of being married to Ronnie, you just let me know."

His brother's response was a jab to the shoulder. Jesse could have dodged it, but then Dylan would have been honor bound to try to hit him again. Philosophically, he figured he deserved it, so he may as well accept the punch and be done with it.

Tyler grinned. "So you thinking about convincing Ronnie that Dylan's tired of her?"

Jesse's gaze shot to Dylan's. The deadly intent in his brother's dark eyes told him just how soon Dylan would be giving Ronnie up—never. That was just fine with him.

"Nope, got my eye on a curvy blonde. Danielle and Lacy will be stopping by this afternoon. I'm gonna give her riding lessons."

"Danielle?" Tyler asked.

He shook his head. "Nope. Lacy."

Dylan seemed to be listening but didn't say anything. Finishing off his meatball, he hesitated, then speared a second one. "So when are you gonna tell us where the money came from?"

Jesse wondered if he should share his news about his win out at Devil's Bowl. Rather than answer, he chomped on the savory ball of meat and shrugged. "Man your wife can cook, Dylan."

Dylan was still watching him carefully, as if judging whether or not Jesse was really going to try to steal Ronnie from him. Yeah, like that could happen in this lifetime. "Give it up, Dylan, you know Ronnie's only got eyes for you."

Dylan finally relaxed and Tyler nudged him. "She's partial to Dylan 'cause he married her to spring her out of jail."

Dylan shook his head as he stuck his fork in another meatball. Taking a bite, he chewed, swallowed, and grinned. "My woman's a great cook, and I hated the thought of seeing her behind bars, but that wasn't why I married her."

Jesse and Tyler shared a knowing look. "Must be some hidden skill that she possesses."

Tyler laughed, but Dylan didn't. "She sure as hell isn't gonna show it, or share it, with anyone else but me," Dylan ground out.

"Hey, no offense, big brother," Jesse said, backing away with his hands up in front of him to ward off the impending attack, "but she's taken the edge off of you. The old you would have planted a fist in my face by now."

"I'm still thinking about it."

Tyler grabbed for the bowl of meat and sauce. "So who's gonna tell Ronnie what happened to dinner?"

The three looked at one another and broke into gales of laughter. Jesse dug into the potato salad and heaped it onto a plate. "She and Emily really take good care of us," he said, looking at the plates, utensils, and cups

Emily had left out for them to use. "I can't wait till Danielle and Lacy get here."

His brothers waited for him to say more, but in the end were left wondering. He wasn't ready to say anything else. By the time the hole in his belly was satisfied, they'd polished off most of the potato salad and half of the noodle salad. "Maybe Ronnie won't notice that we ate some of the meatballs," Jesse said staring at the bowl.

Dylan smacked him on the back of the head. "Some? Hell, we ate half of it!"

Tyler smiled. "It'll be worth catching hell for." He reached for a sandwich and sat at the table.

"Dylan will have to sweet talk her so she doesn't stay mad at us," Jesse said. "I'd hate it if she got mad and stopped cooking for us."

As one, the brothers paused to stare at Jesse as that thought sank in. "Damn," Tyler rasped.

Dylan's smile was just this side of wicked. "I've got a secret weapon, don't you boys worry none."

Chapter 9

DANIELLE WONDERED IF SHE'D EVER SLEEP THROUGH the night again. She'd tossed and turned but couldn't get the memory of Jesse pulling her close and kissing her out of her head. Lord, the man could kiss.

Looking over at her daughter, she smiled. Lacy had been good as gold today, and she wondered if it was because her favorite cowboy had tucked her in last night or because they were headed to the Circle G. "Are you sure you don't want to stay and help Uncle Jimmy?" Although she already knew the answer to that particular question, she still waited to hear what her daughter would say.

She was surprised when Lacy answered. "I promised Unca Jimmy we'd help all day tomorrow. Will cowboy Jesse be waiting for us when we get there?"

Danielle sighed. "He didn't say exactly what time this afternoon he'd be able to meet us, but he will be there. Until then, you will have to learn some patience, sweet pea. Besides," she said, hoping to redirect Lacy's attention, "Jesse called earlier to say that we'll get to meet Ronnie and Emily—his brother Dylan's wife and his oldest brother Tyler's fiancée. They're going to be home when we get to the Circle G."

"I gots to see him, Mommy. I forgot to tell him something."

"Don't worry, you will. Now, pay attention, sweet pea,"

she said to distract her. "I need you to be on the lookout for a big old tree standing all alone right next to the road."

"Why?"

"That's the road into the Circle G."

Lacy was practically vibrating with excitement when she spotted the tree. "There!" she shouted, scaring the life out of Danielle. Before she could remind her not to yell when they were in the car, unless it was a dire emergency, Lacy started bouncing in her seat. "We're here, we're here!"

It was another mile or so before they reached a huge gate.

"Why is there a *C* in a circle?" Lacy asked.

"That's a *G* sweetie. It stands for Garahan."

Her heart was beating just a little too quickly for comfort, but she put the car in park, patted her daughter's hand, and said, "Sit tight and watch me."

Lacy grinned. "OK!"

When she opened the gate and got back in the car, Lacy turned to her. "It's like in the movies, isn't it, Mommy?"

She smiled and nodded. "OK. Now wait here."

Lacy did as she was told and was waiting patiently for her to get back in. "Do you think it's much further?"

"I can't see the ranch house from here, can you?"

Her daughter shook her head so hard, her cowgirl hat flew off. Out of the corner of her eye, Danielle saw Lacy's hand move toward the seat belt-release button. "Don't even think about it, or I'll turn this car around so fast your head will spin."

"But, Mommy—"

"I mean it. You promised to be on your best behavior today. Unbuckling your seat belt before I stop the car isn't behaving."

Lacy hung her head but put her hands back in her lap. "Sorry."

Danielle didn't notice the fork in the road until Lacy was pointing at it. "Which way?" she asked. "I don't see the house."

Danielle frowned. "I don't either. I didn't remember hearing that the road forked." Kicking herself for not getting the telephone number for the ranch house, she turned to the left and followed the road, hoping it was the right direction. If they got really lost, she could always turn around or call Uncle Jimmy.

"Oooohh." Lacy pointed to the pond. "Can we go swimming? I'm hot."

Danielle laughed. "Not right now. I think we've gone too far. We should have seen the ranch by now. Let's turn around."

"Can't we just go over and look at the water?"

The plaintive note in her daughter's voice swayed her. It was a pretty sight, with the grass blowing in the hot afternoon breeze and the water rippling as it moved across the surface. "We're only going to look at it."

"Yay!" Lacy was out of her seat belt in a flash and had her hand on the door latch.

"Wait up!" Danielle called out, but her daughter was already out of the car and running toward the water. Hurrying to catch up, she reached Lacy's side as her daughter got down on her knees and bent toward the water. "I'm just gonna touch it," she said, looking up at her mother. "OK?"

Moved by a similar need, she agreed. "Let's see if it's a cool as it looks."

Running their fingers through it wasn't enough; they

bent farther until Danielle had Lacy around the waist and her little arms were wet up to her elbows. "That's enough for now, or you'll end up head first in the water and then we'll have to go back to Uncle Jimmy's."

Lacy sat up so fast they tumbled over into the sweet smelling grass. Laughing, Danielle hugged her to her heart, and Lacy's little arms wrapped around Danielle's neck as she pressed her lips to Danielle's cheek. "I'm ready to go."

How many more moments would there be before Lacy was too old to want to throw her arms around Danielle and kiss her? Letting her breath go out in a sigh, Danielle gathered her daughter in her arms and got to her feet.

"You don't have to carry me."

"I want to."

Lacy leaned her head against the side of Danielle's. "I like it out here."

Danielle's heart stumbled in her chest at the realization that she did too. "It's pretty special out here by the pond, isn't it?"

Lacy nodded and her hat flopped around from her back to her shoulder. Putting it on Lacy's head, she set her little girl on her feet and opened the door. "Let's go."

Backtracking, they were at the fork in the road again. Danielle marveled at the beauty of the sweeping pastures and trees lining the road.

"There! It's right there!"

Up ahead, the road widened into a huge area that encompassed the driveway and the road that led to the barn just past it. The old two-story farmhouse was picture perfect with its bright white paint and colorful flowers spilling out of pots on the steps and planters on the porch railing. The back door opened and a pretty redhead stood smiling in welcome. "We thought you'd never get here."

Danielle turned to help unbuckle Lacy, but her daughter was already running toward the back porch. She was shaking her head as she got out.

"Me too," her daughter said, grabbing a hold of the woman's hand. "I'm Lacy and that's my mommy."

Laughing, Danielle bent to touch the tip of her finger on her daughter's nose. "Someone was really impatient to get here."

"We were starting to worry that you'd missed the turn off."

Danielle looked up as a beautiful brunette joined them on the porch. "Welcome to the Circle G." She held out her hand, and Danielle shook it.

"Thanks. In case you didn't hear the introductions, this is my daughter, Lacy."

"And you're Danielle Brockway," the redhead answered. "I'm Emily Langley and this is Ronnie Garahan."

Danielle smiled. "It's a pleasure to meet you both. Thanks for letting us visit."

"We've been wanting to meet you," Emily said. "Jesse's been so busy lately that we didn't think we'd get to before the celebration."

"What are you celebrating?"

Emily smiled at Lacy's question and bent down and brushed wisps of hair out of Lacy's face. "Our town."

"Take Pride in Pleasure Day," Ronnie finished for her.

"Can we come too?"

"Absolutely," Emily said, getting to her feet. "I'm going to be making brownies and helping my cousin

with the entertainment for the day." She stared at
Danielle for a few moments and then smiled. "It's going
to be quite a hit with the ladies."

"Sounds intriguing." Danielle figured she'd be hearing all about it before their visit was through.

"I wish I could chat, but I have to fix a second dinner."

"What happened to the first one?" Lacy wanted to know.

"Somebody ate most of it."

"Did they break down the back door?"

Ronnie smiled. "No, they walked right in and helped
themselves."

From the way the ladies were smiling, Danielle had
a good idea who the culprits were. "Did they leave any
clues behind?"

"Other than demolishing half of the meatballs I
made early this morning, so I wouldn't have to cook
in this heat?"

"Oh." Danielle knew what that felt like. She and her
uncle worked hard to do the same. "Uncle Jimmy and I
do most of the baking and prep work a day ahead."

"Me too!" Lacy chimed in.

"You too, sweet pea." Looking up, she saw the un-
disguised interest on the faces of the two women. She
wondered just how much Jesse had told them about her
and Lacy. "We're here a little earlier than planned, but
Jesse said that would be OK."

"So, I hear you want to learn to ride." Ronnie seemed
excited about the prospect.

"Yes!"

Laughing at the way little Lacy jumped up and down,
Ronnie held out her hand. "How about if I introduce you
to a couple of our horses? They love visitors."

"I thought you had to make dinner," Lacy said, taking Ronnie's hand.

"I changed my mind. Jesse and his brothers can have the leftover sandwiches they didn't eat earlier, since they ate half the pot of sauce and meatballs."

"It was cowboy Jesse and his brothers who stole the meatballs?"

Lacy's horrified look had Danielle reassuring her that Ronnie was only kidding when she said someone had walked into the house to steal food.

"I'm sorry, Lacy," Ronnie said. "I was joking. Those men come and go, and eat us out of house and home. It's hard work to keep up with their appetites."

"Especially when they work so hard during the day," Emily added. "They use up every ounce of food they eat by lunchtime."

"But they didn't eat their sammiches," Lacy pointed out.

Ronnie smiled. "Not all of them."

Lacy grabbed a hold of Ronnie's hand and danced along in front of Danielle and Emily.

"I learned to ride when I was your age," Ronnie said, smiling down at Lacy. "And when I was old enough, I learned how to barrel ride."

"Really?"

"Truly. My parents let me take lessons back East."

"I thought you were from Texas."

"I'm from New Jersey," Ronnie said and Lacy started to laugh. "What's so funny?"

Lacy tugged on her hand and said, "There's no cowgirls from there."

Ronnie patted the mini pink Stetson and reminded her, "That's where I'm from, and I can tell you, they not only have horses back home, they have cows, sheep, and llamas."

Danielle watched her daughter laughing with Dylan's wife and felt a sharp tug in the vicinity of her heart. She was grateful that her uncle had invited them to come out for the summer. If they stayed—well, best not to think of that right now.

Wanting to make sure that they didn't wear out their welcome, she said, "If Ronnie said she learned to ride horses in New Jersey, then you should believe her."

Ronnie was laughing as they disappeared into the barn.

"Ronnie's an excellent horsewoman," Emily said as they were walking toward the house. "She won't let anything happen to Lacy."

With one last look over her shoulder at the doorway to the barn, Danielle stopped. "If you're sure."

"She's great with kids and will watch Lacy like a hawk."

They were by the back steps when Emily asked, "How long are you staying in Pleasure?"

There was something open and genuine about Emily's question, so she answered honestly. "I'm not sure, that depends on whether or not I can find a job and support Lacy and myself."

"Ah, so you're not married?"

She tried not to smile at the obvious interest behind the question. "Divorced."

"Oh," Emily said, her tone sympathetic.

Danielle wanted to ask her if she'd been married once before too, but heard a faint whinny from the barn and knew she needed to be with Lacy in case she got nervous around the animals.

"Look—" she began.

"Why don't we go see what they're doing," Emily suggested.

Relief speared through her. "Thanks." Danielle ran the last few feet and entered the cool, darkness. "Lacy?"

"Back here, Mommy!"

Her daughter sounded ecstatic. "We're introducing her to two of our older horses," Ronnie said. "On your left is Trigger, he's eighteen, and on your right is Champ, he's nineteen."

Danielle moved closer so she could rub the blaze between Trigger's eyes. "He kind of looks like the real Trigger, doesn't he Lacy?"

"Uh-huh, just like in the shows Gramma watches."

Emily was smiling when she asked, "Did you meet Champ too?"

Danielle moved to the other stall and scratched the inquisitive beast behind his ears. "Hello, boy."

Champ lifted his head high and whinnied in appreciation.

"What do you think of these two, Lacy?" Emily asked, coming to stand next to Danielle.

"They're big." She stood on her tippytoes and couldn't quite reach Trigger's velvety-soft muzzle. "How am I gonna get all the way up there?"

"I can lift you up," Ronnie offered. "But there are some things you need to learn before you sit on the back of a horse. Are you sure you don't want to wait for Jesse?"

Lacy's eyes opened wide. "He won't mind, will he, Mommy?"

"I don't know." Danielle looked at Ronnie, who shrugged.

While Ronnie talked to Lacy about the different parts

of a horse, which side to approach first, and which side spooks the horse, Danielle wondered if it was going to be too hard for her little one to remember, but Lacy proved to be an excellent pupil.

"So, I'm gonna talk nice to him, be careful not stand by his back legs 'cause if I scare him, he could kick me."

Ronnie smiled. "That's right. You're a fast learner."

Emily and Danielle were impressed by Ronnie's patience. "Have you worked with kids before?" Danielle wanted to know—not that it would make a difference; she had a gut feeling about Emily and Ronnie and trusted her daughter with the women. At least she could read women; it was men that she had a problem understanding.

"I have some younger cousins that I taught to ride before I got divorced."

Danielle was immediately intrigued. "Dylan's not your first husband?"

The other woman grinned. "No, but he'll be my last."

Their shared laughter lightened Danielle's heart. Lacy smiled up at them. "I like it here, Mommy."

Danielle smiled. "I do too. You know, it's funny," she said. "I took a wrong turn and ended up by this beautiful pond. The air smelled so wonderful: fresh, clean, different. It's hard to explain."

Emily and Ronnie shared a glance and a secret smile. Apparently, they shared similar feelings about the pond.

"I hope it was all right that we stopped there. We didn't disturb anything—"

"We touched the water," Lacy added. "It was cool and felt good. Mommy let me reach in up to my elbows."

"It's one of the special spots at the Circle G, and unless you've experienced it firsthand," Emily said, "it's hard to explain about the intriguing scent and feeling of coming home."

Danielle glanced at Emily. "Exactly."

"Now that you've met two of our horses," Ronnie said, "would you like to see the swing and the ranch house?"

Lacy immediately starting jumping up and down again, and in her excitement forgot about the horses. But Ronnie moved to grab Trigger by the halter while Emily did the same with Champ.

Danielle realized a few minutes too late that her daughter had spooked the horses. "Lacy and I will wait outside. We're sorry." She looked down at her daughter. "Aren't we?"

Tears gathered in Lacy's eyes, making them appear bluer. But instead of breaking down and crying, she wiped her eyes with her knuckles and sniffed. "I broke the Code, didn't I? Now cowboy Jesse won't ever teach me to ride." Crestfallen, her little shoulders slumped forward as she quietly walked toward the front of the barn.

Danielle was worried about her daughter's infatuation with the man… *Good Lord, what now?*

They stepped out in the sunshine just as the ground started to rumble.

"Is it an earthquake?"

"No, sweetie," Danielle called out looking toward the sound. "The birds are still chirping and one of the horses whinnied. When it's an earthquake, there is an eerie calm right before it happens."

"So what's making that sound?"

Emily and Ronnie joined them and Emily smiled. "Look's like you'll have a chance to see cowboy Jesse again."

"Cowboy Jesse!" Lacy called out, racing toward the three riders headed their way at a fast trot.

Fearing the men wouldn't see Lacy in time to stop, Danielle raced after her, scooping her up in her arms. But her toe caught on a dip in the driveway, and she lost her balance. Her protective instincts were screaming for her to hurry, as she cocooned Lacy in her arms and twisted so she took the brunt of the fall on her back.

She couldn't catch her breath, but from the way Lacy was squirming, she knew that her daughter was unharmed.

"Hell's fire, woman," a familiar deep voice ground out. "Where are you hurt?"

Jesse! But Danielle couldn't answer, she'd knocked the wind from her lungs and couldn't get enough air back in to breathe, let alone speak.

"Just take it easy." He sounded so confident, the fear that she'd pass out from lack of air dissipated. "It'll get easier to breathe in a minute."

"Mommy's hurt and it's my fault," Lacy whispered. "Can you fix her?"

For her daughter's sake, she willed her eyes to open and wished she hadn't. Jesse's dark eyes, filled with concern, looked down at her while the grim set of his mouth had her wondering if the Lord had a sense of humor. This was the second time they'd met in the daylight and the second time he'd had to rescue her. But that thought slipped away as the memory of their first kiss filled her. They were so close; if she lifted up just a few inches, their lips would touch.

A moan of sheer pleasure slipped out before she could get her scrambled brains to work.

"Maybe she busted a rib," another voice rumbled from somewhere close by.

"I'm checking, damn it!" Jesse ground out, though his strong hands gentled as he probed her sides, checking for any slight variation in the pattern of her ribs.

She winced as his fingers brushed closer to her spine. She'd landed hard enough to have a couple of sore spots that would probably be bruises tomorrow.

"Did I hurt you?" The strangled sound of Jesse's voice had her gaze lifting from where it had gotten stuck—the middle of his chest. When their eyes met, the concern was still there, but it was mixed with another emotion, one she could lose herself in—desire.

Needing to find her balance and not give in to what her body clamored for, she answered, "No, but it hurts where I hit the ground."

"Her ribs are good," he called out, not breaking eye contact. While she watched, the look in his eyes changed, and he was back fully in control of his emotions. She envied his ability to do that. Her belly was filled with butterflies and her body sparking like exposed wires everywhere he touched.

Danielle closed her eyes and willed her heart to slow down and her lungs to work properly, so she could draw in a deeper breath. Thankfully, the men surrounding her distracted her long enough for her body to take over and get its rhythm back. Although the first breath was painful, the next one was easier to draw.

Lacy squeezed around Jesse and was clinging to Danielle's arm like a burr and crying. Before she could soothe her baby girl, Jesse reached out to brush away Lacy's tears. "Your momma will be fine."

"I'm OK, sweet pea," she rasped, agreeing with Jesse. Well, she would be in a few minutes. "I guess this is how it feels to get thrown from a bull."

The intense look in Jesse's eyes softened, as if he realized she wasn't badly hurt if she could joke about it. She tried to push herself up, but a big hand pressed against her shoulder to keep her still. An indefinable sizzle arced from where Jesse touched her, but had it come from him or her? Using all of her willpower to separate herself from the delicious vibrations surrounding this man, she ignored the fluttering in her belly and heady rush of excitement tingling in her shoulder, sprinting through her body.

"Best give it a few more minutes. If you did fracture a rib, it could poke through something important."

Lacy's hands covered her mouth and her eyes grew round as saucers. The strangled sound she made had Danielle shaking off the last of the feelings Jesse elicited with just one touch, and she scooted sideways, glaring at him as she reached out to take hold of her daughter's hand. "I'm fine. I had the wind knocked out of me, but that's all. Jesse's just being overly cautious."

"Can't be too cautious," one of the men warned. "He still has to check your limbs, so lie still."

The deep voice must belong to the oldest Garahan. Although she'd met them years ago, she didn't remember, but it was easy to recognize the familial traits. They were still the spitting image of one another: tall, dark hair, dark eyes, and go-to-hell smiles on their three handsome faces. Good Lord, they were dangerous to a woman's heart.

"I've got it under control here. Ty, why don't you

and Dylan take care of the horses." Jesse turned to speak to Lacy again, reassuring her that Danielle would be fine, and the memory of her daughter throwing her arms around his neck and claiming she loved him filled Danielle. A lump formed, and she had to blink back tears that threatened to fall. She had been just as swept away last night by the man kneeling at her side.

"I'm gonna check your momma's arms and legs to make sure she didn't break anything," he said soothingly. "OK, little darlin'?"

Lacy sniffled and nodded.

Her daughter's permission received, he turned back to Danielle and her heart tumbled over in her breast. The desire was back in his gaze, and for a moment, she was afraid that if he touched her, they'd both go up in flames.

"Jesse, I'm OK—"

In a heartbeat the look in his eyes changed and a feeling of déjà vu filled her. He was frowning down at her—the exact same frown he'd had the day he'd pulled over to help them. "You gonna let me drive you to the hospital for X-rays?"

"No."

"Then lie still and behave."

"Yeah, Mommy," Lacy said, patting her mother's cheek. "Behave."

Digging deep for a calm she surely didn't feel, Danielle snapped, "Fine."

He snorted and she wondered if he was covering up a laugh. Her gaze met his, but he was all business as he warned Lacy to ease back so he could show her how he checked his steer and horses for injuries.

"But she's Mommy, not a cow."

"That's right," he agreed. "But the funny thing is, a leg bone is a leg bone." He slipped his hands around her left ankle and she struggled not to moan. His tender touch set fire to her skin.

He hesitated. "You all right?"

She nodded and he turned back to Lacy. "We have to be careful, but there's no cuts or bones sticking out—"

"Don't scare her—"

"I'm not a'scared, Mommy."

Jesse smiled at his little helper. "Now, I'm going to run my hands along her legs to make sure the bones don't feel like they've separated or cracked." His eyes deepened to a rich, dark brown, reminding her of the bittersweet chocolate she loved.

When she licked her lips, he froze and closed his eyes. He was just as affected as she by his hands smoothing along the length of her legs.

"Did you find something?" Lacy asked, poking him in the shoulder.

Jesse shook his head and moved to test her other leg. The sight of her smooth and supple quads shot right to his core and the heart of his problem. He wanted Danielle so badly he ached. It was next to impossible not to be affected by the beauty lying on the ground before him. Praying for the strength to finish the job, he turned toward Lacy, and said, "Now, we check her arms."

"But I didn't land on them," Danielle protested.

"You won't know just what you hit until tomorrow or the day after, when the aches and pains start making themselves known."

She frowned up at him but relaxed again so he could check her arms.

"Can I try it?" Lacy asked, obviously wanting to help.

"Let me check first."

She nodded and waited. After he was certain nothing was out of place, he eased back and urged Lacy to put her hands on her mother's upper arm, then he placed his on top of hers and said, "Now, close your eyes and imagine your mom's arm bone all in one piece, and then let your fingers tell your mind what's going on beneath the skin."

Lacy's concentration went right to his heart. That she trusted him to take care of her mother added to the growing affection he felt toward the little cowgirl.

"It's good." Lacy's excitement was infectious.

"That's what I think too."

"Can I get up now?"

"We gots to check your other arm first, Mommy."

Danielle sighed and let them finish. It was the hardest thing she'd done in a long time, subjecting herself to Jesse's touch without giving in to the desire that threatened to pull her under. She wanted this man with a desperation that she'd never felt before. Whether or not her mind was ready to accept what her heart was telling her, she knew they wouldn't be able to keep their hands off one another once they were finally alone.

She sat up and pulled Lacy onto her lap. Her daughter had stopped crying but was still sniffling. Before she could soothe her, Jesse ground out, "What in Sam Hill do you think you were doing running out like that in front of the horses? You could have been seriously injured."

Disbelief shot through her system like a bolt of

lightning, blasting all thoughts of lovemaking from her mind. She gave him tit for tat. "Making sure you didn't run down my daughter."

It was his turn to look shocked. Shaking his head, as if he could not believe what she'd just said, he grumbled, "Out here, people give us credit for having a brain and quick reflexes. Lacy would have been far safer running out to greet me and my brothers than you were lying in the road barely breathing."

Her eyes narrowed to slits. It was hard, but she held on to her temper—by a thread. "So your reflexes only work if the target is moving toward you and not immobile?"

His eyes grew impossibly darker, as if his pupils were swallowing his irises and nothing was left but endless black. Her father had a hair-trigger temper, and it looked like Jesse did too. But he surprised her; while she watched, his eyes grew lighter again and his jaw relaxed. It was as if he gained control over his anger one degree at a time. She liked him better for it, but would be damned before she admitted it.

"I broke the Code," Lacy admitted, looking like she'd just confessed to a cardinal sin.

Jesse nodded and patted her hand. "Why don't we get your momma inside and get her a nice cool drink, then you can tell me all about it."

Danielle didn't want him to be kind to either one of them, and she didn't want a cool drink, damn it. Before she could voice her opinion, she was unceremoniously hauled to her feet and into Jesse's arms.

"I'm perfectly capable of walking."

"Best not to take any chances."

"Need a hand?" Tyler called out walking toward them.

"Yeah," Jesse answered. "Lacy, this is my big brother Tyler. You can trust him."

"OK," she said, grabbing a hold of his hand, but instead of walking her back to the ranch house, he swept her up onto his shoulders.

"Look, Mommy!" Lacy called out from her high perch. "I can touch the sky!"

Wondering if she and her daughter were going to get their hearts broken if they got any more attached to the men of the Circle G, she bit back what she wanted to say.

Jesse leaned down and rasped, "Let her enjoy herself for a little while. She might forget how scared she was when she thought you were hurt."

Their eyes met and she wanted to disagree, but Lacy's giggling was infectious, and she realized he was right and thanked Jesse for his help.

Just as Danielle was about to warn Tyler not to bang Lacy's head on the doorjamb, he swept Lacy from his shoulders and into his arms. Her squeals of excitement were balm to Danielle's aching heart.

Instead of Lacy's father making her laugh, it was a family of brothers Danielle'd met years ago, men who were all but strangers to her now… but wouldn't be by the time their visit was over.

Jesse was so gentle with her and kind to Lacy.

"You're quiet." His deep voice summoned her from her thoughts. "Where do you hurt?"

She laughed; she couldn't help it. He set her on her feet by a chair and urged her to sit. When she had, she finally answered him. "All over."

"I could still drive you over to the hospital," he offered.

She shook her head. "It's just sore muscles from

the added weight of falling with Lacy braced against me. Besides, you and Lacy checked, and my bones are all in one piece. I think I'd know if it something else was wrong."

He studied her closely, as if he could see through to her heart and discern whether or not she was telling the truth. He finally nodded, satisfied. "You'll tell me the minute something doesn't feel right?"

"Yes, sir," she answered.

His lips twitched, but he didn't smile; he obviously wanted her to know how serious he was. Finally, he said, "We've got cold tea, juice, or water."

"Water would be wonderful, thanks."

"How about you, little Lacy?" he asked.

Danielle's resolve softened when he smiled down at her daughter. There was an innate kindness in him. Rather than worry about how dangerous it would be, she relaxed and followed her heart.

"Juice, please."

His smile widened as he handed Danielle her water and reached for a smaller glass to fill with juice. "Your momma raised you right."

Lacy sipped her juice as Tyler and Emily were pouring tea into glasses filled with ice. Her daughter was taking it all in, until she finally sighed, a really big sigh for such a little person. "I gots to tell you what I did."

Jesse squatted down next to Lacy's chair. "I'm betting it's not as bad as you think, but go ahead and tell me."

Lacy set her glass down and twisted her hands until Danielle reached out to still the movement. "You aren't going to get into trouble, sweet pea. Just tell him."

"I got excited about learning to ride and maybe

I danced and shouted in front of Trigger and Champ and scared 'em till they scared me back." The tremor in Lacy's voice had Danielle taking her daughter's hand and squeezing it to reassure Lacy.

Jesse pushed his Stetson to the back of his head, and finally said, "Well now, that could have ended badly if they weren't in their stalls. You could have been hurt."

"But what about the horses and the Code?"

The way he paid attention to her daughter eased Danielle's worry that he'd be upset with Lacy.

"You care about Trigger and Champ, don't you?"

Lacy nodded.

"And I think you really didn't try to upset them."

Lacy hung her head, but finally answered him. "That would be mean."

He touched his knuckle beneath Lacy's chin and coaxed her to look up at him. "Then I think we should go apologize by feeding them an apple. What do you say?"

Happiness shone from her daughter's bright blue eyes. Danielle's throat constricted as emotions long buried tried to surface. Lacy started to bounce, and then seemed to change her mind. Her little girl was smart and learning from her earlier mistake. "Can I, Mommy?"

"If you do exactly as Jesse tells you."

"Can Mommy come too?"

Jesse slowly pushed to his feet and frowned down at Danielle. "I think she should rest some more. She's still as pale as flour."

Lacy tilted her head to one side and asked, "Like Unca Jimmy uses for his pies?"

Everyone laughed at the image Lacy planted in their minds... everyone except Danielle. She wasn't happy to be relegated to the kitchen while her little girl went back out to the barn with the cowboy Danielle was too attracted to and Lacy worshipped. But she'd already caused enough of a problem by interrupting the Garahan men.

She kept her troubled thoughts to herself and smiled as Jesse got two apples from the bowl on the kitchen table and reached out his hand for Lacy's. That simple action caused her heart to skip a beat, and in one painful moment, her worst fears were realized—Lacy wasn't the only one who was over the moon about cowboy Jesse... she was too.

The door closed and Tyler sat down across from her, pulling Emily onto his lap.

"Tyler, we have company." Emily struggled to her feet.

He grinned and leaned across the table and confided, "She can't keep her hands off me."

Emily laughed, smacked him on the shoulder, then kissed him before settling on the chair next to him.

Danielle couldn't help but smile. Tyler and Emily were so obviously in love. She thought she and her ex had had something special, but it turned out, she was in love alone. Trying hard not to sink back into that abyss of loneliness and recrimination, she looked toward the back door again.

"Don't worry about Lacy. Jesse will guard her with his life," Emily reassured her.

"So, Danielle," Tyler said, folding his hands on the tabletop, "what the hell were you thinking running out like that in front of our horses?"

She opened her mouth to speak, then closed it. What could she say that wouldn't have her sounding like a shrew?

When he continued to wait for her to answer his

question, she threw her hands up in the air, and asked, "What do you think I was doing? Did you even see Lacy running toward you?"

He nodded. "Ranchers have to have a sixth sense when it comes to what's going on around us. We'd never survive out there otherwise—neither would our herd."

She fell silent. Well, he'd answered more succinctly than Jesse had. "I'd do the same thing again in a heartbeat. It's my mom-radar. Can't turn it off and can't ignore when my gut says Lacy's in trouble or danger."

"So," Tyler drawled, "you planning on getting into more trouble so my little brother will have to rescue you again?"

"Of all the—"

"Tyler don't tease, Danielle," Emily chided. "She's had enough for one afternoon." Turning toward Danielle, Emily added, "The Garahan men have an odd sense of humor." As if that explained it all, she got up and started to clear the glasses away and put them in the dishwasher.

"We should be going," Danielle said getting to her feet. She knew she'd feel worse tomorrow, because she'd been hugging forty pounds to her chest when she landed on her back just now.

"Stay for dinner," Emily offered. "We're having—"

"Sandwiches," Tyler interrupted with a sheepish grin.

Emily's lips twitched as if she were fighting to hold back a smile. Danielle really liked Emily and Ronnie. She missed not having female friends. When she and Buddy first got married and settled in their apartment, she'd been sick for her first trimester; by then, time seemed to pass by at warp speed, and before she knew it, she was raising Lacy and working part-time at a real

estate office. Friends were a luxury she intended to in-
dulge in now that she was here in Pleasure.

"If you're sure you have enough, we'd like that."

Emily seemed pleased with her answer. "Tyler,
please go tell Ronnie that we need to throw something
else together to go with the sandwiches."

Danielle stopped him. "If we're staying for dinner,
let me help."

Torn, Tyler hesitated in the doorway. Finally, Emily
nodded. "You might want to check on your brothers."

Once he was gone, Emily said, "All that man has to do
is stand there looking at me and I forget my own name!"

Danielle smiled.

"So, what else besides potato salad and macaroni
salad go with sandwiches?" Emily whispered.

"Do you have any chocolate and heavy cream?"

"Not sure, hang on." Emily opened the fridge and got
out a small container of cream. "Will this be enough?"

"Perfect, but what about the chocolate?"

Emily rummaged through one of the overhead cabinets and called out, "Got it!" Putting it on the counter
next to the cream, she asked, "So, what on Earth are you
making that goes with sandwiches?"

"My uncle's famous chocolate pie." Emily giggled
and Danielle said, "Pie goes with anything. It's really
the perfect food."

The other woman shook her head. "Actually, brownies
are the truly perfect food. I baked a batch yesterday, but the
guys found them and demolished them before breakfast."

Working and chatting, Danielle had the crust ready
and in the oven and was creating the chocolate filling
when Jesse and Lacy returned.

"Yeah!" Lacy said, running toward the table. "Unca Jimmy's chocolate pie!" Suddenly, the little one stopped and looked over her shoulder at Jesse and then back at Danielle. "Is this an 'I'm sorry we scared you' pie?"

Danielle couldn't keep the smile from her face. With a glance at the tall man standing just behind her daughter, she nodded. "Actually, it's a 'thank you for inviting us to dinner' pie."

"Really?" Lacy and Jesse said at the same time.

—∙∙∙—

Everyone started to laugh at once, and Jesse had the strangest feeling that his life had just shifted on its axis, turning in a new direction. He couldn't quite put his finger on what had changed—whether it was having the life scared out of him watching Danielle scoop Lacy off of her feet, hit the ground hard, and not get up, or the simple fact that Lacy and her mother were here at the Circle G, where he'd wanted them from the first.

Wanting to wipe the smudge of flour off the bridge of Danielle's nose, he started to move forward when Emily turned and noticed the same thing. She handed a towel to Danielle and pointed to her nose, and his chance to touch the delectable Danielle was gone.

Having held her in his arms, he knew how perfectly she fit against him. He'd held other women, but something was innately different about this woman. Maybe it was her prickly nature or her protective streak where her daughter was concerned. Maybe it was the way her eyes deepened to a warmer, darker shade of blue when he'd kissed her last night. He'd felt the shock when their lips met; it felt like that time he'd been too close to a lightning strike.

Ushering her daughter to the sink, he lifted her up so she could reach the faucet and wash her hands. When he was finished and had set Lacy on her feet, he washed his. He could hear her talking to her mother about the pie she'd made. A definite plus in his book. A woman who was kind and caring to her child, pretty as fresh milk, and could cook. Maybe he ought to snap her up and stake his claim now. He was scowling as he dried his hands.

"Something on your mind, Bro?" Dylan stood in the doorway with his hand wrapped around Ronnie's waist.

Jesse narrowed his gaze at the way his brother seemed so relaxed. *Damn.* Dylan and Ronnie had been outside for quite a while before Jesse and Lacy went out—but Dylan and Ronnie had been nowhere in sight. One look at the flush on his sister-in-law's cheeks and he knew why and what they'd been up to.

"No." He shook his head and walked over to hang his Stetson on one of the empty pegs by the back door. As Danielle put the pie in the fridge, he knew he wanted to spend more time with her—in bed or out, didn't matter. He wanted more time with Lacy too. Danielle was a bit skittish around him, and it was either because the hurt from her divorce was still fresh in her mind, or something a whole lot more fun, if he was reading the signals her body had been sending to him.

Willing to test his theory, he walked around the room and opened up the cabinet above where Danielle was standing, washing the bowls in the sink. Their bodies brushed as she backed into him. Hadn't she seen him or was she planning on playing with fire?

She jolted and he had his answer; she'd been

preoccupied. Taking things a step further, he reached out to steady her, pulling her against him—her back to his front. Lord, it was a miracle he didn't spontaneously combust. Every curvy inch of her backside was nestled snug against him.

Her sharp intake of breath was all he had to hear to know she'd been just as affected as him. Relieved, he pretended to lose his balance and wrapped his arm around her middle. The sensation of holding the wasp-waisted woman in his arms went to his head like a shot of the Irish. Reeling from the contact, sizzling along the length of the arm still wrapped around her, he stood stunned. Outfoxed by his own experiment.

"Please," she rasped, pushing against him. "Let go."

He bent low so he could whisper, "Dani darlin', I don't think I can do that." He was delighted when she shivered against him.

"Is my mommy all right?"

The quivering sound of Lacy's voice had him backing up as if he'd been burned. What the hell was wrong with him? They were standing in a room filled with people, and Danielle's daughter, and he was thinking with his johnson! He was lower than dirt… he was pond scum.

"She's fine," Jesse answered. "Aren't you?"

Danielle impressed the hell out of him. She gathered herself together for her daughter's sake when he knew she'd been quivering from his touch. He would never forget the way she felt melting against him; it would keep him awake nights until he had her where her wanted her—in his bed.

Damn it! There were way too many people and too many distractions for him to give in to what his body clamored for—to grab the woman and run! It was actually painful, but he moved a step back from the golden woman, still vibrating from their brief touch.

"Yes, thanks," she said at last. With a faint smile, she stepped around him and walked to the other side of the room. Hiking Lacy up on her hip, she watched him from a distance like he was a poisonous snake and she a frightened filly.

If it took the rest of the night, he would figure out a way to get her back in his arms.

How? He had no idea.

When? He had no clue. All he knew was that it had better be soon.

Chapter 10

WHILE HIS BROTHERS WASHED UP, THE LADIES BUSTLED around the kitchen setting out the smorgasbord of left-overs: salads, sandwiches, meatballs, with the pièce de résistance—Danielle's chocolate pie.

Jesse did something out of character; he watched everyone around him while he ate, not adding to the conversation. Truth be told, the joy filling the Circle G's kitchen tonight touched him deeply. Emily had added so much to their lives when she took Tyler up on his offer to come and live out at the Circle G. They were getting married in the fall, but Jesse wondered if they'd really be waiting that long.

Next came Ronnie, who'd married Dylan weeks after meeting him. The circumstances were special—you could say that Dylan was Ronnie's saving grace, but in turn, she added happiness to his brother's life that had been sadly missing.

"We're staying with my uncle for the summer." Danielle was looking at Tyler, who must have asked the question, and Jesse noticed that her eyes twinkled a lovely shade of crystal clear blue, just like a picture Jesse'd seen once of a lagoon in a nature magazine. Mesmerized, he couldn't look away. The sharp jab to his ribs had him rubbing the spot, but still he watched the woman as if she were a dream… just out of focus and not to be touched or else she'd disappear.

"I think Jesse's done in."

Tyler's voice broke through to Jesse's thoughts. He turned toward his brother. "Just tired 's all."

"So you're staying home tonight?"

Jesse's heart sank; he'd have to leave the cozy scene in their kitchen soon, or he'd be late and Slim would start looking for another driver. Jesse was only as good as his last race, and if he didn't get in enough practice time, he'd lose the edge he had.

It took more than skill to drive a race car; it took guts, desire, and an extra helping of ego. He knew he could do it, but he'd have to work for it. He shook his head. "I've gotta go out."

He pushed his chair back from the table and stood. "Dinner was a pleasure, thank you, ladies." Turning toward Danielle, he asked, "Would you and Lacy like to take a walk with me out to the stables? I'd like to check on Dodge before I leave."

"But you didn't get to try Mommy's pie." Lacy sounded so disappointed, he almost changed his mind and reached for his cell to call Slim. But he'd been dreaming of this chance for so long, it would be like cutting off one of his legs and trying to walk without it.

"If you slice off a piece, I can take it with me. I promised a friend I'd help him out."

"Friends are important," Lacy said looking up at him and then at her mother. "Mommy and I can come back… anytime."

Her smile was so hopeful, he had to laugh. "That would be fine."

He was confident enough in his legendary charm to think that he could woo Danielle and convince her to bring Lacy back soon. By the time he'd gotten a few Saturday night races under his belt, he'd have Danielle right where he wanted her—in his bed.

Lacy had his thoughts moving back to safer territory when she asked, "Don't you have an apple for Dodge?"

He bent down to scoop her up into his arms. "Hey, Dylan, pass me an apple."

Without pausing to see if his brother would do as he asked, he reached up a hand and caught the fruit his brother threw to him and handed it to Lacy.

"Wildfire's gonna get jealous," Dylan warned.

That had Jesse pausing by the back door. "Better toss me a few more. Put your hands around my neck and hang on," he warned Lacy.

Tyler and Dylan picked up apples and tossed them at him. He hadn't expected any less. His older brothers were always trying to outdo him. He caught the first two easily and dropped them down his shirt, and was ready when Dylan tossed one at his face and Tyler tossed one zipper-level. "Thanks."

"Show off," Tyler said, but he was grinning.

When Danielle's mouth dropped open, he grinned. "Played shortstop in high school."

"I thought Texans only played football."

She seemed interested in his answer, so he explained, "Pleasure's not like most towns out here. Yeah, football is big, really big, but we've always had a baseball team too. Garahans like to play both."

With his shirt bulging with apples and Lacy wrapped around him like a vine, he put one arm beneath her to steady her and the other around Danielle, ushering her out the back door.

Outside, Danielle slowly came out of the daze she was in. He couldn't say that he minded all that much, because it had been his quick hands that had captivated her. Was she thinking of what he could do with those hands when they were alone?

Hell, he was!

"Here," she said, holding out her arms. "Let me take Lacy. You'll need to get the apples for the horses."

He grinned down at her and passed Lacy into her mother's waiting arms. He watched the way Lacy leaned into her mother and memories of his mother doing the same thing haunted him. He still missed her and hadn't been ready to lose her. But the Lord had had other plans. That was his grandfather's explanation for the wreck that took his mother's life. Hell, that was what he had said when a dark sedan pulled up in front of their house and two Marines got out.

Jesse didn't actually remember seeing the car or the Marines, but Tyler remembered and had reminded both him and Dylan every year, so that they wouldn't forget that their father had died serving their country. All these years later, they had four days that they observed quietly and in their own way: their parents' birthdays and the day each one was taken from them.

"The horsies really want those apples." Lacy's words jarred him back to the present. It wasn't like him to let his mind wander when he was around their horses. They were big animals and required his full attention.

He shook his head; he had no excuse but didn't have time to sort out why he had now. He could do that later.

"Then let's give them their treat. You want to help?"

"We both do."

Danielle still had a hold of Lacy, and it was a good thing, because the little girl never would have been able to feed the horses their treat otherwise. "I like to cut the apple into quarters before giving it to them."

He pulled out his pocketknife and sliced into the first apple. The tangy scent had all of the horses whickering and stomping in their stalls. They knew Jesse had a special treat for them.

"Are they mad?" Lacy looked worried and had a tight grip on her mother's neck.

So he shook his head. "Just excited. That's how horses let us know what they want or what they're thinking."

"Oh. Can I feed them too?"

"That was the plan, little darlin'." He handed a slice to Lacy and reminded her, "Just like before, hold your palm out and curl your fingers back as far as they can go so none of my friends nibble on your fingers."

"Would it tickle?"

He frowned and held up his left hand. "See this scar?" The fleshy part of his palm right below his fingers had a line that stretched from pinky to pointer finger. "Got this when I was right around your age."

Lacy looked at his hand and then up at him, and asked, "What happened?"

"I didn't listen to my grandfather and curled my hand the wrong way."

"Did a horse bite you?"

He nodded. "But it wasn't the poor horse's fault, and my grandfather reminded me of that as he was putting a butterfly bandage on my hand."

"So their teeth are sharp?" Danielle sounded horrified.

Danielle sounded worried, and he didn't want her to

be. He wanted these two to be comfortable around their horses and at the Circle G. "No, but they are strong."

"Did your grandfather get mad at the horse?"

Jesse laughed, delighted that Lacy seemed to understand and wasn't frightened by the prospect of being bitten. "No, but I sure caught hell—er, heck for not listening. He reminded me that it was my fault for not listening or feeding the horse properly."

"Like this, right?" Lacy held the slice of apple in her hand just like he'd shown her earlier.

"Perfect," he said, as Dodge carefully lipped the treat out of Lacy's hand. She giggled and Jesse smiled. "Tickles, doesn't it?"

"Uh-huh. Can I do it again?"

He nodded. "We've got a few more mouths to feed. I'd appreciate the help."

As they took turns feeding the horses, Danielle asked, "Do you still have that horse?"

He stared at her for a moment to be sure she wasn't just being a wiseass. She seemed to want to know. "Uh, no, that was nearly twenty-five years ago."

"Oh, I didn't realize you were…" Her voice trailed off and her face turned a delightful shade of pink.

So, he thought. *Pretty Danielle is trying to guess my age*. He'd been taken from anywhere from twenty-five to thirty. He didn't mind; it gave him a broader range of women to choose from. Looking down at her, his gut churned remembering the sparks he'd felt from a simple touch and knew that his heart was now spoken for. Time to start convincing her that hers was too.

Her colored deepened and he wondered if she was remembering how perfectly she'd fit against him or if she was thinking about kissing him again. Need to have her pressed up against him again shot through him, singeing him. Hell, he wanted a tongue-tangling, mind-blowing, full-bodied kiss from this woman… and more…

"Cowboy Jesse?" Lacy was standing beside him, holding on to her mother's hand.

Damn, he'd better get his mind where it belonged—in the barn—and out of the bedroom, or else he'd blow his chance to get to know Danielle better. "Yeah?"

"What will the horsies do now?"

Delighted with her question, he squatted down so they were eye level when he answered. "They'll relax once I turn the lights off and drift off to sleep. They know they've got a lot of work to do tomorrow."

"Do they get days off?"

"We do give them a day or so, now and again, but we've only got five horses, so they don't get much more than that." He stood up and turned off the first set of lights at the back of the barn.

"When do you get a day off?"

Danielle's softly asked question had hope swelling inside of him. She had to be just as interested in him if she wanted to know that. "Ranching's a tough business," he said quietly. He didn't want to scare her off, but he didn't want to sugarcoat the truth either.

"My brothers and I work twenty-four/seven, so there's not much time off, 'cept when we're in bed," his eyes met hers and he couldn't keep from grinning when he added, "sleeping."

He watched as her eyes narrowed and her gaze dipped down to the top of Lacy's head. Jesse wasn't stupid; he caught her silent warning that he'd better keep things clean for her daughter's sake. With a shrug, he ushered them toward the front of the barn, turning off lights as they went.

"I'm glad you came today."

Danielle smiled and looked down at her daughter and back into his eyes. "We are too."

"It's a busy time of year for us at the Circle G."

"From what my uncle says," Danielle said, "it's busy all year out here."

"Well, except for twice a year when the cows are calving; that's when it's insane around here."

"What's calving?"

He normally had a quick comeback that was a little rude and a lot crude, but this was Danielle's pixie pink cowgirl asking him. He remembered to think first and told her, "It's when the baby cows are born. Sometimes there's a bunch born all at once."

Lacy's eyes brightened at the thought. "Do they have big horns when they're borned? Doesn't that hurt the mommy cow? Can I play with them?"

Danielle's eyes were bright with amusement, but she held her tongue, waiting to see how he would answer. He'd get even with her later and the look he sent her promised both retribution and passion. Her eyes widened a heartbeat before softening with an answering passion that smoldered in their depths until soft blue deepened to sapphire.

"I uh... no." He tried to remember what the heck Lacy had asked. "They don't have horns when they are born, so it doesn't hurt the mother. You can come and visit the next time we're expecting calves."

Lacy danced all the way back to the house. "Are the momma cows 'specting soon?"

Jesse had to tear his gaze away from Danielle's tempting mouth to answer her daughter. "Uh, not for the next little while. I will let you know in plenty of time, OK?"

"OK." Lacy raced up the steps and smiled up at Tyler, who was holding the back door open. "We fed all the horsies apples, and know what?"

His older brother grinned down at Lacy. "What?"

"Cowboy Jesse said I could watch baby cows being borned."

Their eyes met and Tyler's smirk irritated the hell out of him. He promised himself that he'd punch Tyler later. "What else did *cowboy* Jesse say?"

"That horses can't help biting you if you don't feed them right."

"Then I guess cowboy Jesse knows everything."

"Uh-huh," Lacy said, slipping past Tyler into the kitchen.

Jesse paused and stared at his brother. Tyler's gaze narrowed and he said, "Anytime, anyplace, Bro."

"Except here and now," Emily said coming to stand next to Tyler. "We have company, and besides, I don't like sleeping alone. Do you?"

Jesse laughed, hoping his brother would punch first and think second. But after one last glare, Tyler looked away and tugged Emily inside.

"Thank you for being so nice to Lacy."

He held the door for Danielle and walked in behind her. "It's no hardship; she's a great kid."

Danielle's smile seemed to blossom from the inside. It was one thing he had noticed about her—the way her eyes would light up when she smiled. He really wished he didn't have to leave tonight. He wanted to taste her so badly; his hands ached from clenching them so he wouldn't reach out and simply grab hold of her.

"Danielle, I have to go."

Her smile faded, but a trace of it remained as she nodded. "We should too. Time to leave, Lacy."

"But, Mommy—"

"No buts, remember?" She hated having to be the responsible one alone; it would be easier to share the burden, but that was no longer an option for her. "We have to get back and help Uncle Jimmy finish the food prep for tomorrow."

"Can we make more pie?"

She laughed, delighted that her daughter enjoyed creating pies alongside of her great-uncle. "Count on it, sweet pea."

Lacy raced back over to where Jesse stood in the doorway. "Thanks, Jesse!"

He tipped his hat. "My pleasure, little lady."

"Can I come back tomorrow?"

He glanced from mother to daughter and grinned. "I'll be working with my brothers most of the day without a break. How about the day after?"

"OK!" Lacy was tugging Danielle's hand, but her mother stopped her. "Aren't you forgetting something?"

Lacy stopped tugging and looked up at her mother. "Um… Oh! Thank you for letting us visit and stuff."

Danielle shook her head and frowned down at her daughter. Jesse would bet money there would be a discussion on the ride back to Sullivan's house. "What my darling daughter forgot to say was thank you for dinner and letting us take you away from your chores."

She smiled and turned to leave, pausing in front of

Jesse. "I'm sorry for causing a problem earlier, but I was terrified for my daughter's safety."

He nodded. "You had no reason to be. Ranchers are very alert, watchful individuals; we'd lose half our herd if we weren't."

"I know," she rasped. "Tyler explained it to me. I'm still sorry, but I would probably chase after her again, even knowing that you would stop in time."

Their gazes locked on one another and he sensed a strength that went right down to Danielle's core. Something inside of him clamored to be a part of the life she led with her child. "Being a parent must be hard work."

She agreed. "Hardest job I've ever loved." With one last look, she and Lacy were gone.

"And you can't go chase after that woman, why?" Dylan had his arms around Ronnie and was distracted by something she whispered.

"Can't you call whoever you're helping out and cancel?" Tyler turned and brushed a kiss to the top of his fiancée's curly head.

Rather than answer his brothers, who wouldn't hear him anyway because they were both so wrapped up with their women, he stalked out the back door, got in the truck, and drove away.

—⁓—

"So how did the visit go?"

Danielle smiled at her uncle. "Obviously it went well, since we're getting back so late."

He nodded. "If I didn't know better, I'd think there was something more interesting about the Circle G than its horses."

She laughed, and hollered up the stairs after Lacy, "Make sure to use lots of soap!"

Her daughter didn't answer her, which meant she was probably daydreaming about her new hero.

"I'm going to have to make sure she gets into the tub."

Her uncle frowned down at her. "You know I love you, June bug."

She paused with her hand on the newel post. "I count on it, Uncle Jimmy, and love you back."

He nodded. "That's good because what I'm about to say is guaranteed to piss you off."

She turned to face him. "Won't be the first time."

"You'll only come to heartache if you let yourself fall for another cowboy."

Folding her arms in front of her in a protective stance, she knew it was the gospel truth. "What if I can't help myself?"

He mumbled something she couldn't hear, and then said, "Then I'll be here to help you pick up the pieces."

"He might surprise you." Lord, she prayed he would surprise her too, because she couldn't stop thinking about him and they way he connected with Lacy. "He's wonderful with Lacy, the way he—"

"Will he stick? When things get tough again out at the ranch, and he doesn't have time to spend with Lacy or you? Are you a passing fancy, a reminder of…"

Danielle felt her heart fall to her feet. Digging deep for the courage to uncover the truth, she whispered. "What is her name? Who do I look like?"

Her uncle stared down at his feet and shook his head.

"Mommy, the water's stuck! Can you turn it on?"

"Be right there, honey."

"You'll have to tell me eventually." Turning to go up the stairs, she said, "It would help to know before I hear it from someone in town."

"Give little June bug her bath and then tuck her in. We can talk about it when you come back down."

An hour later, Lacy was clean as sunshine and tucked into bed. Trudging downstairs, Danielle felt old, worn, used up, and worried about what she might hear. Drawing in a cleansing breath, she steeled herself for whatever it was Uncle Jimmy had to tell her.

She walked through the empty downstairs and finally found him on the back porch with two tall glasses of iced tea on the table next to him. "Have a seat." When she did, he handed her a glass.

She sipped slowly, letting the cool tea soothe her suddenly dry throat. "It'll be better if you just tell me."

He nodded. "You look a lot like Lori Jones."

"A former girlfriend of his?"

"Sort of." Her uncle tipped his head back and drank from his glass. With a sigh, he set the glass back down. "It's not too late to cut yourself off from him."

She laughed. "You heard the way Lacy's been talking about him. She was over the moon when I drove out there today. She's hooked."

"Between the two of us, we can keep her busy enough that she'll forget about him in time. Isn't that how it worked with Buddy?"

Her smile faded. "He left us and no matter how young you are, that's something you always remember."

"He was a nice guy but didn't stick, and let his dream get in the way."

Sadness engulfed her. "We were both so wrapped up

in one another, we got careless, but I believed that his love for me would be strong enough to keep up with his dream... I guess I was wrong." She had cried buckets over that realization and had none left now. "Being a bull-riding star was, and will always be, his love and the only thing he'll ever need."

Her uncle rose from his chair and pulled her into a hug. Easing back, he met her gaze and said, "Sometimes a man's dreams are so big there isn't any room for anything else."

She looked out into the night, watching the fireflies rising from the ground to dance in the air. "I know."

"But the right man will make room beside his dream for the woman and child who will make his life whole and his heart's desire that much sweeter."

Later, alone in the bedroom she shared with her daughter, Danielle stared up at the ceiling and wondered if Jesse could be that man. How would she know? Would she have the guts to find out? She'd come to stay with her uncle to start over, not dive right back into a relationship with another cowboy.

Closing her eyes, she let her mind drift and pictured the type of man she should be interested in. He'd be tall, whipcord lean, and look great in a three-piece suit... a banker or businessman.

Her dreams were vignettes featuring a man in a suit who came into her life, robbed her blind, and left just as quickly. Each and every time, a tall, dark, handsome cowboy rode in to pick up the pieces of her heart. Grateful, she took the handsome wrangler's hand to thank him and ended up in his arms, with his lips hovering a breath above hers, poised to kiss her.

Danielle woke with a start and sat up in bed. Moonlight slashed through the darkness of the room. She glanced at her daughter's bed, worried that her own dreams might have wakened Lacy.

She sighed in relief; her little girl was still asleep. Lying back down, she wondered why she couldn't get cowboys off her brain. It wasn't just the fact that she was in Texas; she'd never lived in any other state.

An image of a smiling cowboy, perched in the saddle as his horse stood on his hind legs pawing the air, filled her. "It's all Roy and Trigger's fault." Her mother had always loved the cowboys of the silver screen and had spent early Saturday mornings watching old movies with Danielle. That love had filtered down and formed the image of the perfect man in her young heart. She couldn't think of a time when she wasn't infatuated with men who made their living in the saddle or out on the range.

"Gee thanks, Mom," she murmured, falling asleep dreaming of a handsome cowboy with devastating dimples and a heart of gold.

Chapter 11

LACY SMILED AT MISS DAWSON. "UNCA JIMMY GAVE US his list."

"Well." Pam smiled. "Let's see what he needs." Leaning on the counter by the cash register, she grinned. "Looks like more baking."

"My favorite's his chocolate pie," Lacy confessed.

Pam's laughter was like a warm hug. "Your great-uncle has a way with pie crust, but he won't give me his secret ingredients."

Lacy looked up at Danielle and grinned. "We know it but can't tell."

Pam nodded. "I suppose it wouldn't be right to try to wheedle the secret out of you."

Lacy's hold on Danielle's hand tightened. "I promised."

With an exaggerated sigh, Pam looked back down at the list. "Then I'd better see what he's got on the list, so I won't be tempted to ask you again."

Lacy seemed relieved.

"I hear you two were guests out at the Circle G yesterday."

"News travels fast." Danielle couldn't believe how much faster than back home.

"Did you have a good time?"

Her daughter was grinning up at Pam and helping her stack the dry goods on the counter. "I gots to feed apples to the horsies and ride on Tyler's shoulders and—"

"I thought you went out to see Jesse?" Pam's confusion was obvious and for a moment Danielle considered leaving her floundering, but at the last minute, she couldn't. "We did. He was, um… showing us around the ranch."

"You know what, Miss Pam?" Lacy asked, tugging on the woman's elbow.

Pam smiled down at Lacy. "No. What?"

"Mommy rescued me first, then cowboy Jesse had to rescue her."

Pam's gaze lifted to meet Danielle's. "Really?" Without looking away, she asked, "What happened?"

"I kind of runned out in front of the horses and Mommy scooped me up, but I sat on her chest hard, and she made this really awful sound."

Pam tore her gaze from Danielle's and looked down at Lacy. "How many horses?"

"Just three, but you know what?"

The owner of the store didn't ask; she simply waited to be told. Lacy whispered, "Cowboy Jesse had to pick Mommy up 'cause her legs weren't working right."

"Lacy's exaggerating just a bit." Danielle wondered if it had seemed that dramatic to someone so young and realized it just might have. "I was doing all right until I tripped, that's when I knocked the wind out of myself with Lacy's full weight on top of me."

Pam placed a hand to her breast. "Land sakes, what were you ladies thinking?"

"My instincts to protect my daughter kicked in." The horror of that instant in time replayed in her mind, tormenting her. "How was I supposed to know that the men would see her and pull up before their horses trampled her?"

The older woman shook her head. "You're not from around here, so that would explain things. But, honey, those Garahans would never let one hair on your daughter's head come to harm. They're ranchers—"

"Tyler and Jesse tried to explain that to me last night, but it wouldn't have mattered. I'd still chase after her. I could never just stand there watching if my baby girl was in danger."

Pam nodded. "Well, you two did have quite a day yesterday." She had placed the list on the counter while listening to their story and glanced down at it. "We'd better get this filled so you can bring Jimmy what he needs. I'd bet money that you'll be going out to the Circle G again today."

Danielle shook her head. "Jesse said they'd be too busy today, and he couldn't give Lacy a riding lesson."

"Ronnie could," Lacy whispered. "She was gonna teach me, but I wanted cowboy Jesse to. Maybe she could teach me just a little bit. Then he wouldn't feel bad that I didn't wait, cause he could teach me too."

Danielle rolled her eyes, and Pam laughed and said, "That sounds like a good idea. Ronnie usually closes up her shop around four o'clock. Her shop is called Guilty Pleasures. She sells lovely lingerie and scented oils and such."

"What kind of such?" Lacy asked.

Danielle bent down, lifted Lacy up, and settled her on her hip. "Why don't we go and visit her?"

"Some of her satin and lace confections are very racy. You might want to go alone the first time you visit and decide for yourself."

"Thanks, Pam." The people of Pleasure were helpful

and friendly… just a bit too nosy for her tastes, but then again, it was better than living in a bigger city where no one knew her and no one cared that she and her daughter had been left high and dry.

"But why can't I go?" Lacy wailed.

"You remember me telling you that some things are meant just for grown-ups?"

Lacy's eyes filled and she nodded.

"Miss Pam is being very considerate to everyone's feelings by suggesting I go first to check it out."

"But I want—"

"Sweet pea, life isn't always going to be what you want, when you want it." Brushing her hand beneath her daughter's lashes, she dabbed at the tears and swept them away. "But life is definitely what you make it, so let's do our best to be considerate of Ronnie too. She might get into trouble if her shop isn't meant for children and we show up there together."

Lacy sniffed back the rest of her tears and nodded. "I like Ronnie. Let's not get her in trouble. OK, Mommy?"

Danielle kissed the top of Lacy's head. "I'm proud of you."

Lacy grinned and waved at Pam. "We gots to bring Unca Jimmy his groceries. Can I come back and visit sometime?"

The older woman smiled. "Anytime you like, Lacy. You just come and visit me."

After dropping Lacy and the groceries off at the diner, Danielle followed the directions Pam had given her. Danielle was surprised to find that she remembered being on Main Street and recognized some of the storefronts, and while some of the businesses themselves had changed, the look of the town was the same. Just older.

Pulling up in front of Guilty Pleasures, she was surprised to see how new the storefront looked, but then remembered something about Dylan doing carpentry work for Ronnie. She'd been so busy thinking about Jesse that she hadn't heard everything Emily and Ronnie had said about Ronnie's shop. She'd have to pay closer attention or people would think she didn't care.

She cared... perhaps too much and about the wrong things...

The door was open so she went inside and her jaw dropped. Lacy nightgowns, tap pants, and brassieres were the first things she noticed walking inside. She gave in to the overwhelming urge to touch. Cool silk and smooth satin begged to be held up against her waist to see if the sexy undergarments would fit.

Danielle couldn't remember the last time she'd splurged on underwear. She'd spent the last five years bargain shopping, which meant that she had a sad selection of white cotton, with a couple of pale pastels mixed in.

Pushing that depressing thought aside led to yet another—she had no reason to buy anything so decadent. After all, who would see it but her? *A dark-haired cowboy with broad shoulders, sculpted lips, and a wicked grin... Jesse.*

Shaking that tortuous thought from her mind, she hung the silky things back on the display rack and brushed her hands on her jeans skirt, as if to remove the sumptuous feel of the fabrics, so she wouldn't be tempted to pick them up again.

"Danielle?"

She turned toward the sound of Ronnie's voice. "Hey, I just stopped by—" *Damn.* She couldn't remember why; the silky gowns and lace-edged tap pants had distracted her completely.

Did she look that confused and pathetic? Ronnie walked over to slip her arm through Danielle's. "It must be tough being a single mom. When was the last time you went shopping to buy something just for you?"

Danielle laughed. "Probably six years ago."

Ronnie shook her head. "Isn't it time to treat yourself?" She swept her free hand in front of her and Danielle's gaze greedily followed. The rainbow-colored fabrics were sumptuous, tempting her once again to touch, to savor, to sigh.

But she couldn't. She needed to save every penny they had for Lacy. "I, um… need a job before I can splurge at your shop." Looking around her, she sighed. "You have so many lovely things, I wouldn't know where to start."

Ronnie gave her a tour of her shop, and by the time they reached the back counter where all of the essential oils were displayed, Danielle remembered what Pam had said. "She's right."

"Who's right?"

"Pam said that I should visit your shop without Lacy, because she's too young."

Ronnie smiled. "Well, I could bring a few pretty things home today, and you and Lacy could drop by the ranch and we could show her what her mommy is going to be buying."

Her heart wanted to say yes, but her head wouldn't let her. "I wish I could, but I really don't have the money right now."

But Ronnie wasn't listening. "With your coloring, I think turquoise, black, and periwinkle would be colors that suit you best."

"I can't—"

"I only allow positive thinking in my shop," Ronnie countered. "Now, will you bring Lacy out to see us this afternoon?"

As if she could sense Danielle's hesitation, Ronnie withdrew her arm and stood facing Danielle. "I think Trigger and Champ would like a chance to visit with Lacy out in the corral."

Tempted more by the chance to do something for her little one than the lovely lingerie, Danielle shrugged. "I know Lacy would enjoy the visit, but—"

"I can pick you up on my way home." Ronnie smiled. "Those two don't get ridden as much as they should and would welcome the chance to teach Lacy how to ride."

"Oh." Thoughts of seeing her little girl's face beaming with pleasure as she sat on top of Trigger or Champ filled her until she couldn't imagine anything else. "Do you always get what you want?"

Ronnie shook her head. "Not the first time around."

Confused, Danielle tilted her head to one side. "First time around what?"

The woman flushed a deep rose. "My first marriage."

"We'll have to compare notes one of these days. Maybe we have more in common than either of us realizes."

Ronnie agreed. "Should I pick you up at the diner or Jimmy's house?"

"We usually close up around three o'clock, but we could wait for you there if it's easier."

"I can meet you at his house, that way Lacy won't be too tired; she can have a nap waiting for me to pick you two up." Ronnie paused and Danielle realized she was waiting for her to say yes.

"Thanks, Ronnie. That would be great." She turned to go and glanced at the wisp of a nightgown in periwinkle blue one last time. "See you later!"

But Ronnie wasn't listening; she was too busy planning what to bring for Danielle to try on. Grabbing the nightgown and two sets of brassieres and tap pants, she added a black lace chemise with matching thong for good measure.

She couldn't wait to show Emily and plot out how they were going to throw Danielle and Jesse together while they kept an eye on Lacy. "I almost feel sorry for Jesse… but those two are made for one another."

Tossing the garments on the counter by the register, she hit number two on her speed dial and waited for Emily to pick up. "Em! I just had the best idea."

"The guys will be working through until about five or six o'clock," Emily reminded Ronnie. "But I think that if we play our cards right, we could have little Lacy out by the corral getting to know Trigger and Champ out in the open, where she'll see for herself how important it is to respect their size, strength, and intelligence."

"I've got some fabulous silky things for Danielle to try on while we're outside with Lacy." Ronnie paused and wondered if she could or should try to meddle and finally just threw her idea out there. "Em, what if, while we were outside with Lacy, we have Danielle trying on one of my fabulous silky or lacy gowns, and Jesse just happens to walk in on her." The silence on the other end of the line had Ronnie taking a step back. "But that probably would be a bad idea."

Emily started laughing. "I was wondering how we were going to keep all three of them from walking in on Danielle. We only want Jesse to see her, right?"

"Good point." Ronnie wracked her brain and finally realized there was only one way it would work. "They'll have to be in on it."

"Would Dylan go along with it?"

Ronnie thought about it. "He might, if Tyler agreed."

"All right then," Emily said. "I'll text Tyler and let him know what's going on and ask him to tell Dylan."

"Do you think Jesse will figure out we're up to something?" Ronnie worried about his finding out.

"Probably not," Emily told her. "See you around five."

Chapter 12

"WE'RE GOING TO THE CIRCLE G?" LACY CLAPPED HER hands together and started to stomp her feet.

"Save some of that spark for learning how to ride, little June bug."

"OK, Unca Jimmy. Do you think the horsies will 'member that I spooked them?"

The worry in her voice tore at Danielle's heart. "I don't really know, sweetie, but we'll find out together."

"I gotta go put on my best cowgirl shirt and jeans."

While her daughter raced up the stairs, Danielle flopped down in one of the kitchen chairs. "Sometimes she makes me feel so old."

Her uncle laughed and shook his head. "You're only as old as you feel."

"Right now," she said, closing her eyes, "I feel a hundred."

"Good thing you aren't that old, or else that Garahan boy wouldn't be interested in you."

Her eyes shot open and she glared at her uncle. "Who said that he's interested? Who have you been talking to since we've been gone?"

"No one." But his answer didn't fool her. Living in a small town like Pleasure, her uncle would have to be deaf not to hear the gossip going around town. "Why don't we get started on those pies before I get cleaned up?"

"I think I can handle things," he reassured her. "I've

been doing it all along without you, but it's been a treat to have you and Lacy help me." He nodded toward the doorway. "Git on up those stairs and into a hot shower. By the time you're finished, I'll have the coffee made and something hot to eat."

Love for her uncle swamped her. Tears threatened to spill over, but that would only make him feel bad, and she'd never do that to one of the only men in her life who ever truly loved her—her uncle or her father. Brothers... the Lord knew what he was doing when he created the Sullivan men. But he broke the mold; there couldn't be any other men, anywhere in the world, who were as wonderful as James and John Sullivan... except maybe the Garahans.

Walking up the stairs, her gut clenched as a vision of three handsome-as-sin cowboys crowded closely around her while she looked up at them filled her mind. She just might have to change her mind about that mold being broken. The Garahan brothers were similar in temperament and thoughts to the Sullivans.

"I can't think about that right now. I've got to focus on Lacy and her riding lessons."

A half hour later, she and Lacy were sharing leftovers while her uncle pulled the first batch of pies out of the oven. A car pulled up outside and Lacy was opening the back door, rushing outside before Danielle had a chance to react. "Stay on the porch!"

"Yes'm."

At least Lacy had learned a valuable lesson yesterday at the Circle G—the importance of listening. She'd been frightened when her mother hadn't been able to breathe or speak. It had been hard on Danielle too, but at least for the next little while, Lacy would be paying a lot closer attention to what her mother had to say.

The screen door swung open and Lacy leaned inside. "It's Ronnie!" The door slammed shut and her daughter was calling out a greeting to their friend.

"Are you ladies ready?" Ronnie asked following Lacy inside.

"As promised," Danielle said. Turning to her uncle she asked, "Are you sure you don't need me to stay and help?"

Frowning, he put his hands on his hips and opened his mouth, but Danielle had seen that look and stance before, so she quickly kissed him on the cheek, grabbed Lacy's hand, and waved good-bye.

"What was that all about?" Ronnie asked as Danielle buckled Lacy into the backseat.

"That was Uncle Jimmy's I-told-you-what look. Best not to rile him after he's told you what."

They were laughing as they drove toward the ranch. Lacy pointed out the big tree they'd seen from the day before. Ronnie turned down the long road leading to the ranch. "Here's where we got losted yesterday," Lacy piped up from the backseat.

Ronnie smiled as she turned toward the right and the road that would lead them to the house.

"It's beautiful out here," Danielle whispered. Trees, interspersed with wide open spaces, caught her eye and had her wondering what it would have been like living out here one hundred fifty years ago. "Has it changed much?"

"The ranch?"

"Mmmm... do you know if the house was added on to, or if it's the original structure?"

"I've never really thought much about it," Ronnie admitted. "You could ask Jesse when you see him later."

Danielle's heart dropped to her feet. "Oh, but I thought the men would be working until late and that we wouldn't be seeing any of them today."

"That depends on how the work goes. We might just see them come six or seven."

"Hooray!" Lacy squealed from the backseat. "Mommy?"

Danielle resigned herself to the fact that she'd have to work doubly hard from now on not to fall under the cowboy's spell and be distracted by his hypnotic gaze.

When she didn't answer right away, Lacy asked, "Can we move in with cowboy Jesse and live on the ranch too?"

Ronnie was smiling at Danielle's discomfort, but Danielle was too busy trying to do damage control, to ensure that her daughter wouldn't be asking a certain cowboy the same question when she saw him later... if she saw him.

By the time Ronnie parked the car and they all got out, Lacy was crossing her heart, promising Danielle not to ask cowboy Jesse if they could move in with him. "Can I go to the corral yet, Ronnie?"

"Let's go find Emily first."

Reluctantly, Lacy trailed after Ronnie. Danielle wondered what was up, because she spotted the two horses standing by the fence. They'd noticed the arrival of the car and had watched with interest.

"Be right back, Trigger!" Lacy called out. "See you soon, Champ!" Satisfied that her horsey friends would be waiting for her return, she hurried to keep up with Ronnie. "Will they miss me?"

Ronnie opened the door and held it for Lacy. "I'm sure they will, but we won't be long. Em?"

"In the laundry room!"

"Company's here."

When Emily walked into the kitchen, she was smiling. "Well, we're glad you came back. Things weren't the same without you two."

"Really?" Lacy asked.

"Danielle… are you all right?"

"What? Oh." Rubbing her damp palms on her thighs, she smiled. "Just thinking about something."

"Mommy does that sometimes," Lacy said, taking hold of Danielle's hand.

Bittersweet pain lanced through Danielle's heart. Love for her little girl brought tears to her eyes. Lacy's compassion humbled her. How her daughter had learned to recognize the need in others and respond to that need was beyond her. "We're a team, right, Lacy?"

"Right!"

She bent and pulled Lacy close, hugged her tight, and reluctantly let go. Thank God and His infinite wisdom for giving her a gift beyond compare. Even if Jesse decided he wasn't interested in more than a fling, Danielle had something far more important—Lacy.

"Did you bring the bag in?" Emily's question distracted Danielle.

"What bag?"

Ronnie shook her head. "Would you please go get it? Lacy and I are going to go out to the corral now."

Before Danielle could ask what was going on, Ronnie nodded toward her. "Would you please give Emily a hand?"

"Of course. With what?" But Ronnie and Lacy were already out the door and Danielle was left talking to the four walls.

"You're going to love these." Emily said, walking into the room and laying a bag in the middle of the kitchen table. "Ronnie just asked me to help her down at the corral; Champ's feeling left out and starting to act up."

"I'll go—"

Emily held out her hand to stop Danielle. "Ronnie thought you could use a little alone time, so why don't you just relax. Lacy's in very good hands—ours. Take some time, drink some of the iced tea I left in the pitcher on the counter, and try on some of the yummy underthings Ronnie brought from her store."

"But I—" Danielle was talking to the swinging screen door. "Well," she mumbled, stalking over to the pitcher. Pouring herself a tall, cold glass of tea, she hoped it would cool her temper enough for her to chase Emily down and demand to know what they were thinking and who they thought they were to arrange Danielle and Lacy's lives.

A few sips later, she realized that she was overreacting. Emily and Ronnie were just trying to help ease some of the burden Danielle carried as a single parent. Suddenly feeling very selfish, she sat down and toyed with the edge of the bag.

"I wonder what things Ronnie brought." Remembering some of the lacy confections she'd touched and admired, Danielle gave in to her curiosity and opened the bag. Sheer fantasies spilled into her hands.

"Oh!" she breathed, separating the waterfall of color.

"Lovely." The periwinkle gown with the deep ecru lace hem tempted her until she gave in and lifted the soft satin to her cheek and brushed it back and forth, absorbing the cool, smooth sensation, storing it away for a future time when she could splurge and buy something so decadent.

She set it aside and lifted a pair of sassy tap pants, slit up to the waist band, so that if she turned quickly, her hip and thigh would be totally exposed... but she didn't have anyone who would see her, did she?

The sharp memory of being pulled against Jesse's muscled frame and surrendering to his lips assaulted her senses. Pinpricks of awareness started out low in her belly and shot to her fingertips. With his busy life out at the ranch and her taking care of Lacy, when would they find the time to be together? Unbearably sad, she set the silky clothes in a heap on the table and wandered to the back door. Looking out, she could see all the way to the corral and watched her daughter leaning out of Ronnie's arms tentatively reach out to stroke Champ's muzzle. Lacy's laughter was worth its weight in gold.

She wished she could guarantee her daughter would always be this happy.

She looked over her shoulder at the booty from Ronnie's shop. A swathe of black lace beckoned her back to the table. Pulling it free, she wondered what it was about the dark lace that called to her. A long ago memory surfaced, of her great-grandmother telling her that if a woman wanted to have a baby the first thing she needed was a black lace nightgown.

Letting the material drift through her fingers, she

finally laughed. Unable to resist, she swept the gown off the table and held it against her. "Maybe I could wear it just to please myself."

One more look out the back door reassured her that Lacy would be occupied for a little while longer. Knowing the men wouldn't be home for a while yet, she stepped into the laundry room, stripped out of her T-shirt and denim skirt, and lifted her arms above her head. The swirl of lace settled against her like a glove.

"Oh!" She twirled and watched it flare out around her and then cling. She ran a hand down her side, amazed at the fit of the gown as it hugged her curves, accentuating them. "Maybe I should treat myself."

Wondering how the satin tap pants and bra would fit, she dashed out to the kitchen and grabbed the turquoise satin pants and matching bra. Slipping out of the gown and stepping into the pants had her feeling younger, sassy. She did a little hip shake movement that had the material flaring out and flashing her toned quads. Chasing after an almost four-year-old had its advantages. "Look out, world, trouble's coming!"

Delighted with the feeling of freedom sprinting through her, she took her time mimicking the sound of the brush hitting the cymbals on a drum set as she sauntered out to the kitchen. "Che, de, che che, de, che che, de de de."

She had one more nightgown to try on. The feel of the slinky material as it flared out again and then settled against her hip and the top of her thigh had her wishing Jesse was hers to tempt. She had a feeling he would appreciate what she had to offer. But it had been so long, would she even remember how?

The low whistle of appreciation had her heart stopping in her breast. "You pack a lethal punch, Dani darlin'."

Her sharp intake of breath as she prepared to scream got caught in her throat as the shock of being caught nearly naked mingled with the realization that the man she'd been dreaming about was standing right in front of her.

She couldn't find her voice, so she slid her hand to her throat to reassure herself all of the working parts were still intact. Finally, she finally rasped, "You weren't supposed to be here yet."

His eyes lit with desire—dark, dangerous, and just this side of desperate. "Thank God we finished early, or I would have missed the fashion show."

That's when she noticed he held the periwinkle gown on the tip of his finger. "Were you gonna put this on next?"

Her voice failed her for the second time. His look told her so much more than words. His reaction to her fueled her own. The overwhelming need to be held against him, to touch the tip of her tongue to the hollow of his throat and savor his flavor, had her by the throat. "I… uh… yes."

He closed the distance between them, clutching the gown to his heart. "I'd be happy to wait and give you an honest opinion. But I already know you're gonna look amazing."

The note of sincerity in his deep voice poured over her like syrup on a stack of hotcakes. She shivered.

His eyes widened. *He noticed.*

"Jesse, I—"

"Would love to put this on for you."

His certainty that she would added to the charm of his
crooked smile and hit her hard and deep, but it was the
dimple winking at her that was her undoing. Before she
could think, she was reaching for the gown and back in
the laundry room changing into it.

———————

When she walked back into the kitchen, his eyes swept from
the top of her head to the tips of her toes, and he reached for
her. "You are so beautiful, Danielle," he rasped, moving to
stand beside her. "When I walked in and saw you standing
there—my head went light and my knees went weak."

Fighting the emotions bubbling up inside of her, she
struggled not to be moved by his words. "This is hard
for me," she confessed. "You're the first man to tempt
me in a really long time," she whispered. "I can't seem
to help myself when you look at me like that."

His eyes glazed over and deepened to dark chocolate.
"Darlin', you knocked me flat the first time I saw you.
I don't mean to push you, but seeing you standing here,
all peaches and cream with your tawny blonde hair tumbling free, gets to me. Do you have any idea how hard it
is for me to stand here and keep my hands off you, when
I want so badly to slide them across your shoulders and
around to your back, so I can draw you closer to me? I
want to feel your curves against me to see if we fit as
good together front to front."

His eyes darkened with unquenched desire. "I already
know how perfectly we fit back to front." The deep rumbling of his voice untied invisible knots that had bound
her since the moment she realized her husband wasn't
ever coming back.

Could she take a chance? *Yes.*
Was it the smart thing to do? *Hell no!*
Did she care?

Tamping down her inner conscience, taking a chance to feel alive again, not knowing how long it would last, she met his gaze and took a step toward him. "It's been a long time… I don't know where to start."

"I can help with that." He yanked on her arm and she tumbled against him.

———

Her mouth rounded in a perfect little O that he just had to trace with the tip of his tongue.

The shocked sound she made stroked his ego, so he slid his arms lower, bringing her hips flat against him. Need for this woman nearly swallowed him whole. "Kiss me back, Dani."

He would later swear he heard the sound of something snapping as her hands stole around his neck and she lifted her lips to his. Sweet but savory, tender yet firm, her mouth destroyed him as her tentative exploration flared into a full-bodied, mind-blowing, hellacious kiss.

He didn't remember backing her into the counter or lifting her up, but he reveled in the feel of his hands on the silky fabric and then—oh God—the supple length of her thighs. She tensed, but he soothed. She opened her mouth to speak, and he took full advantage and tangled her tongue with his.

Her moans of pleasure fueled his need to touch, to taste, to take… but he didn't want to scare her off, so he dug deep for control. Instead of gobbling her whole, he brushed the tips of his fingers from her knee to her curvy little backside, and he just had to dig his fingers in to hang on, because once he had her in his hands, his mind blanked of all but one thought—Danielle naked in his bed... He strained against his zipper. Need to be inside of her was tearing a hole in his gut.

The woman in his arms was incandescent, burning with a purity of spirit that added fuel to the sensual fire they'd lit. He had to have more... he had to have it all. "Danielle, come upstairs with me."

She tilted her head back and smiled up at him—all the answer he needed. He swept her into his arms and strode through the kitchen toward the stairs. *Now!* was all he could think.

He took the stairs two at a time and strode down the hallway. His door was partially open; he put his shoulder to it with enough force to have it swing open and then bang shut behind him.

If he didn't slow down, he wouldn't last five minutes. He closed his eyes and drew in a deep breath. When he opened them, she was watching him, her eyes no longer soft blue but a deep sapphire. He recognized the passion simmering in the depths of her gaze.

"I've been wanting to get my hands on you for days. I can't wait."

Her lips lifted in a half smile. "Then don't." She whispered kisses along his jaw and worked her way to the tendon in his neck. He sucked in a breath and knelt on the bed and placed her in the middle before his legs gave out.

He slipped the straps off her shoulders and pressed his lips where the silky strands had been. She shifted beneath him, softening beneath his touch. When her hips lifted toward him, he stared down at her, mesmerized by her beauty.

She grabbed a hold of his shirt and pulled him on top of her. "In a hurry?" he rumbled.

"How long do you think we have?" she rasped, fumbling with the buttons of his shirt.

He eased back and yanked on his shirt; buttons pinged against the walls as the worn fabric gave. She worked his belt free and had him in her hands before the remnants of his shirt drifted to the floor.

"God, Danielle." Her hands were magic. The air sucked out of his lungs as her fingers wrapped tight around him.

"I want you," she rasped, helping him shimmy out of his jeans, but they got stuck on his boots. "I can't wait," she whimpered, kissing his chest and licking a path from his breastbone to his navel.

"Drawer," he ground out, shifting so he could pull his boots off. When she stared at him, he grit his teeth and said, "Condom."

The dazed expression in her eyes changed to determination as she opened the drawer and pulled out a foil packet. Before he could take it from her, she had it open and was slipping it over him from tip to base. The erotic slide of cool latex over his engorged flesh nearly pushed him over the edge, but he pulled back, refusing to come before she did.

—ⵡ—

Danielle didn't think; she simply shifted on the bed, grabbed him by his amazingly taut backside, and lifted her hips. He balked, and for a moment, she thought he'd changed his mind until he rasped, "I'll take the lead now, Dani darlin'."

She wanted to tell him that it didn't matter, but his lips found hers and his kiss had every last thought evaporating.

His hands swept the gown up and over her head a heartbeat before his mouth latched onto her left breast and he destroyed her with lips and tongue. Aroused to the point of pain, she grabbed his hair and tried to make him stop, but he only paused long enough to grin up at her and latch onto her other breast.

Her eyes rolled back in her head as her orgasm ripped through her.

"Dani?"

She somehow found the strength to open her eyes; when she did, he was smiling down at her.

"Hang on, darlin'," he warned, a heartbeat before gripping her hips and filling her to the hilt.

Her breath snagged in her chest as he drew back and thrust home again. But this time she was ready for him, meeting him thrust for thrust. Her hands stroked his back, his shoulders, his amazing backside, all the while whispering words of encouragement.

His head was going to explode. He drove into Danielle with a mindless determination to drive her up and over the edge. Desperate to hear her sweet cry of release as he wrung yet another orgasm from her delectable body, he braced one hand beside her head and slid the other beneath her sweet little backside. He lifted her up off the bed and drove home.

He felt her muscles tighten around him as she came

undone in his arms. Reveling in the madness that still held him by the throat, he followed her up and over the edge into oblivion.

———ᴧᴧᴧ———

"Can we do that again?"

Jesse propped himself up on his elbow, stared down at the rapt expression on Danielle's face, and stifled a chuckle. "Well now, darlin'," he drawled. "I think we'll have to fit some time into our busy schedules, because there is no way in hell I'm gonna wait another few days to make love to you."

She closed her eyes and sighed. He pressed his lips to the middle of her forehead. He wanted to tell her how he felt, but wasn't sure he could put what was in his heart into words. One thing he could do was to let her know she mattered.

"Danielle," he rasped. "I want more... not just this," he said, brushing the tips of his fingers along the line of her collarbone, following the path with his lips. "But you, being here at the Circle G."

She cupped his cheek in her hand and lifted her lips to his. "It's not just me—"

"I know," he interrupted. "I want Lacy here too. I don't know how to work it out just yet so your uncle doesn't come after me with a shotgun, but there's no going back now that I've tasted paradise."

Her cheeks flushed a lovely pink. Enchanted, he hugged her close and knew he'd have to let her go now, so that she and Lacy could come back. "We'd better get dressed before someone comes looking for us."

———— ∿∿ ————

"What'll everyone think?" she said as she slipped the periwinkle gown over her head. Smoothing it into place, she scooted off the bed and started to wring her hands.

"What happened to the woman who wanted to know if we could make love again?" He pulled her into his arms and waited for her to answer him.

She laid her head against his broad chest and sighed. She could get used to having someone strong and solid to lean on... making love with Jesse was definitely going to be a plus. But how would they explain things to her daughter?

"I'm still here, just confused. I don't know how I'll explain things to Lacy if we were to get involved."

"Darlin'," he drawled, "I'd say we are beyond involved. Committed's the word I'd use."

He was frowning down at her and she really loved that about him. He wanted her as much as she wanted him. Definitely a plus. "What will your brothers say?"

"To you and in front of Lacy?" He shrugged. "Nothing. We weren't raised in a barn, despite the fact that we spent a good part of our childhood in one. Did you and your ex talk to Lacy about your sex life?"

Shocked to the core, she gasped. "Of course not."

"Then why would you have to explain ours to her?"

A tingle of awareness shot from her core to her heart. "Ours?"

Yanking her close, he grabbed her shoulders and gave her a shake. "Are you listening?"

"Yes," she whispered.

"Good, because I'm only saying this once more. We

aren't done here, Dani; we're just beginning. You got that?" he demanded, setting her free.

"Yes, sir," she giggled watching him bend over to grab his jeans off the floor.

"You think this is funny?" he asked as he pulled them on and bent back down to find his boots.

"Uh, no," she said softly, as love for this man filled her heart to bursting and overflowed.

"This is going to work," he said as he stood up.

She threw her arms around him and sighed. "Work is a four-letter word you know."

"Come on," he said, pulling her along behind him. "Let's go find your clothes. I'm not sure I want my brothers seeing what I'm seeing right now."

"Jealous?" she asked, reveling in the possibility of having someone care enough to be jealous.

His nostrils flared and his eyes narrowed. "I don't share," he grumbled.

Her head felt light as she told him, "I don't either."

He took her hand and led her downstairs. Fortunately, no one was around when they collected her clothes and Jesse helped her out of the silky nightgown and into her clothes.

She was wrapped around him when the back door opened and a deep voice called out, "Thought you had somewhere to be, little brother."

"Damn," Jesse said, easing out of her hold and taking her hands in his. "Can you stay over?" Her heart tumbled in her breast at the unasked question shimmering in his dark and yummy gaze. She wanted to say yes, but it wasn't just her to consider.

"Maybe next time. Lacy has to get used to seeing

us together… besides, I'll have to explain things to my uncle too."

He rested his forehead against hers. "Stay for dinner at least."

"All right."

Chapter 13

"EMILY SAID RONNIE'S COOKING BURGERS ON THE GRILL!"

Lacy's smile had her smiling. "Your favorite."

"Uh-huh, and know what?" she asked tugging on Danielle's skirt until she bent down to Lacy's level.

"What?"

"Cowboy Jesse's gonna eat dinner with us before he gots to go." Lacy looked up at Jesse and nodded. "He gave his word to go somewheres tonight, so he can't stay long."

"I did," he rumbled, coming to stand next to Lacy and Danielle. "But I'll be back really late, so your momma said you had to go home."

"But we can come back, right, Mommy?"

Danielle smiled. "Yes, ma'am."

"Cowgirls follow the Code," Lacy said, grabbing a hold of Danielle's hand and then Jesse's.

"Yes, ma'am." Jesse's deep voice did funny things to Danielle's insides. "Cowboys and cowgirls should always do their best to uphold the Code."

Danielle let her gaze slide up the long, strong length of his jean-clad legs to his worn cotton shirt—a replacement for the one he'd ripped in his hurry to make love to her. Her sigh was long and low. She'd have to talk to her uncle soon; she didn't think she could stand to be away from the man who'd turned her world upside down in one afternoon.

She lifted her gaze to meet his and the power of his passion hit her hard and had her struggling to remember to breathe. His eyes darkened to molten chocolate and he swept his Stetson from his head, holding on to the brim with both hands.

"I'd like it if you'd come visit me again tomorrow."

"But I don't want to leave," Lacy told him.

He squatted down next to her and touched the tip of his finger to the end of her nose. "I've got to go help a friend, but you're welcome to stay and visit with everybody."

"You really have to go?"

Danielle's heart hurt for the little one who had her daddy leave her, and it looked like cowboy Jesse was going to be leaving them too. "He just said he did, sweet pea. Now stop pestering Jesse."

"Yes, Mommy." Lacy spun around and clamored up onto the swing and leaned against her mother. "Bye, cowboy Jesse!"

He put his hat on his head and tipped it in their direction, and was gone.

Dylan walked back outside, and asked, "Where's he off to?"

Emily got up and looked Dylan in the eye. "I don't know."

Lacy was watching everything with interest, but Danielle didn't want her daughter to get sucked into life out at the Circle G until she and Jesse figured out how they'd make their relationship work "Are you sure it's OK that we stay? I could call my uncle."

Tyler leaned out the back door, and said, "Dinner'll be ready in five minutes. You want to help me set the table, Lacy?"

"Sure!" She flew over to the door and ducked inside before Danielle could remind her to wash her hands and watch her manners.

"She'll be fine," Emily reassured her. "Now, why don't you tell me what happened?"

Danielle sighed and moved over so Emily could sit beside her. "What do you think happened?"

Emily tilted her head to one side and seemed to be carefully considering the options. "Well," she said at last, "knowing those wild-eyed Garahan brothers, anything from stealing a quick kiss to backing you into a corner and scrambling your brains with a kiss that would curl your toes—or the heart-stopping possibility of making love with the dark-eyed cowboy of your dreams."

Danielle couldn't keep from laughing. "I guess they are more alike than I figured."

Emily nodded. "So, which was it: the sweet peck on the cheek, the full-bodied *I can't get enough of you* brain scrambler, or a little afternoon delight?"

Danielle sighed and confessed, "All of the above. I hadn't intended to," she said slowly, "but one thing led to another after he saw me in one of Ronnie's satin and lace getups."

Emily scooted closer and whispered, "Which one?"

Danielle closed her eyes and whispered back, "The turquoise set."

"Oh, the sexy tap pants and bra?"

When she opened her eyes, Emily was eagerly waiting for Danielle to tell her more. She nodded.

"And?"

"What makes you think there's an 'and'?"

Emily shrugged. "He's a Garahan. There's always an 'and.'" As if that explained it all, she sat back and waited for Danielle to continue.

With a worried glance at the back door, Danielle asked, "Can we talk about it later?"

"OK," Emily agreed, getting to her feet. "We should probably help with dinner."

Danielle followed behind and wished she didn't have the feeling that Tyler's fiancée would try to extract every last detail from her.

But to her surprise, no one mentioned Jesse or the fact that he'd left in a rush to go somewhere. Odd that neither of his brothers spoke about where he was going.

Danielle's head was starting to pound from trying to figure out what was going on and whether or not it would affect their newly forming relationship. Finally, she let all thoughts of the tempting man go, and focused on the meal and the way she and Lacy had been accepted with open arms.

The kitchen in the Circle G was filled with warmth and good-natured teasing. Jesse's brothers seemed relaxed and at ease in their company. Although neither brother had any children, they had no problem including Lacy in their conversation or trying to draw her out when she fell silent.

That's when Danielle realized that, although their parents died when they were younger, they had a solid role model in their grandfather. She smiled and tried to catch up on the conversation.

"So then what did Trigger do?" Tyler's question must have had something to do with her daughter because he was waiting expectantly for Lacy's answer.

"He snuffled my hand and then nudged my elbow."
Her daughter's eyes were shining.

"Trigger's smart," Dylan said. "He knows if you had
one piece of apple, you were bound to have more."

"Dylan's right," Tyler added. "Our grandfather used
to keep apple quarters in his pockets. Trigger remembers
and was looking for some."

Ronnie and Emily were quietly watching their men
interact with Lacy and smiling. Danielle had a good idea
of what was going on in their minds. Tyler and Dylan
had the makings of wonderful fathers. They were kind
and paid attention to her daughter, showing that they had
patience as well as intelligence.

She'd seen the same qualities in Jesse, but hadn't
wanted to think of him in that particular role. But after
the way they'd nearly burned each alive with the passion
they both fought to restrain, she might have to reevaluate
the situation.

Emily finally spoke up. "So, when do your cousins
arrive?"

Tyler and Dylan shared a conspiratorial glance and
grin. "At the end of next week. They're going to be helping us move the herd."

Ronnie looked confused. "I thought you were doing
that this week with Timmy and his friends."

Dylan stroked his fingers along the side of her cheek.
"We were, but when Jesse told us that Tom and Mike
were coming in a week or so early, we decided that the
herd could last another week where they are."

"There's still plenty of pastureland where they are,"
Tyler said. "We just didn't want them to overgraze it."
Looking at Danielle, he explained, "Pastureland needs

to be rotated and replanted in order to ensure that our longhorns are getting the proper diet and not some of the weeds that could be dangerous to their health."

"Are your cousins really firemen?" Lacy wanted to know.

Danielle was surprised that her daughter knew about them. Before she could ask Lacy how she knew so much, her daughter added, "And the ones from Colorado are really lawmen, just like Marshal Dillon?"

Tyler and Dylan started to laugh, and Lacy's little chin jutted out. Before Lacy could say something inappropriate, Danielle said, "We're both big fans of TV marshals and cowboys. My mom actually encouraged my fascination, and Lacy sort of carries on the tradition."

"Somebody's been talking about us," Dylan said with a smile.

Danielle laughed. "I don't know who or how, because I only just heard about them coming today."

Lacy leaned closer to Dylan and confided, "Ms. Beeton stopped by the diner today and told us all about it."

"Did she now?" Emily asked. "Well, it must be true if Mavis knows about it. That woman is hardwired to the gossip chain in town."

Ronnie's gaze met Danielle's. "Well, one thing's for sure—we can definitely use your help organizing the All-Male Revue for the celebration."

Danielle's eyes widened, but no words came out. "You don't really mean what I think you mean, do you?"

Dylan and Tyler started to chuckle. The deep rumbling sound was identical to Jesse's. She wished Jesse were here to the point that she actually ached for him.

"This is strictly G-rated entertainment," Emily said.

"The ladies over at the Lucky Star wanted to contribute to the celebration but didn't think the former mayor—"

"He hasn't been indicted yet," Tyler reminded her.

"Well," Emily pursed her lips and continued, "he should be behind bars for what he tried to do to Jolene and me."

Tyler reached over, grabbed her hand, and brought it to his lips. "The truth will come out and he will pay for trying to railroad you and Jolene out of your business and out of town."

"This sounds like the plot to an old-time Western!" Danielle couldn't believe stuff like this was still happening today. "Are you making this up?"

Dylan frowned at her. "No, ma'am. The real crime is that Emerson thought he could get away with it, that he was above the law."

She shook her head. "No one is above the law... well, they shouldn't be."

"Exactly," Dylan agreed. "But it's out of our hands."

"Too bad the sheriff hasn't arrested anyone in the shooting yet."

"Did somebody get shot?" Lacy was riveted to the conversation, and Danielle was worried that her little girl was going to have nightmares. She wanted to change the subject but needed to hear the answer first, so she asked, "Did they?"

Ronnie sighed. "No, but unfortunately, it was the sign hanging outside of the Lucky Star and my shop."

Danielle liked the way the brothers were actually trying to soothe their women. It showed that they were worried about them, that they cared. And then it hit her—they were in love... truly. Ronnie and Emily had the good fortune to have men such as the Garahan brothers in love with them... but then again, now Danielle might too. From what she'd witnessed the few times she'd been out at the ranch, the men worked hard, fought hard, and loved their land, their women, and their animals... and not necessarily in that order.

"So that's why your shop looked so new." She'd wondered about that. "At first I thought your shop was historic, but then parts of the front looked so new, and when I walked inside—"

"With the exception of the very front downstairs, my building is over one hundred years old, and part of the reason I was targeted."

Danielle didn't know what to say to that, but figured there was definitely more to the story than the little bit her uncle had told her the other day. With a glance in Lacy's direction, she turned back to Ronnie, and said, "I'd love to hear more... later."

Everyone seemed to realize that the conversation was headed in the wrong direction, given Lacy's age. In silent agreement, Ronnie changed the topic back to the celebration. "We're also going to have a barrel riding demonstration, and Dylan is going to let me ride Wildfire."

"But that's his horse." Lacy had been sucked in by Ronnie announcement. "Won't Dylan mind?"

He pressed his lips to his wife's cheek. "She wouldn't marry me unless I promised she could ride Wildfire."

Danielle smiled. The Garahans were a constant surprise to her. They seemed so tough on the outside, but inside was a soft center where their women were concerned. Jesse had proven that earlier. "What about your cousins?" she asked. "You don't have enough horses for them to ride, do you?"

Tyler grinned. "Noticed that did you? Most of the ranchers out here have spare horses that don't get ridden every day. It's hard work, but Quarter Horses are up to the challenge and the best breed for ranching."

"We've already lined up four horses for them to use," Dylan said. "Two from the Double M and two from the Bar N."

Tyler nodded. "In exchange, while our cousins are here, we'll be helping both ranchers move their herds as well."

"It sounds as if you live in a very tight community." Danielle was surprised. "I would have thought that ranchers preferred to do things themselves."

"It's true," Tyler said. "We do, but times are tough, and we all need to work together to keep our way of life moving forward and our ranches from going under."

Ronnie and Emily shared a glance, but whatever they were thinking was a mystery to Danielle. Finally, Emily said, "The idea behind Take Pride in Pleasure Day is to draw the community together… ranchers and town folk… and raise enough money to help pay down a few of the ranchers' feed bills and mortgages."

"The town folk depend on the ranchers to purchase their goods from them, and the ranchers depend on the town folk to keep them supplied." Ronnie added, "This was the perfect solution for everyone."

"What else will be happening aside from the barrel riding?" Danielle hoped there would be something else for Lacy to do, because she wasn't going to let her attend the revue.

"We've got food lined up: the BBQ Pitt is supplying ribs and barbecue beef sandwiches; there will be cotton candy, homemade lemonade, and iced tea… isn't your uncle donating pies?"

"I don't know." Danielle wondered why he hadn't said anything, then realized why. "He hasn't mentioned it, but we've been really busy."

"There's a lot to do and we'd love to have you help, if you aren't too busy helping Jimmy make the pies to donate."

"I'd love to."

"Me too!" Lacy practically bounced off her chair.

"You too, darlin'," Tyler agreed. "I bet you could help run the lemonade stand."

"Really?"

"Ms. Beeton is in charge of the drinks. I'm sure she'd love your help."

"Can you call her, Mommy?"

"We could stop by and visit with her on the way back to the diner," Ronnie offered.

"Sounds like a plan." Dylan brought Ronnie's hand close and kissed it again. "Hurry home, darlin'."

Danielle knew it was time to leave. "Thank you all for a wonderful meal, but I need to get Lacy home and put her to bed."

"Awww—"

"We've got to get up early to help Uncle Jimmy."

Lacy's frown turned around and she told everyone, "He lets me help with the secret."

"What secret?" Dylan asked.

"Can't tell." Lacy grinned. "But it goes into his pie crust."

Before her daughter could spill the beans and the family recipe, Danielle started to clear the table, but Tyler got up, grabbed her by the elbow, and steered her toward the back porch. "You and Lacy go sit a spell on the swing while Ronnie says good-bye to Dylan. Emily and I will clean up; Dylan can load the dishwasher."

"But—"

"No buts, now, she'll be right out."

"I really like it here, Mommy."

Danielle settled them on the swing and pushed off. "I do too."

"But I miss cowboy Jesse. Will he be back before we leave?"

Although she was just as sorry he hadn't been there for dinner, she knew the importance of keeping promises. She brushed a lock of hair out of Lacy's eyes. "He would have told us if he was."

Lacy's exaggerated sigh had her swallowing a chuckle.

Danielle was staring off into the distance, down the road, when Lacy asked, "Can we wait right here on the swing for cowboy Jesse?"

She turned to look down at her daughter's upturned face and couldn't help but smile. "Not this time, but maybe next time."

"You say that a lot."

"I don't want to break any promises to you. You know that don't you?"

"Uh-huh… Daddy din't care that he broke promises."

The screen door opened and Danielle was embarrassed to see Dylan and Ronnie standing there. Dylan was frowning and Ronnie was shaking her head at him. "Ready to go?"

Lacy jumped off the swing and ran toward Ronnie. "Can we stay and wait for cowboy Jesse?"

Dylan's frown softened as he bent down and lifted Lacy onto his shoulders. "He's gonna be real late tonight. Maybe next time."

Lacy sighed. "Now you sound like my mommy."

Everyone laughed as Dylan carried Lacy to Ronnie's car and buckled her in. "You can come back anytime, Lacy."

Without missing a beat, she grinned and asked, "Tomorrow?"

He was laughing as he moved away from the car. "That's up to your mom," he said, closing the passenger's side door. "You just have her give us call and we'll be happy to have you visit."

Lacy beamed as Ronnie got into the driver's seat. "Bye, Dylan!" she hollered out the window. "Say bye to Tyler and Emily for me!"

He stood and waved until they rounded the bend and were out of sight. "I really, really like it here," Lacy said to no one in particular.

Danielle knew then that she would have to have that talk with her uncle tonight. He knew the Garahans, but would understand her hesitation to dive into a relationship with Jesse and would help her put everything into perspective. She couldn't complicate Lacy's life by getting all tangled up with another Texas cowboy until she and Jesse figured out how they'd make it work.

Jesse was home by midnight and wasn't surprised to find the light on or that everyone had already retired for the night. Hell, he wished Danielle was waiting on him upstairs.

"Damn." That thought came out of nowhere and rocked his concentration. Frustrated that it took so little to redirect his train of thought, he grabbed the wad of money from his front pocket and tossed it on the table. This time, he didn't bother to leave a note. His brothers would know it was from him.

Heading for the stairs, he felt weighed down by the responsibilities he shouldered. He needed to keep winning out at Devil's Bowl, because the Circle G needed the money and it wasn't right to expect his newlywed brother to keep working late nights at the carpentry jobs he'd taken on.

He needed to find a way to get the Brockway ladies to agree to stay at the Circle G… he needed them in his life. Exhausted, he went to bed, but ended up lying awake, thinking of the paradise he'd tasted that afternoon. "Hell."

It was going to be a long, sleepless night.

Chapter 14

"THAT LITTLE LACY'S A LIVE WIRE." TYLER LIFTED another forkful of soiled hay.

Jesse grunted. He was tired, hot, and horny, and sure as hell didn't feel like jawing with his brother. He wanted to ride into town, kidnap Danielle, and spend the day in bed with her.

"Her mom sure is a looker."

If Tyler was trying to piss him off, it was working. "Yep." Concentrating on mucking out the stalls, he wished it were tomorrow already; his cousins were due in and their help with routine chores would be a relief and might buy him some time to visit with Danielle and Lacy.

"Have you heard the rumors in town?"

A cold chill chased up Jesse's spine. Sticking his pitchfork in the wheelbarrow, he wiped his sleeve across his sweaty brow. "Just get it said, Tyler."

His brother leaned against his pitchfork and nodded. "I heard Mike Baker's taken to having breakfast at Sullivan's Diner."

The cold chill stole around to his heart. He might not have gotten around to romancing Danielle, but in his mind he'd already staked his claim when they'd made love.

"Sadie told Mavis that Mike's been singing Danielle's praises, hinting he's finally found a woman worth changing his workaholic ways for."

"That's poaching," Jesse ground out.

"Only if you're dating Danielle," Tyler said watching him closely. "And I know you haven't had the time."

"I'm making the time now." Jesse spun on his heel and walked out of the barn.

"Hey, we're not finished!"

Jesse heard his brother and paused in the doorway. "I lost a woman I cared about once before because I didn't move fast enough. I'll always wonder if things would have been different if I'd told her how I felt instead of thinking she knew. I'll be damned if I'm making that same mistake with Danielle."

Instead of arguing, his brother grinned. "Good luck."

Jesse just might need that luck. He had a woman to claim before that damned banker could sweet-talk her into forgetting about the slow-burning fire they'd started the other day.

He didn't want to talk to Emily or Ronnie, so he walked around to the front of the house. Listening, he could hear the women chattering in the kitchen amidst the sounds of dinner being made. His stomach growled—he was starving—but he ignored his empty belly and went upstairs to get cleaned up.

While the hot water beat down on his tired muscles, he tried to think of an approach to use; he had hoped to take his time getting to know Danielle, to woo her, so she'd be putty in his hands and fire in his bed. But now he'd have to revise his strategy. It was like what Slim had to do last Saturday night; instead of waving Jesse in for a splash of gasoline, he went on faith in Jesse's driving talent and let him finish the race on fumes. It had been risky, but had worked.

Driving over to her uncle's house right now would be

the same… risky… but he was afraid if he waited, he'd lose the chance to tell her how he felt. Searching his heart, he knew this time, something was off… weird… different. Was it love?

Damned if I know. And he probably would be for thinking that he could just show up and expect her to fall on her knees and declare her undying love for him.

"Damned banker. Can't trust a man who wears a suit." A few months ago, Jesse'd promised retribution for the bank's threat of foreclosure and had walked into the bank, thrown the first punch, and had drawn first blood. But Baker had surprised him and retaliated by giving Jesse a fat lip and tossing him out of the bank. They'd been wary of one another since then.

Drying off, a nasty thought had his stomach turning. "What if she likes him better? What do I have to offer Danielle?"

One hundred and fifty years of Irish pride, blood, sweat, and tears tilled into the soil. They might not be on the verge of losing the Circle G anymore, but they were a long way from being in the black. But she seemed to like the ranch and, more, had fit in, as if she and Lacy had always been here. Having her here, smiling and laughing in the kitchen, had felt like the missing pieces of his life had finally fit into place. It hadn't felt that way since his mom died.

Too tired to run a razor over his face without slicing off something important, he forced himself to think about something other than what life had been like when he was ten. It took some doing, but finally worked when he turned his thoughts toward a certain little cowgirl and her tiny pink boots.

Staring at his reflection, he dug deep for the resolve to see this through. "Only one way to find out."

Danielle was sitting on the back porch when Jesse drove up; she got to her feet and had a hand to her heart. He didn't think he surprised her; she had to have heard the truck driving up. Holding his irritation with the rumors he'd heard about Danielle and Baker in check, he strode over to the porch and was suddenly at a loss for words.

Feeling like the world's biggest fool, he stared up at her, so damned glad to see her—alone—that he grinned.

She smiled. "What a surprise."

"Should I have called first?"

She waited for him to come up the steps. "No, I'm glad you came by."

Her hair was pulled back in a high ponytail and the overwhelming urge to set it free and bury his hands in it had him moving in close. He wanted to ask how she felt about him, if the rumors about Mike Baker were true, and if she'd thought about him as often as he had about her since they'd burned up his sheets and she'd etched her name on his heart.

Giving in to need, he watched her blue eyes widen as he reached to pull the band from her hair. She drew in a breath as it tumbled free and glorious tawny waves fell past her shoulders. Standing in front of him, all he could think of was tangled sheets and tasting her sweetly parted lips.

The hell with asking; he yanked her arm, and she tumbled against him. Her heart was pounding hard, like she'd just crossed the finish line and won a race. Was she worried that Lacy would come outside when he was kissing her, or was it something a lot more fun... the desire they'd barely scratched the surface of? He had to know before he lost what was left of his sanity.

Their lips touched and the frustrated desire he'd been keeping in check since he'd seen her in that damned silky underwear burst free. He drank from her lips, like she was cool, life-giving water, and he'd been wandering on foot out on the range without it.

The sweetness of her mouth broke through the haze of passion gripping him. "Berries," he rasped, deepening the kiss by banding his arm around her lower back and forcing her hips flush against him.

Her soft moan of pleasure shot through him, like crossing that finish line and seeing the checkered flag waving. Wanting more, needing it, he traced the rim of her mouth with the tip of his tongue. She shifted closer, slipping her arms up and around his neck, and offered him more.

Close to the edge of sanity, ready to jump off, he shifted and bent her over his arm. She tightened her grip and he plundered, soothing his need to take, to taste, and to fill the empty well inside of him.

"I'm ready, Mommy!"

Jesse crashed and burned at the sound of Lacy's voice. Digging deep, he fought for control and won. Easing her up, he looked over his shoulder, expecting to see Lacy standing in the doorway, but her little girl must have been calling from somewhere inside the house.

—⁂—

Danielle's legs threatened to give out on her. She reached out to steady herself and ended up grabbing a

hold of something warm, solid, and lethal to her heart—
Jesse Garahan. He'd been in her every waking thought
since they'd made love at the Circle G.

But she had no choice; it was hang on or fall down.
"Be right there, sweet pea."

Staring up at the man who'd destroyed her resolve
not to get involved so soon, let alone with another cowboy, she knew she wouldn't be able to forget the taste
of his lips, the strength of his arms wrapped around her,
or the heavenly sensation of being cradled against the
warmth of his broad chest.

"I have to tuck Lacy in," she said. "Would you like
to help?"

Before he could answer, her uncle walked outside
and said, "I need to talk to Jesse."

"I'll see her tomorrow. Give her a kiss for me."

His expression had her wondering what kind of man
would put a child before himself or his own needs. Her ex-
husband certainly hadn't. Looking over her shoulder, she
realized that Jesse wasn't like other men… he was unique,
special. "I will," she promised, slipping past her uncle.

Normally, the nightly routine soothed her frayed
nerves, but tonight the whisper of a dream haunted
her—a strong man by her side to ease the burden of raising her daughter… one that would love Lacy as much
as she did… someone who would stay because he loved
her more.

"Night, Mommy." Lacy hugged her tight and sighed
as she settled down under the covers.

Danielle pressed her lips to her daughter's forehead
and smoothed the baby-soft hair out of her eyes. "That's
from Jesse."

"He's here?" Lacy was trying to scoot out of bed when Danielle stopped her.

"Yes, but Uncle Jimmy's talking to him. Jesse said he'd see you tomorrow, OK?"

Lacy lay back down and crossed her arms over her chest. "I guess so."

"Sweet dreams, sweet pea." The sound of Lacy's even breathing had her smiling. As soon as her daughter's head hit the pillow, she was down for the count.

Making her way downstairs, she heard the rumble of male voices coming from out on the porch. There was no sense in worrying about whatever her uncle would say to Jesse when he had him alone. She'd talked to her uncle last night and he'd seemed resigned to the fact that she wanted Jesse Garahan in her life. Uncle Jimmy had had plenty of time to unload with both barrels... she just hoped that he hadn't had a change of heart and tried to chase Jesse away before she could say good night.

She opened the screen door and both men turned to face her; neither one smiled.

"Didn't hear you come back down, June bug." Her uncle shot one meaning-filled glance at Jesse. "I think I'll go watch the news." He paused in the doorway and said, "Don't forget what I said."

"No, sir."

"And just what did you say, Uncle Jimmy?"

"Nothing that you need to worry about. Is Lacy asleep?"

She crossed her arms and stared at her uncle, waiting for him to tell her what the two men had been discussing, but he didn't budge. Whatever he'd said to Jesse, he wasn't about to share with her. Obviously, it had to do with her or her and Lacy. "Like a log."

"Did you take her boots off?"

"She wears boots to bed?"

Jesse's question had her smiling. "Every night."

"And you let her?"

"Until I go to bed, then I take them off her and put them by her hat, so she can put them both back on in the morning when she gets up."

He chuckled. "Must be quite a sight first thing in the morning."

Uncle Jimmy shook his head. "Took me by surprise the first morning I saw little June bug standing in the kitchen with her little ruffled night gown, tiny pink boots, and cowgirl hat." His eyes misted. "If I hadn't already loved her to pieces, I would have fallen right then and there."

Danielle hugged her uncle. "She loves you back… we both do."

He hugged her close and nodded to Jesse before going inside.

"Your uncle is a good man."

Surprised by his comment, she turned to make certain he wasn't being sarcastic, although he had sounded sincere. "Yes, he is."

"You're lucky." Jesse watched her from where he stood on the bottom step.

When he made no move to join her on the porch, she invited him to do so. He surprised her by shaking his head. "You should turn in. Don't you have to be up early?"

"I'm always up early." What was going on here? Ten minutes ago, he'd been ready to devour her whole.

"Just another work day for me," he said with a grin.

"Why don't you and Lacy come and visit tomorrow afternoon? I'd like to start those riding lessons."

Testing a theory, she walked toward him until they were face-to-face and eye-to-eye, with her on the top step and he on the bottom with their lips lined up just right for kissing. His eyes darkened to that delectable shade that reminded her of chocolate at the melting point, but he didn't move.

Licking her lips, she watched his jaw clench and the muscle beneath his left eye start to twitch, but he kept his hands locked at his sides and his lips to himself. "What did my uncle have to say while I was gone?"

His gaze flicked to the screen door and back. "He's worried about you and Lacy."

"We're doing all right," she said. "All I need is a job. I have to help pay my uncle back for feeding us and giving us a place to stay until I get on my feet."

"He probably won't take the money."

It must be a man thing because she couldn't even begin to reason out how Jesse had come to that conclusion. She frowned at Jesse. "How do you know?"

"I wouldn't if I were him."

"What if I insisted?"

"There's some things a man's got to do; taking care of the women in his life is just one of them."

"He's my uncle, not my father."

Jesse looked like he was trying to find the right words. Instead of interrupting and blasting him with her opinion of his last statement, she found the patience to hold her tongue.

"All the more reason to do whatever he can while you and Lacy are living under his roof."

"But that's—"

The sweep of his fingertips on her cheek was tentative, when earlier his mouth had been possessive. She
wanted to tell him what she thought of interfering males,
but he brushed his knuckles against her face and his
touch distracted her.

"Your father is three hours away."

"How do you know that?" She had a sneaking suspicion that her uncle had warned him off; she didn't figure
much would scare Jesse away. Eyes narrowed, hands on
her hips, she asked, "Did he tell you to leave?"

Jesse's hands clenched and unclenched. "He's
smarter than that." Her confusion must have showed on
her face because Jesse added, "He asked me."

"So you'll just leave even if I don't want you to?"

He shook his head and turned to go. "Not a lot of
choices here, Dani darlin'. We don't want the gossips to
start talking about what we have that's special and twisting it around until it's tawdry. Lacy wouldn't understand."

His determined strides ate up the ground between where
she stood and where his truck was parked. Launching herself off the top step, she nearly did a face plant but managed
to find her footing without eating dirt. "Jesse—wait!"

Hand on the top of the driver's door, he paused but
didn't turn around. "I've got to go."

Going with what was in her heart, she touched his
shoulder and whispered, "Don't I get to say good-bye?"

He vibrated beneath her hand. Was he angry or was
it something else? A man like Jesse Garahan wouldn't
tremble at a woman's touch, would he? "I'm hanging on
to my control by a thread here, Dani, please don't make
it harder for me."

She dropped her hand and he got into the cab. But before he could reach for the door handle, she slipped under his arm, cupped his face in her hands, and pressed her lips to his. He didn't have time to react as she stepped back and closed his door. "We'll see you tomorrow afternoon. I hope you're ready for one excited little girl."

The heat in his gaze seared her. "I'm always ready." He gunned the engine, backed up, and spun his tires while she stood there trying to figure out why he would leave when it was so obvious he wanted to stay.

And then it occurred to her—*the Code.*

Her mother was right to wean her on silver screen legends; the men of the West were strong, hardheaded, and loyal to the bone. They loved the land, the animals, and the way of life they'd chosen, and although life out west was a testament to those strengths, there were times when only the love of a good woman would keep a man going.

She'd found the cowboy she'd always dreamed of… and damned if she was going to let him walk away because of some misplaced sense of duty. She wanted to be the woman Jesse depended on to keep him going when his back was to the wall. Because she knew in her heart that Jesse Garahan was the man who would ride straight into hell for her… and damn the consequences.

She turned around and saw her uncle standing on the top steps. His slow smile pushed her over the edge. "What did you say to him?" she demanded, stalking over to the porch. "Why did he leave?"

His smile slipped a little, but he was definitely still pleased by the fact that Jesse hadn't stayed. Danielle asked, "Do you really still hold that pie theft against him?"

"Is that what you think?" Her uncle shook his head. "I was wrong then, but I'm not wrong now. That man has a good head on his shoulders and the brains to do what's right, no matter the cost to himself."

He hadn't admitted to telling Jesse to leave yet, so she asked, "And how would I ever find that out if you keep scaring him away?"

"June bug, if you weren't so tied up in knots over that man right now, you'd see that he just proved how much he cares about you and Lacy by leaving!"

"But he wanted to stay… I wanted him to stay."

Her uncle ground out, "Exactly!"

"Buddy wouldn't have left," she rasped as tears filled her eyes. "That's what you wanted to find out, wasn't it, Uncle Jimmy?" She brushed her tears away and her anger fizzled out. "You wanted to see if he was the type of man who would grab whatever he could and to hell with everyone else—"

"Like that good-for-nothing rodeo cowboy," he ground out.

"Like Lacy's father," Danielle said softly.

"And that's the only good thing Buddy Brockway did in his whole sorry existence," her uncle growled. "Fathered the most beautiful little girl on God's green Earth."

"Well," Danielle said with a smile. "On that at least we agree."

Watching the way her uncle's throat worked, she could tell he was holding back things best left unsaid. Glad that he had a handle on his anger, she closed the distance and hugged him tight. "I love you, Uncle Jimmy."

"I promised your daddy I'd watch your back," he said rubbing his hand on her back, as he had when she was a little girl. It soothed her then; it did the same now. "And I mean to honor that promise."

She had no doubt that her uncle would keep his word. She depended on it. The realization that Jesse was a lot like her uncle and her father made Jesse's leaving just now a little easier to take.

"Do you think he'll be happy to see us tomorrow?"

"Count on it."

"But he seemed so angry—"

"I think he was mostly frustrated and not wanting to leave without sampling a little more of what I'm trying to protect."

She pushed out of his arms. "Uncle Jimmy!"

He shook his head. "No use trying to pretty it up. That man's gonna be hurtin' until he has a cold shower… maybe two."

Shaking her head at her uncle's plain way of speaking, she sighed. "I'm going to bed. See you in the morning."

"You and little June bug can sleep in tomorrow."

She laughed. "Not if we're going to help you over at the diner before we head on out to the Circle G for the afternoon."

"So come over to the diner around eight o'clock. Sadie'll be there to help me, so you don't have to rush. All right?"

Love for her uncle had her smiling. "All right, but no more tests or interfering. Deal?"

He looked like he was about to refuse but then shrugged. "Deal. Night, June bug."

She laughed softly. "Night, Uncle Jimmy."

Jesse thought about what Danielle's uncle said all the way back home. He got out to open the gate and wondered if she and Lacy would still come for a visit tomorrow. "I want to be the one to teach Lacy to ride, and a hell of a lot more. I want to be there for Lacy… all the time."

With his hand on the latch, he looked up at the wrought iron and marveled that his great-great-great-grandfather had been the one to forge the huge circle with a *G* in the center of it. Proclaiming to all that this land was Garahan land, and come hell or high water, Indian uprisings, or battles over water rights, a Garahan had held on to this land for generations.

He'd never lacked for pride and knew it all stemmed from his roots—solid Texas roots. But there was one thing he lacked, he thought as he got back into his truck and drove to the house. He needed a woman to stand beside him and help him keep the family going strong.

He wanted to do his part working the ranch alongside his brothers, but more, he wanted to settle down, marry a good woman, and watch her grow round with his child. He was certain tonight when he'd kissed her that Danielle Brockway was that woman.

Putting it in park, he marveled that he'd already have a head start on his brothers—he'd have a daughter… a little pixie pink cowgirl.

He hung his hat on the peg by the back door and, for the first time since Emily and Ronnie had come to live out at the Circle G, took care not to make any noise to wake anyone up.

Chapter 15

"I THOUGHT YOU'D STAYED OVER IN TOWN LAST night." Ronnie smiled and flipped the steak she'd been frying. "I didn't hear you come in."

Jesse walked over to where she stood and kissed her on the cheek.

She tilted her head to one side and asked, "What was that for?"

"Caring about me," he said and meant it. And it was that simple. Both she and Emily loved his brothers enough to let that love spill over and care about him. "I'm one lucky bastard."

"You'll be a bleeding bastard if I catch you kissing my wife again."

To prove a point to himself and his brother, he hugged Ronnie close and kissed her forehead. "The womenfolk don't like to see blood spilled before breakfast." He winked at Ronnie and shocked the hell out of Dylan by pulling him in for a quick brotherly hug. And just to make sure his brother didn't think he'd completely lost his mind, Jesse turned around and punched Dylan in the shoulder.

Dylan grunted, walked over to his wife, swept her into his arms, and kissed her like he'd never see her again.

"Damn," Jesse mumbled. "Wished I'd done that just once more last night."

"You get lucky last night?" Tyler asked walking into the room.

Dylan finally came up for air and said, "I'm thinking he must have."

Jesse pushed down hard on the lid to his temper. He didn't want to start a fight today of all days... he was going to see Danielle and Lacy today and get behind the wheel of Slim's race car tonight. Nothing and no one was gonna do anything to ruin his good mood.

Just as he was about to speak, Emily put her hand on his back and poured his coffee. "Stop picking on Jesse."

Jesse winked at Emily; she was smart and knew that once the men had that first cup of coffee in their hands, they were less likely to pick a fight with one another. Tyler was just as fortunate in his choice of woman as his other brother. The more he paid attention to the subtle signs of affection between his brothers and the amazing women who loved them, the more he realized that what he wanted out of life wasn't what he'd thought he wanted when he was eighteen and could only think of racing cars...

What he wanted was going to be visiting today, and if he didn't set the record straight right now with Emily and Ronnie as his witnesses, his brothers would probably say something stupid that *he* would end up regretting. Not that they would intentionally say anything mean.

He set his mug down and set the table. "Danielle and Lacy are coming out to visit today."

Tyler's mug froze halfway to his mouth. He glanced at Emily and then at Jesse. "That a fact?"

Jesse shrugged. He didn't have time to figure out what was going on in his older brother's mind. "I'm gonna need some time to spend with them." He looked at both of his brothers when he asked, "Will that work for you?"

"Is she who you were with last night?" Tyler's question hung in the air.

Jesse clenched his hands into fists but kept them at his sides. Gradually, he eased them open again and picked up his mug. The kick of caffeine cleared his brain and he answered, "I drove into town last night and spent some time with Danielle, but not the way you're thinking."

"How do you know what he's thinking?" Dylan asked.

"Breakfast is ready, boys," Ronnie interrupted. "Come and fill your plates." When Dylan walked over, she smacked him in the back of the head with the spatula.

"What the hell was that for?"

She grabbed him by the front of his shirt and kissed him. "Because it's none of your business what Jesse's doing."

"Why should he care what we say—" Tyler began only to be interrupted by Emily.

"Because Jesse treated Ronnie and I with respect from the moment we met him, and we expect no less from either of you where Danielle's concerned."

"But that would mean—" Dylan began only to fall silent when Ronnie lifted the spatula and shook it at him.

"That she is every bit of deserving of your respect and if we find out any different—" Ronnie began.

"There will be hell to pay," Emily finished.

His brothers, smart men that they were, looked at their women and then over at Jesse before they shrugged and sat down at the table.

"Will they be staying for lunch or dinner?" Ronnie asked.

Jesse finished chewing before answering. "I have to leave by five o'clock, so unless you ask them to stay, she won't want to wear out her welcome."

Emily was opening and closing cupboards when she said, "Danielle and Lacy are always welcome here."

"What are you doing?" Tyler finally asked.

"I thought I had another box of brownie mix. I guess I'll have to go into town and buy some more."

Concern etched his brother's brow and he got up and drew Emily into his arms.

If Jesse hadn't been straining to hear what his brother was saying, he might have missed hearing Tyler ask her if everything was all right.

Emily didn't answer him with words; she lifted her lips and Jesse looked away, but not before he saw the look in her eyes. A look that reminded him of what he'd glimpsed in Danielle's blue eyes last night—love.

He started choking until he felt a strong hand pounding on his back. He held up a hand to indicate he was all right. By the time he could draw in a breath, his brothers were looking at him like the time that two-headed calf had been born.

"Is there something you're not telling us, Jess?" Tyler asked.

"Aside from where you go at night and how you're earning whatever money you leave on the table?" Dylan added.

He shook his head. "Nope. I'm good. Thanks for breakfast, Ronnie." He rinsed his dishes, put them in the dishwasher, and headed for the stairs. "I'll be right down with my laundry."

Ronnie and Emily exchanged a knowing smile. "He's got it bad," Emily said.

"What?" Tyler demanded.

Jesse could hear the sound of delighted feminine

laughter as he walked back through the kitchen to the laundry room. "Did I miss anything good?"

His brothers watched him with an intensity that had him wondering just what they'd been talking about while he was upstairs. Probably about him and Danielle.

Emily put her arm through his and asked, "Are you sure you have to go out tonight? Ronnie and I wanted to make a special dinner."

He looked at the four expectant expressions and shrugged. "Maybe next week."

"How about Friday night?" Ronnie asked. "Your cousins should be here by then."

He shook his head. "I'm busy Friday night."

"We'll plan for Saturday, then," Emily said with a smile.

He paused with his hand on the back door. "Can't do it Saturday unless we eat around three o'clock."

He had to get out of the house, before they asked him for another night that he would be out at the track either practicing or racing and his temper burst free. Damn, it was hard to be considerate. If it had been his brothers asking him, he could have told them both to go fuck themselves and be done with it. But he'd never say anything like that to their women.

"Damn," he grumbled. "Women complicate everything."

Once Jesse left, Dylan and Tyler followed him, leaving Ronnie and Emily alone in the kitchen.

"So," Ronnie said slowly, "got any ideas?"

Emily grinned. "We're going to interfere."

Ronnie laughed. "Good. Did you see the way Danielle kept staring at Jesse, when she thought no one was looking, with an all-too-familiar shell-shocked expression on her face?"

Emily nodded.

"Once they're here, we can tell her we need Lacy's help in the gardens or for a secret project that we're doing for Take Pride in Pleasure Day."

Emily dried her hands on a kitchen towel and asked, "What secret project?"

"Hmm?" Ronnie asked getting out the ingredients for the marinade she was planning for their dinner.

"Ronnie?"

She turned and laughed at the way Emily was frowning up at her. Finally the light went on and Emily was laughing right along with her. "You just made that up."

Ronnie agreed. "Think it'll work?"

Emily's laughter died. "They need more time together, but because of Lacy, they're putting their own needs aside."

Ronnie scored the steak and poured the marinade over it. "Jesse seems really distracted." She covered the dish with plastic wrap and put it in the fridge.

"We need to give them a push."

"I want Jesse to be happy too," Emily said.

"He will be, Em."

"Danielle and Lacy too?"

Ronnie reached for the phone. "Why don't I call Danielle and give her the heads up."

Emily nodded. "I need to run into town for a couple of things. Tell her I can pick them up on my way back… it'll be easier to convince them to sleep over tonight if they don't have a car."

"Danielle might say no," Ronnie warned.

"Maybe we'll get lucky and Lacy will answer the phone."

—~~~—

"Mommy! Ronnie's on the phone. She says we can help her with stuff and sleep over."

Danielle held out her hand and Lacy gave the phone to her mother. "Cowboy Jesse's gonna teach me to ride today."

"Hi, Ronnie, what's this about a sleepover?" She thought Lacy had been making that up, but to her shock, Dylan's wife started to explain the reasons it would be a good idea.

"The guys are really behind schedule and need to make some repairs to the barn before their cousins arrive to help them move the herd."

"It sounds like we should wait until after they do that." Danielle didn't want to disappoint Lacy. Then there was the fact that she'd actually spent the night staring at the ceiling reliving Jesse's devastating kisses—and their mind blowing, orgasmic lovemaking.

"We really need Lacy's help, though."

"Really? With what?"

"There's a super secret project that we need her help with."

"You can't even tell me?"

"Well," Ronnie said slowly. "I could tell you, but then…"

Danielle laughed. "I'll let you two keep your secrets. We'd love to come over—"

Lacy tugged on the hem of her T-shirt and asked, "Can we sleep there too?"

Danielle nodded. "We're going to help my uncle until after lunch. We can drive over later."

"Emily's going to be at Dawson's later. She can come by and pick you up at the diner."

"Well—"

"It'd be easier for us; that way, we'll have all of the help we need all day and Lacy can get a riding lesson this afternoon and then again right after breakfast."

Lacy was watching her closely, but for once, she didn't hesitate. Lacy wasn't the only one who wanted to spend more time out at the Circle G. Danielle couldn't wait to see more of the ranch... and spend a few stolen moments in Jesse's arms and find out if he felt the same connection on as deep a level as she did.

"We'll be ready."

"Emily will stop by around one thirty."

Danielle disconnected and bent to lift Lacy into her arms. "Pack your backpack, sweet pea, we're going to be camping out at the Circle G."

"Yay!" Lacy hugged her tight and kissed her cheek before squirming to get down. "I'll right back."

The morning flew by with Lacy asking every ten minutes when Emily was arriving. Between her uncle and Sadie, they managed to keep Lacy from driving her crazy.

Lacy called out "She's here! She's here!" and ran to the door.

"Hey there, Lacy," Emily said, getting out of the car. "Are you ready for some fun?"

Danielle joined her daughter outside and smiled. "We are. It's been a really long time since we did anything for fun." She reminded Lacy about her backpack, giving

her time to speak to Emily alone. "I'm not sure what surprise project you want Lacy to help you with," she said
quietly. "She's so smart, it's hard to remember she's just
a little girl."

"No problem."

"So is Jesse going to be there?"

Emily smiled and nodded. "He… uh… doesn't know
that you and Lacy are staying over."

"Is that going to be a problem?"

"No. You'll find the Garahans are an affable bunch
for the most part."

"They seem to disagree a lot."

Emily laughed. "They're just brothers." She turned to
open the back door when Lacy reappeared with her pink
hat and matching backpack.

"Did you say good-bye to Uncle Jimmy and Sadie?"

Lacy nodded. "Unca Jimmy wants to tell you something."

Danielle wondered if it would be a continuation of
their discussion from the night before. "I'll be right
back. You mind Emily now."

"She won't be a problem. We'll be right here."

Danielle walked inside and reached for the overnight
bag she'd left in the corner behind the cash register.

"There you are." Sadie smiled. "Your uncle's in the
kitchen."

When she walked in, he turned and smiled. "Emily's
probably got a list of errands a mile long, so I won't
keep you." When he just stared at her, she wondered
what was up.

"Is there something you wanted to say?"

He shook his head. "I'm going out on a limb here,
June bug." He stacked his saucepans and brushed his

hands on his apron. "Not all cowboys are like the one you married." Before she could respond, he folded his arms across his chest and frowned. "I may not have approved of him as a kid, especially when he and his brothers stole—well it's best if I don't get all riled up again. What I'm trying to say is that Jesse turned out all right and proved it last night."

"Good to know," she said, putting her bag down to hug him.

When he set her back from him, he said, "Those boys are doing everything they can to keep that ranch. Don't say as I approve of the way Tyler or Dylan started out making the extra money they needed, but it isn't for me to say."

"You know that I love you, don't you?"

Her uncle opened his mouth to speak, closed it, and then started again. "Well now, it's always nice to hear the words said." He touched the tip of his finger to the end of her nose. "Best you remember that and get a going."

"Thanks. We'll see you tomorrow."

"Take tomorrow off," he said as she opened the kitchen door. "Sadie and me are used to the Sunday crowd."

"Thanks," she agreed. "It's not easy prying Lacy away from the ranch."

"Have fun!" he called out as she walked through the diner.

"We will. See you tomorrow."

"Kiss that cowboy for me," Sadie said with a wink.

Danielle shook her head and walked outside. Emily and Lacy were chatting up a storm, but her daughter jumped up and grabbed her backpack off the steps and opened the back door to Emily's car. "Can we go now?"

Emily's conspiratorial smile had Danielle feeling like a kid going on an adventure. "The guys will probably be coming in for a break by the time we get back." She got in the driver's side and waited until Danielle was buckled in before adding, "They work long hours and don't stop for regular meals."

"It must be hard to keep their energy level up when they're working so hard physically."

"Ronnie and I keep after them and load their saddle bags with snacks and a big jug filled with plenty of water or iced tea."

"How do they carry a jug in their saddlebags?" Lacy wanted to know.

Ronnie laughed. "When they're working in the far pastures, one of them drives the truck."

While Emily drove, Lacy settled down in the backseat, content to be headed back to the Circle G.

By the time they'd arrived, Danielle was anxious and wondering if Jesse's interest had really been more than just physical or if she had imagined the whole thing. Sometimes when you want something badly enough, your mind plays tricks on you. It had where her ex had been concerned.

"Can I open the gate?" Lacy started to unbuckle her seat belt, but one look from her mother and she stopped. "Please?"

Danielle relented. "Lacy and I will open the gate for you." They got out and pushed the big gate open together. She held tight to Lacy's hand as Emily drove through and they closed the gate behind her and got back in the car.

"Can we go to the pond today?"

Danielle looked over at Emily. "That's not up to me, sweet pea. Let's wait and see what's going on up at the ranch house."

Emily nodded as she turned to the right and followed the road that would lead to the Garahan's back door.

Danielle rasped, "Does it always feel like you're coming home?"

Emily parked the car and patted Danielle on the arm. "It does for me." While Lacy fiddled with her seat belt, Emily asked, "Do you believe in fate and destiny?"

Without missing a beat, Danielle said, "Absolutely."

"Sometimes, they need a little push."

Emily's cryptic remark had her wondering what was going on, but Lacy didn't give her a chance to respond; she bolted out of the backseat, dropped her pink pack on the porch steps, and dove onto the swing.

Danielle shook her head. "Lacy, you can't just leave this here, someone might trip over it."

"But—"

"No buts, young lady. We're guests here, and if you don't want anyone to send us home early…" Danielle let her words sink in and from the expression on her little one's face, her daughter would be sure to listen. Neither one of them wanted to go home before seeing Jesse.

Following Emily into the kitchen, her thoughts returned to the handsome cowboy. She hoped he was interested in more than just a quick tumble between the sheets. She didn't want Lacy to be hurt if and when he lost interest in them. So she focused on the prospect of watching Lacy's first riding lesson, knowing it would be like watching her little girl open presents on Christmas morning.

"The men should be back soon, and when they get here, they'll try to eat anything that isn't nailed down," Emily warned.

Ronnie was pulling a huge casserole out of the oven. Savory spices filled the air as the scent wafted toward Danielle on the afternoon breeze. "Smells marvelous."

The other woman grinned. "It's my grandmother's lasagna recipe." Ronnie turned at the thunderous sound of horses riding hard toward the ranch house. "Batten down the hatches, ladies, the storm's about to hit."

"I don't like thunderstorms." Lacy moved to stand behind her mother.

Danielle patted her shoulder. "That sounds like horses to me."

Lacy's worry changed to wonder. "Is it cowboy Jesse?"

Ronnie and Emily laughed. "And his brothers too."

The tantalizing thought of being this close to Jesse again had her hands shaking. Needing to do something with them, she asked, "What can we do to help?"

Emily pointed to a drawer and said, "You could set the table."

Finally having something to do to still the trembling, Danielle set out the flatware and dishes and kept an eye on her daughter, who was standing by the screen door watching for the men. "They're coming!"

She raced over to the table and then back to the door. "Can I go out, can I, Mommy?"

With a look to make sure there were no loose horses, she told her, "You can go stand on the porch and wait for them."

"But—"

"If you step one foot off that porch, we are going home."

Lacy stared at her for a moment, but the sound of horses whinnying and deep voices talking had her dancing from foot to foot in anticipation. "OK."

Using her most stern voice, she cupped Lacy's face and lifted it gently so their eyes met. "Promise me."

Lacy crossed her heart and solemnly said, "I promise."

Danielle pressed her lips to Lacy's forehead, her daughter's signal to go ahead. She chuckled watching her daughter blast through the back door and rush to the edge of the back porch, gripping the railing. "Cowboy Jesse! We're here!"

Unable to stop herself, Danielle followed her and waited.

"Looks like you got yourself an itty-bitty cowgirl waiting on you, Bro." Tyler grinned.

Dylan poked Jesse in the ribs and nodded toward her. "Looks like she brought her fine-looking momma with her."

Jesse stopped in his tracks and shifted his gaze until it collided with hers. She could feel the instant the banked heat in his eyes flared to life. Need slashed through her outward calm as her skin warmed by degrees... more than a match for the fire that was slowly beginning to burn inside of her.

He was close enough for her to get lost in his velvet dark eyes. She licked her suddenly dry lips and couldn't help but become captivated by the way his pupils dilated, his nostrils flared, and his jaw clenched.

He wanted her.

Tingles of awareness electrified her skin as the need to touch, to taste, arced through her system. She had to swallow the saliva pooling in her mouth—no way was he going to see her drool.

Instead of the greeting she'd begun to imagine, he winked, shifted his gaze to her daughter, and said, "I can see that, little darlin'. You ready for a riding lesson?"

"Yes!" Lacy screamed, prepared to leap into his arms. But a quick look over her shoulder and she must have remembered her promise. "But I gots to stay on the porch."

Jesse's eyes brightened, and she would swear he wanted to laugh out loud but didn't. A feeling of contentment filled her along with the realization that he was trying to spare Lacy's feelings by not laughing at her.

"Well then, hang on," he rumbled. "I'm coming."

When had her ex ever treated either of them with that kind of consideration? Lost in thought, she didn't notice that Jesse had reached the edge of the porch. "Let's go, little darlin'."

Lacy grinned and leaped off the top step and into Jesse's waiting arms.

Danielle smiled at the sight of Lacy's bright pink cowgirl hat flying out behind her as she jumped, but it was the joy in her daughter's eyes reflected back at her that caused Danielle's heart to lurch. While she wrestled with yet one more aspect of the cowboy she was falling for, his brothers walked over.

"Nice catch, Bro," Tyler said, patting him on the shoulder.

The three of them were a solid unit. Although she'd seen them scuffle and ride each other's case, at the end of the day, it all came down to family and sticking together.

"Be sure to pay attention to Jesse," Dylan reminded her daughter. "He's a good teacher."

Dylan's words redirected Danielle's thoughts. She asked, "He is?"

Jesse's shrug wasn't the answer she was looking for. But her chance to ask disappeared as he lifted her little girl up onto his shoulders. Lacy tilted her head back and gave a rebel yell that would have made her grandmother proud.

"Where'd you learn to do that?" Jesse was smiling as he set Lacy back on her feet by the split-rail fence.

"My gramma."

"My daddy would have loved to hear you do that."

"I can do it again." Lacy beamed. "Where is he?"

Jesse's wistful expression had Danielle's hands itching to grab a hold of him and hug him until every trace of sadness disappeared, but she hesitated when he said, "He died when I was younger than you."

Lacy wrapped herself around Jesse's leg and held on tight. "I don't gots a daddy anymore either."

The walls around Jesse's heart shattered, as Lacy's confession touched him deeply. No one had been able to breach the gap that had widened when his mother died and grew even more when his grandfather passed away.

Unable to trust his voice to speak, he reached down and rubbed Lacy's back. When she looked up at him, her baby-fine hair blew into her eyes. He loosened her hold on him so he could squat down and smooth the hair back off her forehead. Setting her hat on her head, he knew his life would never be the same.

Women had come and gone in his life, and he'd been so focused on one in particular that he had ignored others. He was Irish enough to believe in fate and destiny. But a tiny part of him still questioned—would he have found something as precious as this woman and her child if he hadn't had his heart broken?

Was this love or his desperate need to find the kind of love his brothers had? He heard the soft sound of someone clearing their throat and knew that Danielle was waiting for him to say something to her daughter.

They'd both gone up in flames when they'd finally let their hearts lead them into bed. But he needed to find his footing again, or else he might misstep by saying the wrong thing and making light of something so wonderful as this little bit of a thing offering her compassion.

Lacy probably didn't understand what she had confessed to him, but Jesse did. Whoever her father was, the dickhead had thrown away this little girl... and for what? Garahans weren't stupid, and he intended to embrace the chance to fill the gap Lacy's father had vacated.

"My daddy built that swing over there for my momma."

Lacy nodded.

"When I'm missing him, sometimes it feels good to just sit and rock and remember him." He didn't add that he usually drank whiskey while sitting there, but hey, a man could change, and besides, he didn't have to confess all of his secrets. "If we swing there later, maybe I won't miss mine so much."

He hugged her tight and felt like he'd been surrounded by sunshine.

She giggled. "You're squishing me and I wanna ride Trigger."

He laughed and set her back down. "Well then, let's see if your mommy's ready to watch you learn how to ride."

"I'm ready!"

Jesse's gaze shifted from daughter to mother and the breath whooshed out of his lungs. Her eyes were filled with unshed tears, but she was smiling. A blue so pure, and a smile so sweet, he'd later swear he heard the angels singing. Shaking his head to clear it, he asked, "Will you ladies wait here? I'll go and get Trigger."

Danielle blinked back her tears and nodded.

Leading the horse out of the barn, he had a moment to watch mother and daughter. So many things about Danielle reminded him of what he missed... that loving touch only a mother could give. He'd had his grandfather and his brothers, but it wasn't the same. Need to have Danielle brushing a lock of hair from his eyes or cupping his face in her hands and pressing her lips to his cheek filled him to bursting, as the maelstrom of emotions churning inside of him threatened to drag him under.

This wasn't what he usually felt for the women he dated, and it scared the hell out of him. He needed to get control of the situation, forcing those weird thoughts aside; he led Trigger into the corral. "He's happy to see you."

The horse walked over to where Lacy and her mother stood and lipped the brim of Lacy's hat.

"Sometimes he forgets his manners," Jesse said, telling the horse to quit it. Trigger eyed Jesse, but finally lifted his head up and down as if he was agreeing to behave. "Now. Let's see if you remember what Ronnie told me she taught you the other day."

As they talked about the different ways to approach a horse, good and bad, and how and where to pet a horse,

Jesse knew he had an apt pupil. "You're pretty smart for a little bitty thing."

"I'm not that little," Lacy replied, looking up at the saddle and then back down to her toes. "Can you lift me up?"

Danielle's laughter was infectious, and he was amazed that he wanted to hear it again, but under different circumstances—when it was just the two of them. Knowing better than to lose concentration around one of their horses, he focused on his star student and asked, "Ready?"

She grinned up at him and nodded. As he lifted her and set her down on the horse, she started to throw her arms open, but stopped and frowned. "Sorry."

He was not sure what had happened to her happy mood, so he asked, "For what?"

"I almost scared Trigger," Lacy confessed.

Suddenly, Lacy's bringing her arms down to her sides made sense. "Is that what happened the other day?"

Lacy nodded again. "I din't mean it; it was an accident."

"I think he knows that, sweet pea," Danielle added. "Why don't you let Jesse tell you what to do now that you're up there?"

After warning Lacy about making sudden movements near Trigger's ears or eyes and to be sure to hold on to the saddle horn, they were ready for him to lead Trigger around in a circle while Lacy got used to the feel of being in the saddle.

Danielle watched the man who'd turned her inside out with his kisses and the strength of his passion leading the horse by the reins while her daughter listened intently to his instructions. The concentration and focus her little girl exhibited didn't surprise her; Lacy had been asking for riding lessons for a while now.

Jesse's gentle way with both her daughter and the horse eased some of the tension that not sleeping had left behind. It was always harder to get through the day when you were tired, cranky, and irritable. Relaxing for the first time today, she leaned against the split rails and rested her chin atop her hands.

The deep rumbling sound of Jesse's voice was a sharp contrast to the higher pitch of her daughter's. For a moment, she closed her eyes and wondered what it would be like it to have a man like Jesse Garahan in their lives.

"Dinner's ready!"

She opened her eyes in time to see Ronnie standing in the doorway with her hands on her hips, waiting for someone to respond. "We're coming," she called out. Ronnie nodded and turned around.

"OK, little Lacy," Jesse said, bringing Trigger to a halt. "We'd best not keep Ronnie waiting. Why don't you two go on in?" he suggested, lifting Lacy out of the saddle. "I'll take care of my buddy here." Setting Lacy on her feet, he waited for her to join her mother outside the corral.

"Aww, can't I stay with you?" Lacy would have said more, but the way Jesse shook his head and nodded toward the house stopped her from whining quicker than anything Danielle might have said. She could use help like that on a day-to-day basis.

"Come on, sweetie. Jesse will be right behind us." Not giving Lacy a chance to complain, she held out her hand and waited for Lacy to take it. "See you inside," Danielle called out over her shoulder.

"Can I ride again after we eat?"

"We're hungry." Dylan swept Lacy off her feet and hauled her inside.

Surprised, Danielle hesitated on the porch. "You coming?" Tyler asked, opening the screen door.

"Oh… yes, sorry, I was just thinking about something."

Tyler waited for her to walk inside, then looked past her toward the barn. "My brother's a good man." He pitched his voice low so only she could hear.

Her gaze met his and she slowly smiled. "He's wonderful with Lacy."

Tyler frowned but didn't say anything else. She wondered what he'd been thinking, but just then Emily called her name.

"I'm not sure who had a better time out there," Emily said. "Lacy or Trigger."

Danielle thought about it and grinned. "I think it's a tie. Trigger seemed happy to have Lacy riding on him."

"He's used to kids learning how to ride on him," Dylan added.

Tyler mouth twitched like he was fighting not to smile. "He only threw you off once."

Dylan's grin was quick and lethal. "Tossed Jesse off twice."

"Not true," Jesse called out as he walked inside. "He only threw me off once… I fell off the other time."

"That's his story," Tyler said with a knowing look.

"He's sticking to it," Dylan finished.

"Come on guys, my lasagna is getting cold."

"That'd surely be a crime," Dylan rasped, pressing his lips to Ronnie's temple.

The longer she was around the two couples, the more

she was convinced of their commitment and love for one another. The bond between the brothers and their women was titanium strong, and she glanced at Jesse, wondering if she'd be lucky enough to forge something like that with him.

Their eyes met and the warmth in his gaze had butterflies dancing in her belly. Lord, that man made her feel so many different emotions all at once, her brain couldn't seem to process any of them, leaving her bewitched, bewildered, and befuddled.

She hadn't realized that she'd been staring until one side of his mouth quirked up, highlighting the deep dimple that tempted her to touch her tongue to the corner of his mouth.

"How long can you ladies stay today?" he asked, letting his gaze slide from the top of her head to the tips of her toes.

Rattled by the attention and sensual tension surrounding them, making it hard to breathe, Danielle cleared her throat to answer, "Emily and Ronnie invited us to sleep over."

His head whipped around to stare at the other women and then snapped back so he could lock gazes with her. "Is that a fact?" His lazy drawl couldn't hide the fact that he was taking shorter breaths. His nostrils flared more than once, as if he were a stallion sensing a mare in heat.

That analogy had her tamping down the desire curling up from her toes. She no longer wondered what it would be like to taste more of him—she knew and couldn't wait to follow where her heart and his heat were going to lead her.

Ronnie must have sensed that Danielle was having

trouble putting two words together and said, "We thought it would be good for Danielle and Lacy to spend more time out here at the Circle G."

Emily agreed, "Jesse's been working too hard too, so we thought it would be a nice change for him to give Lacy those riding lessons. You two can handle things in the morning, can't you?"

Jesse was shaking his head at her. "I'm leaving in a little while. I know I told you I wouldn't be here past five o'clock."

Ronnie and Emily exchanged a knowing glance before Ronnie said, "That's why we're having our big meal now."

Jesse pulled out the chair for Danielle, and when she looked up to thank him, she saw irritation in his gaze. Surprised at way he seemed to be holding back, she wasn't sure if she should ask him what was wrong.

"So you and Emily are going to be entertaining Lacy and Danielle while I'm working tonight?"

"Just where did you say you were working, Bro?" Tyler's voice was soft but firm.

He blew out a breath. "Can we talk about this later? I was hoping to drive on down to the pond with Lacy and Danielle before I leave."

Dylan looked at Tyler before shrugging. "OK by me."

And as quickly as that, the subject was dropped, with Danielle left to wonder where Jesse spent his nights working and why his brothers didn't really know what was going on.

"I like riding Trigger," Lacy said. "Dinner's good."

"He's taking a liking to you too." Jesse told her before asking Ronnie to pass the garlic bread. "This is awesome with the sausage, Ronnie."

Danielle watched the other woman's slow and easy smile, and she sensed that Jesse complimented her often.

"I'm glad you like it."

Dylan grumbled, "Get your own woman."

Jesse shook his head. "Don't need to. You and Tyler found women who can cook and do laundry, what do I need a woman for?"

The teasing way he said it took the sting out of his question, but it still smarted that he would even tease about not needing a woman when her heart was so close to being captured by his. As if he could sense her unease, Jesse patted her hand and added, "But if I could find one that had a pretty little pixie cowgirl, I might think about it."

"I'm a cowgirl!" Lacy exclaimed. "Can we be your women?"

Laughter filled the kitchen and it felt as if someone had given Danielle a gift. Despite feeling so at home with the Garahans, Danielle shook her head at Lacy and said, "I think Jesse's too busy for one woman in his life, let alone two."

"You'd be wrong." The rasp of his voice sent shivers up and down her spine. "I could make time for two special ladies."

"Can we ride Champ tomorrow?"

Danielle laughed and told her daughter to finish her supper. "But, Mommy, cowboy Jesse din't answer me yet."

"Yeah, cowboy Jesse," Dylan drawled. "Can Lacy ride Champ tomorrow?"

The brothers sent silent messages that Danielle suspected had more to do with actions than words… those actions having more to do with fists than a friendly smile. Jesse finally shook his head and said, "Not a problem, little darlin'. But what are you going to do tonight?"

Ronnie smiled and got up to serve more lasagna. "We've got a secret project that we're working on for the celebration."

"And I'm helping," Lacy announced, clearly pleased with the prospect.

"So what's the project?" Tyler asked.

Lacy rolled her eyes and sounded exasperated. "We can't tell… it's a secret."

While the men polished off a second helping, the women ate their salad. Jesse pushed back from the table and cleared his place before helping to clear Lacy's and Danielle's. Anticipating his next move, Danielle started to fill the dishwasher. His smile added another layer of excitement to the thrill she felt every time he glanced in her direction.

Lord, she had it bad.

"Are you ladies ready to go?"

Lacy was out of her seat and reaching for his hand before Danielle could hang the dish towel on the oven handle. "We're ready."

Closing his hand around Lacy's, he surprised Danielle by reaching for hers. "Come on."

Desperately fighting to keep her equilibrium, Danielle let herself be led.

Chapter 16

With Lacy between them, Jesse drove to the pond; it would have been too far to walk, since Jesse had to leave soon.

It was a good thing that her daughter was chattering nonstop; Danielle found that she didn't know what to say that wouldn't end up making her either sound like a prude or a nymphomaniac. She was so twisted and conflicted where Jesse was concerned. He was kind to her daughter and really listened to what Lacy had to say, but all she could think of was losing herself in his arms.

"Do you like bugs?"

Jesse's laugh filled the truck cab. "Depends on the bug."

"I like 'em all," Lacy confided.

Lacy tugged on Danielle's arm and pulled her closer, but in a stage whisper said, "I really like him."

Jesse's chuckle had her relaxing. It was a lovely afternoon. The temperature had already peaked and was starting to cool down just a bit, and she looked forward to spending some time, just the three of them.

Jesse pulled off the road next to the pond. "Let's go check out the grass by the edge of the water; we might find some frogs."

"Or bugs?"

He walked around the front of the truck and had Danielle's door open before she'd finished unbuckling the two of them. "Thanks."

He held out his hand and didn't let go of hers until he'd stroked the back of it with his thumb.

Her skin tingled and her step faltered. Aware of her misstep, Jesse slid his other hand around her waist to steady her. Pinpricks of awareness shot straight through to her core, making her head spin and her heart pound.

"Mommy, I wanna come out."

Danielle felt the heat staining her cheeks. "Sorry, sweet pea." She held out her hands and helped Lacy down.

Jesse was quiet as he led the way over to the pond. Standing on the bank, he breathed deeply. "Smell that?"

He seemed to be waiting for them to do the same, so Danielle squeezed Lacy's hand and said, "Take a big breath, sweetie."

Danielle breathed in the heavenly scent of sun-warmed dirt, grass, and something she couldn't identify. Jesse seemed to be waiting for her response, so she said, "It's beautiful."

"It smells like outside." Lacy tugged on her mother's hand so she would let go.

Jesse nodded. "That it does, but there's something special about out here." He locked gazes with Danielle and asked, "Can't you smell it?"

Even if he hadn't wanted to know what she thought, she would have felt compelled to answer. "We noticed it the other day, when Lacy and I took the wrong road and ended up out here."

Jesse urged her to take another breath. "What do you smell?"

Danielle closed her eyes this time. "It's hard to put into words."

"Try."

She sighed and let her imagination take over. "Lacy's right, it smells like outside—"

"You can do better than that," he grumbled.

Why the answer seemed so important to him she couldn't say, but she did as he bid and cleared her mind and tried again. "I can smell the dirt, warmed by the sun, and the grass, stirred by the breeze." She hesitated, still unable to place the other scent she'd noticed. "There's something more—"

"Yes?"

She caught his excitement and wanted so badly to describe the indescribable. "I don't have the words," she rasped. "But there's just something different about the air here, when the breeze blows over the water, rustles the tall grass, and teases the dirt..." Shaking her head, she opened her eyes and said, "It smells like home."

Jesse's smile was blinding. The beauty of the man before her went soul deep... *no*, she thought, *deeper*... He was grounded to the very land on which they stood. Heart in his eyes, smile lifting his lips, he surprised her by asking, "Can you dance, little Lacy?"

"Uh-huh... I can two-step."

Bowing to the both of them, he asked, "May I have this dance?"

His words reminded Danielle of an old Anne Murray song. As the refrain filled her head, she lifted Lacy onto her hip and held out her free hand.

His hand was callused and his grip strong. Before she could process the fact that she'd always feel connected to this man whenever he touched her, Jesse had settled Lacy on his hip and pulled Danielle closer.

He began to hum a tune that her grandmother used to

listen to. She tilted her head back and smiled. "I love the 'Tennessee Waltz.'"

His eyes darkened with emotion. "Sing it with me?"

"Me too!" Lacy crowed, bringing them back to reality.

"You too," he agreed.

As the sun glinted off the water and the breeze rustled through the grass, they danced and sang the words to a song that would forever bind them together in Danielle's heart.

Years from now when her daughter was grown, Danielle would remember dancing in the meadow by the pond at the Circle G and wishing with all her heart that Jesse Garahan would ask them to stay.

"Can we look for bugs now?"

Lacy's question and Jesse's answering chuckle broke the spell and brought Danielle sharply back to the present.

"Well now, I was hoping we'd be looking for frogs."

Lacy patted him on the shoulder. "We can look for them too."

He set her down and said, "We have to be real quiet."

"So we don't scare them off."

"Exactly." He smiled down at her. "You're pretty smart for a cowgirl."

"Mommy says it's 'cause we like to read."

"Frog hunting always reminds me of a book my grandpa liked."

Entranced, Danielle watched the way Jesse talked about his grandfather's favorite Mark Twain story, complete with hand gestures.

"Mommy, we gots to get that book."

"We'll see if they have it at the library the next time—"

A loud beeping interrupted what she had been about to say.

"What's that?" Lacy asked staring at Jesse's shirt pocket.

"My phone alarm." He reached into his pocket and shut off the alarm. "I've got to go."

The fact that he seemed to want to stay wasn't lost on her. "Come on, Lacy."

"But we din't catch any bugs… or frogs…"

"We can try again tomorrow morning," Jesse told her.

"Aren't we gonna ride Champ tomorrow?"

Jesse grinned down at her and held out his hand. "We can do both if you want. I'll drive you ladies back to the house before I go."

The ride back ended all too soon. Danielle's feelings were all jumbled together; it was probably a good thing that he was going to work… even if no one seemed to know where he was headed.

"See you in the morning." He waited until they'd stepped back before putting the truck in reverse and driving away.

"I miss him, Mommy."

"I do too."

"There you are," Ronnie said, coming out onto the porch. "Are you ladies ready to work?"

The distraction was just what the both of them needed. "Absolutely."

Reluctantly, Lacy let her mother tug her inside.

Emily was waiting for them at the kitchen table. "Oh, good! We were wondering when you'd be back."

"Jesse had to go to work."

"Um… at the—" Ronnie began.

"He didn't say." Danielle hadn't wanted to pry, but she did wonder why the secrecy. Did he have something to hide? She really had no reason to ask, and asking might send out the wrong signal and scare him away, so for now she'd keep quiet.

"What're you doing?" Lacy asked, walking over to the table where tiny boxes were scattered among muffin tins.

"This is the secret project."

Lacy's eyes widened. "I can keep secrets."

Ronnie and Emily looked at one another and then Danielle. Sensing they were waiting for her agreement, she said, "I can too."

"All righty then," Ronnie said. "We want to have a cupcake decorating contest for the kids."

"The boxes are pretty." Lacy pointed to a bright pink one. "Can I have that one?"

Emily smiled. "Absolutely, but don't you want to wait until you've decorated a cupcake?"

Danielle shook her head at Lacy. "Let's wait and see what they need us to do."

Ronnie nodded. "We were hoping to test out our idea on Lacy. There will be prizes for the different age groups, but we wanted to see if someone her age would be interested. We've got a few different mediums to work with and wanted to see which one would be right for the little ones."

"Can I eat it?"

"After you decorate it," Emily said. "Want to give it a try?"

"Like making pie with Unca Jimmy!"

Danielle smiled. "Only you don't have to bake the cupcakes, sweet pea, just frost them."

Lacy squirmed until her mother told her to be still or she couldn't help. Her daughter frowned but finally listened, and carefully used a butter knife and smeared frosting on her hand and the top of the cupcake.

"Hmmm," Ronnie said. "Let's try the icing in a tube."

While Lacy worked, the women chatted about the celebration and the arrival of the Garahan cousins.

"It's going to be pretty crowded here at the ranch once they get here, but the guys are used to bunking together."

"How many bedrooms are upstairs?" Danielle had only seen the ground floor.

"Four bedrooms," Emily answered, "but there's a bunkhouse on the other side of the barn."

"Can we sleep out there?" Lacy wanted to know.

Ronnie smiled but shook her head. "I thought you two would like to sleep in the front bedroom; it's so pretty when the sun comes up."

"Are you sure we aren't putting anyone out of their room?"

Emily smiled and said, "Why don't we clean up and we can show you the upstairs?"

"And the bunkhouse?" Lacy asked.

Ronnie and Emily laughed. "And the bunkhouse."

―∾∾―

Adrenaline still pumping through his system, Jesse drove home with his pockets full. Life just couldn't get any better than this. He and his brothers were still chipping away at their debt and hanging on to the ranch, he'd been given the chance to fulfill a childhood dream, and there was a curvy little blonde waiting for him at the ranch.

He drove up to the house and wondered if she would be awake. He hadn't had a chance to ask her, but surely she knew he wanted her. He could still taste that explosive kiss they shared the other night and feel her trembling at his touch.

He was going to be careful not to make any noise, but then on the outside chance that Danielle was asleep, she wouldn't know he'd arrived home if he was too quiet. With a grin and a plan, he opened the screen door and let it hit the frame behind him as it closed.

Not sure if she would hear the back door from the front bedroom, he hung his hat on the peg and walked around the kitchen table three times. The sound of his boots should be echoing upstairs right about now.

Satisfied that he'd made enough noise to give her a chance to wake up, he headed for the stairs. Taking them two at a time, he made it to the top as the door to the front bedroom opened. There, in the doorway, stood his sleep-tousled angel. The neckline of her T-shirt slipping off one shoulder, exposing creamy, smooth skin he just had to taste.

Drawn to her like a magnet to true north, he locked gazes with her and slowly walked toward her. "Were you waiting for me?"

She combed a hand through her hair and tucked it behind her ear. "Uh… no. Did you just get home?"

Deflated but not defeated, he smiled. "Why are you up if you're not waiting for me?"

She shook her head as if she was trying to clear it. "I don't know… one minute I was sleeping and then something must have woken me up." Her befuddlement was endearing. He closed the gap between them until the toes of his boots were snugged up against the prettiest little feet. Damn, he had it bad if he was rhapsodizing over her feet.

It was his turn to shake his head, but the sight of her coral-painted toenails started his guts to churning with want, and there was no way he could just walk away from her tonight.

"Dani darlin', I—" What could he say? *I want you so bad it hurts.* Like that would entice her into his arms. He never had a problem talking a woman into bed before… why now? *Because she matters.*

He was silent long enough that she started to shift from one foot to another. Finally she asked, "Can I make a cup of tea?" When he just stared at her, she offered, "I could make one for you too."

His johnson was so hard he didn't think he could walk, and she wanted to make him a damned cup of tea? The door frame was enticingly close; he could start banging his head on it to ease the ache inside of him.

She faltered. "You're probably tired and not interested in talking…"

Her voice trailed off and he kicked himself for making her uneasy. If he could get her into the kitchen, maybe he could talk her into sitting outside on the swing… that could lead to some serious necking and maybe something more.

"Sure." He held out his arm and she grabbed a hold of it.

When they got to the stairs, he straightened his arm, and when she would have let go, he held her hand and led her downstairs.

"It's so quiet," she mused, reaching up to get two

mugs out of the overhead cabinet. "Do you really want hot tea?"

He shook his head. "I'd rather have something cold." While she heated water in the microwave, he rummaged around in the fridge and finally settled for iced tea, sensing that cracking open a cold one might not fit the mood he was going for.

When she had her cup in her hand and moved toward the table, he asked, "Want to go sit on the swing?"

Her eyes widened, but she didn't hesitate. "I'd love to."

Holding the door open, he waited for her to pass through before quietly closing it.

"It's so beautiful out here."

He wasn't sure if she meant the porch or the ranch so he asked her.

Laughing softly, she told him, "Both. I'm not used to the wide-open spaces, but it's awful pretty. The quiet is unnerving at first, but I could really grow accustomed to it."

"You lived in the city before?"

"Well, not quite big enough to be a city, but we had sidewalks and streetlights."

He snickered. "We don't need streetlights out here." Lifting his glass high, he gestured to the sky. "We've got something better."

The moon was three-quarters full and shining brightly over the corral.

"We couldn't always see the moon from our house."

He sensed there was something more she'd been about to say, so he asked, "Do you miss it?"

Danielle shook her head and a lock of hair brushed against his shoulder. Unable to resist, he lifted the lock and brushed it against his cheek. "It's like silk."

It was impossible to see the color of her eyes, but he remembered how they'd deepened to sapphire before she'd come apart in his arms. Leaning toward her, he waited a moment to give her a chance to refuse. She set her mug on the floor and he pulled her hard against him.

"Dani darlin', you're making me crazy." His lips covered hers gently at first, slowly increasing the pressure and angle until she moaned low in her throat. The moment he'd been waiting for, his tongue tangled with hers and amped up the pressure building inside of him.

Coming up for air, they held on to one another, her eyes misty with passion. "Are you gonna make me beg, Dani?"

When his lips traced the line of her cheekbone, finding the sweet spot beneath her ear, she melted against him. She turned in his arms until they were face-to-face. "I want you so badly, Jesse, that it scares me."

He brushed the hair back from her forehead and did something he'd never done before—talked when all he wanted to do was delve deep into her welcoming warmth. "You shouldn't be afraid of me," he rasped. "I'd never hurt you, darlin'."

She shook her head. "I've heard that before—"

He fought to keep a lid on his temper. "Not from me."

She looked up into his eyes and sighed. "No, from the man I thought I'd spend the rest of my life with… look how well that turned out."

Jesse tipped up her chin with his knuckles. "I'd say pretty well. That daughter of yours is something special."

Tears filled her eyes and spilled over. "I've never regretted, Lacy… she's the best thing that ever happened to me."

"Your ex must be an idiot to let the two of you just walk away."

She hunched her shoulders forward and hung her head. "We didn't."

"Then—" The haunted look in her eye had him changing the subject. "I don't know how we got started talking when all I want to do is kiss you." He nipped the edge of her jaw, then soothed it with a kiss.

She leaned closer. "Let's not talk anymore."

Jesse vowed he'd get to the bottom of Danielle's story, but not right yet...

Smoothing his hands over her shoulders, slipping the shirt down so both shoulders were exposed, he sampled the satin-smooth skin from nape to shoulder and back again, until she was vibrating beneath his touch, moaning softly.

"Tell me what you want, darlin'." He nipped her collarbone and teased it with his tongue.

"You," she rasped.

He drew in a breath to keep from devouring her. With a choke hold on his libido, he stroked his fingertips up and down her spine, each time getting closer to the hem of the T-shirt she wore. Just when she started to writhe beneath his touch, he moved his hands, cupping her tantalizing backside.

"Oh God," Danielle rasped, arching her back like a cat, pressing her breasts against him, stretching his control to the breaking point. Shifting her onto his lap, he captured her mouth and kissed her hard, deep, as he slid her legs so they straddled him and her warm hot center was pressed against his zipper.

"Let me love you, Dani," he rasped, stroking his

hands from her shoulders, along the length of her spine to her curvaceous backside.

When she squirmed in his lap, he slid his fingertips along her taut and toned thighs, down her calves to her ankles. Scooting forward to the edge of the swing seat, he gently tugged until she locked her legs around his waist and pressed her sweetest spot against him.

He moaned low in his throat as her heat tormented him, tempted him to lose himself in the woman in his arms.

The last shred of his control held him back, waiting for her to answer.

"Jesse, I…" She couldn't speak as his lips teased her and his hands tormented her, driving her higher.

"What?" he rasped, pressing a kiss to her heart. "Tell me."

"What if someone hears us?" They were on the back porch and in full view of anyone who happened to look out the back door.

He nodded and slowly stoked the fires burning just beneath the surface with lips, tongue, and hands until she wanted to scream out in frustration. She wanted to revel in the strength of him as he took her over the edge.

As if sensing her withdrawal, he ground out, "Hold on tight," and stood. With one large hand cupping her backside and her legs locked around his waist, he strode over past the barn to the bunkhouse. He opened the door and closed it, enveloping them in darkness broken only by a thin shaft of moonlight coming in the far window.

"We've already made up the beds for when my

cousins arrive. What do you say we try out that one over there?" He pointed to the last bunk… the one by the moonlit window.

Overcome by need, desperate with want, she laid her head on his chest.

Taking that as a yes, he walked over to the bed and wrapped his hands around her ankles, urging her to let go. When she did, he swept her onto her back on the bed. While she watched, he toed off his boots, pulled off his socks, and undid his button fly jeans… one button at a time.

Her eyes were glued to his hands; she couldn't look away. When the last button slid free, his jeans slipped down to his hips, but got caught on his erection.

She giggled and he lifted a brow. "You laughing at me, Dani darlin'?"

"No, never… it's just that I didn't get a good look the other day and you're so… um… impressive."

He grinned down at her and shimmied the rest of the way out of his jeans. Crawling up the bed until he'd pinned her to the mattress, he rasped, "You ready to be impressed, darlin'?"

The words tumbled down her throat as the heat of him pressed against her belly.

He kissed her until she curled herself around him and begged him to ease the ache inside of her.

"Soon," he promised a moment before he sat back and reached for his jeans. Fishing in the pocket, he held up the small square foil packet and ripped it open with his teeth. "Gotta protect you first."

Fascinated, she watched him slip the condom on from tip to base, already knowing how good it would feel when

the length of him stretched inside of her. She nipped his
chin with her teeth and teased his mouth with quick little
bites followed by tender-soft kisses. He moved again and
she hesitated, confiding, "You're beautiful."

His snort of laughter caught her by surprise and had
her insecurities roaring back. "Are you laughing at me?"

"Hell no, woman. No one's ever told me that before."
He grabbed a hold of her shirt and pulled it over her
head. His short, sharp breath and groan of desire arrowed through her. "I just didn't expect it right now."

She shifted beneath him, and he pressed his full
weight against her, trapping her. His gaze devoured her
as he rasped, "I can't wait to fill you."

The strain in his voice sounded surprised her. "Are
you in pain?"

"Darlin', you're killing me." He lowered his head to
the valley between her breasts and placed tantalizingly
soft, sweet kisses along the fullness of her curves.

His mouth heated with each press of his lips, burning
inside of her until it threatened to flare out of control.
The tip of his tongue flicked first one nipple and then
the other.

Lost in the sensations rocketing through her, she
reveled in the sensation of his callused hands cupping
and molding her breasts. "Jesse," she rasped, spiraling
downward into a maelstrom of desire that threatened to
swallow her whole.

He lifted her hips off the bed and stripped her panties off.

Sliding her hands down, she gripped his muscled
backside with both hands, dug her fingers in, and pulled
him closer, to where she ached for him to fill her.

"That's it, darlin'," he groaned. "Take what you want."

He shifted and slid into her welcoming warmth, losing himself even as he gave to her. Picking up the rhythm, he drove her up onto the ledge, stretching her out on a rack of passion, until she'd thought she'd explode.

Desperate for release, needing to take him with her, she pressed her lips to his neck and bit down as she drove her hips up and he took her over the edge into madness.

Lifting her hand had never been this difficult after making love, but she had to know… with her thumb and forefinger, she pinched the amazing backside she'd held on to as her world shattered into a thousand pieces.

"Hey!" Jesse placed his hands on either side of Danielle's head and lifted up. "What was that for?"

She stared up at him and licked her lips. "I'm not dreaming!"

The rumble coming from deep inside of him sounded suspiciously like a laugh. She frowned, but before she could say anything, he lowered himself onto one elbow and brushed the tips of his fingers along her cheekbone. "Dani, if this is a dream, I never wanna wake up."

His words and his tender touch eased the worry that had started to surface when she thought she'd been dreaming.

"Is it always like this for you?"

He paused, a wrinkle forming between his dark brows. "Define 'like this.'"

Suddenly shy, she closed her eyes. Searching for the right words, she drew in a sharp breath as his lips touched first one eyelid and then the other. Contentment spread from her belly to her toes. When his lips touched her forehead and then the tip of her nose, it spread all the way to her heart.

Ignoring the warning signals her head kept trying to

send, she wrapped her arms around his back and pressed her cheek against his broad chest and sighed.

"You can't hide forever, darlin'. Sooner or later, you'll have to answer me."

"I'm not hiding... exactly," Danielle confessed. "I just don't want to sound naive."

Wrapping his arms around her, Jesse rolled until they were on their sides. Trailing the tips of his fingers from her shoulder to her hip, he waited, watching her until she realized he was waiting for her to explain.

"I'm not that experienced and the last time we didn't exactly go slow... but still..." His lips twitched, but he didn't smile, which was a good thing because if he had, she was out of there. "Not that it's any of your business, but my ex was the second man I'd been with." *And he didn't think to protect me.*

He lifted her chin with his knuckle and gently pressed his lips to hers. The kiss was as soft as a sigh. "Darlin', that wasn't what I wanted to know. I wanted to know which part of our makin' love surprised you. Did you enjoy it as much as your body tells me?"

She looked away from him, but he turned her face until she had no choice but to answer him. "All of it," she whispered. "No one's ever made me feel wanted and desired like you have—twice now."

He closed his eyes for a moment and when he opened them, the heat in his gaze had her belly twitching and her core weeping. "The thought of makin' love to you has had me twisted inside out and backwards since the day I saw your curvy little backside bent over the hood of your car on the side of the road."

She cleared her throat. "Really?"

He rolled on top of her and kissed her long, hard, and deep. "Let me show you."

Instead of settling between her legs, he shifted and leaned over the bed again.

"Do you seriously have another condom in your pocket?" Danielle couldn't believe it.

"Yes, ma'am," he rumbled. "That's the beauty of a three-pack."

Chapter 17

SO MANY THOUGHTS SWIRLED AROUND IN HER BRAIN, but one kept surfacing—Jesse wanted her, but he also wanted to protect her. Reveling in the newfound feeling of being the sole focus of Jesse Garahan's desire had her giddy with pleasure.

"Why hasn't any other woman staked her claim on you?" It didn't make sense. He was such a handsome man, but more, he was dedicated to his family and saving their ranch; he was hardworking and the very devil in bed.

"How do you know they haven't?"

That threw her for a loop. "OK," she admitted. "Why don't you have a woman in your life?"

"I'm working on it, Dani darlin'." His eyes gleamed and the passion in his eyes had her heart singing.

He grinned, eased back, and opened another foil packet. With his hands on her hips he held on to her as he dipped his head to taste her mouth. "So what do you say? You want to be my woman?"

"Yes!" She threw her arms around his neck and pulled him close as he lifted his hips and thrust so deep, she felt him touching her womb. Her moan of ecstasy was quickly followed by his groan of desire.

"Come with me, baby," he urged, picking up the pace, filling her, and then sliding out until just the tip of his erection remained inside of her.

Rolling his hips, he teased her until she grabbed a hold of his hair with both hands and demanded, "Now!"

He tilted his head back, gripped her backside, and filled her to the hilt. The heat of his body and strength in his hands sent her shooting over the edge. He hung on as his body emptied into hers.

With his palms spread across her cheeks, he tilted backwards and they fell onto the mattress.

"Darlin'," he rasped, breathing hard. "You pack a lethal punch."

She snuggled against him and closed her eyes. "Same goes, darlin'," she whispered, drifting off to sleep.

The kiss to her belly felt so wonderful she moaned and reached for him. "Mmmm... you still have energy?"

He nipped her hipbone and soothed the skin with his lips. "I can't get enough of you, Danielle. You're like a drug in my blood... addictive... I've got to have you—just once more?"

She knew she should probably go back inside so Lacy wouldn't wake up to find her momma gone. "I should probably go back."

His answer was to slide his tongue from her belly up an invisible line to the hollow of her throat. Tasting and teasing, he gorged himself on first one breast and then the other. Suckling and then sucking until she cried out for him.

Sheathed and ready to please, he paused at her heated entrance, waiting while she trembled with want, need for him twisting her into tight, taut knots until she thought she'd go mad. "Jesse," she rasped.

He didn't make her beg; he pounded into her like a man desperate to mate to ensure the survival of his race.

She met his powerful thrusts and was rewarded as he whispered her name a heartbeat before she came undone.

———

"I don't think I'll be able to walk," she confessed.

He lifted his head and couldn't resist just one more kiss. Her lips tasted like honey, her mouth felt like silk, and her lovin' went to his head like twelve-year-old Irish whiskey.

"I'll carry you back."

She shook her head. "Aren't you tired?"

"I feel like I could climb a mountain," he admitted. "Your lovin' makes me feel energized, ready to roll."

She looked up at him. "I hate to ask you, but I don't know if my legs will work… it must be from wrapping them around your waist for so long."

His gut clenched as want for the woman in his arms spread from there to his fingertips. Digging deep for control, he eased back and smiled. "I'm gonna be sore later."

Concern filled her gaze. "Did I hurt you?"

He leaned in for a swift kiss. Tempting him to do more, but it was late, and he didn't want anyone asking questions… well, more than they probably would when he walked downstairs with a shit-eating grin on his face. "Not a bit. I'm just out of practice 's all."

Her smile warmed him from the inside out. "We'd better get dressed."

She reached for her T-shirt and pulled it over her head, and he wished they'd had more time. There was this little mole beneath her right breast that he hadn't had a chance to taste.

Slipping into his jeans he thought, *There's always*

tonight. Reality and the simple fact that she lived in town and he lived almost an hour away had him swearing. "Damn, Dani, when can I see you again?"

"Well," she said, bending over to look for her panties. "It'll be light in a few hours and you'll be giving Lacy another riding lesson…" Her voice trailed off as she found what she'd been looking for slung across his boots.

Picking them up, she shimmied into them and wobbled on her feet. He reached out to steady her. "Here hold these." He handed her his boots and lifted her into his arms. "Hang on, Dani darlin'."

"I'm not too heavy?"

"You don't hardly weigh more than a kitten."

She snorted and buried her head in the crook of his neck. "Flattery will get you everywhere."

He kissed her as he carried her outside. Careful not to misstep in the semidarkness, he made his way over to the back porch and set her down. "I want to take you upstairs to my bed."

She shook her head, "Not yet, Lacy—"

"I know," he said. "Tomorrow night?"

She smiled up at him and placed her hand in the middle of his chest and nodded. "Good night, Jesse."

After an all too brief kiss, she disappeared inside. Steeling himself not to chase after her and cart her off to his bed, he sat down on the back step, pulled his boots on, and swore—he'd left his socks in the bunkhouse. Not only that, he had a bed to strip and sheets to wash.

Making his way back, he found his socks, toed off his boots, and put them back on. He noticed his shirt lying on the floor next to the bed and shook his head. "Damn, but that woman packs a lethal punch."

Stripping the bed, he noticed a faint glimmer reflecting off the window. Not enough time to wash the sheets. What the hell would he do with them? Looking around, he realized he couldn't stash them here. Wadding them up, he hauled them back to the house and dumped them on his floor. Exhausted, but satisfied beyond his wildest dreams, he fell face-first onto the bed.

He had two hours before he had to get up and he was gonna use both of them to recharge.

His last thought before he drifted off to sleep was that he had to convince Dani and Lacy to stay at the Circle G for a few more days.

***

"I picked up the mug and glass you left by the swing last night."

Ronnie looked at Emily and shook her head. "Dylan and I didn't sit outside last night."

"Oh, well then, who..." Emily started to say and then she smiled. "Hmmm... sounds like someone else was making use of the swing last night."

Ronnie grinned. "It's so romantic sitting out there in the moonlight."

Emily was staring out the back door. "Ronnie, do you think we should bring blankets out to the bunkhouse?"

Ronnie thought about it and added a dash more milk to the batter and stirred briskly. "I'm not sure if their cousins are used to East Texas weather, but we might as well bring them over later, just in case they need them."

***

"Hey, Ty, were you over in the bunkhouse this morning?" Dylan wheeled the wheelbarrow into the barn, picked up the pitch fork he'd been using, and started on the next stall.

Tyler paused and looked over at this brother. "No, why?"

Dylan shrugged. "The door's open and we usually keep it closed to keep varmints out."

Tyler leaned on his pitchfork. "Did you look inside?"

"No. I noticed it while I was dumping the straw, but it didn't sink in. Hell, Tyler, you know I'm not that sharp until I've had that second cup of coffee."

"We're almost finished up here," Tyler said, forking up another load of soiled straw. "Then we'll go check it out."

Dylan put his back into it and then paused. "Have you seen our little brother this morning?"

Tyler nodded. "Damn fool was whistling while he was tearing apart the fuel pump on the tractor."

"And you didn't think that was odd?"

"We're talking about our little brother here." Tyler hefted the wheelbarrow and wheeled it outside. Dylan put the pitchforks away and followed.

When Tyler had stowed the wheelbarrow, they walked to the bunkhouse, steering clear of where their brother was working on the tractor. "Door's usually closed."

Standing inside the doorway, Dylan mumbled. "Looks like everything's as it should be."

Tyler shrugged and turned around. "Pat's not coming, right?"

"Yeah, why?"

"Just checking to see if the girls made up enough beds." Tyler stared down the row of twin beds and noticed the last one was pushed off to the side and devoid of sheets. "They must have been in a hurry."

Dylan had been about to leave, but he turned around to ask, "What makes you say that?"

Tyler pointed to the last bed. "Every other bed is lined up perpendicular to the wall and made up, except that one."

"Is that so?" Dylan stepped around his brother to investigate. When he got down on one knee, Tyler started walking toward him, but when his brother started to laugh, Tyler hesitated.

"What's so funny?"

Dylan held up an empty foil packet. "Seems like somebody got busy out here last night."

They shared a smile as Dylan tucked the packet into his back pocket. "I need coffee if I'm gonna lay into our brother about taking advantage of a certain little blonde divorcée."

Tyler straightened the bed so it matched the others and they headed to the house for breakfast.

They were still chuckling when they opened the back door. "Morning, darlin'." Dylan walked over and kissed the side of Ronnie's neck. The wooden spoon dropped to the floor as she swayed toward her husband.

Tyler swept his fiancée into his embrace and kissed her. "Whatcha making, Ronnie?"

"Hmmm?" His sister-in-law was too wrapped up in kissing his brother to pay Tyler any mind.

"What's in the bowl?"

"Oh," Ronnie said, pushing out of Dylan's arms. "Pancakes."

Dylan grinned and pulled her back for a quick but meaningful kiss. "She means flapjacks."

Ronnie shook her head. "Why do you call them that?"

"What do you call them pancakes?" Tyler countered.

Emily laughed. "How about we agree to call them breakfast?" Turning toward Tyler she asked, "Are you ready for more coffee?"

"Desperate enough to hold off ravishing you until I get one."

The first thing Danielle heard as she walked down the stairs was Emily's laughter. Still smiling herself, after the late night rendezvous with the dark-haired cowboy who had turned her world upside down, she hurried to the kitchen to make sure Lacy hadn't been getting in the way.

She froze in the doorway. Tyler and Dylan were sitting at the table drinking coffee while Emily and Ronnie were making breakfast... Lacy was nowhere in sight. "Oh, I thought Lacy was helping you."

Ronnie looked up and smiled. "She was, but when Jesse came in for coffee, she tagged along after him. Since he said he'd watch out for her, we didn't think you'd mind."

"Uh... no." Danielle tried to cover up the fact that she was feeling left out.

"He's behind the barn." Tyler lifted his mug, but then didn't take a sip. Danielle had the odd feeling that he was waiting for her to say something. When she didn't he added, "By the bunkhouse."

Heat rushed up from her toes as memories of last night's loving filled her to bursting. Her cheeks felt warm, and she hoped no one noticed.

Tyler's grin was just this side of wicked and mirrored by Dylan. The brothers lifted their mugs to her, as if in silent salute, and drank.

"OK," Ronnie said, hands on her hips. "What's going on?"

"Yeah." Emily crossed her arms beneath her breasts and stared at the men.

"I, uh, think I'll go find Lacy." Danielle couldn't get out of the kitchen fast enough. Did they know how she and Jesse had spent the last part of the night? Walking briskly across the yard, she bypassed the barn and practically ran past the bunkhouse as memories of last night filled her.

"So what's that for?" Lacy was asking Jesse from where she sat perched on an overturned bucket next to the tractor.

"It's the gas line," Jesse answered. "And probably the real problem—it's clogged." He shook his head and pulled the one end free. "Damn, and I just finished re-building the fuel pump… should have checked the gas line first."

Lacy got up and walked over to Jesse. Leaning close, she whispered, "You just said a bad word."

His delighted laughter warmed Danielle's heart, but the sight of his black Stetson bent low next to her daughter's hot pink one had her stumbling and nearly pitching to the ground.

Jesse looked over his shoulder and grinned. "Hey there, gorgeous."

At a total loss for words, Danielle stopped and stared at him.

He frowned. "Don't tell me no one's ever told you how beautiful you were before?"

Lacy laughed. "Unca Jimmy tells her, 'cept he says prettier than a June bug."

Jesse's look turned thoughtful. "That a fact?"

"Uh-huh," Lacy said. "But I think she's beautiful."

He nodded. "She sure is," he said. "And that's why you're beautiful too."

Lacy seemed to be hanging on his every word. "I am?"

He laughed and pulled Lacy in for a hug. "Yes, ma'am. Your momma must have looked just like you when she was your size."

"Is that why Unca Jimmy calls me little June bug?"

Jesse nodded as he let her go. "'Cause you're pretty just like your momma."

Not used to being the center of attention or being talked about as if she wasn't standing two feet from them, Danielle cleared her throat and told them, "Uncle Jimmy's partial to bugs."

Lacy started giggling. "He is, 'cause you know why?"

Jesse brushed his hands on his thighs and waited for Danielle to join them. "No," he rasped, staring at her mouth. "Why?"

Lacy shrugged.

Danielle had to laugh at the expression on Jesse's face. He hadn't known Lacy long enough to know that half of her questions were really meant as statements. Taking pity on him, she said, "We don't know. He just is."

When he didn't look at her like he had last night, like he was ready to devour her, she started to worry. Needing a distraction, she wracked her brain to think of something to say that didn't have to do with the breadth of his shoulders, the strength in his hands, or the devastating power of his kisses. She finally said, "Ronnie's making flapjacks."

Jesse grinned. "That woman can cook." With a dark and dangerous look that had her shivering in response, he asked, "Do you like to cook, Dani?"

"I do," Lacy piped up. "I can make pie."

He looked from mother to daughter and grinned. "Then I'm right glad you're a team. I surely won't starve."

Danielle stared at the two of them as the realization that they just seemed to fit swamped her, threatening her control. Her hands started to tremble, so she clasped them behind her and tried to think of something to say, but all she could think to ask was did last night have the same meaning to Jesse, did he want to build on the love they'd made? Was it the beginning of the relationship she wanted to build with him? Not one of those questions was appropriate right now.

"What's your favorite pie?" Lacy asked, while Danielle wondered if Jesse was in it for the long haul.

"I like 'em all," Jesse rumbled, glancing at her with a question in his eyes. Did he really want to know what she was thinking or was he just biding time until she and Lacy left? Would she have the guts to ask him outright?

Probably not.

Would she try to get him alone to ask him about last night?

If I could, I definitely would.

She'd spent too much time over the last few years worried about how long her ex would stay, knowing from the moment he'd said he'd marry her and give their unborn baby his name, it would only be a matter of time before he left.

"What do you say we go get some breakfast before my brothers eat all of those flapjacks?"

"OK!" Lacy reached up to take Jesse's hand and the rest of whatever reservations Danielle held in her heart evaporated as Jesse reached down and took Lacy's hand.

When they stopped in front of her and he offered his other hand to her, Danielle knew she was lost.

Walking back to the house, Lacy kept jumping while hanging on to their hands, so Jesse looked over Lacy's head at Danielle and mimicked to tug Lacy up with his free hand. Danielle smiled and the next time Lacy jumped, they lifted her up off the ground. Her delighted laughter surrounded them.

They lifted her high so she could land on the top step of the porch. More giggles had the screen door opening and Tyler stepping outside. "I wondered who was making that racket. Hey there, Miss Lacy."

"Hi, Tyler. Can I have flapjacks?"

Charmed, he bent down, lifted Lacy into his arms, and carried her inside.

"Hey." Jesse pulled Danielle up the back steps. "Give me back my little cowgirl!"

"Not until we feed her."

Following the sound of her daughter's laughter, they walked into the kitchen and found her already sitting at the table with a plate in front of her.

She grinned and lifted a forkful to her mouth. "Look, Mommy, I gots my own plateful!"

"I can see that." Danielle shook her head. "Are you sure you can eat all those?"

"Don't you worry none, darlin'," Jesse said. "I'm sure I can eat whatever she can't." Turning toward the two women standing by the stove, he smiled. "Morning, ladies."

Ronnie shook her head and handed him a plate heaped with fluffy, golden-brown cakes. "There's sausage and bacon." She set a platter in the middle of the table. "Help yourselves."

"Coffee, milk, or orange juice?" Emily was watching Danielle rather intently, making her wonder if Emily could see the echo of last night's passion shimmering around Jesse and herself… either that or *Jesse and I did the wild thing* was tattooed in the middle of her forehead.

"Can I have juice?" Lacy asked, still shoveling in the pancakes.

"Better slow down, sweet pea, or you'll get a tummy ache."

With her mouth full, her darling daughter nodded and waited until she swallowed before reaching for the glass Emily set by her plate.

"Here, why don't you two sit down and while I fill your plates," Danielle offered. "After all, you made breakfast and the coffee. It's the least I can do to thank you for being so wonderful to Lacy and me."

Once she'd set a plate in front of Emily and Ronnie, she sat down and started to eat. "These are great, Ronnie, thanks."

"So," Dylan drawled, "sleep well, Danielle?"

She inhaled instead of chewing the bite of pancake she'd just put in her mouth. When she finally stopped choking, she reached for the glass of water Emily was holding out to her.

"Better?"

Danielle cleared her throat and could at last breathe. "Thanks."

"Are you all—Ow!" Before Dylan could ask, he was frowning down at his wife. "What was that for?" he demanded.

But before Danielle could ask what was going on,

Tyler was saying, "I hope you didn't have any trouble sleeping last—Oomph!"

Danielle suspected that Ronnie and Emily were either pinching or kicking their men beneath the table so that they wouldn't keep asking about what happened last night. Somehow the women must have figured out what had happened.

Tyler had turned toward Emily and was about to say something when Jesse ground out, "Could I see to the two of you outside for a moment?"

Dylan and Tyler got up so fast their chairs rattled against the wide-board floor.

"Shouldn't you go see what's going on?" Danielle asked as the sound of angry male voices carried into the kitchen.

Ronnie shrugged. "They're just having a family disagreement."

"It doesn't sound pleasant. Maybe I should go out there. I'm a good mediator," Danielle offered.

Emily shook her head. "They should be finished up in a few minutes."

As the deep voices increased in volume, Ronnie reconsidered. "Maybe you should go."

Danielle told Lacy to sit still and stay in her chair. Pushing open the screen door, she saw them standing just off the porch. Tyler and Dylan were standing side by side with their backs to her, while Jesse stood alone, facing them with his back to the barn.

"That's just not fair," she murmured walking toward the steps. Before she could tell them to cut it out, Jesse whipped his bright white T-shirt up and over his head and the words got caught in her throat as she was spiraled back in time to the night before, when he'd taken off his shirt in his haste to make love to her.

But something looked different. Maybe it was because he stood vibrating with anger instead of need... staring at Jesse, marveling at the beauty of the man who'd loved her until her eyes crossed, she realized it was the flash of brilliant green on his left pec that caught her eye.

Jesse's fist shot out at the same time she asked, "Is that a shamrock?"

The men hadn't noticed her standing on the porch, but her question gave the older brothers the distraction they needed and used to their advantage; each one grabbed a hold of one of Jesse's arms.

"Hey," Jesse shouted. "Lemme go!" He struggled against their hold, but was trapped like a fly in a spider's web.

Incensed that his brothers would gang up on him, Danielle flew off the porch and poked her pointer finger in Tyler's broad chest. "You let him go."

His eyebrows raised in question, Tyler waited a moment before glancing in Dylan's direction. "This is a private fight."

Hands on her hips, Danielle let her temper loose. "Well, it sure as hell isn't a fair fight with you two goons holding on to poor Jesse's arms so he can't defend himself."

"He took the first swing," Dylan said, calling her attention to him, and that was when she noticed blood trickling from the corner of his mouth.

Danielle crossed her arms in front of her to keep from striking Jesse's brothers. "You must have done something to deserve it. Jesse would never just punch somebody without a reason."

When the three of them just stared at her, she realized that she'd have to try to reason with the brothers. "Lacy and I were going to stay for another riding lesson, but if you two beat the crap out of Jesse, there's no point in us hanging around. We may as well leave now and let you get to it."

She spun on her heel and stalked back over to the porch.

"Man, did she just tell us to go ahead and beat you up?"

She could hear Jesse struggling against their hold a moment before she heard him say, "I can't just let her leave."

She fought against the need to turn around, instead slowing her steps in the hopes that the brothers would see reason... hers... and let Jesse go. She'd reached the top step by the time he grabbed a hold of her arm and spun her around into his arms. "Please don't go yet."

His lips were a breath away from hers, but she knew if she gave in and let him kiss her, she wouldn't find out what the argument was about. She couldn't explain why, but somehow she sensed that it was important that he tell her.

Leaning back away from him wasn't what he expected. "What's wrong?"

"That's what I'd like to know." She managed to slip out of his embrace. Once free, she took two quick steps back. "I came out here to put a stop to whatever you three were arguing about."

Her gaze slipped below his collarbone and settled on the shamrock tattooed over his heart. How had she missed that last night? "When did you have time to get a tattoo?"

The confusion in his gaze matched what she was

JESSE
265

feeling. He shook his head and mumbled something about women that she couldn't quite make out. "A while back, why?"

"I... um... didn't notice it before." Her confession had him grinning.

"That's because you were desperate to make love with me, darlin'."

She narrowed her gaze at him. "Desperate?" The fact that he was right irritated her, but what was worse was that her body started tingling from head to toe the longer he stood there looking down at her with desire swirling in his dark brown eyes. "You make me sound like some lovesick teenager."

Before she could turn her back on him, he had her locked against him, with his lips a breath from her own. "Dani darlin', you made me feel like one last night," he whispered so no one else could hear. "Standing here right now in front of God and my brothers, I want to strip you bare, toss you on the ground, and have you all over again."

Caught up in the image he'd painted for her, she had no choice but to lift her lips and press them to his. His taste was a potent combination of want, need, and desire. The memory of last night had an answering warmth spreading through her.

"Are you two through arguing?" Tyler asked.

"Go to hell," Jesse ground out a moment before claiming Danielle's lips in a kiss that promised passion and something more.

"Maybe you two ought to get a room," Dylan suggested.

Jesse pulled back and sighed. "Hell. Can't get no privacy around here."

His brothers were standing right behind him and

Danielle sensed that whatever had been wrong wasn't any longer. "Are you through fighting?"

"Hell," Tyler snorted. "That wasn't a fight."

"Yeah," Dylan added. "More like a misunderstanding."

Jesse pressed his lips to the top of her head. "We're good."

She didn't believe them. "Just like that?"

"Yes, ma'am," Tyler said.

"Can't get any work done around here if we stay mad," Dylan explained.

"We've got to work as a team," Jesse said. "Like you and Lacy."

Ronnie stepped out onto the porch, eyed the brothers, and then glanced over at Danielle. "Is everything all right?"

"As rain," Dylan agreed, slipping around behind Jesse and Danielle to take Ronnie by the arm and steer her back inside.

Tyler walked past them and grinned.

When the door closed behind him, Danielle asked, "Did I miss something?"

Jesse hugged her tight and kissed her cheek. "My brothers like you."

"OK." She wondered how they'd act if they didn't. "And was that part of what you were doing out here? Defending my honor to your brothers?"

Jesse slipped his arm around her and reached for the door. "I'd go to the wall for you, darlin'... never doubt it."

She couldn't say why she needed to hear him say the words just now, but she did. "Why?"

His hot gaze raked her from head to toe. "I protect what's mine."

That wasn't quite what she wanted to hear. "Yours? Branded like your tattoo?"

He let the door close. "Yeah. You got a problem with that?"

"I am my own woman," she bit out. "Not any man's shiny toy or possession." Incensed that he would even think that way, she poked her pointer finger into the middle of his chest. "I can take of myself and my daughter, you got that?"

He had the nerve to grin. "Yes, ma'am."

Tracing his fingertips along the line of her jaw, he tipped her face up so he could kiss her. Every last thought just melted away as his lips devoured hers. Boneless but energized, she couldn't wait to get her lips on his bodacious body again. Steeling herself to push back from the temptation of being in his arms, Danielle shook her head at him. "I have to think of Lacy."

"She's a spunky little girl," he said, tilting his head to one side as if studying her. "A lot like her mother."

"Flattery will get you—"

"Everywhere?" The impish grin on his face undermined her need to keep him at arm's length until she and Lacy went home. The man had her contradicting herself and doubting her own good sense. If they didn't leave soon, she'd be in a puddle at his feet.

"Come on." He opened the door and pulled her inside. "I've got a lesson to give before I head on out with my brothers to ride fences and check the herd."

Chapter 18

DANIELLE WAS HAVING TROUBLE CONCENTRATING since they'd returned from the Circle G. Jesse filled her thoughts and had them wandering back to the stolen moments they shared in one another's arms.

It had been four days since she'd seen him, but the phone calls in between had reassured her that he'd meant what he'd said about her being *his*. She understood that he had a ranch to run and no spare time… well, other than wherever he spent four nights out of the week and earned a couple hundred dollars. But after spending Saturday night making love with Jesse, she couldn't stop thinking about what it was going to be like the next time they would be together.

His lips would be commanding, his hands callused and firm, while he—

The ringing of the phone jarred her back to the present and her responsibilities; she answered it.

"Darlin', I miss the hell out of you."

Jesse's voice smoothed over her ragged emotions like butter on a stack of hotcakes. The deep rumbling pitch eased the knots between her shoulders. "I was hoping you'd call. How are you?"

"Busy. Would you like to meet my cousins?"

She almost asked if Lacy was invited too, but figured he would have mentioned her if he wanted her there. "Yes. I would. Will you be driving into town?"

He chuckled. "Hell, darlin', we're exhausted from moving the herd." He paused and asked, "Can you and Lacy come out to the Circle G?"

Warmth filled her. "Absolutely, what time?"

"We should be finished up early. How about four o'clock? We'll be firing up the grill... sort of a competition between cousins. Our New York cousins think they can grill meat. We need you and Lacy to help judge."

"We'll be there with bells on." As she hung up the phone she felt giddy. He wanted to see the both of them, and unless she misunderstood him, it sounded as if he wanted to include them in their family gathering... as if she and Lacy really mattered.

She told her uncle about the call and he had everyone hustling so they could close up on time and head back to the house.

A little while later, Lacy called out, "I'm ready!"

Danielle smiled at the picture Lacy made in her denim skirt, T-shirt, and matching pink boots and hat, and couldn't help but wonder what Jesse's cousins would think when they met her. Well, no time to worry about that now. She hugged Lacy and raced upstairs, changing into a sleeveless black shirt, denim skirt, and boots. Laughing at her reflection, she realized all she needed was a hat and she and Lacy would have matching outfits. She thought about changing into jeans, but it was still too warm.

"Mommy?"

"Coming, sweet pea." When she made it downstairs, she asked, "Are you ready to go meet Jesse's cousins?"

"Yep, but Unca Jimmy gots something to give you first."

Intrigued, she let Lacy lead her into the kitchen. "Hey, Uncle Jimmy."

Her uncle smiled. "You know that I believe a man should be given a second chance if he proves he's worth it?"

She had an idea of where this conversation was headed and braced for another lecture.

"Well, Jesse and his brothers proved they're worth it a while ago, but I never had the chance to tell them I was wrong about them... so here." He handed her two large baskets covered with green and white-checkered dish towels, holding out a third to Lacy.

The scent of berries and apples mixed with a hint of chocolate filled the air around them. "You made them pies?"

He grinned. "Yeah, figured they'd get the gist of what I was saying if I gave them what they took in the first place."

She blinked back tears. "You're one in a million, Uncle Jimmy. I know they'll appreciate the gesture."

"See that they share those pies with their cousins."

Peering beneath one of the towels, she realized her uncle had used his special pie baskets with the footed dividers so each basket actually carried two pies. "Did you seriously make a half a dozen pies for them?"

He nodded. "Two chocolate, one apple, cherry, blackberry, and buttermilk."

She hugged her uncle and whispered, "I love you."

He squeezed her tight and rasped, "I love you back, June bug. Now go on and have a good time."

The drive over to the ranch was filled with laughter as they tried to decide if any of Jesse's cousins would look like *real* cowboys or the city slickers he'd described. When they drove up to the gate, Lacy waited without being told, content to hold one of the baskets on her lap… the ones with the chocolate pies she was hoping to get a piece of.

Once Danielle had driven through and closed the gate behind them, they made their way to the ranch house. A couple of pickups were parked on either side of the one Jesse usually drove. Not knowing where else to park, she pulled up behind Jesse's. Before she could open her door a tall, good-looking stranger with bright blue eyes and blond hair was opening it for her.

"Hey there, sweet thing," he rumbled. "You must be Danielle."

She was about to agree when she heard a voice on the other side of the car. She turned in time to see an auburn-haired man with a devilish grin smiling at her from the open passenger's doorway. "I'll just help little Lacy here with her basket." Lifting it closer, he sniffed and smiled. "Smells like heaven." Setting it on the roof of the car, he helped Lacy with her seat belt and held out his hand.

Lacy smiled and told him, "It's Unca Jimmy's chocolate pies."

"Don't mind my cousin, Mike," the man told her. "He's got nephews her age. He's good with kids."

She watched Lacy walking hand in hand with the powerfully built man and noticed the way he slowed his pace and bent down in order to hear whatever Lacy was chattering about… probably the pies.

"Thanks. It's just that I don't normally trust my daughter's safety to strangers."

"A wise woman." He grinned. "My name's Ben"—he held out his hand to her—"let me help you with those."

She handed over one basket and hung on to the other.

Trying not to be obvious, she hurried after Lacy. His low chuckle had her smiling up at him and missing the bottom step, but as she lost her balance, strong hands pulled her close. Before she could thank him, hard hands pulled her back against a heavily muscled chest. "Find your own woman."

Ben met Jesse's look with a challenge. "What if I want this one?"

Danielle felt every muscle in Jesse's body tighten— good Lord, would he really fight his cousin over her? "I might decide that I'm not interested in either one of you." That ought to give them something to think about. She retrieved both baskets and stomped up the stairs and into the kitchen.

"Men," she grumbled as she lifted her gaze and nearly dropped her baskets. Dylan and Tyler were talking with two more gorgeous men. "Are all of your cousins this good-looking?" The low chuckles that followed were her first clue that she'd asked that question out loud; the second clue was the angry voice behind her that said, "Not after I get through with them."

"Hell, Jesse," the light-haired giant standing next to Ronnie was shaking his head. "Can't we eat first?"

"Yeah," the other auburn-haired man said, "don't worry, we'll still want to fight later."

Emily and Ronnie were shaking their heads and Danielle would later swear that the testosterone was so thick in the air, it was like peering through fog.

"OK," Ronnie began, "listen up, because there are a couple of new house rules since you guys were here last."

The men turned and waited for her to speak. "The house has been declared a fight-free zone."

"Well, hell, how can I sneak up on Dylan if—"

Ronnie put her hands on her hips, but before she could speak, Dylan cleared his throat. "I thought Jesse told you things had changed."

"Just because we can't beat on a married man doesn't mean we can't go a couple of rounds with Tyler and Jesse while we're here... does it?"

"If you want to eat, you aren't going to fight." Emily moved to stand beside Ronnie.

"Geez, Jesse," one of the auburn-haired men said, "you should have told us that before we agreed to come."

Jesse muscled his way through the group and looked like he was ready to spit nails. Sensing that the tension in the room was about to escalate, and needing to bring it back to a level that wouldn't scare her little girl, Danielle spoke up. "Well, now that we know there won't be any fighting, why don't you tell me who's who while Lacy and I show you what my Uncle Jimmy baked for you?"

Jesse stopped dead in his tracks. "Your uncle made us pie?"

She smiled up at him and uncovered the first basket. "This one's got an apple and a blackberry pie in it."

"Whoa! Two pies in each basket?" Tyler's words had the men gathering around the table to watch the unveiling.

"This basket has a cherry and the buttermilk pie," she continued, trying not to laugh at the sight of so many handsome faces captivated by the prospect of unveiling baked goods.

"Mine gots two chocolate pies," Lacy announced.

"So," Danielle said quietly, knowing she had everyone's attention. "I met Ben outside," she said turning to the other fair-haired man. "You must be his brother."

"Yes, ma'am," he said. "Name's Matt."

"Are you the Colorado cousins or the New York City cousins?"

"No offense, ma'am, but can't you tell by the way we talk?"

She felt her cheeks heating with her embarrassment. "Actually, I wasn't paying attention to your accents."

"That's because she's distracted by the better-looking Garahans from New York." The man who walked inside with Lacy held out his hand. "I'm Mike Garahan," he said. "This is my brother, Tommy."

Danielle nearly laughed at his words until she saw the look in Jesse's eyes... a look that promised retribution. "So you're the firemen from the East Coast?"

"My brother and I are lawmen up in Colorado," Ben said quietly, drawing her attention back to him.

"Are you on the local police force there or with the U.S. Marshals?"

"A cop's a cop, Dani darlin'," Jesse said quietly. His voice still had a dark edge to it that had her looking up into his eyes.

"Nothing's ever black and white," she told him. "People are complex and not always what they seem."

"We're marshals," Matt told her.

"Do you ride horses like Marshal Dillon?" Before anyone could answer, Lacy added, "My daddy rides bulls." Lacy climbed up onto one of the chairs and sat down. "He gots a new RV 'cause he took all the money."

Danielle wished the floor would open up and swallow her whole; that way, no one would be able to see the hurt and embarrassment she felt at Lacy's innocent declaration.

"Has he missed any child support payments?" Matt asked.

"I could track him down for you," Ben offered.

"Garahans stick together." Jesse nodded to the group and then looked down at Danielle. "We'd be happy to arrange a trip up to San Angelo and track him down for you."

"He might not be riding for a bit after we—" Mike began, only to be interrupted by his brother.

"Uh… visit with him," Tom finished.

"Are the coals ready yet?" Ronnie asked, changing the subject. "I've got marinated steaks just begging to be grilled."

"Lacy, honey," Jesse said, "you want to go for a walk?" Her smile was her answer. "Come on with your momma and me, then." Jesse took them by the hand and led them through the house to the front door. He opened it quietly and walked along the path that wound down toward another building.

"I didn't know you had so many outbuildings here." Danielle would do anything not to talk about her ex and the truth she'd been hoping to keep to herself for a little while longer. She didn't want to dredge up the hurt all over again.

"It takes a few to house everything we need to keep the ranch running." When Lacy started to lag behind, he lifted her up and carried her. "We've got a shop filled with tractor and truck parts, and anything we need to keep our machines going. It takes time to drive all the way into town; time isn't something we have a lot of around here."

While Jesse explained about the other buildings

they walked past, Danielle got caught up and let him distract her.

———∿∿∿———

Jesse felt relieved when Danielle finally lost that haunted look. He wanted to wrap her in his arms and promise that no one would ever hurt her again, but they hadn't had a chance to talk about things. It had been a few days and he was still trying to squeeze in the time to be alone with her. He had so much he wanted to say.

Walking in the late-day sun, with Lacy in his arms and Danielle holding his hand, he couldn't figure out how her ex could have been such a piece of shit. The stark realization that he'd do just about anything for Danielle and Lacy washed over him. The tour of the Circle G took on a whole new meaning as he admitted to himself that he wanted them to stick around for more than just a few weeks.

Danielle was more than a distraction from the tough life he led ranching. Yeah, he wanted her in his bed, but not just for a couple of nights—he wanted to be there when she grew round with his baby and be there to hold her hand while they watched Lacy walking up to receive her diploma. He wanted the whole package… and he wanted forever.

Now all he had to do was convince Danielle and Lacy they wanted him too. "Want to see the honey tree?"

Lacy patted the side of his face. "Trees don't make honey," she laughed. "Bees make honey."

He laughed and hugged her tighter. "Yes, ma'am, but there's a hive in an old tree just over that rise. Want me to show it to you?"

"Yeah!"

A few minutes later, he stopped and pointed to a huge old oak that had been struck by lightning.

"Is it dead?" Lacy wanted to know.

"The tree is, but the hive isn't." He pointed to a couple of bees that were flying around the top of the tree. "See up there?" When she nodded, he told her to watch where the bees go. "Right there is where the hive is, tucked inside the tree."

"Is the honey in there too?"

"Yes, ma'am. Want to get a closer look?"

"No," Danielle said. "We can see fine from here. Besides," she said, looking at her watch, "we should get back to help Ronnie and Emily with dinner."

"But we brought pie."

Danielle paused to ask, "And what did I tell you about being guests?"

"We should always help," Lacy answered.

"Because?" Danielle prompted.

"It's like saying thank you." Lacy grinned at her mother and Jesse melted watching the way Danielle smiled down at her daughter. This wasn't the first time he wondered if he was attracted to Danielle because she was such a wonderful mother and he missed having one or because she was a curvaceous, spontaneous, and everything he wanted in a woman.

By the time they got back to the house, the steaks were being pulled off the grill. Tyler smiled at them. "Did you show Lacy the honey tree?"

"I wanted to get closer," she said, for once eye level with Jesse's brother. "But mommy said no."

Tyler chuckled. "Mom's are like that. Are you hungry?"

Lacy nodded. "Can I have pie?"

Jesse looked around but didn't see anyone else. "Where is everybody?"

Tyler was watching him closely when he answered, "Dylan's showing them the bunkhouse."

Danielle's face flushed a delicate pink. Silently vowing to rip Tyler a new one later, Jesse tugged on her hand to get her to follow him and Lacy into the kitchen.

The moment Lacy saw Ronnie and Emily she asked, "Can we help?"

Ronnie smiled. "Wash up and you can help set the table."

With Danielle at his side and her daughter still in his arms, he headed toward the kitchen sink, but then detoured to the bathroom down the hall when he saw that Emily was washing tomatoes and lettuce.

Hoping not to sound like a fool, he said, "I know that Lacy likes it here, but what do you think of the ranch now that you've seen more?"

Danielle grinned. "I can't believe how big it is. Do you ever get used to the fact that it's yours?"

He shook his head and set Lacy down in front of the sink and turned on the taps, holding his hand under the stream of water until it was the right temperature. He nodded and let Lacy get her hands wet. When she started to wash up, he said, "We wake up every day and work the land just as our ancestors did, grateful for every waking moment that we get to spend under the bright, blue Texas sky, knowing as far as we can see is ours… land that we will plant with grasses so that our herd will graze."

"You really love it." She paused to help Lacy reach

the hand towel to dry her hands. "I mean, it's not just the responsibility, is it?"

He felt a clutch in the vicinity of his heart and realized that everything he wanted was standing right in front of him. If he could walk on Garahan land with Danielle and Lacy at his side, his life would be complete. Would he be able to get up the nerve to tell them how he really felt?

One day soon… real soon… he hoped he could convince Danielle and Lacy that they wanted to spend the rest of their lives with him at the Circle G ranch.

"Hey," they heard Ronnie call out. "Where are my helpers?"

"We'd better hurry up, or they might not save any steak for us."

Lacy laughed. "They have to wait for us, 'cause we din't set the table yet."

With Lacy in the lead, he followed behind the two women who'd restarted his heart only to capture it and hold it captive.

Walking back into the kitchen was like walking into bedlam, either that or a nonstop frat party. His cousins were drinking beer and charming his brothers' women. "Damn," Jesse grumbled. "Quit poaching."

Dylan glanced at Tyler, who nodded to Jesse. "We're going outside in five minutes."

"You never did like to share." Mike was grinning at Dylan but nodded at Tyler, letting Tyler know that he would be willing to go a few rounds.

Danielle tried to ignore the undercurrents, worried that the men would go outside to fight before they ate. Burying her worry, she set out the plates and Lacy put the napkins and silverware by each one.

"I'm finished," Lacy said. "What else can I do?"

"Not a thing, little darlin'," Jesse told her, lifting her onto a chair. "Let's eat."

Chapter 19

"HAVE YOU LIVED IN PLEASURE LONG?"

Danielle looked at Ben and said, "Lacy and I are staying with my uncle until I can find a place to live."

"Our house is gone."

Before her daughter could bare any more of their misfortunes in front of the Garahans and their cousins, Danielle took Lacy's hand in hers and said, "Why don't you tell them about the pies?"

It was just the distraction Lacy needed; while she went into detail about what went into the pies, Danielle blew out the breath she'd been holding, hoping that the ruse would work. Damn her ex for putting them in this position, and damn her for her foolish pride.

She turned to ask Jesse a question and noticed the mix of emotions in his warm brown eyes… compassion laced with understanding. "I have to leave soon."

She leaned closer to ask, "Where are you going?"

His eyes turned colder a moment before he shook his head, apparently all the answer she was going to get to that question. Why wouldn't he tell her?

Was it a woman?

Good Lord, was it something illegal?

She was contemplating whether or not she should try to trick him into telling her when he got up and cleared his place. "Who's ready for pie?"

Everyone joined in the discussion of who was going

to try which pie, and had pretty much decided what they wanted until Lacy announced, "I'm gonna have some of each one."

"That's a lot of pie for a little person like you," Matt said and grinned.

Without missing a beat, Lacy said, "I'm gonna be four and my Unca Jimmy lets me have slivers of each kind."

"Does your uncle have a spare room?" Tommy asked. "I could get used to living in a house where there's always dessert."

"My uncle runs Sullivan's Diner in town; his specialty is pie."

Lacy was nodding her head like a little bobblehead doll. "But the bestest is chocolate!"

When the table had been cleared, Danielle helped Jesse set out the pies and a stack of plates while Emily and Ronnie poured hot coffee and cold drinks.

"Whose idea was it to bring all these pies?" Jesse asked. "Not that I'm not grateful you did."

Danielle rested her hand on his forearm and said, "My uncle wanted you and your brothers to know what fine men you turned out to be. These pies are his way of letting you know that he didn't hold the pie-napping incident against any of you."

"Well, I'll be," Tyler rasped as slices of pie were served and devoured.

"Son of a—" Dylan began before he remembered that a little lady was present.

Then everyone started to chuckle. When Jesse and his brothers joined in, the chuckles deepened to full belly laughter.

"We'll have to stop by and thank him soon," Tyler said.

"I've got to get going," Jesse announced, pushing back from the table.

"Where are you off to?" Ben asked.

Jesse bent down to press a kiss on the top of Lacy's head and then one on Danielle's cheek. "See you later."

With that he was gone.

"So what's he up to?" Matt asked, watching the screen door slam.

"He's got a night job doing something," Dylan said, digging into a second sliver of pie.

"We haven't tried to beat the truth out of him yet." Tyler nodded toward Danielle and said, "Certain people would take exception to us beating on our little brother."

"But that's our job." Tommy's matter-of-fact statement had Danielle wondering if all brothers accepted that as the way it is, or if it was just this family.

She was about to ask when Ben shook his head. "Matt perfected the fine art of beating me without leaving too many bruises years ago."

The Justiss brothers started to argue, but Danielle didn't worry because there wasn't an edge to their threats; it seemed to be good-natured.

"It's either illegal or there's a woman involved," Matt said quietly.

The silence that followed had Danielle wondering if they all knew something that she didn't. Was there another woman, or was she the other woman? Before she made herself crazy, she glanced over at Lacy who'd stopped eating and was watching the adults and said, "We should probably be going too."

Ronnie shook her head. "There's no need to leave just because Jesse did."

"Besides," Emily said, "Lacy's not finished with her first piece of pie."

"I feel like a pelican," Lacy said, sitting back in her chair. "I'm full."

Mike and Tommy were laughing; they'd obviously heard the childhood rhyme about a pelican's eyes being bigger than his belly, but their Colorado cousins seemed baffled.

While Danielle explained it to them, Lacy asked, "When's cowboy Jesse coming back?"

There was a brief moment of silence before Matt snickered and Ben elbowed him.

"Hey, Danielle." Jesse stood in the doorway. "Can you move your car?"

"Be right there." And before she could tell Lacy to wait, her daughter was out of her chair and running to the door. With a huge sigh, she followed her daughter.

Jesse was sitting on the steps listening to something Lacy was telling him, but when Danielle closed the door behind her, he smiled up at her. "Lacy's reminding me that I forgot to let her hug me good-bye."

Danielle's belly flipped over. Did Lacy remember that her father had left without saying good-bye? Sadness engulfed her as she watched the way Lacy kept chattering while Jesse paid attention to her, really listening. *Women develop their memory skills at an early age... they never forget.*

"If you'll watch Lacy, I'll move my car."

When Lacy asked, "Can we swing?" Jesse called out, "Catch!"

She glanced up in time to snag his keys. Jesse got to his feet and walked over to the swing with Lacy. While they sat and chatted, she got into her car to move it. After she moved his truck, she decided she and Lacy should go, so she asked Jesse to wait one more minute. Saying a quick good-bye to everyone, she hurried over to where they still sat on the swing.

"Jesse said that we can come back anytime," Lacy told her.

"Really?" Danielle asked, staring up into Jesse's eyes. Watching closely for a reaction, she said, "Maybe we can come back tomorrow night."

He frowned. "Actually, I'm working tomorrow night too."

Wondering what the big secret was, and thinking maybe his cousin was right and he was either doing something illegal... or worse... that there was a woman involved—she screwed up her courage and asked, "Where exactly is it that you're working?"

His jaw clenched at the same time his hands curled into fists. Not a good sign. When he didn't answer her, she knew where she stood... on the outside of his life. He wasn't willing to confide in her, but he'd taken her to bed. Too bad he'd been too busy at his job... whatever that might be... and moving the herd to sweet-talk her back into bed.

Maybe there wasn't going to be another time. The thought made her stomach churn and her head pound. "Time to go, Lacy." Grabbing her daughter by the hand, she whisked her into her arms and had her buckled into the seat belt before Jesse had moved off the porch.

Gunning it, she peeled out and had the immense satisfaction of seeing Jesse throwing his arms in front of his face to protect it from all of the gravel her tires spit out as she floored it and headed down the drive.

Lacy didn't say one word until the second time Danielle got out to close the gate to the ranch.

"Why are you mad at cowboy Jesse?"

"It's a long story, sweet pea," she said. "But it comes down to Jesse not trusting me."

"Oh." Lacy was quiet the rest of the ride home. When they pulled up outside, her uncle was waiting on the porch.

"Had a phone call a little while ago," he said, getting to his feet.

"Who from?"

"Tyler." Her uncle waited until they'd walked over to the porch. "He wanted me to let him know when you got home."

"Why?" *Why couldn't it have been Jesse who was worried about them?*

"He said Jesse had called him from work, worried about you and Lacy, and wanted Tyler to find out."

"Did Jesse leave a number where he could be reached?" Not that she expected that he would after the way he refused to divulge any information about where he worked.

"He told Tyler he'd call him back on his next break."

"Is there anything you want me to tell Tyler?"

She laughed. "Tell him thanks. Lacy and I had a nice time. Oh, please tell him that we'll be by to pick up the baskets tomorrow."

Her uncle frowned down at her, but she ignored him and said, "Lacy go on in and get ready for your bath."

"Do I have ta? I'm not dirty."

"Yes," she said. "You do."

Clomping through the house and up the stairs, Lacy let her displeasure at having to have a bath be known.

"She's an awful lot like you were at that age," her uncle reminded her. "What happened at the Circle G?"

"I learned that I'm not as important in Jesse's life as I thought."

"And you know that because?"

She sighed. "I don't want to talk about it."

"Then how will you ever reason through whatever problem's weighing on your mind?"

"Don't worry about it." She kissed him on the cheek and told him, "I've got to get Lacy in the tub."

A little while later, Lacy was tucked in and sleeping peacefully while Danielle was still all churned up and couldn't settle down. She'd tried reading a book, but when she realized she hadn't turned the page in a half hour, she closed her book and headed downstairs to the back porch.

"I didn't know you were still up."

His gaze met hers and didn't waver. "You ready to talk?"

She was the first to give in. "You win," she groaned.

"What?" he asked. "The stare fight or the contest of wills, which means you're gonna spill your guts?"

Danielle rolled her eyes. "All of the above." Slumping into the chair next to him, she put her feet up on the railing and crossed her ankles, then crossed her arms in front of her.

"Not exactly proper body language for someone who's ready to talk. Your body says you've already closed your mind." When she still didn't say anything, he grumbled, "Just spit it out, June bug; you'll feel better for it."

Maybe he was right. She didn't have anyone else to talk to at the moment, and he'd always been a good listener. "Jesse works nights."

After a few minutes of silence, he said, "And—"

"He won't tell me where."

He chuckled, then cleared his throat. "And this is a cause for concern because?"

"What if he's not telling me because it's illegal?"

"That might be a cause for concern, but probably not the reason he won't tell you."

"What if it's another woman?"

"A man'd have to be superman to work that ranch all day, fit in visits with you and Lacy, and another woman besides. Has he slipped up and called you any other woman's name?"

"Well, no, but—"

Her uncle held up one hand. "Has he treated you any differently than he has from the first?"

"No, but—"

"Do his brothers know where he's working?"

"Well, no, but—"

"June bug," he said softly. "Give the man a chance. He's had it the roughest, being the youngest. He was two when his dad died and ten when his momma died. His granddad raised those boys, which is why they ran wild for a time, but they all settled down and turned themselves into upstanding members of this town. He deserves your patience… and your trust."

"I trusted blindly before," she rasped. "Look what it got me!"

He nodded. "Divorced, but with the cutest little cowgirl this side of the Mississippi."

Deflated, she sat there and stared down at her hands. "Maybe there's something wrong with me…"

"Now, don't go barking up the wrong tree. That man's crazy about you and my grandniece. Give him time to come around. It's probably not my place to tell you, but since you're convinced otherwise, let me tell you that that boy had his heart broke by the same woman… twice!"

That got her attention. "Recently?"

"Couple months ago. It's a long story, but the point is that the woman he thought loved him ran away and married the same loser… twice. You think on that while you're sitting out here feeling sorry for yourself."

The screen door banged once before it settled in the door frame. Great, she'd made both Jesse and her uncle angry with her, all in the same day. Shaking her head, she closed her eyes and let her mind drift. Crickets started singing; maybe it was because she and her uncle had finally stopped talking. A few minutes later, the call of a whippoorwill brought tears to her eyes, reminding her of her mother's favorite Hank Williams song. But she wasn't really lonesome; she was heartsick. Not sure which was worse, but not sure there was anything she could do but listen to her uncle's advice and give Jesse a chance to come around.

She started to add up all of the things she liked about him; when she got to honest, she paused… because he hadn't lied about where he worked… he'd refused to tell her… that was a whole other ball of wax.

While she sat, the bird called again, this time an answering three-note call had her smiling. She'd give Jesse a chance. After all, the only thing he'd done wrong was not tell her where he worked.

She was being ridiculous... and selfish... *and bitchy.* She sighed and nestled back into the chair until she was more comfortable. Her breathing deepened, and while the crickets and whippoorwills serenaded her, she fell asleep.

The phone woke her. She couldn't believe she'd fallen asleep in the chair on the porch. Not sure what time it was, she dashed inside and grabbed the phone, surprised that it was Ronnie.

A glance at the clock told her it was almost midnight. "What's happened? What's wrong?" And then it hit her. "Is Jesse all right?"

Ronnie's voice broke as she told her, "Jesse's hurt... he was in an accident."

"Oh God, what happened?"

"We don't know. His friend Slim called and said Jesse'd been rushed to the hospital in Mesquite. He's asking for you."

Her stomach wanted to rebel, but the need to find out everything Ronnie knew kept her focused and the contents of her stomach where it belonged. "What can I do?" The need to see for herself that he was in one piece threatened to push her over the edge.

"Tyler and Em just left for the hospital. Dylan and I can swing by and pick you up."

"What about the Circle G?"

"Their cousins will hold down the fort and wait for news."

"I'll be ready when you get here." She hung up the phone and dashed upstairs and knocked on her uncle's door.

"Who was on the phone?"

"Jesse was in an accident. He's asking for me."

Her uncle got out of bed and raked a hand through his hair. "Little June bug'll be fine with me. You stay as long as you like." He gave her a long look and shook his head. "You've got a little time before they get here. Why don't you put on some coffee?"

She hugged him tight and hurtled down the stairs and started a pot of coffee, pacing while she waited for it to brew. Unsure if anyone had had time for coffee, she searched through the cabinets until she found a thermos. It wasn't big enough to bring coffee for everyone, so she kept poking through her uncle's cabinets until she found what she was looking for—a carafe with a screw top.

She couldn't find paper cups, so she wrapped a couple of mugs in paper towels and put them in a brown paper bag. Then she poured coffee into the thermos and the carafe and added milk and sugar.

She looked at the clock and started to fidget. They wouldn't be here for a little longer. What else would they need while they waited, to keep their minds occupied?

She heard her uncle's footfalls on the steps. He walked into the kitchen and said, "Why don't we make some sandwiches? Hospital food is lousy… waiting's lousy… this'll give you something to do with your hands."

Danielle looked down and nodded. She'd been wringing hers. Working together, they had a half a dozen sandwiches wrapped up and ready to go when they heard a vehicle pull up outside. "Keep the faith, June bug." He hugged her and reminded her, "He's worth praying for."

Dylan's fingers tapped the steering wheel while waiting for Danielle to hand off the coffee to Ronnie and close her door. He turned Ronnie's truck around and put the pedal to the floor and didn't let up until they screeched to a halt outside the emergency room. Ronnie pushed him out and told him to get on inside, she'd park the truck.

The look in his eyes had tears filling Danielle's eyes again. Blinking furiously, she vowed she would not shed one tear; she had to be strong. No one knew what kind of shape Jesse was in and she wouldn't add to their worry while they waited to find out. "Let's leave the food and one container of coffee out here."

Emily looked up as she and Ronnie rushed into the waiting room. "They're talking to the doctor." Reaching for Danielle's hand she said, "They asked me to wait out here."

Danielle handed a cup to Emily and one to Ronnie. "We've got sandwiches in the truck, but my uncle thought you'd need decent coffee while we wait."

The heat from the cup warmed her ice-cold hands. Wishing they knew more, she struggled with the need to get up and start pacing. Sipping slowly, she was the first to see Dylan walking toward them. His head was high and his eyes clear. *OK… this would either be really good news or really bad.*

"He's stable."

Ronnie nodded. "Good. Now what's the rest of it?"

Dylan's mouth quirked up on one side. "Bumps and bruises so far."

She set her empty cup down and got to her feet.

"He's in X-ray right now and might have a broken wrist and ankle," Dylan explained. "The doctor said that we can go in for a few minutes at a time." He looked at Danielle. "He's asked for you a couple of times."

Danielle drew in a deep breath and asked, "Can I see him now?"

He nodded and held out his hand to her. "He looks bad, but it's the swelling and bruising. Thank God for safety glass. The cuts on his face are superficial… nothing really deep."

"Thanks for the warning, but I won't fall apart when I see him."

"You sure?" Dylan waited for her to answer. "He's got enough to worry about right now… he doesn't need to worry that we aren't telling him something important."

Worry gnawed at her gut. "Are you hiding something from him?"

Dylan's gaze met hers. "No."

Chapter 20

JESSE CAME TO SLOWLY AS PAIN RICOCHETED THROUGH his body. His head ached, and he sure as hell wished he couldn't feel his ankle or his wrist. Both might be broken—like Slim's car. He remembered getting hit from behind and going into the first roll—then his car had flipped over like a gator in a death roll.

"Hell," he rasped, struggling to open his eyes. A redheaded nurse was poking a needle in his arm. He hated needles, so he closed his eyes and told her, "That felt good."

Her chuckle told him what he needed to know. He wasn't on deathwatch; he might feel like he should be, but the nurse seemed relaxed, not like the time with his mother—

Pushing those thoughts aside, he waited until the nurse was finished drawing blood before he opened his eyes.

"I thought you were asleep." She checked his vitals and made notes on his chart.

"Nope. Hate needles."

"Well, you should be needle-free for the next little while. Your brothers have both been here to see you."

He thought he'd been dreaming, hearing Tyler and Dylan firing questions at the doctor until they'd gotten the answers they wanted. "Garahans stick together."

"The doctor wants you to rest," she was telling him, but his eyes were already closing of their own accord.

He opened his eyes and blinked. But Danielle didn't disappear. She looked good enough to eat. He must have said so because she smiled and sniffed and that's when he noticed her eyes were glassy. "Am I that bad off?"

"No," she reassured him. "How do you feel?"

"Like I survived a car wreck."

She needed to talk so that she wouldn't stare too long at the battered man lying in the hospital bed. "Did you see the other car? Did the sheriff haul his ass off to jail?"

He chuckled and swore. "Don't make me laugh," he told her. "It hurts."

She bit her lip. "Sorry."

"What makes you think the other guy was at fault?" He liked that she had that much confidence in his driving. What would she say when she heard the whole story?

"Oh." She shuffled her feet and placed her hand on the bed rail. "It doesn't matter. What matters is that you'll be OK and the other guy will too, won't he?"

"I got hit from behind."

"We can sue his ass. I have a cousin who's a lawyer."

He groaned and swore. "Damn it, I told you, don't make me laugh."

"I'm sorry, it's just that I want to find the bastard and wring his neck, then I'll let my cousin at him."

"Bloodthirsty… I like that."

She grabbed a hold of his wrist and pain shot right through to the bone. Her grip tightened as she told him, "Just tell me his name and I'll take care of it."

He nodded and she eased her hold on him. He wanted to tell her to let go of his mangled wrist, but got distracted by the sadness in her eyes. He reached for her hand and asked, "Why are you here?"

"You don't know?"

"After the way I treated you earlier… You asked a simple question and I let my pride keep me from answering."

"I should go."

"Not happening."

Deciding to humor the patient, she stopped struggling and told him to close his eyes. She'd leave when he was asleep.

"So you can slip out as soon as I'm asleep?" He tugged and she fell across his chest, right where he wanted her. "No way."

Their lips were close, but her nose was closer. He kissed the tip of it and confessed, "I almost messed up big time."

Her breathing was ragged and she was trying to shift so she could wiggle out of his grasp. Wise to her, he squeezed her hand and said, "I've been racing cars out at Devil's Bowl."

Her eyes widened. "Are you crazy?"

He tried to smile, but the left side of his face hurt. "I've always wanted to race cars. When my buddy Slim asked me to fill in for him, I jumped at the chance for two reasons: a chance at a teenage dream, and an opportunity to contribute toward the Circle G's mountain of bills."

"So that's the job you didn't want to tell me about?"

"Ranching is my life and in my blood, but I've dreamed of racing since I was a kid and wanted to give it a shot."

"I thought you were doing something illegal."

"Like what?"

"I don't know… running shine—"

"You've been watching reruns of those Duke Boys," he told her, hoping to take her mind off the fact that he hadn't been willing to tell her.

"Sometimes dreams can be shared."

"I managed to make enough money that we're further out of the red and leaning toward the black. I'd do anything to keep our ranch from going under. We all would."

"So, your pride kept you from telling anyone?"

He searched her eyes for a clue as to what she was really thinking. "Will you hold that against me?"

She shook her head. "Lacy and I have been struggling to get by since my ex cleaned out our savings account to buy that damned motor home."

His grip on her hand was painful. "When I'm healed… I will kill him."

"Maybe I'll let you," she said, patting his hand so he'd loosen his hold on her.

"Danielle, I've been ten times a fool for not telling you straight out when you asked. I never thought you'd really be worrying over where I was going or what I was doing."

"I was hoping there wasn't another woman," she whispered.

"I'm good, but not that good." He lifted her hand to his lips. "I told you, you pack a lethal punch."

"I was beginning to wonder if you'd had enough of me…"

"Hell, when I screw up," he told her, "I screw up big."

"What else could I think?"

"That I've been spending four nights out of the week

practicing and one night racing. I spend my damn days working myself right into the ground out at the Circle G to keep the herd fed, healthy, and happy, moving them to a new grazing pasture. When would I have time to even think about another woman?"

Before she could say anything else, he used his good hand to tilt her chin up, so her eyes were looking right into his. "I've never been this crazy over a woman before. You damn near killed me that night at the bunkhouse… I've been walking around all churned up inside, feeling like I've just gone three rounds with both brothers!"

"Jesse, I—"

He shook his head and then moaned. "Damn that hurts."

"Are you sure you don't have a concussion?"

"Garahans have really hard heads."

"Tell me about it," she grumbled. "Let me call the nurse."

"Not until I tell you what I realized earlier. I've gotten used to seeing Lacy and you out at the Circle G… you fit."

"We fit?"

"Yeah," he said. "Will you and Lacy move in with me?"

———

Danielle couldn't believe what she was hearing. He's crazy over her, he loved making love with her, and she and Lacy fit the mold… so move in?

"Why do you really want us to move in?"

He paused as if struggling to come up with an answer. In that split second, her healing heart broke. She'd wanted him to be the right one so badly that she'd ignored all of the telling signs. God, when would she learn that cowboys and she just weren't a good mix?

Wondering how she would tell Lacy that they wouldn't be able to visit Jesse anymore, she hadn't noticed that he'd drawn her closer until his lips were pressed against hers.

"Tell me I haven't messed up," he rasped. "My head hurts and I've got so many aches, I don't know where to begin." When she tried to resist, he kissed her again, softly, coaxing her to listen. "Dani darlin', I love you so much I don't want to spend another hour without you… and hell if I'm gonna give up that pint-sized, cotton-candy cowgirl."

"You really love me?"

"Hell, woman, have pity on a man in pain. I. Love. You!"

When she smiled at him, half of his pain was forgotten.

"Will you marry me first and then move out to the Circle G?"

Her smile had the angels singing in his head again… well, maybe that was a ringing in his head from smacking it against the side of the car as it rolled…

"Lacy and I are a team… I have to check with her before I say yes."

Relief seeped into his aching bones. "But you want to?"

"Hell yeah!" She kissed him until he started to groan. "Oh God… did I hurt you?"

He moved her hand across his thigh and onto his rock-hard erection. "Woman, you're killing me."

"Good," she said with a grin. "Now we're even."

"Damn it, Danielle," Tyler growled from the doorway.

"Jesse might have fractured ribs," Dylan grumbled. "You'll break them if you don't get off him."

"Quit yelling at my bride-to-be," Jesse rasped.

Tyler and Dylan stopped in their tracks and looked from their brother to Danielle and back. "Your what?"

"I just asked her to marry me."

Tyler turned and motioned behind him. "You've got to hear this!"

Emily and Ronnie stepped into the room and Ronnie asked, "What's going on?"

"Our boneheaded little brother is getting married," Tyler told them.

"He's not so boneheaded," Emily said, walking over to place a kiss on Jesse's cheek.

"Sounds pretty smart to me," Ronnie agreed, taking her turn kissing Jesse.

"What the hell does that mean?" Tyler asked Ronnie.

"Don't swear at my wife," Dylan warned.

Before they could start shoving one another, Danielle spoke up to redirect the conversation. "Thanks, but I didn't say yes yet," she warned him.

"What are you waiting for?" Tyler demanded.

"What's wrong with our brother?"

Emily and Ronnie were trying not to laugh. Danielle knew then there was just something about the Garahan brothers that was by turns annoying as hell and endearing. One minute they were yelling at each other, and the next defending each other.

Jesse explained before she could. "She's got to check with Lacy."

"Is that all?" Tyler asked.

"Damn," Dylan rumbled. "You're a shoo-in with little Lacy."

Jesse grinned at his brother and pulled Danielle back in for a kiss. "She's partial to cowboys... just like her momma."

"Since you seem to be doing so well," Ronnie said,

"why don't I leave Danielle here with you? We'll come back in the morning."

Jesse let go of Danielle and tried to sit up, but ended up groaning and holding the side of his head. "I'm not staying here tonight," he ground out. "Hate hospitals." His gaze met Tyler's and then Dylan's. "You know why I can't stay."

His brothers nodded and Tyler closed the gap between them. He grabbed a hold of Jesse's hand, looked down at his brother, and finally said, "I'll talk to the doctor."

Danielle wanted to do something, anything, to ease Jesse's frustration and worry even if she didn't understand the reasoning behind his not staying overnight at the hospital. "There's more coffee in the car... and some sandwiches."

Dylan grinned. "I could eat." He tugged Ronnie behind him. "Be right back."

Emily looked over her shoulder and said, "I'll go make sure your brother doesn't try to bulldoze the doctor."

Waiting until everyone had gone, Danielle asked, "Why can't you let them take care of you tonight?"

He closed his eyes and cleared his throat. "Our mom died here... I was just a kid, but I'll never forget what it was like"—Danielle grabbed a hold of his hand and held tight—"waiting through the night... hoping that she'd cheat death."

Leaning over the bed rail, she looked into his eyes and saw the pain he was in. His pupils looked OK, but she still worried that the doctor might have missed something important, like a concussion. He brushed the back of his hand along her cheek. "You could come back to the Circle G with me and keep an eye on me. Of course, you'd have to come to bed with me."

The floor shifted beneath her feet as her world narrowed down to this one man, in this defining moment. "I guess you don't hurt all that badly if you're thinking what I think you're thinking."

His lips lifted into the crooked smile she loved. "Darlin', I hurt all over, I'm tired, and I want to go home... but I'm not going without you."

"What about Lacy?"

"Your uncle could drop her off when she wakes up."

"The gossips would have a field day if we were staying out at your ranch."

"Are you worried about your reputation?"

She shook her head, and he smoothed the hair back off her forehead and said, "I've got an idea... but I need to talk to my brothers alone first."

Danielle wanted to ask what he had in mind but didn't want to press him. He'd been through so much.

"All right. Why don't you close your eyes while we wait?"

"Just for a few minutes," he said as he closed his eyes.

With a silent prayer of thanks that he'd survived the accident, she held his hand. They didn't have long to wait. His brothers walked back in with their women in tow. "I talked to the doctor," Tyler said.

"What did he say?" Jesse reached for Danielle's hand and waited for the news.

"Badly bruised and sprained, but nothing's broken—including your hard head."

"And?" Jesse prompted.

"The doctor will stop by to release you after he makes his rounds."

He squeezed Danielle's hand and brought it to his

lips. "I need to speak to Tyler and Dylan alone for a minute. Will you excuse us, ladies?"

They looked at one another but agreed. Danielle led them out into the hallway where Ronnie asked, "What's up?"

"I don't know," Danielle admitted. "He said he had an idea but that he had to talk to his brothers first." Worry ate at her until she asked, "So the doctor really thinks he'll be OK?"

Emily put her arm around Danielle's waist. "Our men might be stubborn, but they wouldn't do anything to put one another in danger."

Ronnie agreed. "They might beat on each other, but that's different."

Relief started to ease the noxious roiling in Danielle's stomach. "I guess we'll have to wait and see what Jesse's got in mind, then."

"You can come back in." Dylan was grinning at her, but when she started to ask what was going on, he shook his head at her. "Jesse's got something he wants to say to you."

Tyler's smile mirrored his brother's. "We'll be right back."

Hesitating on the threshold, not sure what was going on or what to expect, she finally called out, "Hey."

He turned to look at her and held out his hand. "Hey, yourself."

She dragged a chair over to the side of the bed, reached for his hand, and sat down.

"Do you trust me?"

She tilted her head to one side and studied him. His face was covered with bruises and tiny cuts from the safety glass; his left wrist and left ankle were both immobilized. He had to be in intense pain and should be resting, yet he wanted to know if she trusted him?

"Not exactly the response I was hoping for," he grumbled. "I already told you, I'd let my pride get in the way of telling you—"

"Yes," she said softly, knowing that it was the truth. "I trust you with my heart and with my daughter."

"Then come on back to the Circle G with me... I need you, Dani darlin'."

She got up, leaned over the bed, and kissed his cheek. "Let me call my uncle."

Chapter 21

IT WAS A TIGHT SQUEEZE, BUT EVERYONE PILED INTO the two pickup trucks and headed back to the ranch. "Easy," Tyler said as he helped his little brother out of the cab.

The back door opened and their cousins walked out. "We're just about ready to feed the stock and muck out the stables."

The look that passed between the Garahan men and their cousins added to the feeling of rightness that filled her every time she was at the Circle G. While they discussed the day's list of chores and the order in which things should be done, Danielle felt like she belonged, was accepted, as if they'd been waiting for her and Lacy to come along and slip into the fabric of their lives. She was doing the right thing.

She had followed her heart once before, but she'd been too dazzled to look beyond what she thought was love to accept that what she felt for her ex didn't go below the surface. How could it, when he never gave her the chance to see beyond the bright and shiny veneer he showed the rest of the world when he was competing for that silver buckle?

"We'll go see about breakfast." Ronnie said. When Emily and Danielle caught up, Ronnie added, "We'll divide and conquer."

Emily grinned at Danielle. "I'll start the coffee and

set the table if you can make up the couch with sheets from the basket of clean clothes in the laundry room."

Working as a team, they had food for everyone and a bed for Jesse by the time the brothers walked inside with Jesse braced between them. "You ladies ready for me?" Jesse called out.

"I am." She walked over to where he stood and got up on her toes to kiss his cheek. "Now, let's get you to bed."

"Darlin', if I wasn't in such sad shape, I'd make it worth your while."

She laughed and it felt good. "Later, darlin'. Come on."

"I can take it from here, guys," he told his brothers.

Bracing herself on his injured side, she took as much of his weight as she could and helped him through the kitchen to the living room. "Can you sit by yourself?"

"Yes, ma'am."

Once he was on the couch, she eased him back and couldn't keep from kissing him again. "I've never been so worried in my life."

"You sure about that?"

"I've been through a lot with Lacy, but nothing like this."

"Life's not always easy, Dani, especially a rancher's life."

She knelt on the floor beside the sofa. "I don't need it to be easy."

He was fighting to keep his eyes open. "What do you need?"

She brushed the tips of her fingers across first one of his eyebrows and then the other and whispered, "You." She watched his smile bloom and his eyes slowly close. The sound of his even breathing was music to her ears. With a glance at her watch, she mentally started the timer. The doctor said it wasn't a concussion, but she wasn't taking any chances with Jesse's headache.

———————

The kitchen was a mess by the time the men filed out to get on with the rest of their day. There were fences to mend, the herd to check, and the never-ending list of chores that were all part and parcel of ranch life.

"Why don't you and Emily go lie down for a bit? I'll load the dishwasher."

"You were up all night, same as we were," Emily protested.

"I'm going to go sit with Jesse when I finish up here."

"If you're sure," Ronnie said slowly.

She nodded and bustled around the kitchen while the other women headed upstairs. She'd been checking on Jesse every ten minutes or so, and had been relieved that he'd seemed to be resting comfortably.

With one last look around the room, satisfied that she hadn't missed any dirty pots, pans, or dishes, she checked the coffeepot. It was ready for someone to come along and press the brew button. She wished she'd thought to bring a spare shirt; she looked like she'd been rolling around in her T-shirt.

Shrugging that thought aside, she went to check on Jesse. Rousing him wasn't as easy as it had been the last time she'd tried. He was sleeping so deeply, fear edged its way into her heart until she had to take a deep breath to settle her nerves and the need to call for help. He was just tired, she kept telling herself.

Inspiration struck and she got down on her knees and moved close to press her lips to his. Jesse's soft moan was music to her ears, but he hadn't opened his eyes yet. "If a simple kiss could rouse you this much, I wonder what would happen if I added a little oomph to it?"

Gently cupping his battered face in her hands, she tested the fullness of his bottom lip with her tongue, swirling it around the rim of his mouth before taking his in a devastatingly erotic kiss.

The arms banding around her were a testament to her powers of persuasion. "You wouldn't wake up," she whispered against his lips.

"I'm up now," he groaned. "Want to see how much of me is up?" he teased.

"And take a chance that your brothers or your cousins will end up walking in on us? I think I'll wait a bit until we can be alone."

"I'm glad you woke me up. I made some plans for this afternoon."

His dark and dangerous gaze had her juices flowing and her hot spot doing the hoochie coochie. "You are supposed to be resting... doctor's orders."

He didn't like the reminder. "I already rested this morning. Besides Tyler and Dylan will be here in case I need a hand."

"What about the herd?"

He smiled. "Now you're thinking like a rancher's wife."

She liked the way that sounded, but couldn't help but wonder if he would still think so a few months down the road. "I might not be what you need, as far as a wife goes, but I'm real glad to be what you want, because you are definitely the man I need in my life."

He stared at her for a moment and then struggled to sit up. "What type of a wife do you think I need?"

She didn't hesitate to tell him. "One without baggage, one who can focus all of her time, talents, and love on you."

"I'd be crazy not to make enough room in my life for you and Lacy," he rasped. "I think your heart's big enough to make room to love Lacy and me." The look in his eyes told her how much he wanted this to work.

"It's not that I doubt you, it's just that I've—"

"Been hurt by a no-good, lying, son of a bitch who didn't know a good thing when he had it. His loss is definitely my gain, and I'm not going to let anything stand in the way of making the most of the fact that you and Lacy love me back."

Danielle knew there were many types of love: love for a parent or grandparent, love for a child, love for the father of your child... but she'd been blindsided, not realizing that there was such a thing as a second chance at love.

Her momma didn't raise no fool; she was grabbing this chance and holding on to it for all she was worth. Hell or high water, as soon as Jesse was able, they'd set the date and get married.

"So when were you thinking we should get married?" Her mind was already creating the to-do list; so much went into the perfect wedding.

"I'm thinking the sooner the better." He toyed with a lock of hair that had slipped free from the elastic band she'd wrapped around it on her midnight dash to the emergency room. "Are you flexible?"

She laughed. "I'm a mother... it's part of the job description."

His smile was slow and easy, reminding her of the second time he made love to her. "Your lips are too far away," he whispered. "Come 'ere."

Need for this man overwhelmed her, but she needed to be careful of his injuries; needing him whole was more important than satisfying her raging libido. Promising herself to go slow and easy, she leaned closer until her lips met his.

His kiss was sweet, his touch tender, lulling her into a state of contented bliss. She gently eased back and sighed. "It's going to be hard to wait until you heal," she confessed. "When all I want to do is climb up on that couch and—" She shook her head. "Can't go there right now, or I'll tie us both up in knots."

Jesse stroked the lock of hair that had slipped free. The gentle movement hypnotized her so that she wasn't prepared for the shock when he wrapped her hair around his finger and tugged her close. "I ain't waiting that long to have you, Dani darlin'."

His lips molded to hers, and her breath caught in her lungs. He took full advantage of her gasp of surprise, tracing the rim of her pretty mouth with the tip of his tongue. He felt her softening by degrees, and when she was putty in his hands, he took full possession of her mouth in a tongue-dueling, heart-pumping, soul-wracking kiss.

He was so hard he hurt. Reaching out, he wrapped his good arm around her and hauled her up on top of him. When he had her heat nestled against him, he pressed his hand to the curve of her backside to bring her even closer. Her breathy moan of need sprinted through him. He could feel her heart pounding, echoing the frantic beat of his own.

"I'm not waiting for all the bells and whistles, Dani."

He ached to be inside of her but wasn't eager for the audience that would be guaranteed the moment he threw caution aside. If things went his way, he'd have her in his bed tonight.

"Did I mention that Garahans aren't long on patience?"

She laughed and rested her forehead against his. "I kind of figured that out on my own."

"Tell me you'll love me no matter what life brings: good or bad, easy or hard."

"You know I will."

"Convince me," he rasped, pulling her mouth back to mate with his. When she started squirming on top of him, he rolled them off the couch and onto the floor. She was pinned beneath him.

"Perfect." And she was; her lips were rosy and moist and begging for more. Her eyes held the promise of heaven and the need to take them both there had him bracing his good hand beside her head and nudging her legs apart. Now that he knew they fit like a hand in a glove, the thought tortured him.

He wanted her now but needed to rein in his libido if he was going to get through the rest of the day. "I want to make love to you, right here… right now."

The passion in her slumberous gaze nearly undid his resolve to wait. He shook his head, but with what he had planned, it would be worth it. "I need you to promise you won't be angry with me today."

"You are a hard man to say no to, Jesse Garahan." She kissed him lightly on the lips. "I promise."

"Have I told you I love you yet today?"

"Mmmm." She smiled. "But tell me again."

His eyes met hers. "I love you, Dani darlin'."

"What the hell—" Tyler broke off what he was going to say when Jesse got to his feet and held out his hand to Danielle. "I thought you needed to rest."

"You know a better way to relieve stress?"

His brother's laughter was a welcome sound. He'd been afraid he'd never hear it again. Pushing those thoughts aside, he tugged Danielle close to his side and wrapped his good arm around her. His head was starting to pound again, but he ignored it asking, "Is everything ready?"

Tyler glanced at Danielle before answering. "Yeah."

"What's going on?"

He shook his head at his brother and told her, "You'll see."

"But—"

"You going back on your promise already?"

She laughed. "No, I promised I wouldn't be mad at you today and I meant it."

Tyler's chuckle had Jesse glaring at his brother, but Tyler ignored him and asked, "Did you have a chance to rest yet, Danielle?"

She smiled at Tyler and shrugged. "I'm used to getting through the day with little or no sleep."

"She's going to lie down with me for a little while," Jesse told him. "We're going upstairs."

She pushed out of his arms. "I don't think that's a good idea."

"You will," he promised. "There's aspirin in the bathroom upstairs," he said, tugging on her hand. "Come on."

"But I—" Her protest was cut off when he silenced her with a kiss.

"I'll call you when it's time." Tyler turned and walked away.

"Time for what?" Danielle asked. "And why did you let your brother think you were taking me upstairs to make love with me?"

Jesse chuckled and tugged her toward the stairs. "You just think on it while we're walking."

Halfway up the stairs, she gasped. "I am not—"

He cut off her words with another kiss. By the time they'd made it to the top, she'd stopped protesting, but he figured she had more on her mind. Sure enough, when his hand was on the door to his room, she blurted out, "You're not up to it."

With a grin and a tug, she was in his arms and the door was closed. Just to show her he meant business, he locked the door and backed her up against his bed. "You underestimate my stamina, darlin'."

He pulled off her shirt one-handed and yanked her close. Whispering kisses along the side of her neck, he rasped, "Your skin tastes like wild honey." Nipping the spot beneath her ear, he inhaled her womanly scent and trailed kisses along the edge of jaw. When he got to her chin, he nibbled it, drawing a gasp from her.

"I'm going to love you in the daylight, Dani."

She started to protest, but he pressed his fingers to her lips. "When I got hit and my car started to roll, I thought I'd never see you again, never be able to be with you like this again." He ran his hands up and down her sides, ignoring the twinge of pain shooting through his wrist. "Let me lay you down and love you."

Her sigh was one of acquiescence; he eased the top button on her jeans skirt open and slid it down over her hips, the rasp of the denim fabric a contrast to the silk of her skin. Everything was brought sharply into focus by the near-death experience he'd had. If the car hadn't had a superior roll cage, he wouldn't be here, about to make love with the woman he was going to spend the rest of his life with.

"I don't want to hurt you," she whispered, trembling as he hooked his fingertips in the waistband of her panties.

"You couldn't." With a tug, she was naked from the waist down. He closed his eyes and let his hands whisper over the curve of her waist and around to her back, molding the apex of her sweet backside with both hands. The pain in his wrist and ankle faded, along with the ache in his head, and were forgotten as he lost himself in the satiny feel of her skin beneath his hands.

His lips followed the path his hands had forged. When they touched the baby smooth skin of her backside, he knew he couldn't wait much longer unless he reined back on his desire. Changing tactics, he traced the tip of his tongue along the lacy edge of her bra. With a glance up, he could tell she was right there with him, on the edge of reason.

He licked beneath the lace and let the tip of his tongue rasp against her nipple. Her body's response had him desperate to take her. "I thought I could take my time…"

"Don't."

She was on the bed, her bra pushed down beneath the bountiful breasts he'd just set free. Feasting on first one and then the other, he sucked and suckled until she was writhing beneath him begging him to take her.

He tried to flip open the top button of his jeans, but his hands were shaking—he'd never trembled for a woman before. "Help me?"

Urgent hands freed him and shucked his jeans down

his legs until he could step out of them. "Now!" she demanded falling back on the bed and pulling him with her.

He slid into her liquid warmth and lost himself in the overwhelming need to make this woman his. He set the pace, lightning fast strokes, delving deep, pumping hard, taking them higher and higher until he thought he'd go blind—and then he came, hot and fast. His lips captured her cries of ecstasy as he emptied his life-giving essence deep inside of her, triumphant knowing that it mingled with her honeyed warmth, as they tumbled over the edge together.

The knock on the door woke him. When he looked down, Danielle's beautiful blue eyes were watching him. "Hey, handsome."

"Hey, yourself." He had to remind himself just how good she tasted; dipping down, he captured her lips, tormenting himself with a long and lazy taste.

"Jesse, open up!"

"Go away, Tyler." He wrapped his arms around Danielle and shifted so they were back to front... her delicious backside cuddled in his lap.

"Can't. Just got the phone call that company'll be here in fifteen."

"It's too early—" he began until he heard his brother's laughter.

"You've been up here a couple of hours, Bro, time to get cleaned up... I'll hold them off till you two come downstairs."

A hint of suspicion clouded her gaze when she asked, "Who's here?"

"You heard my brother—company." He pushed her

toward the edge, delighted that she was fighting him to stay in his bed.

"Maybe I don't feel like being around anybody right now."

He laughed. "You will. Come on, let's get a quick shower."

She finally relaxed against him and let herself be pushed out of bed. "OK, but under protest."

Tossing her his T-shirt, he pulled on his jeans, zipping them partway so they wouldn't fall off while he was walking to the bathroom. "Come on, darlin', you're about to have a quickie in the shower."

"I don't think—"

"Now you're talkin'," he said, tugging her along. "We don't have enough time for thinkin'."

"What about your wrist?"

Jesse unwrapped his wrist and his ankle and grinned. "No problem, darlin'."

They were slippery with soap and panting by the time someone knocked on the door. "Go away!" he grumbled, turning her back around to kiss her just once more.

"Everything's ready when you are." Normally, Tyler's laughter would have irritated him, but making love to Danielle had taken the edge off.

"Be there in a few," he promised. Turning off the water, he reached for a towel and started to dry her off. "Dani darlin', don't forget your promise."

She picked up the other dry towel and started to dry him off. "Not to be mad?" She giggled. "Are you kidding? I'm way too relaxed to be mad. Besides, I've just beat my all time record."

"For what?"

"That would be telling," she said, pressing her lips to his neck and trailing kisses down to the shamrock tattooed over his heart. "Have I told you how sexy your tattoo is?"

He groaned. "God, woman—tell me later. There's a surprise waiting downstairs for you."

She pulled back from him. "What kind of a surprise?"

"How the hell many kinds are there?" He couldn't believe she was going to make this difficult.

"Two," she told him. "The good kind and the bad kind."

"Oh." He grinned down at her. "It's the good kind."

With towels wrapped around them, they walked back to his room. She looked over her shoulder and said, "The bed's made."

He nodded, urging her into the room. "Looks like it."

"Someone left clean clothes… great! I didn't really want to put on the same clothes I'd been wearing since yesterday."

"I, uh… thought you might be worried about that."

"Is this dress Ronnie's or Emily's?"

"Emily's. Will it fit?" Hell, he hoped it would, or else the rest of his surprise wasn't gonna work.

Her hand froze as she reached for the pale blue sundress, and he realized she'd noticed the turquoise bra and matching tap pants. "Are these what I think they are?"

"Yes, ma'am." He pulled her into his arms. "Will you wear them for me today?"

"OK," she said, "but only because I keep my promises."

Relief speared through him as she wrapped her arms around his neck and pulled him close for a tongue-tangling kiss.

So far everything was going according to plan.

Knowing he wasn't strong enough to watch her getting dressed without sampling the satin doll skin she'd be covering up, he put a hand to his temple, and before he could even say it hurt, she was saying, "You forgot to take the aspirin."

He tried not to smile. "I got distracted."

"I'll get it—"

He held up his hand. "I've got pants on, I'll go get it."

He was out the door before she could protest. Tyler answered his text before he got the bottle of pain-reliever opened. He sent a reply, opened the bottle, dry-swallowed the aspirin, and smiled all the way back to his bedroom.

Danielle knew Jesse was up to something, but she was in too good of a mood to wrangle the truth out of him. If he wanted to surprise her... with the good kind of surprise... then she'd be willing to let him.

Stepping into the satin tap pants, she reached for the bra and was fastening it when he knocked on the door. "It's Jesse. Can I come in?"

She grinned and slipped the dress over her head and smoothed it into place. Amazingly, it hugged her curves and belled out softly around her knees. "Yes." She was turning around when he opened the door.

"You're so damned beautiful," he rasped, taking her into his arms, pressing his lips to her temple. Easing her out of his arms, he held out his hand. "Are you ready to go?"

She reached for his hand and smiled. "About your surprise—"

"You'll like it," he promised, tugging her toward the stairs.

"Hey," she said stopping at the top, "we're still barefoot."

He grinned. "So we are. Come on."

When they reached the foot of the stairs, she heard voices coming from the kitchen. "Are your cousins back from making their rounds?"

"Sounds like," he said, tightening his grip on her hand. A few feet from the kitchen Tyler was walking toward them, calling out over his shoulder, "I'll go see what's keeping them."

"We're here," Jesse said.

His brother turned and smiled. "'Bout time." Tyler paused and smiled down at Danielle. "Did my bone-headed brother tell you how beautiful you are?"

"Yes." She grinned at Jesse.

Tyler nodded. "Everyone's waiting."

She planted her feet. "Who's here?"

Jesse kissed her to get her moving again. Tyler walked ahead, and as soon as she could see past his broad shoulders, she started to smile. Her uncle and Lacy were standing by the table.

Before she could say anything, she noticed that Jesse's brothers and his cousins were awfully clean for having just finished a half-day's worth of work.

She tilted her head to one side as she stared up at Jesse. "What's going on?"

Lacy looked up at her uncle. When he nodded, she shouted. "Yes!"

Danielle shook her head. So that was his surprise, bringing her daughter her. "Yes what, sweet pea?"

"Please marry cowboy Jesse."

The smiling faces surrounding them had her laughing.

"You didn't have to go to so much trouble planning an engagement party." She hugged Jesse tight. "But thanks."

"Hold that thought, June bug," her uncle said with a grin. "We're waiting on two more people."

Confused, she looked in the direction her uncle had, and had to shake her head. Mavis was walking in the back door with a man dressed in a black robe. "Sorry, Jesse," Mavis said. "Judge Gambling just finished sentencing someone."

"Judge?" Danielle said looking first at her uncle and then Jesse.

He took her hands in his and lifted them to his lips. "Lacy said yes, Dani darlin'."

Everything clicked into place. "But I thought we were going to wait—"

"Life's too short, darlin'." He pulled her back into his arms. "Marry me."

Bruised and battered, the cowboy she hadn't wanted to fall in love with waited for her answer. Love filled her to bursting. "Well," she drawled, "since Lacy said it was all right with her…"

Jesse tilted his head back and laughed. "I've just gotta have another taste of your smart mouth. Come here, darlin'."

"But the judge didn't say the words yet," her uncle reminded her.

Jesse's kiss made her head spin and her knees weak. "He's got five minutes to get it said."

"Do you, Jesse Garahan—"

"Yes, sir, I do."

The judge chuckled and turned to Danielle. "And do you Danielle—"

"I do."

"You may kiss your bride."

Jesse sealed their promise with a kiss that had her forgetting all about their audience. Deep rumbling chuckles brought them back to Earth and the reality that they couldn't escape back upstairs just yet. There were hands to shake, people to hug, and cake to eat.

Chapter 22

"WHAT DO YOU MEAN THEY CAN'T GO ON STAGE shirtless?"

Emily and Jolene Langley stood with their hands on their hips and fire in their eyes, but Sheriff McClure wouldn't budge. "I told you ladies, SIPs lead to FIPs. This is a family celebration, and I'm not having anyone stripping in public."

"But they're not stripping," Jolene told him.

"They're just shirtless," Emily added.

"And not getting on this stage until they've put their shirts back on." He crossed his arms over his massive chest and frowned down at them.

Danielle hadn't wanted to step in, but in order to avoid the possibility of a fight breaking out and her new husband aggravating his injuries, she spoke up. "Sheriff McClure is right. This is a family event." She stared at Emily and then slowly winked.

Emily nodded. "All right, Sheriff."

"You win," Jolene agreed.

Backstage, Danielle pulled Emily and Jolene aside and told them, "We've got a couple of options: we could have them wear their shirts unbuttoned, or we could have them wear form-fitting white T-shirts that we cut a big slash in, so all of the ladies can see their matching shamrock tattoos."

Jolene and Emily looked at one another and started

to laugh. "Either of those ideas will work," Jolene said, "but I think we should give Sheriff McClure a run for his money and have the guys go out on stage shirtless."

"The sheriff's going to be really upset," Emily warned.

Jolene laughed. "Cousin, did you forget that my give a damn's busted?"

Their laughter had the guys looking over at them. Tyler was shaking his head when he walked over. "All right, ladies, what are you all up to?"

Jolene just smiled up at him. "Nothing to worry your pretty head over, cowboy."

He laughed at the nickname she'd given him when he worked at her club.

"What did the sheriff want?" Dylan asked, joining them.

"We're already married," Jesse said to Danielle. "So I can't invoke the Donovan Marriage Ordinance to keep you out of jail."

"Who's going to jail?" Matt and Ben motioned for Tommy and Mike to join them.

Surrounded by a wall of testosterone that had her fanning herself, Danielle slipped her arm around her husband. Lord, she was a lucky woman. "It seems we have a problem with your portion of the show," she told them.

"The sheriff has strict rules about no SIPs—"

Matt and Ben were shaking their heads. "But we're not stripping."

"How did you know what that meant?" Danielle hadn't.

"We're not acronym challenged," Matt told her.

"Like some people," Ben added.

"Is it against the law to go shirtless in Pleasure?" Mike asked. "It isn't in Central Park… for men or women."

"Yeah, but there's a time element involved," Tommy reminded him.

"I'm not sure," Ronnie answered. "But we can insist the sheriff look it up while you boys get on with your show."

"It's up to you," Emily said. "But we'd hoped to raise enough money to help pay down Zeke's feed bill and put a dent in old man William's mortgage."

"Isn't that why we're getting out there and dancing?"

Jolene spoke up, "It is, but there's a busload of women who arrived just to see the Garahan clan and their hunkalicious cousins flexing their fabulous glutes, pecs, and abs while showing off their Irish pride, matching tattoos. I want them to get their money's worth."

"It would be false advertising otherwise," Emily reminded everyone.

Jesse eased his arm free, and using his good hand, pulled his shirt over his head. "I'm in," he ground out. "Who's with me?"

His brothers and cousins pulled their shirts off and Danielle's mouth went dry.

Seven of the best-looking cowboys she'd ever had the pleasure of seeing stood shoulder-to-shoulder, each one six foot tall or taller. Blond-haired and blue-eyed on one end, auburn-haired with green eyes on the other, and three handsome-as-sin, dark-haired, dark-eyed cowboys in the middle. Lord help her, their form-fitting jeans cupped glutes to die for. Shirtless, their abs distracted, but it was their pecs that she could not look away from; every last one of them had an emerald-green shamrock tattooed over their hearts, calling attention to their sculpted muscles.

"Well?" Jesse demanded, obviously not happy that she was looking her fill.

"There's just something about a tall, dark, and handsome cowboy," Danielle said, walking over and pulling him out of the line up. "That just gets a lady's heart pumping."

"Quit looking at my cousins," he grumbled yanking her against him.

She smiled and lifted her lips until they were a breath apart, the devil in her teasing, "I was looking at your brothers."

He swore and when he would have let her go, she wrapped her arms around his neck and pulled him close, kissing him till his eyes crossed and she heard his low moan of pleasure. "Just so you never doubt which Garahan brother I love."

He slid his hand down the curve of her spine and held her pinned against him. When their eyes met, his darkened, desperate with desire. He dipped his head until their lips were a whisper apart. Every fiber of her being cried out for him to kiss her; when he didn't, she opened her mouth to protest, and that's when he laid claim to her mouth. Plundering then savoring, devastating then worshipping—until her knees gave out and she clung to him.

"Danielle!" Jolene called out. "No manhandling allowed until after the show."

"You're just jealous," Jesse teased, steadying Danielle until she got her balance.

She drew in a calming breath and brushed the hair out of her eyes. Her man packed a lethal, sensual punch that had her body tingling with awareness and begging for more.

He pulled her close and whispered, "You all right, Dani darlin'?"

Love for this man filled her to bursting. She leaned her forehead against his heart and heard the steady beat of it. Pressing her lips to his tattoo, she rasped, "I will be, as long as you love me."

He hugged her tight. "I love you more than yesterday—"

"People," Jolene grumbled, interrupting him.

He pressed his lips to her forehead and Danielle looked up at him and smiled. "But less than tomorrow."

He grinned and they both said, "Forever."

"Can we please get on with this?" Jolene sounded seriously peeved, but everyone laughed until Jolene reminded the guys not to forget the steps they'd been taught.

Tyler nodded. "Relax, Jolene, we'll remember."

"Come on, ladies," Emily said. "There are a couple of front-row seats waiting for us."

Danielle, Ronnie, Emily, and Jolene sat front and center waiting for the curtain to go up. When it did, Danielle's jaw dropped and her blood started pumping; standing center stage was the cowboy of her dreams.

He picked her out of the crowd and tipped his hat to her. Her husband was the best-looking one in the lineup.

When the music began to play, all eyes were glued to the long-legged, broad-shouldered cowboys while the crowd went wild, singing along about saving a horse and riding a cowboy.

Danielle's eyes filled with tears as Jesse struggled to dance on his sprained ankle. The Garahan brothers and their cousins were small-town heroes who set aside their reservations to get up in front of the crowd to fulfill their promise to help their neighbors.

Jesse was her hero—Danielle couldn't wait to get her cowboy home.

Read on for excerpts from the previous books
in The Secret Life of Cowboys series
by C.H. Admirand

Tyler

Dylan

Available now from Sourcebooks Casablanca

From *Tyler*

HARDWORKING MAN WANTED.
MUST HAVE A STRONG BACK
AND EVEN TEMPERAMENT.
APPLY IN PERSON.
334 LOBLOLLY WAY
PLEASURE, TX

TYLER GARAHAN CRUSHED THE NEWSPAPER ADVERtisement in his hand. Staring at the building across the street from where he'd parked his pickup, he dug deep for a confidence he sure as hell didn't feel.

"I don't have time to waste."

He needed this job. Hell, he needed any job, but this was the last one he'd circled in Sunday's paper. His last chance or he and his brothers would lose the Circle G.

He tried to swallow past the lump forming in his throat but couldn't muster an ounce of spit. Facing down the longhorn bull that tore ass toward him, wanting to skewer him in the part that made him praise the Lord he was a man, was the closest he'd come to being this scared.

He gritted his teeth, braced his arm against the door, and pushed it open. "I'm not scared."

You shouldn't lie, Tyler.

His gut clenched.

Trust in yourself, son.

Was it wishful thinking or had he just heard from

his grandfather on the other side? Shaking his head, he brushed his damp palms against the front of his jean-clad legs and closed the door.

Stalking across the street, he glanced up at the sign above the building. *The Lucky Star.* As if called up by a long ago memory, the lyrics to an old Kenny Rogers tune his mom loved played through his mind as he crushed the unease he refused to give in to and reached for the door.

The scent was the first thing that hit him, right between the eyes. Rain? How could it smell like a warm summer rain?

Focus on the goal. Get the job first.

But his concentration wandered when he noticed the mirrors on both sides of the entryway. What the hell was that about? He sneered. *A guy doesn't want to see himself walking into a bar. He wants to see the bar, check out what's on tap, and maybe if his luck is running high, flirt with his choice of curvaceous sweet things perched on a bar stool.*

He grinned, savoring the image, because he hadn't had the time lately to get out on a Saturday night in search of a little female companionship. A knot of need started to form in his gut, but he ignored it and strode forward down the hallway lined with mirrors.

Tyler stopped dead in his tracks and stared. "Damn. What's the owner thinking?"

His gaze ran the length of the hallway and back—he wasn't seeing things—there were benches in front of the mirrors.

"Red velvet."

He didn't have to touch the seats to know what they

were covered with. His mother had a favorite lady's chair in her bedroom. A red velvet lady's chair.

"Hell," he muttered. They needed to hire him, if only to suggest a few major changes to increase business. No self-respecting bar owner would have mirrors or velvet in their place.

At the end of the hallway, a long, sleek ebony bar gleamed, and damned if every one of the bar stools didn't have a red velvet cushion to sit on.

"Shit," Tyler muttered aloud. "I can't see myself working in a place like this."

"Well now, handsome," a husky voice purred to the left of him, "I can see you working here just fine."

He turned and felt his mouth drop open. *Beautiful. Stunning. Drop-dead gorgeous.* All of the above fit the little lady walking toward him with her hand outstretched.

"Name's Jolene Langley," she said. "Welcome to The Lucky Star, cowboy."

Lord, she was a looker. Belatedly, Tyler removed his Stetson, ran his hand through his still-damp hair, and grasped her hand. "Tyler Garahan."

Satin. Damned if her hand didn't feel like one of his mom's nightgowns. He'd done his fair share of laundry over the years and ought to know.

Her grip surprised him. It was firm. His gaze drifted from the top of her wavy red head to the tips of her fancy blue boots—a color only a female would wear.

"Emily!" she called out though her gaze never left his. "See something you like, cowboy?" She returned the favor by letting her gaze slide from the top of his tousled dark brown head to the tips of his worn leather boots. Her gaze lingered on his boots. He glanced down and swore beneath his breath; he'd forgotten to polish them.

"Em?" she called a second time.

"I'm coming," a soft voice answered. "Give me a minute."

He glanced in the direction the voice seemed to come from—somewhere just beyond the bar—and noticed small tables scattered in front of a stage.

"You have live entertainment in here?" He imagined some whiny soft rock band standing on stage, playing music that would get under his skin and have him reaching for a shot of whiskey instead of his usual longneck bottle.

Her laugh was as smooth as her skin. "You could say that, cowboy."

Irritation began to burn in his gut at the way she'd sneered when she called him cowboy. Hell, he was one and proud of it, but that wasn't as important right now as landing the job and saving the ranch. "Name's Tyler, ma'am."

"What's up, Jolene?"

The pretty redhead walking toward him had to be a blood relative to the one currently staring at the third button down on his worn denim work shirt. He hoped Jolene didn't look lower and notice the tear he tried to hide by rolling up the sleeves. The woman was getting under his skin—and not in a good way.

"Trouble, Em?"

Tyler finally tore his gaze from Emily's face and noticed what Jolene had: the huge splat of chocolate dead center between Emily's breasts. Firm and proud, cupped lovingly by a form-fitting, cropped T-shirt.

The saliva pooled in his mouth. He swallowed. The urge to devour the chocolate-covered confection caught him off guard. Digging deep for control, he realized he'd been too long without a woman: two months, three weeks, and four days... if he were counting.

He may be damned for it, but he let his gaze feast on the bounty before him. The two inches of exposed skin was tanned and taut. His gaze dipped to the hem of her denim mini skirt, and he had to swallow again. The woman had legs—curvaceous and toned, not toothpick thin—and Lord Almighty, bright green nail polish on her toes.

Emily smiled at Tyler and answered Jolene, "The spoon got caught in the mixer."

Jolene had a good three inches on Emily and an in-your-face beauty and sexuality that challenged him on every level, but there was something about the barefooted redhead with chocolate smeared across her cheekbone like a slash of war paint that tugged at his gut.

He had to fight against the urge to smile and replied, "Looks like the mixer won."

Emily lifted her right hand and the mangled spoon she clutched. "That's the second spoon today." Her sigh was long and low.

Jolene patted Emily's shoulder. "Why don't you just quit while you're ahead?"

"You know I can't until I beat the stress out of myself and this batter." Emily looked over at Tyler and asked, "Are you here to fix the sink?"

He shook his head. "Although I have been known to wrastle an ornery pipe into submission, I'm actually here about your sister's ad in the paper." For a split second disappointment clouded her pretty face and had him offering, "Maybe I could take a look at it before I leave."

Her smile blossomed slowly and was surely like a flower opening its petals to catch the rain. Before he could untangle his tongue, she said, "That's right neighborly, but I'll wait for the plumber. Oh… and she's my cousin."

"Really? You look enough alike to be sisters." Now that she was close enough to touch, he could see the subtle differences: the shape of their eyes—Emily's were long-lashed and almond shaped—and the curve of their lips—Emily's were fuller, and there was something indefinable about the barefooted redhead that went a whole lot deeper, straight to her core, a sweetness he hadn't found in long, long while.

If he were gifted with words like his New York City cousins, he'd have said there was something special about Emily and the way she seemed to smile from the inside out. But Tyler'd probably mess it up and compare her to one of the Circle G's milk cows.

Neither woman looked like they'd ever set foot on a ranch, and Emily sure as hell wouldn't believe him if he told her that certain breeds of milk cows had beautiful eyes and sweet faces. The steer he and his brothers raised for beef weren't pretty—well, they probably would be if he were another steer.

Shaking his head to clear it, he asked, "So did you save any of the batter?"

Emily's smile was slow and achingly sweet. "Enough to fill half the pan."

"Are you really going to bake half a pan's worth, Em?"

Emily grinned at her cousin. "No. That's why I

decided to get another spoon and just eat the batter after I nuke it for a few seconds. Then I'll start over with another batch."

Tyler could handle cooking meat and potatoes. Baking was a whole other ball game, but he was pretty sure it would take longer than a few seconds to cook brownies in the microwave. "That wouldn't be long enough to cook them, would it?"

Her slow, sweet smile eased under his worry about getting the job. "Brownies taste better half-cooked," Emily said. "Imagine how great the batter would taste warm and freshly whipped."

Tyler couldn't keep from grinning at the thought. Standing this close to her, he couldn't help but notice that without boots, the top of Emily's head would hit him mid-chest. He'd have to work at it to line up their lips, but if they were lying down—Whoa! Hold on there. Time enough to go there later, after he'd landed the job. *If he landed the job.*

"So, you're here about the position."

The hard edge in Jolene's voice had Tyler looking at her. Hell, a few positions came to mind and stubbornly got stuck there, making it hard to focus. Man, if he didn't need the money, he'd be looking for a nice quiet place to sample the chocolate-covered redhead. Head to toe and every luscious inch in between. Had she noticed him drooling over her cousin?

"I think you should hire him, Jo," Emily said, heading back the way she'd come. "See y'all later," she called out over her shoulder. "If you need me, I'll be upstairs whipping these brownies into submission. Bye, Tyler."

Lord, he'd get arrested if either woman could read his

thoughts right now. One of Grandpa's favorite expressions came to mind watching the gentle sway of Emily's hips. The hitch in Emily's *git-a-long* was as delectable as the front of her had been, and damned if a line from a Trace Adkins song didn't start running through his brain, *We hate to see her go, but love to watch her leave.*

Damn, get your mind on the job, son.

Jolene asked him a question, but he was too preoccupied to pay attention. "I'm sorry, ma'am… what did you ask me?" *Lord, don't let Jolene wonder if I'll be able to keep my mind on the job and off her cousin. I need this job!*

Jolene was watching him closely. Finally the corner of her mouth lifted into a smile. "Are you here to apply for the position?"

"Yeah. I mean, yes, ma'am. I'm here about the job."

"You a hard working man, Mr. Garahan?" She reached out and brushed at the front of his shirt.

He shifted from one foot to the other, uncomfortable now that she'd touched him. Had she meant to? "Excuse me?"

"The person I need to fill the position has to be willing to work hard."

He rubbed his fingers along the brim of his hat and wondered how to convince the woman that he'd work until he dropped. *Doing's smarter than jawing.* "I give one hundred percent to everything I do."

Damned if she didn't reach out and touch him again, this time he twitched as her nail flicked unerringly over his left nipple. *Holy Hell!*

He stepped back. Had she meant to touch him like that, or did she simply have dead-on aim? Unease roiled in his gut. He couldn't flat out ask her. If he was wrong he'd look like a fool, blow the interview, and lose his chance at the job. "Ma'am?"

"What about your temperament?" she asked, taking a step closer to him, easily closing the distance.

"I'm easygoing most of the time." His eyes narrowed. Was she coming on to him, or was it some kind of test?

"So far, you have all of the qualifications I need. How's your back… strong?"

"Yes, ma'am."

She stepped around behind him, and he wondered why she couldn't take his word for it that his back was strong and had to see for herself. The small palm cupping the seat of his Levis was all it took to answer his unasked question and end the interview.

He spun around to face her. "I don't know what kind of game you're playing or what kind of *position* you're hiring for, but I don't think I'm the man for the job."

Hell, usually he enjoyed an aggressive female, given the fact that free time was next to nonexistent and getting down to the good part right off meant more time in the saddle, but he'd been attracted to Emily, not Jolene, and totally missed the fact that Jolene apparently had other things in mind. At least Emily had been honest in mistaking him for a plumber. He couldn't imagine what Jolene had mistaken him for.

"I believe you're just what we're looking for." She smiled, and he wondered if anyone ever told this woman flat out no.

"Take off your shirt."

From *Dylan*

DYLAN GARAHAN NARROWED HIS GAZE, TRYING TO focus in the glare of the spotlight, searching the crowd for her face. It was time for the big move in his act—the showstopper.

Where was she?

Jolene would kill him if he messed this up, but he'd made it through the last two nights and would make it through tonight. The redheaded owner of the club should have no complaints about the middle Garahan brother not keeping his word or holding up his end of the bargain. Damn the woman and her tests!

Controlling the urge to turn on his heel and walk off the stage, he dug deep and found the grit to stick it out. *Hell, if Tyler could handle this job, so could he. Garahans went down fighting!*

Oblivious to the adoring gazes of the women around him, he moved toward center stage, bent, and picked up the coiled rope. He looked up as a blonde, a brunette, and a redhead walked into the bar… right on schedule… but there was something different about the brunette. Maybe it was the blindfold. He struggled not to laugh, but he couldn't keep from smiling, wondering why the cloak-and-dagger bit.

Looping the lasso in his hands, he started the slow circular motion. Getting the rhythm going until it was smooth and sweet, he raised it above his head and locked

gazes with the blonde. When she nodded, he let the lasso
fly, as the blonde whipped the blindfold off the brunette.

The woman's stunned expression as the rope slipped
around her upper body didn't stop him from tugging on
the rope and reeling her in. The patrons of the Lucky
Star hooted and hollered, encouraging him to pull faster,
but he didn't want the little lady to trip and fall on her
pretty face.

Glad that the focus of the crowd wasn't totally on
him, he gently pulled her toward him. The brunette's
gypsy-dark skin, full red lips, and almond-shaped eyes
captivated him. The promise of pain-filled death in her
dark green eyes, as she struggled against the bonds that
held her, had his lips twitching, fighting not to smile.

She dug in her heels, but he used his strength to
subdue her. Undeterred, he yanked on the rope. When
her eyes widened in shock, he used her surprise to his
advantage and reeled her in the last few feet. When they
were a few inches apart, he tipped his hat, smiled, and
rumbled, "Happy birthday, darlin'."

Her eyes narrowed, and her nostrils flared; Dylan
recognized the signs of a fractious filly about to raise a
ruckus. Not a problem, he was ready. Wrapping his free
hand around her, he hauled her in close, pinning her to
him before she could let loose and kick him.

The crowd roared its approval.

"Let me go," she demanded, her sweet breath tickling
the hollow of his throat.

Enjoying himself for the first time since he'd hit the
stage, he chuckled and bent his head closer to her full
red lips. "Why?" His gaze locked with hers. "So you can
have more room to do more damage?"

"I don't like being manhandled."

Her vehement protest didn't deter him; he had a job to do and an act to finish. "Well now, darlin'," he drawled, "that's not what your friends said."

Her eyes sparkled with temper, and her willowy body trembled with anger. Dylan's body stood up and said *hell yeah*! It'd been a long time since he'd had a woman tempt him. The sultry brunette in his arms looked like she wanted to tear a few strips off of his hide... right before she killed him.

Damn, but that turned him on.

Perverse. That's what his grandpa would say. He grinned and would swear he heard her grinding her teeth in frustration.

"Let me go." She struggled against him, but he'd trapped her slender curves against him so not a breath of air was between them. "I'm not one of those desperately lonely women, or buckle bunnies coming in here looking for some eye candy."

Lord, he really loved the husky sound of her voice. Even angry, it sounded sexy. He fought against the instant attraction he'd felt and shrugged. "I'm not the one whose friends blindfolded me."

She closed her eyes and stopped struggling. Dylan could feel the anger leaving her by degrees.

"They're just trying to help."

"With a face like an angel and a body made for lovin', why would you need any?"

Tears gathered in her eyes. "None of your business."

Well, hell. His one weakness cut him off at the knees. *A woman's tears.* "I'm about to make it my business."

Acknowledgments

In our family, both the good and the bad come in threes, so once the first crisis hit, we braced for two more. Through it all my best friend—my rock—my husband stood firm beside me offering me the chance I never thought I'd have: the opportunity to write full time, and thank God for that, because without that gift, *Jesse* would still be a work-in-progress.

While writing *Jesse* I gained a son-in-law, a wonderful man who loves our daughter, dances with her, and makes her laugh. Now we have three sons. We are truly blessed and looking forward to the birth of our first grandbaby… life is good.

There are so many people at Sourcebooks to thank, but first and foremost, thank you to my wonderful editor, Deb Werksman, for her vision, attention to detail, and amazing ability to push me to dig even deeper, helping me to become a better writer.

A special thank you to our publisher, Dominique Raccah. How amazing that she really does know who I am and what I write—she gives the best hugs!

Thank you to Cat, Susie, and Danielle for your hard work pulling everything together and making it work; you ladies totally rock!

Although I do mention him last, it doesn't reflect the importance he has in my writing life. A very special thank-you to my fabulous agent, Eric Ruben, who has taken the helm and is steering my career in the right direction. While I'm sad to be leaving Pleasure, Texas, I cannot wait to start writing about the Mulcahy sisters and small-town America! Without Eric's guidance, none of this would be possible.

About the Author

C.H. Admirand is an award-winning, multi-published author with novels in mass-market paperback, hardcover, trade paperback, magazine, e-book, and coming soon in audio book format.

Fate, destiny, and love at first sight will always play a large part in C.H.'s stories because they played a major role in her life. When she saw her husband for the first time, she knew he was the man she was going to spend the rest of her life with. Each and every hero C.H. writes about has a few of Dave's best qualities: his honesty, his integrity, his compassion for those in need, and his killer broad shoulders. She lives with her husband and two of their grown children in the wilds of northern New Jersey.

She loves to hear from readers! Stop by her website at www.chadmirand.com to catch up on the latest news, excerpts, reviews, blog posts, and links to Facebook and Twitter.

Cowboy Crazy

by Joanne Kennedy

———

Sparks fly when sexy cowboys collide with determined heroines in a West filled with quirky characters and sizzling romance. Acclaimed for delivering "a fresh take on the traditional contemporary Western," Joanne Kennedy's books might just be your next great discovery!

From stable to boardroom...

Sarah Landon's Ivy League scholarship transforms her from a wide-eyed country girl into a poised professional. Until she's assigned to do damage control with the boss's rebellious brother Lane, who's the burr in everybody's saddle. He's determined to save his community from oil drilling, and she's not going back to the ranch she left forever. Spurs will shine in this saucy romp about ranchers and roots, redemption and second chances.

———

Praise for Tall, Dark and Cowboy:

"Another steamy, suspenseful offering from
the popular Kennedy."—*Booklist*

"A sassy and sexy wild ride that is more fun than a
wild hootenanny!"—*The Romance Reviews*, 5 stars

For more Joanne Kennedy, visit:

www.sourcebooks.com

Tall, Dark and Cowboy

by Joanne Kennedy

—⁓—

She's looking for an old friend...

In the wake of a nasty divorce, Lacey Bradford heads for Wyoming where she's sure her old friend will take her in. But her high school pal Chase Caldwell is no longer the gangly boy who would follow her anywhere. For one thing, he's now incredibly buff and handsome, but that's not all that's changed...

What she finds is one hot cowboy...

Chase has been through tough times and is less than thrilled to see the girl who once broke his heart. But try as he might to resist her, while Lacey's putting her life back together, he's finding new ways to be part of it.

—⁓—

Praise for Cowboy Fever:

"HOT, HOT, HOT... with more twists and turns than a buckin' bull at a world class rodeo, lots of sizzlin' sex, and characters so real you'll swear they live down the road!" —Carolyn Brown, *New York Times* and *USA Today* bestselling author of *Red's Hot Cowboy*

www.sourcebooks.com